"Deranged police procedural me
in Wild Wild Wessex. Utterly me
        JAKE ARNOTT, AU

"*Pornography* by the Cure is the ultimate brown acid album; the magic mirror from Hans Christian Andersen's *The Snow Queen*, held up to the idea of the 60s & the summer of love: all optimism, joy, energy and compassion foreclosed only nihilism, horror and collapse ahead. *Disintegration* by the Cure is a stately review of the wreckage, which, ironically, suggests an attempt at reintegration, though there has been too much decimation for this to work. Both albums are powered by total immersion in LSD, the powerful hallucinogen which (arguably) constituted humanity's last roll of the dice in terms of us achieving a powerful, wide-ranging and effective consciousness shift, and are soaked in the sense that we are too late. The disaster has already happened. Both albums provide some unique structure to Tariq Goddard's latest thrilling novel, set in a significant 2016, which (I believe to be) a psychedelic, philosophical, political police procedural black comedy in a wider, solidly weird fiction universe. A Wilshire/Hampshire *True Detective*. The hardest of hard recommends."

        JOHN DORAN, *THE QUIETUS*

"Here, as in all of Tariq Goddard's fiction, the ordinary and the uncanny, the mundane and the metaphysical — above all, the sardonic and the profound — merge with one another in some mysterious borderland that he alone seems to have explored. And *High John the Conqueror* may be his most entertaining novel yet."

        DAVID BENTLEY HART, AUTHOR OF
   THE EXPERIENCE OF GOD: BEING, CONSCIOUSNESS, BLISS

"A fantastic mix of high and low literature that just flies. The sense of place is just impeccable — I've never read anything that's so unflinching in its portrait of the real rural England, I loved the tattiness of everything. The final scene is utterly burned on my brain — a truly original piece of work."

MAT OSMAN, AUTHOR OF THE RUINS

"A wyrd & eerie tale for wyrd & eerie times, High John the Conqueror is, like High John de Conqueror itself, 'a genuine hybrid and a one-off,' crafting & grafting police noir, folk horror and occult parapolitics into an altered States of the Nation novel of monsters past and present. P.D. James meets M.R. James!"

DAVID PEACE, AUTHOR OF GB84 AND THE DAMNED UNITED

"It's going to be every outsider's beach read, a doorway into the future."

MARK STEWART, THE POP GROUP

"Tariq Goddard has written a masterwork of the uncanny. High John the Conqueror is a trip into fresh, bizarre, thrilling new territory. Reading it is almost a hallucinatory experience — it takes daring swerves away from what we call reality, but stays close enough to life to get under your skin. By the end you'll be altered on a cellular level, questioning what you thought you knew."

ELVIA WILK, AUTHOR OF OVAL

"Enchanting. A novel of acute and weirdly energetic downland Shamnism of a distinctive Wessex Variety, a Hellbent English Pastoral. Goddard here comes into his own as the GrisGris man of English fiction."

PATRICK WRIGHT, AUTHOR OF
THE VILLAGE THAT DIED FOR ENGLAND

HIGH JØHN
THE CØNQUERØR

HIGH JØHN
THE CØNQUERØR

A NOVEL

TARIQ GODDARD

Published by Repeater Books

An imprint of Watkins Media Ltd

Unit 11 Shepperton House

89-93 Shepperton Road

London

N1 3DF

United Kingdom

www.repeaterbooks.com

A Repeater Books paperback original 2022

1

Distributed in the United States by Random House, Inc., New York.

Printed and bound in the UK by TJ Books

To Margaret Glover;
we live in the country but were built in London.

BOOK ONE

What can you see elsewhere that you cannot see here?
Thomas à Kempis

There is nothing wrong with inherited wealth if you melt the silver yourself.
The Auteurs

I can take anything. I think about Nietzsche a lot. I know what the Overman is... But how much of my balls do I have to chop off to be this new guy?
Mike Tyson

Eventually all things are known. And few matter.
Gore Vidal

BOOK ONE

I always wanted to be a writer, but I became a policeman instead. I sleep badly, which allows me to brood over my capitulation every morning. Between the hours of three and five in the morning, I consider the coy wife, admiring sons, daughter that looks a little like me and the modernist new-build, on a chalk bank overlooking a view that encapsulates as much of the universe as anyone needs to see, that I blissfully inhabit. Later I read my reviews. I am shortlisted for prizes. I enjoy healthy sales, and I accept the self-assurance and self-respect, the emotional closure and intellectual finality, the lasting satisfaction and deep sleep that are the gifts of being able to sum up everything perfectly in words. Meanwhile my baser needs are met in the adulation, temptations, retreats, opportunities and openings that I accept with stoicism as the social return for being so generous with myself. As the morning chorus commences, I welcome the sliver of sleep that lasts only seconds, knowing that my readers will have to wait until I next close my eyes for the literary carousel to turn again.

Before that, I choose to belong to the world, not record it, to carefully mind and ration the hell I live in, not share it, to manage and understand truth, not tell it, and revel in the vanity of knowing that I carry my own water and give nothing up. I wanted to be a writer, but I became a policeman instead.

PROLOGUE

'It doesn't matter if we all die.'

Iggy had no idea why he had just said that, but it was too late to take it back and, unfortunately, wholly in keeping with a number of other disturbing developments in his life. It had taken him several weeks to realise that his belongings really were being moved round his room at night. Once the sun descended over the cul-de-sac at Hanging Hill, Iggy's trailer was transformed into a limited-run play in which each showing was different. On the first morning of the performance, Iggy discovered his iPhone in the sock he liked to pretend was Wonder Woman's pumping fist, instead of the device's usual spot on the floor with the other detritus he emptied from his pockets. As he was still mashed, he found the incongruity funny, though it got him thinking.

The next manifestation of a sneaky presence, to accompany his own, was at least still amusing: a festering bowl of Frosties turned upside down at the bottom of his uninhabited fish tank, brown bubbles and shredded glitter gyrating about its murky sides. In languor he sat and watched the mouldy cereal crud rise patiently to the top, grinning at his reflection, the sock now reunited with his most treasured possession.

The ripping noises were a warning that this was not all going to be fun: eight volumes of A Song of Ice and Fire shredded and scattered by his mattress, the sixth page of each book intact and stuffed into his UGGs like papier-mâché cannon balls. And soon after, other less entertaining messages arrived, not bothering him *at once, but slowly turning sour after the novelties of his morning pipe blended into the day's habitual paranoia. His Ikea storage drawers, instead of being left ajar, with T-shirt and underpants acting as a buffer between the canvas and plywood, were closed, the clothes inside folded with an exactness he was incapable of. The orderly arrangement of these garments seemed to be posing a question about himself, or about what he was not. Iggy knew it was dangerous to make the connection, to draw the conclusion and somehow collude in the process, but he sensed he was being leerily shown up. His feelings were the real target, as they always were when an adult said he was not very good at his life, yet this was not the work of any adult; rather, it was that of a childish mind like his own, reflecting his own sinister ideas of cleverness.*

And then all hell broke loose. Items he was ashamed of and had long since banished the memory of appeared outside by the step ladder, amidst the old teabags and cigarette butts, there for his auntie to find and bring in with his breakfast tray. Transformer Rescue Bots, supposedly lost in the fire that he could never remember starting, assembled round his dwelling like DEA agents closing in for a bust, followed by his cousin's knickers that he had filched from the laundry basket, and finally his father's pornographic magazines, with felt pen-redacted genitals — his mother's well-meaning attempt at censorship should they fall into his hands.

His panic was assuaged by confusion, forever the dominant influence in his life. Most nights he was so smashed he would not have noticed if his room had been taken apart and put back together, as what could be more normal in the life of an aspiring romantic than remembering nothing before going to bed? He was always up for anything after all: jumping into tubs of weedkiller, painting his toenails with varnish. He was the first of his friends to get studs, tattoos and piercings on every coverable surface. Chaos was his master. Could not all of this be consistent with the usual madness? Like most comforting and flawed ideas, Iggy cleaved to this one long after it ceased to be sensible to still do so. Besides, despite all his complaining, he was not yet used to bad outcomes in life or of things, finally and irrevocably, actually turning out for the worse.

And then, in the lonely moment of the last instance, he was woken up by something hitting him, he was sure of it, a hard slap to the face, and there, on the bed, was a boot that he had lost at the party. This party had been unlike any he had attended, culminating in his unrobing and joining the 'old ones' in the silver hot tub, the night it all went wrong and he met High John the Conqueror, a lifetime ago, just six weeks earlier.

The chains that dragged Iggy from appearance to disappearance were fastened unobtrusively while he was daydreaming of everlasting things: fantasies in which he saw himself as a rock star photographer, persuading his harem to show a little more flesh, or as a ripped stuntman abseiling into a blast furnace of snakes, watched by everyone who had ever doubted his courage. That he had never used a camera that wasn't part of a mobile phone, was terrified of heights and physical risk in general, and could still believe in the possibility of greatness few are touched by, came naturally from an anodyne self-confidence bequeathed by a mother who thought he was beautiful and told him so regularly. If life would just let him be more himself, let Iggy be Iggy, then the rewards of hard work would appear, perhaps without him even having to toil for them. This hope saw him through his last summer at school — or 'fuck-about-time', as he liked to call it — the final few weeks a glorious riot of getting noticed, insolence and attitude. The party continued into the summer holidays, moving from his parents' place to the trailer in his auntie's garden, which provided his wrecking crew with a base for operations and the necessary privacy for intimacy with a couple of classmates who were in a hurry to accrue experience.

Autumn was the start of another story and it hit Iggy hard: a slurry of buddies taking off to university, apprenticeships and, where their parents could afford it, a year out in the sun. It seemed that behind the lively clothing, bids for attention and hopes for a better world, his companions had their eyes set on conventional routes out of Wiltshire after all, but then so, according to what he told them, had he. With the arrival of the coldest winter on record, Iggy still hadn't heard from his friend's dad who had promised him work at a recording studio, and was left behind instead with a couple of headcases, a cluster of slow readers and the banshee at Greggs that had already given him the clap. It was a betrayal of his teenage hopes, but as everyone had always suspected he lacked character, there was no one short of his mother he could complain to, and even she was beginning to change her mind now that he was no longer so beautiful but, rather, a whining man-child, approaching twenty with an unfulfillable sense of entitlement. What was so puzzling is that on paper it seemed to him like he had enjoyed himself, without ever actually being happy — the curious space between his activity and the desired state that remained as yet unattainable, his life's sole accomplishment.

The loneliness of existence in the trailer, depressing odd jobs that he could not get the hang of, arguments with his family, and always waiting — for what, he did not know — corroded away at his surly and foundationless self-assurance. Gravitating towards an older set, already reconciled to a life of paralysing inertia, Iggy accepted mascot status: running errands to the off-licence, rolling joints and preparing needles for those too old and wasted to get their act together. Quietly, he collected the credit for being on round-the-clock call. He knew what he was doing was not exactly fun, in fact no fun at all, but it was at least proof that he still existed. Occasionally, rumours seeped through of bigger and better things, parties where posh birds danced and disrobed on hay bales and millionaire swingers paid to watch unemployed scruffs shag their wives, amongst other, darker happenings in the woods, but there seemed little way into these from the swamp that had now claimed him.

That all changed with 'the barbecue' at Sebastopol House on New Year's Eve. Nick the Well, whose claim to exceptional status at the squat hung on his being part of a road crew in the Eighties, was looking for someone to help him flip gourmet burgers at Toad Hall. This prominent building, whose proper name was Sebastopol House, overlooking the dual carriageway to Ringwood, was sat in the midst of a large estate given to the first Earl of Cardigan for being near a battle in which thousands of men under his command had died. It was now occupied by Mr Toad, Mungo Masters, a hedge fund manager with an interest in young men, astral physics, pagan myth and alternative energy. The Well let it be understood that frying offal and washing lettuce was not all that was going to be required of Iggy, not by a long way, without actually getting into the specifics of what would be. In his present circumstances, the invitation, even if it were no more than signing on as hired help, was nothing short of a summons to the palace, and Iggy did not wait for it to be issued to anyone else before accepting. Besides, he could feel that increase in momentum that graces a vague life, as it churns towards a specific conclusion that it really should have nothing to do with, sensing the redemptive possibilities of cutting into someone else's destiny, and ignoring all the danger.

The reality did not disappoint. Iggy had never seen a place like it. A Christmas tree that ought to have stood in Trafalgar Square, surrounded by mountains of unopened presents, resided beside a giant staircase that ascended high into the skull of the domed building. Forming a welcoming phalanx, girls in tights, dressed as elves, and boys in Speedos and Santa caps, handed round stockings overflowing with pills in seasonal colours. Iggy did not do much cooking that night, but his mother's promises came true. He was there for days before he even knew what had happened. Since then he had returned to Toad Hall in his dreams, his recollection of a heavenly ecstasy slowly turning into the fear that a presence had followed him home. And it was not going to leave without him, as what else were these strange goings on in his caravan if not evidence that being scared of the dark is safer than becoming it?

There was a shadow moving across the walls of his room — of that Iggy was sure — closing in and preventing him from physically rising and running away. It was coming for him, and he wanted to scream loudly enough to wake up, but he was too scared to because he knew he was already awake and that life, disappointing as it often was, would still be there in the morning, whereas he no longer would be.

'It doesn't matter if we all die,' he yells, and then the room is quiet. There is no one in it anymore.

CHAPTER ONE

ONE HUNDRED YEARS

Wessex, 2016

I always wanted to be a writer, but I became a policeman instead. On mornings like this the writer is crawling round reality warily, the detective taking credit for turning up — one trying to grasp what days are for, the other putting these insights inexpertly into practice. Today the struggle takes place stood in the careworn bungalow of a missing person's family: the sixth youth to have disappeared this year from Hanging Hill, our city's least fondly spoken of housing estate.

'How long is it since you last saw Iggy?' asks Detective Chief Inspector Tamla Sioux for a second time, pouting slightly, a sign that she knows she is not being taken seriously, and that short of breaking a nose or two, she has lost her chance to make an authoritative first impression. This is not her fault. We both look like central-casting detectives, put-upon and pretty, which may give the public something nice to look at, but annoys our less telegenic colleagues, suggesting that if we are the lead actors, they are minor characters in the same drama.

'Mr Lockheart,' Tamla continues, 'it's important that we can establish, as close as we can, the time of your son's disappearance, his last known whereabouts, when he went missing. That stuff... Mr Lockheart?'

Mr Lockheart snorts, eyeballing me as though I should be ashamed of bringing this tiny northerner in a red overcoat and bleached peroxide hair, neatly parted, into a realm as serious as his. His dogs are growing restless in the kitchen, where they are thoughtfully shut in with his wife, and judging by his popping eyes, he cannot wait to be rid of us.

'Yeah? Go on, I can hear you.'

Tamla clears her throat. 'We need to establish the golden hour...'

'Golden what?' Lockheart splutters, a shy god embarrassed by his genius. 'Didn't think you lot needed to moonlight on your salaries...' he leers. 'Oh come on, are you thick or what? I'm only taking the piss...'

Observing that we do not find him funny, Lockheart closes his eyes with the exasperation of one who is too clever to be appreciated in his lifetime. I know the feeling myself, but I lack his self-belief.

'Come on, Inspector. Tell her to get to the point...'

He and I are men and, until I arrest him, natural allies. I facilitate him with my mute assent, burying my natural impulses and wondering if he can resist the temptation to bury himself with his.

Lockheart has booze burning through his nostrils, an aroma of indigested smoke leaking out of the corners of his mouth, and is long and heavy in the wrong places. I doubt he has seen a dentist since he was old enough to rub amphetamine into his gums, and were it not for his trying to be so fucking funny, I might be disposed to hear him out with sympathy.

'This is the point, Mr Lockheart,' I say. 'Asking you questions is the whole point.'

'And there I was thinking it was all about golden showers,' he sneers, returning to his theme.

'A golden hour is what we call the sixty minutes following a misper's disappearance...'

Lockheart's eyes are at it again, and Tamla heads him off this time: '*Mispers*. Lost boys like your son. The golden hour begins the minute no one can see our missing person, and encompasses the first sixty minutes in which they are lost. Knowing when that is is our best chance of finding them because their traces are still fresh.'

Lockheart sits down and folds his arms, denied of his opportunity to contribute.

'If we don't know when that is, we lose valuable evidence, which in this case means that it will make finding your son much harder than it would be otherwise.'

'That right?' He looks across at the blank television screen, perhaps out of habit or in search of a lost programme still transmitting. 'I never knew...'

'Of course, sir. Tapes get wiped, records are lost, memories become confused...' Tamla pauses, 'Was it you who called emergency services to report Iggy missing?'

Lockheart raises an eyebrow. His face is flushed and the flush deepens.

'No. I thought not.'

Lockheart thrusts his chest out with the dangerous kind of pride that believes itself to be innate rather than the valorisation of failure. 'If you must know, it was his bloody mum that did, that called you. I wouldn't have cared if he had fucked off and gone to live in the woods, not after how he has treated this family. Like shit we are to him. After all we've done, he threw it back in our face and went two doors down, didn't he? We weren't good enough for him, so he shacked up in his auntie's garden. And that's probably where he'll be when you find him, the little slag.'

'When did you last see him?' Tamla asks.

'Might have been a fortnight, might have been more...'

Tamla tips her head slightly and I take my cue.

'Fourteen days?' I ask, allowing the question to sink in. Until now I have been staring at Lockheart with stoic inexpressiveness, a face I pull to confound and unsettle civilians, which certain colleagues find condescending and aloof. With hard cases it is most effective when used in contrast to snapping suddenly, and I take a step closer to the armchair he is sat in, so that I am standing directly over him.

'He lives next door, and you haven't seen him in fourteen days?' I press. 'Two weeks have gone by, and you haven't even seen him come or go? Two weeks? Is that how it normally is between the two of you? Two weeks pass, and you don't think a single thing of it?'

'What you getting at?'

I hold my response down to: 'At what I asked.'

'Your trouble,' he grunts, 'is that you don't know the first thing about living here or understand us. We're not all tied to each other's aprons sitting down to family dinners. We don't have time for that. We have to work to survive, but you wouldn't get that, would you? A nice plainclothes salary and that pension to look forward to, and what with neither of you being from round here anyway...'

'You always this talkative when you're allowed to change the subject?'

'No, I'm not finished yet, and don't you lie to me. I can tell a mile off you're not from round here, either of you. And that's another thing,' Lockheart growls, not finding us so boring now. 'Why'd they send us you and not some local plod anyway? What d'they think he's done or got mixed up in for us t'deserve you, a posh cockney and a Scouse! And those expensive threads, you must be on the take to afford those. Why haven't they sent round an ordinary bobby, eh? Why you two, CID or whatever you are, with your fuckin' weird accents and threads?'

'I can see that not much is lost on you, but that's a nasty chip you have on your shoulder, Mr Lockheart. You ought to visit Harrow on the Hill one day. I'm sure you'd find we're a lot more like you than you think.'

I speak in what used to be a London accent, when people in London sounded like me, tethered to received pronunciation. In a cathedral city, twinned with Tartu, of just 50,000 people, with a half-open door policy to strangers, it does not go unnoticed any more than my fitted suits or Tamla's snakeskin ankle boots.

'That's a matter of opinion,' Lockheart snarls.

I hold his eye until he looks down. The county is divided by a plain that constitutes a Mason-Dixon line between north and south: the top, the beginning of the Midlands; the bottom, the start of the West Country — distance matters, and to these people we are unwelcome harbingers of another world.

'I'm from Yorkshire. Scousers are from Liverpool,' Tamla corrects our host, 'and I look nothing like one. We're ready to speak to your wife now.'

'Where do you get off? She can't speak to you now. She's knackered, isn't she?' Lockheart has got to his feet again, and needs to lean over me to get at Tamla. Gently, I press back against him so our chests are squeezed together like partners about to start a slow dance.

'We're being courteous, sir. We don't need to ask you permission,' Tamla flashes a false smile. 'You said she was in the kitchen?'

'You're not listening to me,' Lockheart says slowly, grinding his teeth. 'She is otherwise *disposed*.'

I keep my funny reply to myself and motion with my head to Tamla to do what she thinks best.

'Oh, for God's sake. Why not?' Tamla shoulder-barges past us and is about to open the adjoining frosted glass door that leads into the kitchen, when Lockheart barks over the dogs.

'Keep your nose out! You don't know what yer gettin' us into! Or what you're gettin' into yerselves... You can't just go in there. What about your bloody protocol?'

Tamla looks at him for a moment, winks at me and mutters, 'This isn't television, Mr Lockheart. You're in real life now,' and pulls the door open. Two barrel-shaped red labradors bowl out, followed by three children. The two boys are perhaps ten or eleven, and brain-dead at a glance. The girl, younger and livelier looking, may go on to more promising things, providing she leaves home before it is too late.

'Oh my days,' murmurs Tamla and disappears into the kitchen, reappearing some seconds later as the physical support of a plump lady in a purple mohican wig, which failing to fall off her head, may even turn out to be her hair. She is dressed in a translucent nightie that would have been several sizes too small for her new, and nothing else.

Lockheart, vindicated, steadies her and guides his wife towards the lounger, allowing her to slump at a graceless angle.

'I told you to let her be,' he coughs. 'You people never fuckin' listen, do you? Leave well alone is all you've got to do, and you can't even do that!'

'Mrs Lockheart,' Tamla attempts. 'We're the police. Remember? You called us earlier? We have a duty to ask you questions, so please don't listen to your husband. You rang us a few hours ago about your son, Iggy... Remember?'

Up until now it has not been clear whether Mrs Lockheart finds the room too bright to open her eyes, or simply prefers to get about with them shut, but as she starts to snore, matters are settled.

Releasing the sleeping woman's hand, Tamla asks her husband, 'What was the occasion?'

'Occasion?'

'Yeah, occasion,' I say. 'Between now and six this morning when your wife called 999 she's gone and got absolutely wasted. I imagine it wasn't a surprise birthday party you'd planned all along. You don't seem to be the type to hold back like that...'

'Doesn't need to be an *occasion* with our Cait.' If there was ever any colour other than red in his face, I can't see it now. 'Every day is the greatest show on Earth as far as she's concerned. Alcohol helps her change her mind quickly, and she doesn't like to stay thinking the same thing for long. If she'd woken up at her normal time, she probably wouldn't have called you at all.'

'But she did. Because she was scared,' says Tamla.

'Listen to me and listen good, because I am tired of repeating myself. That boy wasn't built for anything and she filled his head so full of stardust he thought he was king-shit, and now he's buggered off like a filthy ingrate, and you lot come here asking questions like we'd know the answer to 'em. If you want to waste any more time, go and talk to Eileen two doors down. She's his fairy godmother. We're just the mugs that got down and made him, aren't we?'

'There's no disagreeing with that,' I say. 'Thank you very much for your cooperation and time.'

*

Outside, Tamla sucks on a vape, and I turn to the bungalow and notice that Lockheart has not even bothered to glare out of the curtains and watch us shamble away, which shows a level of confidence that borders on contempt.

'That wasn't very satisfactory,' I say. 'I reckon we'd probably have grounds for obstruction of justice on the back of that performance alone.'

'At least!' Tamla snorts. 'Can he really be that much of a dick, though? If I did it, I'd at least pretend to be nice and ask us how many sugars we want in our tea instead of going for that full Bill Sykes routine.'

'He seems too guilty to really be guilty.'

'If he hasn't done for his kid, he's forced a litre of vodka down his missus's throat the minute he found out she called us, without a doubt. He's frisky enough to. And he's used to pushing people around. You can see that, a born bully.'

'Our friend does appear to be fairly indulged. He'd call that commanding respect though,' I venture.

'He might. But what about Iggy? It has to be him behind it, right?'

'Well he's certainly made the shortlist.'

'It has to be him, Terry. Mummy has been asking what the matter is with the bottom of their eldest boy, and Daddy panicked. Why else would Junior go and skulk in a caravan at his auntie's when he's got a perfectly nice house to be molested in?'

'So where do you put him now?'

'Under the patio. Lockheart did for him because he wanted to cover up his disgusting proclivities.'

'Boom, bang, bosh. If you believe that, then why don't we just go back and read him his rights?'

'Your heart is chaste, Terence. Do you really think it could be anyone else?' Tamla taps some imaginary ash off her vape. 'I mean, really?'

'Maybe.' Lockheart is brutal but would just as soon as ignore his son as kill him, if not want him alive to give him something else to complain about. 'Lockheart needs pain in his life, and Iggy provides him with that. Why cut off the supply?'

'Oh come on! Why do you think he was such a prick? Nobody's that crass. He's shitting himself and can't control his p's and q's. His nerves were all over the place. As yours would be if you were about to be sent away for being a nonce.'

'Perhaps he's a gent of the old school.'

'Come again?'

'One of the never-explain-and-apologise types who doesn't talk to the police.'

'Yeah, right. Of course he's guilty, I don't know why we're even talking about it. Use Occam's razor. Look hither and embrace all you survey. This isn't a place of greater refinement, is it? Our Mr Lockheart is a paid-up member of the scummy-side mafia. Just look at this place, for God's sake. It's notorious. How many disappearances is it this year?' Tamla asks, tapping the thin fingers on her free hand impatiently.

'Half a dozen... from here, this estate.'

'Exactly, at least ten going missing in this city every day, and most of them show within twenty-four hours. But here, on this estate, all of them teenagers, and not so much as a sniff of them. They just disappear. It has to be connected with life on this hump. Cause and effect, Terry.'

Tamla gestures with her vape, bellowing out great clouds of menthol at row upon row of roughcast bungalows descending down the hill in concentric half-circles, like graves in a military cemetery, continuing to the giant roundabouts and ring roads that separate this world from the other. 'It's the pebble-dashed sunken cunt of the world, isn't it? Fathers roast their own families for insurance claims...'

'That only happened once, and he didn't realise they were in the house.' My heart quickens as it always does when I am asked to make a formal defence of what I do not love, but feel obliged to protect.

'So what, Terry? It's of a piece, the grubby mentality behind it. La Famiglia lived along here too. Remember them? Wheeling and dealing and spreading their devilish mischief!'

La Famiglia were the first case Tamla and I worked, and our original claim to crime-fighting excellence. An extended community of distant cousins, restricted to crutches and electric buggies, lived along this road and tortured one another for their pin numbers and bank details. The police looked undeservedly competent when the serial denunciations began, the local news confusing their eagerness to incriminate each other for our good investigative work.

'And we should just sit back and let them pick each other off?' I try to keep the irritation out of my voice.

Tamla appears to consider the possibility. We both know where this conversation is going. She and I are part of a civil war waged within the working class, between the street cleaner and rioter, the employed and the vocationally challenged, the deserving and undeserving poor, our inconclusive skirmishing taking me back to breakfasts with my father. He would start on his eggs, a benign look of amused tolerance hidden under his moustache, and wait for my next assault on common sense. His dismissal of the *lumpenproletariat* and my defence of them was situational; I had spiky purple hair and played drums for Dirty Protest; he ran

Croydon Removals, convinced that there was always work for anyone who could lift, shuffle and break for tea. He and Tamla, whose mother turned tricks in Gipton, a detail she is never afraid to remind me of every time I exercise compassion for the idling poor, would have enjoyed one another.

'So? So stop trying to pretend we're dealing with ordinary folk here, Terry!' Tamla points the vape at me like a gun. 'They're not like you. They're not even like me, for fuck's sake. They're not Homo sapiens; they're trolls that breed and breathe and steal things and hurt real humans, and that's it. They've never fully developed into what we are. It might not be their fault. Perhaps they lack the necessary stimulus.' She grins. 'The point is Iggy must be at least the seventh adolescent to go missing from this monument to misery this year, and we're still in February.'

'Since February last year, you mean.'

'Same difference. Forget Englewood or the Bronx. This is the jungle right here.'

It is frightening how persuasive people who actually believe what they say are, as I find myself about to involuntarily nod in agreement. Their truth *is* the truth, and they will have you believing it right up until they stop talking, a point I try and remember in interrogations or when listening to Tamla revel in the occasional bitterness of her soul.

'You're forgetting about the normal people who live here.'

'*Normal*! What would normal people be doing round here?'

'They'd be here because they couldn't afford to live anywhere else.'

'Dwelling somewhat out of sight, eh?' She makes a show of looking around lest someone is hiding nearby.

'No, more like they're too ubiquitous to notice,' I say, scanning the houses. 'They're here, but you wouldn't necessarily notice them.'

'So, off the radar of law enforcement, then?'

'Exactly. Scraping ice off windscreens, stepping over empties to get their kids to school on time, wondering what the hell happened to the area they grew up in — boring things like that. Not as exotic as the milieu we normally move in.'

She smiles at me, enjoying the diversion. 'I joined the Force because I had to, as a job, and that's what I still treat it as. A job, not a crusade. I didn't study classics at Cambridge. I came up the hard way. Okay, I know you didn't go to Cambridge either, or study classics, but that's not the point. For you, the job is a sport and pastime. Why else would you enjoy the luxury of caring so much?'

She has a point. Inner necessity did not lead me here. I did not have to be a policeman. The police were neither a cool or natural option at my job club unless you were one of those punks who hated people and saw the law as a natural continuum for nihilist activity. For my peer group, they were at best a cry for help that ought not to have been issued, a French Foreign Legion for the unadventurous. Even my father thought I could do better and tried to encourage me to go to university.

What he could not see is that I lacked the courage to unveil myself in words that I admired in real writers. My prose style was a decorative confidence trick, helped by a quiet and intense charisma that persuaded the band to ignore the evidence of their senses and believe I could keep time, whereas in actual fact my drumming was all over the place, and English teachers to say I should write, when my notebooks were full of plagiarised squiggles. Self-respect demanded that I should do a practical thing well and follow that thing through to the end. It was an aesthetic pose that I was in some ways too young for, or too young for anyone else to think I was ready for, but my only hope of attaining moral seriousness. If I threw my whole life behind an unpopular vocation, I might find a way of spending time with myself and not consider that time wasted. Beginning as a worn-out cynic in uniform, I slowly progressed to a bruised idealist in plainclothes, both postures coming naturally to me in a way that a career in the arts never could. Tamla is right: I did not have to be a policeman. I became one because I thought I was already in a book.

'They're the *victims*,' I say, 'our natural constituency. The ones that haven't made it good in the system, but don't call us pigs, filth or cuntstables, who feel relief when they hear the sirens coming.'

'I'm not sure I know who you are talking about,' she laughs.

'You do, Ms Sioux. The punters who don't get pissed for breakfast and don't end up on daytime telly because they've made their nieces pregnant. The frightened majority who have the misfortune to look like their serial killer neighbours. Their taxes are why we form the thin blue line, Tamla. We do it for them.'

Tamla's ocean-blue eyes twinkle with merriment, and she tries to look embarrassed for me.

'Terry, Terry, Terry! *Passion!* I love your passion, Terry — it's what men lack nowadays. Oh well, I suppose it isn't that bad round here, just ugly and a bit eventful. Right. Shouldn't we be talking to the auntie of our misper?'

We walk three doors down in an easy-going silence, the kind that glues our days together; two buccaneering public servants going about their duty as the world around them falls apart.

'You be the one to knock, please. A virtuous woman is bound to prefer your aftershave to my lipstick. Especially one with taste. This place looks a cut above the local average, don't you think?'

The signs are that Tamla is right. The house has its own name, 'Cair Paravel', and is lathered in a minty-green paint, a bold decision on a road where standing out is not to be encouraged. To take temptation further, there are two panpipe-playing fauns balanced on their hind legs in the front garden, issuing an irresistible challenge to local vandals.

'Hello, Mr Tumnus,' says Tamla, touching one tenderly on the nose.

A cloying waft of vanilla gushes forth from under the door,

more The Body Shop than a decomposing body: overripe, rich and fruity. The sort of sweetness that usually disguises something sour. I forget to proceed to where this line of detection might go, as the door swings open before I have a chance to knock.

'Mrs Pertwee?'

'Mmm...' The woman who answers the door appears to have risen from a broken sleep, or some vague waking approximation of it. In spite of appearing in what look like a shop assistant's overalls, there is a dreamy sensuality about her that I would welcomely follow back to bed. My professional filter stops this going any further, and I introduce us both.

'I'm Detective Chief Inspector Balance, and this is my colleague DCI Sioux. Would you mind if we...'

'I know, you'd better come in, my brother rang ahead. There is no Mr Pertwee, just me and my daughter and my mum here,' she yawns. 'I'm sorry. I've just finished a night shift at the Esso. I usually try to have a power nap when I get back and then sleep in the afternoon.'

'We appreciate you making the time for us,' I say stiffly in a voice that is not quite my own.

'That's alright. I can't imagine my brother-in-law being very much help. Not where police or even people in general are concerned,' she replies, addressing me, looking at me, yet keeping something in reserve for herself.

'You're not wrong.'

Mrs Pertwee's formal outward presentation does not appear to be geared towards finding a mate. I try not to inspect her on irrelevant criteria, but years of finding women attractive make this as hopeful as it is disingenuous: she is no longer the sum of her possibilities, and perhaps even less than them. Nothing noteworthy about that in a postal code not overbrimming with opportunity, were it not for the suspicion that songs were written about her once, an electric current of fading vitality still humming in her ash-brown eyes. My expression gives me away, and she begins to fiddle with her fringe, as though it could make something significant happen or change.

'Yes, he doesn't like the police or anyone much else for that matter.'

She pats down her hair, which is arranged sensibly in tandem with clothes worn like a prime minister's wife; any lingering sex appeal a secret between her and a past she does not want anyone else to discover. It would be hard to place when the self-neglect started, but by her early twenties she may have already decided that making an effort was too self-regarding. My silent attention is bothering her, and she allows us to pass through the only half-open door. I pretend to find the short walk across the threshold interesting and try not to look at her.

'Your nephew. He lived out the back in a caravan. Is that right?' I ask, trying to find my rhythm.

'Yes, that's right. I suppose you haven't found him yet, have you?'

Slightly taken aback, and feeling like we are not about to, I reply, 'No, not yet. We're not exactly spoiled for leads as things go. But it's early days.'

'His dad didn't give us anything at all,' says Tamla. 'In fact, he suggested there isn't anything off about him vanishing like this. That it's quite normal for him to go off grid for a bit.'

'He said that, did he?' Mrs Pertwee lifts her knee up and scratches her thigh. I flatter myself to think she does this for me, but the possibility that it could be itching has at least as great explanatory potential.

'Yes,' I reply. Usually I have a fair idea of what someone is going to say next, yet in this case, I feel less sure than normal of my ground. And this must be because I care about what this person might think of me; never a good position to be in as an investigating officer.

'He's an arsehole. Though you'd already know that, being detectives, and quick on the uptake.'

This is a little sharp, but I make light of it. 'He actually said that you might be a more profitable line of enquiry.'

'That was good of him.'

'When did you see Iggy last?' I ask.

'I don't know. I mean, I know he's been out there in the caravan... but I didn't exactly have to see him to know that, if you know what I mean.'

'So you don't have a definite last sighting?'

'No, I'm sorry, I don't.' She draws up to her full height, my height, eye level with me. I lift my chin a little but cannot see over her. 'That's not very helpful of me,' she adds, clicking her tongue. 'But I did notice that the cups of tea I'd leave outside for him were collecting. That may have been a couple of days ago.'

'And then what did you do?' I say.

'I asked his mum, my sister, if he was with her, and she said she hadn't seen him in ages, and that might have been why she called you. I'm sorry. Perhaps I should have done something earlier, but his dad is right. He does take off on his own a lot.'

'So he has vanished before?' Tamla interjects.

'Yes, but never in a way that I lost sleep over...'

'So you are worried this time, then.' Tamla looks at me amused, not quite sure what to make of this woman. She is not 'nice' enough to be innocent, but too careless in her replies for anyone trying to hide their guilt or complicity.

'Yes. I suppose I am.' Mrs Pertwee bites her thumb, perhaps thinking better of going on. 'The thing is, he seemed to be going before he had even gone, disappearing in front of me, little by little. We had stopped talking and... well I was always so frightened for him because I could see this coming, you know, like something approaching from far off, and you know *you* can get out of its way, but the one you're looking after *can't*. And it's your fault for not doing anything all that time you saw it coming, when there was still time to do something, before it was too late.'

'You think he might have been into something dangerous?' Tamla asks, adding, 'Locally, I assume?'

'Very locally,' Pertwee laughs. 'You police. I've never been able to tell whether you know the half of it or are in the dark about it all.'

'In the dark about what?' Tamla presses, digging her heel into the carpet at angle that is bound to leave a mark.

'To what's going on here, here on this hill, with people living in their homes in broad daylight like they're hiding in the deepest darkest part of the woods.'

Tamla raises an eyebrow. 'It's as bad as that, is it? But that doesn't tell me all that much. Why's it so dark here?'

'This is where all the ley lines, the negative ones, you know, meet.'

'Yes, I think I have heard that.' By her tone I can hear that Tamla is running through the mental calculation of whether our interviewee is a little touched or not, as knowing my partner's intolerance for cosmology, this kind of talk will not make Mrs Pertwee a new friend.

'So you think these lines are influencing behaviour around here? Yours as well, perhaps?'

'Why not? I can feel the blood rush through my toes up into my tights when I walk upstairs sometimes, right into my thighs.' Mrs Pertwee rubs her shapeless olive slacks. 'Anyone decent feels the bad energy about the place. It's the best way of finding who the good people are, the ones that notice it and are appalled. I've felt it since I was little, this road. It's the hill of death. It's why the Romans called it Golgotha. You'd have to be very brave not to be a little scared.'

Mrs Pertwee glances at Tamla before meeting my eyes, confident that I will not be put off by her reverence for folklore or witchery. Her eyes seem to have changed into different colours, her left a downpour of ocean rain and its neighbour a plume of coruscating sunshine. Before they return to mellow-brown again, I decide she must be wearing weird contacts, a private desire to beguile hiding behind the exoteric reflex to fit in with the neighbours.

'There is no point looking for Iggy unless you are ready to find them all,' she says, her voice suddenly sharp and wakeful, the dream she was waking from now over.

'I'm sorry?' Tamla asks.

'Iggy's not the only one, you must see that,' Mrs Pertwee replies, and straightens the sleeve of her blouse. 'Come on, do you mean to say that you people have noticed nothing?'

Hearing this sounds the death knell of my first impressions, and I realise I have to quickly revise everything I thought I knew about Mrs Pertwee. Hers is a face that needs to be seen in motion to be properly appreciated, as once she loses her buttoned up aspect, it is clear that she has been borrowing someone else's appearance. She is a leading lady playing the part of a frump to avoid being typecast as the heroine.

'And what are we supposed to have noticed?'

'The other ones, of course.'

There is colour in Mrs Pertwee's face now, a hard-earned redness to her cheeks that gives her the ruddy glow of a farm worker having come off a strenuous shift, and just a trace of moisture about her temples. It is quite a transformation, she has lived between the parts for years, her injured core filtered through all her disguises. I feel the impulse to protect her from the horrors that necessitated this subterfuge, but I am afraid to. I might be going mad and merely have imagined the whole thing.

'I could give you the names,' she adds. 'But seriously, you must already have those, and would you really do anything about it if I did?'

'That depends,' says Tamla, glancing at me nervously. 'If we had a better idea of what you're alluding to, Mrs Pertwee. I am afraid at the moment we're having a little trouble keeping up. Terry?'

'You think we should be speaking to several people, not just you?' I say. 'About other disappearances and not just this one, is that it?'

'It's no use asking anyone else to help you. They're all too frightened. And I should be too. But if you can't make the connections for yourself, then nothing I say is going to help you.'

'You say other people are afraid, but you aren't.' I ask her, 'Is there a reason for that, something you know that they don't?' My interest in her answer is not simply professional, I realise knowing more of this woman is rapidly becoming an end in itself for me.

'Come on, Inspector. For the fearful, what they fear most will always happen. They'll be proven right again and again. Better to not care too much, and that way give yourself a chance, eh?'

Tamla looks at me and shrugs. The speed at which a person can change before your eyes is alarming. Our hostess is now standing with her legs slightly astride, hands on hips, literally daring us to head into the trees with her, an ancient and terrible priestess slathered in mud and woad, her hands slowly closing round the neck of intelligible discourse.

'I've seen you both on the local news. You crack cases.' She smiles. 'But it's selfish to go only for the easy ones, ones that cost you nothing if you solve them. What's happened to Iggy won't fit inside that box...'

Before I have time to reply, she adds, 'Don't tell me you can't take risks. You can afford to. You're not like the other police I've seen up here.'

'How's that?' I ask unwisely, trying not to be distracted by what I am afraid is rising lust.

'You don't have families to go back to. God knows you're both gorgeous enough, but you have that single look to me.'

'I beg your pardon?' Tamla exclaims. 'I'm sorry, but you can't say that!'

'Forgive me, but lonely people always give themselves away.'

I am not going to deny it. She is right. Enforced self-sufficiency is a detective's lot and each of us carries the taint of separateness. Tamla transferred here because her partner wanted to live amidst the green fields, then left a year into the experiment for a fireman. I have not fared better. Despite falling in love with every interesting girl I've slept with, my fear of normality, turning into a soap opera, or having someone get from one end of me to the other and find out that there was nothing there, kept me single until that classification aroused suspicion. My desire for praise and admiration, divorced from love and companionship, is the author of professional triumphs and personal misery; immaturity and narcissism helping me pretend that I prefer it this way, since, as tiring as loneliness is, I know I am not a man people can feel sorry for. Mrs Pertwee seems to sense this, and I can imagine my life having taken a very different turn had I the self-confidence to let her in twenty years ago.

'I don't see what that's got to do with anything,' says Tamla.

'You've nothing to lose.' Mrs Pertwee turns to me. 'Either of you. You don't have to fear losing your position in a community you don't belong in, or a part of the world you'll be well out of when all this is over. No children or loved ones to uproot. Destiny sent you here for a reason, I figure. Can't you see that?'

What I see is her and I living in this house and getting ready for work together every morning, she at the Esso garage and I on the industrial estate, changing tyres or unloading barrels for the brewery, happy but not brilliant, she satisfied and not scared, and Iggy, my nephew, safe and snug in his caravan. At this moment, whether through overwork or her hypnotism, I could almost say yes to this; all she need do is brush my hand, and I am afraid that I could embarrass myself.

'I can see that you want to suggest a great deal, but are going light on the specifics, Mrs Pertwee,' I reply.

'Iggy is not the only kid around here to "take off", is he?'

'If you mean the recent disappearances in this area, say so. You're implying that they might be linked?' asks Tamla. 'Is that it?'

'What else could it be,' answers Mrs Pertwee, and then,

addressing herself to me, asks, 'When does a coincidence become a pattern?'

I am again distracted by the smell I first noticed when I came in, but as I scan the room, I have no idea where it is coming from; her place is a prissy rebuke to poor hygiene. It is almost as if the excessive cleanliness provides protection from fears that cannot be banished by other means. The place is replete with familiar objects: competently assembled flat pack shelves, an unloved row of books that someone who does not read might acquire, compact discs that were bought in charity shops, prints that came free with the lustreless furniture, and behind them all — nothing... just the flat single dimensionality of surfaces. Yet the funky aroma I noticed is growing stronger. The same sweet rot as before, if anything, richer and more sulphurous, concealing something pickled and preserved, that repulses just below the surface. Again I envisage myself and Mrs Pertwee together, walking hand in hand into the fields that lead to the ancient mazes and hill forts, naked and aroused, in a lovers' pact, knowing that when we wake, we will do so elsewhere, far from here. It is like falling asleep on the tip of a spear, and I pull myself out of it.

'I'm afraid we're not oracles or telepaths. If you think there is somewhere we should be looking for Iggy and the others, we'd appreciate it if you just told us.'

'It's too late for looking. The young ones here on this estate, they're not coming back.'

'Why aren't they?'

'Because...' Mrs Pertwee pauses and shakes her head like it doesn't really matter if I believe her or not. 'Because posh people are taking our children.'

I draw a breath and wait for the punchline.

'And we're letting them with our silence.'

'Shit...' mutters Tamla, turning to me. 'I think she means it.'

I nod. I know this will not end in my fast-track promotion, in a photo shoot with our local MP, or with the hero triumphantly returning home. It is the kind of case that will end only when the suffering finally ceases.

'Thank you,' I hear myself say, 'Could you please elaborate on that?'

CHAPTER TWO

A SHORT-TERM EFFECT

Nana Pertwee listens to the voices and is reassured that one of them belongs to a man. The bungalow houses three generations of Pertwee woman, bitter bitches all, not counting the boy outside, who hardly counts as anything. They all miss a man who could make them laugh, even if she is the only one that says so. Whenever she mentions this they groan and tell her they are sick of hearing it, making her feel like a drunk that repeats the same stories, which perhaps she does, as they look fed up and angry, not like they're enjoying a good wind up. Often they lose their tempers, then say they love her, and she wonders whether they mean it, before losing track of matters and falling asleep again.

Why is she still in bed? The wisps of grey light peeping through the curtains bewitch her. There is certainly something off about her being naked — she'll tell her daughter that when she comes in; she usually wears a nightie in bed like a decent woman — but before this can happen, Nana Pertwee turns over and promptly forgets what she was making a point of remembering. For a few moments she is blissfully happy to be warm in her sheets and comfortable and safe, before it all starts again, and she panics as she does not know what is going on, or who the man's voice belongs to, nice as it would be to have one about the place again.

'Myrtle,' she croaks, the dryness in her throat sticking whatever resides in her painfully together. She has heard lots of voices recently, some she recognises, others not. Many are men, none are women, and some are neither, and while appreciating the chats, most of which are far better than anything she actually says aloud to anyone anymore, the places they lead conversation to worry her. She would like to join in, as despite resembling a largish foetus, having forgotten how to eat much of the time and starved herself, her desire to communicate persists long after there is nothing left to say, just as a skeleton endures the loss of its fleshy coating. Contributing would be a way of remembering she is still here, as so much of her no longer is. Elements vanish as friends and loved ones die, which may have made her passing easier, were it not for how happy she sometimes is; her soul remembers what the mind forgets, the distilled essences of the past: sounds, inflections, smiles and kisses. When people say they have no idea what she is going through, she wants to tell them that it is not all bad! They can't see her husband gardening as a thousand autumn days loop and plunge like birds cartwheeling in the sky, or the twins playing knee-deep in knotted green algae, their little hands carrying tadpoles that are about to be released into a great brown river she forgets the name of.

Nana Pertwee shudders, completely awake now, an avalanche of melancholy awaiting her whenever she recollects too well, an ordinary day if she forgets. Time takes that which should never be taken from you away. Blank incomprehension has its uses. It was never easy trying to understand things, having to have everything explained to her twice. Now at least they don't bother, because it is not her fault, at last. The permanent acceptance of less prepares the way for acquiescence with annihilation; life and death being outcomes of equal value that initiate similar states every time she turns over in bed.

Why is she still even here? Because she hasn't died yet, but she will, and soon. She knows she is in danger — they all are. She edges closer to the wall so she can feel her back pressed against its reassuring hard coldness: there's nothing there. She really does not know how she got here, the bed she was asleep in moments earlier, *the one she has slept in every night for the past forty years, her bed. It seems suspended in space; she is in an invisible box. And why have they put this thing in here, in here with her! A realisation occurs; it is ghastly — she is in its house and not her own! Why else isn't her husband here (dead, as he may have been these past seventeen years)? Where is her lovely little granddaughter (long and lithe as she is now)? Or her daughter, when she needs her (falling in love with a policeman in the living room)? Why aren't they here, protecting each other from this menace that forces her to forget everything? She has failed in her responsibility to defend her own. What was it that took them away from her and watches her lying awake in this unrecognisable place waiting for her to disappear?*

Nana Pertwee reaches for the clump of packed moss stuffed helpfully into her pillowcase, her nerves are nature's way of telling her she won't get a second chance, and as quickly as she can, she swallows the crumbly biota whole before she can forget anything else.

*

There are five of us rammed into the trailer with space just for four. Together we are the ruling junta of South Wiltshire Police, a cross section of talent, if not the best this county can muster in times of crisis. Tamla, myself, Chief Constable Desmond Grace, who takes up enough space for us all once his body language is accounted for, and Detective Sergeants Max Orridge and Dexter Christopherson — the former our longest-serving and most jaded operative, and the latter our youngest and most desirous to please. As befits a discussion on our systematic failures, the Chief is doing most of the talking.

'It has most of the merits of a theoretical puzzle, but it is hard to feel particularly moved by this unfortunate turd's fate. Whatshisname, Reggie...?' Grace asks.

'Iggy. Iggy Lockheart. Should be a piss-take name. But isn't,' I reply.

'Iggy? Right, *Iggy*. Not an easy sell, the rivers of acne and all those spears pinned to his lips like flagpoles. I'm not saying he is a product of incest, but a face to launch a thousand appeals? I think not. And what did he do apart from keep the local tattooist in ink? He festered and dawdled, lacking the wit or industry to bugger off and waste his life somewhere less crappy, somewhere further away from us. One more unpromising specimen who has added absolutely nothing to humankind by turning up. Thank you very much for bringing him to my attention, Inspector Balance.'

'I expect he has his finer points too, sir, once you get to know him properly,' I suggest.

'Doubtless he has, but we need him to be a cross between Jo Cox and Madeline McCann, don't we? And what have you given me, DCI Balance? An unlucky berk with Celtic crosses and drawings of goblins on his arms.' He chuckles and wipes the sweat off his temples with the impatient calculation of a man about to devour a meal. 'And then you say there are the makings of an even bigger problem that our boy is but one part of... and if you are right about that, and I pray that you are not, then we are in the shit, aren't we?'

'I concur.'

'Good man, of course you do. And a Royal Visit at the end of the week, which I am beginning to think may even be a good thing. I'll take anything over reality now.'

We all would. Grace's face is an imperial purple, a creamy-white kiss curl stuck to his forehead, and a clumsy passion to make life less miserable for the weakest, disguised by the embarrassment such an admission would cause a policeman of his generation, the reasons for his verbosity.

He brushes at his temple and misses the curl again. 'What I don't understand, sorry, one of the *many things* I don't understand, is how did we not see this coming? Don't we have systems in place to automatically flag this kind of hulla-goola up? Computers, databases, all that carry on? I thought we were a twenty-first-century operation...'

'We were, or were pretending to be. However, we've struggled to centralise information since we lost our IT team.'

'Centralise —what a foul word. Try not to use it again. Still, at least I know what that lot did now.'

'A good chance for a bit of old-fashioned coppering though, sir?' offers Sergeant Christopherson, who would wag his tail if he had one, his enthusiastic face a reminder that we are all being undermined by time when even the policemen are getting younger.

'It may come to that, Christopherson. God help us.'

'If it does come to that, God help us!' Detective Sergeant Orridge snorts. 'Most of our lot's legs give way the minute they leave a Fiat Panda.'

'Then you'll have to be there for them, Max,' says Grace. 'Mother Duck for all her little ducklings, taking them all under your strong and capable wings.'

As an ex-para, but a believer that any system that cannot allow for a bit of anarchy does not deserve a police force, Grace is not a typical Chief Constable. He survives and occasionally thrives in the role because after nine years of austerity no one else wants the job, or to manage us and this crumbling nest of unconventionality. In his tenure, the 'Millennium' Police Station has been converted into retirement flats, the holding cells now comprise four Fiat Pandas tucked behind the leisure centre, and our current headquarters is a website, supplemented by four Nissen huts and a large trailer on an industrial estate, donated by a local radio station, that we are presently squeezed into. Whether all this is temporary or the future of provincial law enforcement will hopefully be settled at the next general election, but if the left wants to abolish the police, they had better get their plans in order while there is still time, before the right finish the job themselves.

'But are we sure, absolutely *sure,* that the evidence is leading us towards some seriously sinister balls, Balance? Is there any lingering possibility that this might not be so bad as you and this woman say it is beginning to seem? Mightn't this lad, I don't know, have found Yahweh and buggered off to a retreat with some foxy piece in robes? Or countless other explanations for his disappearance that could be proffered by common sense, no?'

Free will is the often hypothetical knowledge that you could reply with something other than what you know you are going to say. 'Unlikely,' I reply.

Grace waves me away. 'That was what I was afraid of. Always the melodramatist, Balance. DCI Sioux, please, you're working on this too?'

Tamla proffers, 'I'm with Terry, sir. It's the age and type of misper that stand out for me, and the numbers of course. None of that conforms to the usual pattern for disappearances. You only have to dig a little to see that.'

'Which means we can't have been doing much digging?'

'We've been spread pretty thin.'

'That's a bloody given.'

Grace pulls out a handkerchief and rubs the outlines of spit that collect at the corners of his mouth. 'This is terrible, absolutely terrible,' he mutters, a warning that a civilised intelligence lurks beneath the repartee of an outraged misanthrope. 'This isn't how things should be.'

'I quite agree, sir,' I reply.

'Of course you do.' Blinking slowly, he asks, 'So, numbers and context, DCI Sioux. Where does the usual pattern stop and the unusual one start? Tell me that.'

'Right. So, missing people, we average ten a day countywide. Last year we had 300 reports, 193 kids and 107 adults, which is consistent with the numbers reported elsewhere. We ignored most of them, mainly because we don't have the manpower to follow through, and also because there's usually nothing to respond to. Young kids mostly return from the woods within a few hours, and the old ones, the dementia cases, come to their senses shoplifting packs of frozen cod from Iceland, then ask the cashier the way back home. That's the general pattern with mispers: the ill, the old and the very young. Even teenage tearaways check in for their tea. Hardly anyone actually *disappears*. It happens, but it is a tiny minority of all reported cases. And even with them, only very few stay vanished.'

'Except now they're beginning to?'

'It's starting to look that way,' Tamla replies.

'I see.' He closes his eyes and eventually opens them again as if he hopes something significant may have changed or come to our aid in the brief interval. 'And so I return to this. These disappearances haven't given *any of you* cause for suspicion until now? Even without some Dilbert collecting stats on a database, I'd have hoped South Wiltshire's finest might have detected the makings of a spike. It's not as if we're talking about missing bicycles, is it?'

'In an ordinary year we would have, and in a quiet one we would have been all over it, but I don't think any of us are old enough to remember when we last had one of those. Since last Christmas we've already had the poisoning mystery...'

'And an ex-prime minster to grill over little boys,' scoffs Detective Sergeant Max Orridge. As a self-identifying Tory, Orridge detests anything that compromises pageantry and performance, especially questioning a political hero on matters pertaining to buggery and the age of consent.

'Which with the last run of retirements, redundancies and transfers,' continues Tamla, 'makes it easier to overlook the rising phenomenon of population reduction in our local communities...'

'You're barrack room lawyers, all of you.'

'Just saying, sir. Anyway, we're noticing it now.'

'So who are the rest of these mispers, are they so different from the usual waifs and strays?'

Tamla nods. 'They're all in their late teens or very early twenties for a start. And as Terry said, they're all from here, not drifters, crusties or tramps. Mostly from Telegraph Hill and the Heath, and bumming round at home, like Iggy. None of them were sleeping rough or in shelters. They're all traceable to fixed abodes.'

'Which of course makes it eerier. I see that.'

'And they're going in quick succession,' Tamla adds.

'Do we have any cause for optimism at all, then?'

'None yet. As far as we know four more have already gone missing this year — one from Fairfax Battery, another from Poet's Way, and two more from Hanging Hill. Iggy, if he stays dark, brings it to five.'

'Girls or boys?'

'Six lads, three lasses, all of whom would have had to have known each other, or at least known *of* one another, even if they weren't mates.'

'Right. Not good.'

'It's too much to hope they're not connected. As I say, I think Terry's right, sir...'

'Thank you, Tamla,' I interrupt. 'As I was saying, sir...'

'Oh shut up, Balance. Carry on, DCI Sioux. I'd rather hear you than him.'

'Well, like Terry says, we have to take statements again, review everything we think we know, and treat this as one single investigation.'

'Balance, so you agree with every depressing word of this, I know. Sioux, you'll support your partner of course. What about you, Orridge? And you, Christopherson? What do you make of our body-snatching apocalypse? Spontaneous self-combustion used to be all the rage round here, are we looking at turbulence on the ley lines, crop circles gobbling up our young, or has darkness descended on our happy land? Come on, don't be shy!'

Christopherson looks at me, issuing a silent appeal, and then at Orridge, for reassurance, before mumbling, 'I wouldn't say it was circles or combustion, sir... What was the other one?'

'Let's knock this *Close Encounters* bullshit on the head, eh? This isn't *The X-Files*.' Orridge scowls, ever the pragmatist. 'It's all well and good coming on the full Thomas Magnum, hogging headlines, acting flash, and donning the deerstalkers, but we need to grow up a bit and hang fire, eh? Before we start knocking on doors making pillocks of ourselves, we should secure our lines of information, be sure of what we're wandering into. You follow? Let's just make sure we've done all the sensible stuff first before we see the hand of the devil in this. Whatever happened to trying to tick the obvious boxes, eh?'

'You've got me there,' Tamla says. 'I don't see anywhere obvious to tick.'

'You wouldn't, Tamla, because you're looking for a master crime, alien abductors or a deep state conspiracy, whereas in all probability there isn't a felon to find. This lot, Iggy and company... well come on, just look any them! Couldn't they have all just gone on a, well, you know, a beano, a jolly, you know, a pikey's picnic someplace?'

'Please!'

Undeterred, Orridge continues, 'Or a secret chav package tour abroad? Honestly, I would give this lot the full Jeremy Kyle referral. You know what I mean? I wouldn't be surprised to find them all in some massive bum'ole time share in Magaluf they've all signed up to, and why would they bother to inform us first?' he grins, the sun glints on his fillings. 'I just don't see it, anything suspicious about a group of no-marks taking off like this. And if not Spain, who's to say they'll not all be found putting tents up at a bloody festival this summer, and then we'll all feel right tits, won't we? Let's wait this out, they'll show, there's no rush. Patience is the overlooked part of police work, to be honest.'

'Another one to chalk up to the long arm of coincidence,' I say.

'Why not?' Orridge shrugs his shoulders. 'Like you say, before this nutty woman came out with her accusation, none of us had even noticed anything. And there's a reason for that, Terry. Because there was no bloody thing of value or importance to have noticed.'

'Actually the reason lies a little closer to home than that, Max; it's that no one gives a damn,' I reply.

'I don't know about that, boss. They might be doing it themselves, on purpose like, hiding I mean, to get one over and make arseholes of us, you know, so we look bad,' Christopherson interjects, 'I mean, you drive over there, get out of the car, and it's "pigs" this, "pigs" that. It's a game, basically. They might even think it's a harmless prank, making us look like tits, like Max says.'

I like it when Christopherson acknowledges my seniority by calling me boss, though I like it less when he talks shit. Fortunately, Tamla, who is far nicer to me in front of other people than when we are on our own, is at hand.

'Textbook complacency,' Tamla replies. 'I'm not saying I am not guilty of it myself — I was when I first looked at this thing — but like I say, you dig a little and a different picture emerges.'

'Perhaps the picture before you dug is the right one. Deep isn't always right — it overthinks. Stay shallow and on the surfaces and you see most things for what they are. Life isn't all that complicated, Tamla,' grumbles Max.

'A score of kids vanish into the ether, not even simultaneously, and you don't see anything sinister emerging, Max? Come on!' I goad.

'That's the trouble.' Grace coughs into his arm. 'Because I can't see anything emerging, innocent or sinister, plain or simple. Nothing either of you are saying coheres for me yet. Yes, the numbers are totting up and the pace is accelerating, but if we accept foul play, why hasn't a single body been found anywhere? We're talking about nearly a dozen missing people for God's sake! Where are the headless corpses in shallow graves, found by a dog-walker, waiting to claim our attention? Missing bodies eventually turn up as dead bodies — that's the law of conversion. We could be looking at a murder investigation, and while I can believe that there are no search parties being organised, are you telling me that there aren't even any worried parents asking questions? Wouldn't there be if they believed their children were in danger? These kids just vanish and not even the bloody *Journal* notices, it has me thinking, does everyone know something we don't?'

'They're all secretly on the bloody razzle somewhere, sir. That's what I'm trying to say!'

Although I do not like it when people laugh at opinions they do not agree with, the superiority it implies too like the aloofness I actually feel, I chuckle at this and look at the floor with sympathy.

'That would make life easier, wouldn't it? But it makes just as little sense as their going in the first place,' growls Grace. 'Who's ever heard of a group of kids going anywhere quietly, Max? Especially these days. They'd be sightings, for Christ's sake, even if they were being walled up in a *cellar* they'd still be tweets and photos all over the internet. No one under forty does anything privately now. It's all online.'

Tamla curls her lip. 'Your first reaction nailed the question, sir. The stuff about Iggy being a loser. These mispers aren't the type of kids to attract a lot of attention by taking off. Think of where they are from. Four weren't even reported lost by their families. The exception appears to be Iggy's aunt — we'll tell you more about her later — but as for the others, maybe those responsible for them are just relieved. Relieved and passive...'

I pick it up from her. 'These people see this as the way things are and the kids, well, they're too old to be cute and they take up space. You said it yourself, these aren't faces that anyone in the wider world would necessarily care are no longer with us, sir, however wrong that is.'

'Not all that wrong,' laughs Orridge.

'Perhaps the families think that too, for now,' I continue. 'Think of the missing girls in care that end up fronting for grooming gangs. Most of them are from places like Hanging Hill, aren't they?'

'Your point, Balance?'

'We're not talking about old-fashioned communities here — this is society's dark ocean floor. It shouldn't be, but that's the way it is...' I look at Tamla, who is nodding with enthusiasm. 'My guess is that wherever these kids have got to, they went of their free will, but once there, the doors closed, and now they're shut in.'

'And it hasn't registered because whoever has been charged with their care gives as little of a damn as we appear to,' adds Tamla.

'Unsubstantiated conclusions!' cries Orridge. 'And demented conjecture! I tell you, this isn't foul play, it's just...'

'Of course it's foul play,' snarls Tamla. 'It's just that no one, not the families, social workers, teachers or us, gives a shit.'

'Gives a shit yet,' I say.

Grace lumbers over to the tiny stove and frowns angrily at the kettle. 'I can't think of anything sadder. At this point tea can't actually do any harm.'

*

I nod and lift the dented kettle off the gas hob, then carefully edge my way round Grace's protruding bulk to the sink, mindful that he does not like to be touched by other men, even those innocently squeezing past him. His potent aroma, a plummy cologne picked to disguise the fumes of brandy, reminds me of the summer my parents first suggested I use mouthwash, sharing close quarters on a caravan holiday in Whitby. That did not stop my drinking but taught me that a transparent effort to please, however hypocritical, could exculpate any sin in civilised society.

Edging open the tiny overhead cupboard, I choose him a mug with a pair of petting dinosaurs on what is at least made of bone china, the rest of us making do with farm show freebies that feel like concrete pots with handles.

'Are you taking sugar again, sir?' I ask.

Glancing absently at a daddy-longlegs gliding through the refracting light, Grace suddenly brings his fist down on the worktop, crushing the spindly-limbed Pholcidae. 'You're right, you both are. Yes, yes, I think I am beginning to see it now. They, or whoever they are, knew we'd *agree* that the boy is an ugly brute and that investigating him, or anyone like him, would be hopeless. They relied on it. Moreover, they know if a strapping beauty, let's call her Prunella, vanishes with her horse box, I'd hunt her abductors down like dogs, with the help of the *Mail on Sunday* and every salmon-pink-corduroy-clad retiree in the shire.'

'This is what we've been trying to get at, sir,' I say, trying to disguise my impatience with the speed of my boss's deductions.

'But if they go for the progeny of our *proles*,' Grace goes on, 'found congregating in our supermarkets and car parks, with mothers and sisters but never their fathers, all looking a bit alike, and fagging and boozing and eating the wrong things, daytime television and self-respecting society will give them a free pass. Of course, bleeding hearts and artistes like you, Balance, will say I've just evoked a stereotype, but our victims know better and so does whoever is preying on them. No one gives a damn about a missing *stereotype*... Some lives are more important than others, and they've got us there.'

'Maybe whoever is doing this thinks they're doing society a favour, then?' Orridge grunts. 'Not that I think anyone is *doing* this.'

'If you were a vigilante, they'd be juicier targets,' I say.

'What about a sicko who thinks he's a vigilante?' Christopherson shoots. 'He might even be keeping them all alive someplace and harming them?'

'No,' Grace replies. 'This isn't a serial killer, crazed psychopath or vigilante taking out oiks as a public service because he hates them. There's something else at work here even though I don't know what it is yet. Whoever is vanishing some of our most vulnerable people is familiar with our attitudes. So far just testing us, I fear, wondering where we'll finally draw the line. Once they've run out of stereotypes they'll start on ordinary civilians, and then work their way up the food chain to the rest of the natural order.'

'And take someone you actually care about,' I say to Orridge.

'Quite. Eventually it might be the Prunellas we can't find. And why not? As professionals we have already collectively shown we are not only incapable of *preventing* what's been happening under our noses, we're incapable of even bloody *noticing* it. The point is: do we actually care, then, care enough to go after these unfortunates? Or will this be another of those mysteries that excites conspiracy theorists until it suddenly doesn't, petering out like it never was? Whoever is behind this may even be clever enough to know when to stop. The whole thing is forgotten entirely until it all starts again, far enough away for it to not be our problem...'

'Press indifference and police inactivity,' says Tamla. 'I can see the documentary in ten years, asking why nothing was done at the time. Your face and mine flashing across the screen, Max, as they shame the hopeless twats that were charged with public safety, and who ended up letting everyone down and fucking the whole thing up.'

'Batshit crazy,' Orridge protests. 'We have yet to ascertain whether anyone has even been harmed, and you want to turn this into the hunt for the Ripper!'

'You weren't there, were you,' sighs Tamla, 'when we searched the River Severn for a missing rock star in Dunlops, that went missing at the height of his success? We didn't move quickly, we figured it was a publicity stunt, or something to do with drugs, or a perhaps he'd just run off with the tour manager's wife. Yep, it would be fair to say we didn't take it too seriously, but once we got going we saw some things that changed our minds. Not our misper, we never found him, but unreported black bodies in Nikes dredged up in mud that I'll never forget the colour and consistency and smell of. I close my eyes and still see those dead kids covered in that river shit every time I think I am not doing my job properly.'

'I don't see what that has to do with anything,' says Orridge, reddening. 'I'll be honest. I've seen this coming for a while now. We're all having it taken out of us with stress. I mean look at it this way, we can barely keep the peace on a Saturday night, and yet we're seriously suggesting we begin an investigation that has waste of police time all over it. With the Queen, I mean *Her Majesty* the Queen for crying out aloud, coming here on Friday? We'll look back on this and think we were mad!'

'In short, I am suggesting that a proper investigation is what we do,' says Grace, 'and I don't care how big this gets or what resources need to be called in. I take full responsibility. It's going to be different this time. On our watch no one, understand me, doesn't matter. These are our own people,' his voice is trembling, 'so we'll investigate every disappearance because we're police, even if this has us going down in history as the first force that priorities the disappearances of scabby little gits and troglodytes over kissing the royal arse! Let it, I say. I honestly don't care. I don't have long to go anyway.'

I put down the cup of tea that no one now appears interested in laying claim to and watch to see how this plays out. Our exchanges are often hyperbolic and bad-tempered but, ultimately, signify nothing. This time we all sense it is different — what is decided here may set a precedent.

'Sir, please, the *Queen* is coming on Friday!' repeats Orridge rallying round the House of Windsor like a faithful bannerman in a medieval battle. 'We need to establish some sort of objective order of priority here...'

'That's what we are doing, Max. I'm ready to turn this county apart to find out what has happened to these kids, and I'll enjoy doing it,' thunders Grace. 'And if, by the time we've finished, our dainty shire no longer resembles the best-kept village in England, but Stalingrad, it'll have been worth it. I've a year left before I die trying to tie my laces, or am finally fired, and I'm sick to my guts that we have a well-deserved reputation for doing nothing for the expendable half of this community.'

'Something's just struck me, sir,' interrupts Christopherson. 'Does anyone think these disappearances may be connected to the Queen's visit, you know, that her Royal Highness is the real target?'

Grace closes his eyes.

'Alright,' says Orridge. 'Let's suppose there really is something going on here like what you are saying. If there is, then there's only really one place to look. It's gangs, it has to be... Eastern Europeans... They've been turning up all over town, emptying charity boxes, begging on the streets. If there's anything to this, then it has to be the Eastern Europeans.' He draws his face up close to mine. 'And we've been turning a blind eye to them because of so called political correctness for too long. They're mixed up in everything now. Sod all this woke bullshit. That's who we should be going after.'

I laugh at him, lift the unclaimed cup of tea, and sip the lukewarm mixture like I am enjoying it.

Tamla looks like she wants to bite Orridge's jabbing finger. Unlike us, Max Orridge is very much the public's idea of a rural policeman insofar as he resembles a gardener heading to a funeral party, ready to address the citizenry in the stilted jargonese of a 1970s industrial dispute. As a self-identifying realist, his job should be to stop squaddies pushing and sometimes hitting each other outside our city's single nightclub, but as a patriot determined to fight the Brexit wars by any means, his obsession is Eastern European gangs. To that end, he leaves tractors and quad bikes with their keys in them in the hope they will end up at a farm sale in Poland, confirming his fear that we have been invaded. Meanwhile my and Tamla's longevity upsets him: he never expected us to stay. She is a 'breeder' who failed to settle, and I a careerist who should only have been here for a few months — why are we still here?

'Trust me on this, friends. There's no way this caper, if a caper it be, is homemade.'

'So let me get this straight,' I say. 'The Romanians, Bulgars and Albanians are so desperate to steal our jobs that they're kidnapping our unemployable youth just in case they end up interviewing for the same openings?'

Orridge looks hurt. 'No, for God's sake, of course not. Use your loaf for once, Terry. For a clever guy you say some stupid things. This is more likely a sex thing. That's what I reckon. Sexual stuff.'

Tamla shrieks with laughter, 'You are honestly trying to tell us that Eastern Europeans are sex trafficking kids off the Heath? Because ours are good with languages maybe? Please!'

Orridge goes quiet, and looks to Christopherson for support.

'Of course, the other thing is our gangs, you know, county lines,' Christopherson suggests. 'I mean, they're everywhere now, so why not here? We could be being targeted by the big cities. This has at least some of the hallmarks, right? The right age and background and everything, these kids look just right to be mules. What do you think, Terry?'

'I'm not sure, but it is not impossible.'

'They're the wrong colour, for a start,' snorts Orridge. 'This isn't the only black person killing the only other black person in the village. This is white kids going missing.'

'Jesus, Max. There's just no need.'

'Don't pretend you don't know what I mean, Terry. We touch one and they're protesting nationwide on all their marches and all that, but they keep killing each other at a regular rate, and it's still somehow our fault.'

'A gang is going to work with whoever lives in the locality, Max,' says Christopherson, 'and they come in all colours.'

Next to Orridge, Dexter Christopherson, a sweet boy, could be the future of community policing; the blinding turquoise suit that conducts electricity, a sense that police work is compatible with charity fundraising, and a floppy centre parting worn like an ambitious estate agent, fulfil the minimum criteria of reassuring the public. But his fear that he may be too nice for the job, and that only loyalty will stop him being sacked, means that he must echo our obsessions, and remain a stranger to his own instincts. Renting houses and leaving bugged laptops to be stolen and tracked pleases reality television, who have given him a ten-minute spot on *Police, Camera, Action*, and he is popular on the school and college circuit, the smiling face of our local 'copaganda' campaigns, which of course feeds his fear that he is not real 'police'.

'The urban gangs are coming here,' Christopherson ventures. 'That kid knifed in Southampton shows we had a gang problem as early as last year, and now this. It could be a recruitment strategy or something like that, right? They caught those blokes up in Swindon, that they nicked with all that money and watches and knives. This could be like that, bribing and turning local kids to become their soldiers.'

'Exciting,' says Tamla, watching Grace, who is now stood with his eyes closed shaking his head, 'inventive, au fait with the news cycle, and very of the moment, Dexter. I'm not buying, though.'

'Come on, Tamla,' he pleads. 'Knife crime is pandemic, endemic, you know what I mean. Kids are dropping all over the place, even if real gangs aren't here perhaps country-mouse has decided to copy city-mouse, and settle the usual carry-on with blades?'

'This is more persuasive than the Hungarian Mafia taking over,' I say, 'but not much more.'

'Come on, boss, why not? Think outside the box!'

'Let me lay it out for you, Dexter. You think the dregs of Leyton, instead of bullying kids to come over and sell drugs to bumpkins, are actually kidnapping or persuading our kids to sell drugs in their or other cities? Seriously? Our lot are so hopeless they couldn't sell bread to the starving.' I watch his face slowly collapse.

'You may not like it, but drugs in this city are mainly the domain of posh dropouts and landless labourers. And while they might be getting it into their heads that carrying a knife completes the look, there's no way even an unserious criminal enterprise is going to think our wurzels are recruitment material. They'd stand out a fucking mile in Battersea and be chopped into squares in Tottenham. And if it's the other way round, and they're kidnapping our kids to deal their drugs here, why aren't they on the streets dealing? Where are they? Sorry, Dexter. I just don't see it.'

I feel for Christopherson. He tightens his lips in what looks like an effort to stop them wobbling, the fatal first step in the casual chain to tears. It is a face he has made before and it occurs to me that this is a childhood pattern destined to be repeated until he finally experiences the validation we have contrived to withhold from him — which he may yet do when we stop being such arseholes.

'Criminality seeks the path of least resistance and your version is just too much like hard work, Dexter,' I tell him.

'So we should take his aunt's accusations seriously?' Orridge says. 'That some rich folk are behind it all?'

I look at Tamla, who appears quite happy for me to do the next bit on my own. 'I was going to come to that,' I say. 'I feel like the aunt is sincere, not mad and not a bullshitter, but may have brought some of her existing prejudices to this... mystery.'

'So basically an unsubstantiated and vague accusation without the slightest shard of evidence,' says Orridge. 'A woman's intuition! Go on, I'd like to see you rescue this lost cause.'

'Albeit a more intriguing one than yours about cheap package holidays and gang warfare... Your gut really tells you there is something to this, Balance?' Grace asks.

I am about to see if anyone wants to microwave the tea, to allow me time to make a case, when the caravan shakes like cheap scenery, the banging on the door only stopping when Tamla shouts, 'Just come in, won't you!'

PC Lydia Holiday, a rangy gazelle dressed in combat trousers, boots and a peaked cap, missing only a machine gun to complete the paramilitary look, cries excitedly, 'We've just had word, sir.

Another one has gone missing, and the same place too. The misper's nan... She's been snatched from her bed...'

'What? Iggy's... *grandmother*?' I ask.

'Yeah, yeah, his auntie, Eileen Pertwee. She's just called 999, she says their nan has been... taken.'

'*Taken*? You have got to be joking...' Tamla shakes her head. 'We were only just up there...'

Grace cracks his knuckles. 'Internment of all posh people will have to wait. Look lively. You lot are on your way back up to Hanging Hill, and I don't want any of you coming back down here again without a misper.'

CHAPTER THREE
THE HANGING GARDEN

I glance briefly at my reflection in the rear-view mirror before getting out of the car, adjust my hair in a way no one apart from me will notice, and forget to close the door as I get out, doubling back clumsily to shut it. This is the second time I have been up here this morning, and while I want to remain sensitive to decorum in a house of grief, I grin as Mrs Pertwee acknowledges me, in the time-honoured tradition of allowing those we are pleased to see know involuntarily. Rather than upgrade me with a correctional scowl, having lost a nephew and now her mother in a matter of days, Mrs Pertwee appears to be inviting brash familiarity. Standing guard at the threshold of 'Cair Paravel', her long fingers tapping on her thighs and mousy hair bundled in a stack like a Palaeolithic warrior-queen, I wonder what else has changed, before registering a pair of raspberry leggings and an aquamarine crop-top that were not there before. This alone is enough to arouse suspicion, but unlike Christopherson, who looks genuinely puzzled by her perky bonhomie, I am carried away by the suddenness and ease of seeing someone in a new light, again.

'Preparing for another Spice Girls reunion, Mrs Pertwee?' I say, unable to help myself, conscious that I may be being played for a fool.

'Yoga, Inspector. Anything to take my mind off all the shocking stuff that is happening. It's the only way I can see God in this madhouse.'

'It'd be difficult for him to miss you.' She is stood blocking our way to her front door with an imperious disregard for the cold and propriety.

'That's what I thought. Better he watches me practise the pelvic tilt stretched over the floor in this get-up, than tip a bottle of cheap white down my throat in those horrible work clothes you saw me in earlier.'

'God must have seen worse.' I can feel Christopherson breathing heavily behind me, and I step off the path into the garden, so he can at least see what the delay is all about.

Ignoring him, Mrs Pertwee replies, 'Not if he is watching me. You're probably a good drunk — I'm not. I change completely and start talking loudly and swearing and making up stories about people that aren't true to show my friends I know things they don't. And if I am by myself I get so pissed that I just stare at the sink, and after a while don't even know I am there.'

'Isn't getting into that state the point of yoga?' I take a step towards her and stop, as she does not move back, and I do not want to be standing on her toes.

'It might be, but I'm talking about getting pissed, Inspector. Yoga I do for the Lycra. I have a sort of fetish for it — I like the way it clings to my arse and makes it look bigger. A second skin.' She slaps at her femur. 'Drinking, especially in my family, is a different sort of exercise altogether.'

'I met your sister earlier. It looked like she'd overdone it on the breakfast wines. You struck me as being the more cautious type.'

'Oh, boring you mean? She's nothing compared to me when I get going. Exhausting trying to figure me out, isn't it?'

I am in danger of being professionally embarrassed. Neither of us appears to be in a hurry to get to the point, but I have to, as this is getting out of hand, and there is no such thing as appropriate flippancy when dealing with missing persons.

'I don't try and figure people out, Mrs Pertwee. And when I do, only as much as it is necessary to know whether they are serious or not.'

I cannot tell whether Mrs Pertwee is hissing at me, or if running her tongue across her teeth quickly is simply her way of suppressing laughter. Christopherson is stroking his goatee impatiently beside me, Tamla having driven up to Iggy's school with Orridge, and a muttering line of neighbours are respectfully forming a vigil round her gate. We have an audience she seems completely unaware of, and I put this down to shock rather than having eyes only for me, much as I would like to believe it.

'I'm sorry your bad luck is holding out, Mrs Pertwee. Iggy and now your mother? You must think you're in a waking nightmare,' I offer, careful to not sound too jaunty.

'Any excuse to see you again, Inspector,' she says, brushing her elbow into mine as she turns. 'I must just be enjoying the attention.'

Adjusting my smile, so that my face looks like it is trying to make the best of a painful accident, I check the desire to sway unsteadily into her, and trying to look no further ahead than one foot in front of the next, follow her into the house.

'At last,' whispers Christopherson. 'If you ask me, she's buying time for someone.'

With a thud, he walks straight into my back. Mrs Pertwee has stopped again, blocking us into the corridor. My first thought is she has just thought of something she wants to share on an impulse, but as she dropped her hand to her hip again, and leaning on the wall with her elbow, it seems as though this is where she would like our interview to continue for the time being.

'You told the operator she was, "*taken*"?' I ask.

'Yes. I think I said something like that. I didn't know what to think at first, but what else could it be?'

'Forgive me if this sounds silly, but taken in what way? Are you saying someone came into your house and literally took her away with them, snatched her as it were?'

'Well, I don't know. I mean she was gone, just gone, just like that,' she snaps her fingers. 'I went into her room, and basically, she wasn't there. She can't walk without help, her knees and hips are completely buggered, so she couldn't have got out of there herself. She has Alzheimer's as well. It's got pretty bad. That's why I said to the operator "taken", or whatever it was I said. I know that sounds dramatic, but I didn't know how else to describe it. Or what else to make of it. Somebody must have got her is what I thought.'

'And practically, how could they have done that do you think?'

'Through the window in her bedroom? There's no other way out of the house without my seeing her leave.'

'Right, what I'm trying to get to is this: did you actually witness an abduction?' I feel Christopherson shift uneasily behind me, as once again our physical position precludes him from partaking in the interview or seeing our witness.

'Oh no, that's why "taken" was all I could think of by way of an explanation. That is, unless you can see something I can't, and think there was another way she could have left?'

'Not unless she could move of her own free will.'

'Impossible, and as I say, I would have seen her.'

'And there's no one else that you might have spotted around here, looking suspicious, that could have... "taken" her?'

'No one. Only that lot coming and going.' She points at her neighbours. 'And what would they want with my mum?'

'Then it isn't so much that she was taken, but that she actually *vanished*? Isn't that what you're actually saying happened?'

'Am I?'

'I think you are.' I try and put it as helpfully as I can, 'If you haven't seen her being "taken" by anyone, or physically leaving here of her own accord, what else would you call it?'

'I guess you're right... but when you put it like that, vanishing, you know... it starts to sound like something from a fairy story, doesn't it?'

I smile uncertainly and Christopherson clears his throat loudly. Standing on his tiptoes, he is a foot shorter than me. Bringing his face over my shoulder like a waiter forced to communicate through a service hatch, he asks, 'Do you think she may have taken off herself? I mean are you sure she can't get about on her own, that she's never popped out before without you knowing and thought that she might like to again... There's a window in her bedroom? Couldn't she have got out that way by herself?'

'Absolutely no chance of that. She hasn't been out of the house on her own in years.'

'You don't think she might have tried to make a break for it, show her independence for one last time?' Christopherson persists, 'No offence, but old people can be crafty and stubborn. They were young people once.'

Mrs Pertwee shrugs her shoulders, and slides backwards and then sideways into the sitting room, allowing myself and Christopherson to cut in so we are both facing her at last. 'Like I say, she can't walk without help. And there's no way she would have got through that window on her own.'

'No one else has been in the house? Not your daughter or any other witnesses you saw who could corroborate what you think has happened here?'

'No. Annoying, isn't it?' she laughs.

Christopherson looks at me with bemusement.

'You actually told the operator "they" had taken her,' he says. 'Funny figure of speech, that, if you didn't see anyone do it. I'm guessing an old lady like your mum couldn't have had that many enemies.'

'Did I say "they"?' Mrs Pertwee touches her lip with her finger. 'I don't remember that. I was in shock, you know. I remember making the call, but I don't remember speaking those words. Sorry.'

I have no control over what goes on in other people's minds, but if I did, Mrs Pertwee is regarding me in a way I would like her to if this were a far-fetched dream — one I would wake warily from. The pleasure she appears to derive in my standing here, from my existence itself, and I from her need, is too close to what I desire to be trusted. Trying to snap out of it, I ask with as much tight-lipped rigidity as I can feign, 'When, then, did you actually see her last?'

'About five minutes before you and that pretty little girl you arrived with earlier came to the house.'

'She was still in your house when I was here with DCI Sioux?'

'Oh yes, as far as I know.'

'And you didn't hear anything later, before you came in to check on her, no sounds of her being "taken", or commotion of any kind?' Quickly I try and work out the timing for myself.

'Absolutely nothing. That's the strangest part, really. Unless it happened when you were here, but then we would all have heard, wouldn't we?'

'We would have. And how long was it after we left that you went in to check on her?'

'You know, not that long. I think... maybe half an hour or forty minutes at most.'

What she says is just about plausible, but with the kind of margins that only work if you are already inclined to give her the benefit of the doubt.

'So whoever took her did so noiselessly and in something like record time for moving old ladies?' I ask, wishing there was some way this could look less bad for her.

Christopherson shakes his head at the floor ruefully. 'While you, Mrs Pertwee, were in such shock that you waited a further half hour before calling us so you could fit your yoga in and see God?'

'Be nice, Sergeant,' Mrs Pertwee replies. 'I called right away. It's not my fault it took so long for you to find out or come. It was nothing like half an hour, and the yoga I did waiting for you. Something awful might happen to you one day. It's not like you can plan your response to things.'

'You may be right,' he says, walking past her into the little open-plan dining area, 'but with all due respect, Mrs Pertwee, I have to say that if it did, and I were you, I would be more worried about how this looks. And I would act a whole lot more concerned too.'

'I think I'd better have a look at her room, and Sergeant Christopherson will check all the exits,' I say, trying to keep things friendly.

'Of course, Inspector. I was going to suggest the same thing. You'll be much better at knowing what to look for than me.'

She turns away from us, and I am conscious of the effort it takes to look away from her backside, which appears to be moving in time to music played at a frequency no one except us can hear, evoking desires so simple as to insult the intelligence of anyone who cannot accept that desire is sometimes so obvious. 'The weird thing is...' she mentions over her shoulder, stopping abruptly — I stumble into her and harden instantly, '...is the window in her room,' she says, resting against me firmly enough to be aware of my anatomical reaction. 'Sorry,' I murmur, aware that at this moment she knows me better than I would want anyone to.

'What about the window?' calls Christopherson from the lavatory, where he is banging against glass.

'What's weird is how they... I'm sorry, I am back to "they" again, how they or even she could have got through the window,' she continues, acknowledging with a smile what we both knew seconds earlier — that my erection was pressed against her arse. 'It was locked from the inside when I came in with her tea, actually locked, if you'll credit it...'

'That is weird...' My judgement is a meek and flimsy thing; intimacy creates trust, but if she is having us on it is with the natural aplomb of a practised and seasoned liar. 'And that's the only way out of her room if you didn't see her, right?'

'I am afraid so, Inspector. A bit hopeless, isn't it?'

'You sure it was locked?' asks Christopherson over my shoulder.

'Positive. Another reason why her going doesn't make sense. It's just bizarre.'

Christopherson grumbles behind me, 'Hard to believe a word, boss.'

Replying to him, but talking to me, she sighs airily, 'I suppose you think I should be acting differently. People complain I'm a cool customer, that I don't do feelings...'

I would contradict her, but before I can open my mouth I notice it again: the odour from earlier; meat ripening in the blistering sunshine, a target for enterprising flies to lay their eggs in, reaching everywhere at once, like the breaking of bad news. I lose the tightening in my loins, and try not to wretch, hanging on until the stench lifts so suddenly that I suspect it was banished by my revulsion. As with the first time I sensed it, the episode is over in a twinkling. I want to ask Christopherson if he noticed it too, and I wonder why I had not mentioned it to Tamla earlier, but he tugs my sleeve, whispering sceptically, 'She's hiding something, boss. Her attitude's all over the place. And look at her — she's dressed up for yoga! Unless she's a nutter, it's county lines. It's got to be. Snatching a woman and kid — it's got to be a warning...'

Mindful that Mrs Pertwee has uncommonly good hearing, I cut him short, 'Maybe.'

'They've got to her. Please, can I...?'

I groan. While all things are futile, some things are more futile than others, and I realise that Christopherson will not be denied today. 'Go on. Permission to take your best shot.'

'What are you two nattering about?'

Christopherson tries to wink at me, and instead squints with both eyes, reminding me of a suspect attempting to disguise the effects of the drugs he has just swallowed to escape arrest. I allow him to move past me so that for the first time he is standing in between Mrs Pertwee and myself, and thanks to this distance, I begin to feel more like a policeman.

'Mrs Pertwee, there's something we have to ask you,' he announces haltingly, a little nervous having to do this for real. 'You alluded to goings-on in this area to the inspector and DCI Sioux, "dark" goings-on, but wouldn't say exactly what they were. We want to stop anything worse from happening, but we need to know what you were talking about to do that. And if you'll forgive me, I'm going to come right out and say it for the record, and that's that I'm not buying any of this stuff about posh people. That line you gave earlier.'

'What will you buy then, Sergeant?'

'Well, I would be receptive to a little bit of candid honesty. Drugs, for example. Have you seen much movement of them recently?'

'Drugs? There have always been drugs here,' she replies, pursing her lips.

'I don't mean Hells Angels or crusties. I mean new faces, pushing new drugs.'

'I'm not sure I understand what that has to do with an old lady going missing, Sergeant...'

I can sense her trying to peer round Christopherson and reconnect with me. Ignoring the impulse to come to her aid, I peel off into the missing person's bedroom, which has the desolate feel of an unoccupied cell despite the magenta bedding and fluff-flannel rug, which I catch in the door. The bed has been pulled away from the wall to either make the room look fuller and less lonely, or because Mrs Pertwee has been playing around with the window when conducting her own investigation. The window itself is bolted from the inside by a nasty-looking latch. That observation is welcome; I want things to be just the way she says they are. But my next discovery disconcerts. The span of the old woman's window frame is too pokey to push a pensioner with dementia through without at least occasioning a struggle that anyone with hearing would think of mentioning to an investigating officer. I nudge the catch. It won't move without considerable force from the inside, and the glass would have to be broken from the outside for anybody to get in that way.

On the bedside table is a cup of water with bubbles forming round the inside of the glass, and next to it a tiny knotted ball of stringy green hair. I pick it up. It has the consistency and feel of homegrown skunk but smells of stale mint with just a touch of the odour that made me gag earlier. Stuffing it into the small cellophane bag I carry round for treats like this, I notice the bedding is unruffled and that nothing in the room has the look of having been disturbed. There is also no sign that the old lady's assailants thought of clothing her as they dragged her into a cold Wiltshire winter: her dressing gown still hung on the door and cupboard door closed. As a crime scene, it does not add up.

An unwelcome possibility presents itself: Mrs Pertwee is capable of lying to me, even as she likes me — as devastatingly obvious as it is painful. Of course, anyone who does not relish the challenge of being lied to, all the time, has no place being a detective, yet my disappointment has the raw quality of teenage rejection. *Not her*, I mouth silently.

My phone plays a burst of Philip Glass. It is a message from Tamla: *'Beware of our lady. Even if she is right about them poshos.'*

*

Re-entering the living room, Christopherson, faithful to his own fantasies, is making painful progress in his production of a Wessex *French Connection*. 'It isn't the drugs in themselves,' he stresses. 'They're not really what I want to know about.'

Exchanging glances, I shake my head.

'It's the gangs that are running them.' Without missing a beat he elaborates, 'The innocent lives that are being destroyed. Evil people who aren't scared of using desperate kids to get what they want. Not the sort of people you want to be protecting, by the looks of things.'

'But who am I meant to be protecting?' she appeals to me, evading her interlocutor. 'Am I being accused of something here? Are you saying I've got something to do with this?'

'I think you have just got to hear him out, Mrs Pertwee,' I say.

'With respect,' Christopherson insists, mopping his hair back, 'I'm having trouble reconciling your attitude in your earlier interview, which my colleagues inform me was extremely cryptic and knowing, with these protestations of naivety. You have to be frank with us, Mrs Pertwee. Lives might be at stake.'

'I'm trying to be!'

Christopherson blinks, a sign that he is thinking and prepared to raise his game. 'Alright. Just try looking at this from our point of view for a minute, and imagine what you'd think... if you were us listening to you.' He adds, 'Wouldn't you think your behaviour is just the slightest bit suspicious?'

'Well my mum certainly wasn't in one, a gang,' she exclaims, 'and nor am I, if that is what you are getting at!'

'*Iggy*, Mrs Pertwee. He's the one we're talking about. Iggy. Your nephew is the link, the sausage in the roll, not you or your mum. He's the one that's drawn you all in, and what's more, I think you know it. I repeat, you could be leaving him in harm's way by being evasive with us.'

'I've tried being frank with you, but you don't want to know!'

'Money, did he suddenly come into any?'

'Definitely not that. He was a borrower.'

'Were there any mystery trips to places, visits to cities he had no cause to go to before?'

'Nothing like that.'

'Did you ever go into his caravan?'

'Sometimes. When it really needed a clean.'

'Weapons, expensive watches, nice clobber, ever see any in there?'

'God no!' She laughs dismissively. 'No way!'

'Tattoos then,' Christopherson asks with a pathetic kind of

desperation. 'He had them, apparently. How about any new ones, or any new markings of any kind?'

'Tattoos,' she caresses the o's mockingly. 'There I might be able to help. There was an ugly monster thing with its name underneath, Pussycrook or Tin Cock, something silly like that...'

'Be specific please?'

'Um, no, noooo, The Iron Giant, that was it. And a scrawl in a sort of sign language. Hobbit writing maybe? Are those the sort of specifics you're looking for, sergeant?'

'Not exactly, no.'

'Then what exactly is this interrogation in aid of?'

Christopherson looks to be having trouble with his lips, which are twitching soundlessly of their own accord, perspiration forming like dew over the bristles of his goatee. 'Probably not gang markings then, Dexter,' I intervene. 'Perhaps if...'

'Just a minute please, Terry. I haven't finished,' Christopherson gathers himself, ready to commit everything to one last line of enquiry. 'Mrs Pertwee, have you heard of cuckooing?'

'I'm sorry?'

'Cukooing. Is it a term that means anything to you?'

'Is that like dogging?'

'Please do not try and be funny with me.' Christopherson's voice is unsteady and I am afraid that he may be about to either cry or completely lose his cool. 'You do realise that we're police officers trying to save members of your family from the threat of imminent violence or worse?'

'I know. You've already said as much.'

'Mrs Pertwee,' I interrupt, 'teasing us isn't going to find Iggy or your mother. Nor is behaving like a hostile witness. The sergeant's questions are fairly reasonable. You should answer them.'

Christopherson reddens as Mrs Pertwee shuffles from one foot to the other like a girl waiting for a chance to go to the toilet. 'Did I hear you just confirm that I've become a suspect, Inspector?'

Her voice is softer when addressing me. 'Don't I have a right to a phone call if that is the case?'

'The term he used is *hostile witness*', snaps Christopherson, 'and you don't get a phone call until we've arrested you. Let me break cuckooing down for you. A group of ruthless and completely immoral people move into an area with the aim of establishing a base to sell hard drugs from, and once having established their base, turn the area to shit. It's happened in Swindon, it's happened in Marlborough, it's happening in Trowbridge and in Warminster too. And we're as close to being sure that it is about to happen here. You may find that funny. We don't.'

'I didn't say I did,' she smirks.

'These scumbags', Christopherson is het up and allowing it all out now, 'target people that they perceive to be vulnerable. The young, alienated and lonely, living in the least auspicious of circumstances. Next they establish a bridgehead in the local community by taking over the mark's house, and then use it as a base to supply product from. A bungalow is better than a caravan for that...'

'You mean here, sergeant? This actual house?'

'Why not?' Christopherson concludes. 'Listen, Mrs Pertwee, you couldn't get Iggy or your mum into any more trouble than they're already in. Every minute now is precious. Remember, you are perfectly safe saying anything to us, whatever you share will remain confidential, no one else need know, and we can put a guard on your house if it comes to that,' he adds, even though it is not in his nature to lie, 'but we have to move *now*. And no more games. We're running out of time.'

'Alright, Sergeant,' Mrs Pertwee replies, standing straight, an anaconda preparing to engage in cannibalisation with a smaller mate. 'That's quite a story and like all stories I'm not saying that there isn't a good deal of truth in yours. But it still bears no relevance to me, this house, my mum, or my nephew.'

'I thought we'd stopped playing games...'

'No, let me finish. I'm sorry. I'd love to reward you after all that effort, but I can't in good conscience do so, no matter how preposterous, crazy, or half-arsed you think my version of events might be.'

'I don't think you have been listening to what I've been saying here...' Christopherson wears the look of a man who, having felt the earth move for him, does not want his hard-earned orgasm upstaged by an earthquake.

'I'm sorry, Sergeant, but you need to hear me out. The very idea that Iggy, or myself, are being used, as you'd have it, as contacts for serious drug dealers or addicts or gangsters or whoever they are, is so... I don't know... *so stupid*, I could wet myself laughing, were your insinuations not so crazy and offensive.'

'Mrs Pertwee, the sergeant is...' I try and interrupt.

'None of what you're saying has happened here. I want my mum back, of course I do, but *cuckooing*, and all the rest of it, oh come on! You should listen to yourself. Are these gangs meant to be kidnapping a pensioner, riddled with dementia, for insurance? And if they want a ransom, why haven't they gone for my daughter yet? She leaves the house every morning, is far easier to get hold of, works at the arcade, is a much better prospect as a hostage in every way. But in your telling, Sergeant, they go for a granny that can't remember her name and a boy who's of so little value to the world that even his dad won't trust him to wash the car. Some collateral they'll have there!'

'Drugs make for strange logic,' Christopherson mutters, but I can feel the fight leaking out of him.

'Drugs? Don't talk to me about drugs!' Mrs Pertwee cries, clapping her hands. 'They're too easy to get round here to bother with any of your *Top Boy* nonsense. With the number of users in this place, no kingpin needs to go to the trouble of establishing a monopoly by kidnapping random members of the public. It's ridiculous. There's just no need.'

'So you admit that then at least,' Christopherson's voice is sheepish, and I have to allow him to finish this in his own way to rescue something of his dignity.

'Admit what?'

'Admit that Iggy was connected to the buying and supply of drugs in this area?'

'Of course, anyone could tell you that. Who isn't?' She points to the front door. 'It's a users' paradise out there: cocaine from the Albanians at the carwash, pills at the pub, ketamine at the vets, mushrooms from the hippies, anything you want from the students, and heroin from the losers on the roundabout. I mean, they sell wacky baccy-infused lozenges and hash oil at the National Trust shop if you ask them nicely! Is that what you want to know? Seriously, anyone wanting control over that lot would be fighting over scraps with our entire community infrastructure. The only lowlifes Iggy hung round with were the same lost boys he knew at school and some broken down old rockers that lived in the Purple Hearse. As for drugs, sure. I even went to him for them when I needed them, but there's no way he'd have the courage to get involved with serious people — far less face them down and instigate a turf war!'

Christopherson has the look of a man beaten on his specialist subject at a pub quiz, and instinctively edges closer to me, jutting his chin out, so as to conceal the overworked blood vessels in his cheeks. 'Mrs Pertwee...' I say.

'Eileen, please.'

'Eileen, I appreciate that you think our grasp of the facts of life fall well short of your own, and that we might not be very good at our jobs, but what have you really given us to work with? You present us first with the story of a kidnapping, plausible enough, as we don't believe this is a hoax, only to go on and then demonstrate how such a thing would have been completely impossible in practice. Unless, that is, we're to leave the world of facts behind and embrace supernatural explanations. You then rule out the possibility of your mother acting on her own initiative, but shoot down the sergeant's well-intentioned efforts to identify a plausible external actor that could offer you a way out, and you do this with something approaching relish. You're right — shock does strange things to people, but you appear most at home at rearranging expectations and keeping us guessing, which, in the circumstances, is nothing short of bizarre. I honestly don't know how we can even do the paperwork on this without bringing suspicion on ourselves. Really, it is that crazy.'

'There's no stopping you when you get going, is there, Inspector?'

I want us to be more than good friends, but she has left with me with no choice. 'I haven't finished yet. The only thing protecting you from becoming our prime suspect is a lack of motive. And the fact that anyone trying to hide their guilt would have to be mad to carry on as you have.'

'Mad... how do you know I am not?'

'I don't think so, not you.'

Mrs Pertwee knocks her toe against my shin and whistles with mock exasperation. 'I can't believe you're making me out to be the criminal here. You've got me thinking that I'd have been better off not calling you.'

'Not reporting a crime is itself a criminal offence,' says Christopherson, finding his voice again.

'But the inspector has just said that I don't have a motive, and I haven't, have I?'

'You haven't, Eileen. But unfortunately for you, this particular mystery hasn't occurred in isolation. Regardless of whether the sergeant is right about the encroachment of gangs in this area, your postcode is rife with disappearances, after all you were the one who told me that we can't solve one without looking at them all, weren't you? Why else the remarks about the posh people that you still haven't given us a proper explanation for? As things stand, you are the closest thing we have to a link connecting the weirdness together.'

She pulls at her hair, ruffling it and allowing it down. 'How so?'

'Unlike anyone else who has gone missing in this area, you've actually mislaid two people known to you, and whereas we don't know where they are, you're still here, aren't you? You see, lightning has struck you twice. It's the only break we have, and when we find one, we start to push, because we might just then establish a pattern, which is the kind of thing we go crazy for. I believe you know that.'

'It does look incriminating when put together like that, doesn't it?' she says, toying with her hair. 'You'll have to be careful not to lose me next... But what about the motive? What about that?'

'To be honest, we don't need one yet; reasonable suspicion that you're a bird that doesn't fly straight is enough to take you in for questioning. And before you put words in my mouth, we're not suggesting you're a criminal mastermind or even an accomplice to a crime, only that you need to think very carefully about what you are trying to achieve when you decide next to not be completely frank with us.'

'I was telling you the truth about posh people.'

'That's where we started, and unless you can substantiate it, which you have yet to, I would ask you not to deflect again. Even if I believe you, no one else will.'

'But how do you know they're not? If you would help me, I could prove it!'

'Oh that's just balls,' Christopherson snaps. 'Here we go again. I've had enough of this, boss. She's either lying or on the meds.'

Mrs Pertwee looks at me. 'Inspector, you know I am just as much of a victim here as my mum or Iggy.'

'That's why I am still giving you the benefit of the doubt, even if you do think I have been hard on you. But as things stand, unless your mother leopard crawled across the living room whilst you were in a yogic trance, the tale you've told is basically magic. What else can I say in my report?'

'But what if it was *magic* they used? If the answer to this involves magic.'

'Then we'd have... a problem.' This is a woman whose own version of reality is more important than grabbing a lifeline, and I admire her for it.

'She's taking the rise,' says Christopherson. 'We shouldn't be encouraging this, boss...'

The front door bell rings and we jump as one. Fear — of different things, I suspect — is a great leveller.

Mrs Pertwee asks, 'Can I answer it? Don't worry, I feel safe knowing you're both here to protect me.'

'Go on,' I say. 'But slowly, please.'

*

An ordinary woman once again, Mrs Pertwee opens her front door and allows a small troop of children to file past: two boys exchanging meaningful glances, the keepers of secrets; and a girl who understands the outside world is something to be reckoned with, judging by the way she gave me the same dark look in her parents' house just a few hours ago.

'It's okay, Stella. These are policeman.'

Stella bursts into tears, not reassured. The two boys look straight past us towards something riveting occurring just over our heads, the fun having gone out of the game. I search their faces for anything I can base my first assumptions on and find a diffident and impenetrable distance; even at this age youngsters have layers, or want them. Experience will fill in the desire for depth and complexity, and these two will have no lack of it.

'Mum,' Stella says through her sobs, 'she's *gone*. I don't know where, but she's gone.'

Mrs Pertwee draws the child to her and hugs her tightly. 'But where's your dad?' she asks.

'He's gone too!'

'No,' exclaims Christopherson, 'this can't be possible.'

'They're here. They're not making it up, Dexter,' I say. I get down on my knee beside their aunt. 'Did they go together or one by one? On their own or did someone collect them? There's no hurry. We'll find them wherever they are.'

'Mum, she went somewhere first... When we left her she was asleep.'

'Left her where?'

'Upstairs in her room. Mum and Dad's room. Dad took her there. But later she was gone, and we couldn't find her anywhere.'

'So you didn't see her leave?' I ask.

'No, she just wasn't there when we went in to look.'

'She vanished from her sleeping place?'

Stella nods.

'And Dad,' I say, 'did he vanish as well?'

'No. He went out to look for Mum. He told us to come here and wait until he gets back.'

'Did you say anything to your brother about your mother vanishing?' I ask Mrs Pertwee. 'Did he know we were coming back here?'

Acting like she has not heard me, Mrs Pertwee addresses her niece, 'Alright darling, there's nothing to worry about now. You're not in any trouble. You haven't done anything wrong.'

She beckons to the boys, who join her and their sister in a group hug. With the exception of the girl, who seems miserable enough, no one in this family appears to have consulted the manual on how to behave when bereaved, the boys appearing to enjoy the novelty of the situation. Not wanting them to get too comfortable, I ask the group, 'Did your father tell you where he was going to look for her?'

The children pay no attention, huddling closer together.

Question time is over and Christopherson, who may dine out on this unprecedented calamity for the rest of his career, starts to chatter excitedly in my ear, 'This tops it all, eh, boss? Complete madness.'

'So it seems.'

'Didn't you say their mum was stage drunk and incapable of speech when you left her? And now she's meant to have dematerialised too? It's got to be a trick of some kind, right? But what are they trying to pull here? It doesn't make any sense, all of them vanishing. I mean, what for...'

'Cuckooing?'

Christopherson looks down at Eileen. 'Sorry?'

'Cuckooing?' she repeats. 'Kind of lost its lustre now, hasn't it, Sergeant? You think they are now holding three, maybe four, members of my family? Perhaps we should enquire after the dogs. They'll be the next to go.'

Christopherson reddens. 'There's no need for that. We're all on the same side here.'

'Oh, that is good to know. Where is that nice music coming from?'

Philip Glass is performing in my coat pocket again, and I pull out my mobile and answer it. 'Hi, Tamla, where are you?'

'I swear to God, Terry, you're not going to believe this...'

'Try me.'

'Okay. Our friend, Lockheart, we've just seen him run past us waving a fucking hammer, or some kind of small axe, towards Station Row. We're in active pursuit. I've already requested backup.'

'On our way.'

'Boss?' Christopherson is looking at me hopefully.

'What's going on, Inspector?' Mrs Pertwee asks, 'Is everything okay?'

'I think I can safely say it isn't,' I say. 'We've found your brother-in-law. Now we just need to catch him.'

'Just him?'

'Yes, he's on his own.'

'What about me, then? I thought the plan was that you were going to take me away and throw away the key.'

'Oh come on, Mrs Pertwee. We're just trying out different possibilities for size. There was never any danger of that happening.'

'So I am safe for now, then?'

'Unless you're planning on running onto Station Row with a weapon, yes.'

'Station Row? Didn't you mention the Purple Hearse earlier?' says Christopherson to Mrs Pertwee, 'Iggy worked there or something?'

'Yes, he went there sometimes... not working, exactly.'

'That's what I thought. It's not where I'd expect posh people to hide kidnapped kids, but it gives us somewhere to start, doesn't it? I'll bet you anything that's where your brother is headed.'

Christopherson nods at me and heads towards the door, back on the front foot again.

'Someone will be here later,' I say to Mrs Pertwee, not wanting to leave, as I fear our bond along with everything else will have disappeared by the time I come back.

'I hope so,' she replies, watching Christopherson hurry along the path to the car, 'and I hope it is you.'

'It'll more likely be community support officers and social services...' I reply in what I realise is not exactly the language of high passion. She holds a finger to my lips and turning round quietly asks the children to wait for her in the sitting room. Then she steps up and straightens my lapels, the sort of thing a wife might do for her husband, and a challenge to move away, which I ignore.

'Who are you the rest of the time, when you aren't being this?'

'I am this. There isn't anything else.'

'That's what I thought you'd say. But I don't believe you.'

Eileen adds something further that I like and waits for me to act on it, which I do. Attraction is a zero-sum game and always stupid. If you are looking to develop or apply finishing touches to it, it is already too late.

'Goodbye, Inspector. Don't be a stranger.'

Outside I try not to think of fucking Eileen, her legs pointing like plinths towards blackening skies. The urgency with which I want this, then deny it, only to find I cannot imagine it without it happening, a portent that Cupid is playing with his quiver and arrow again and that I have already fallen in love — salutary compensation for still having no idea where her nephew is, what happened to her sister, why her mother was taken, or whether her brother-in-law will be careful with that axe or not.

'She's as mad as they come,' Christopherson says, revving the engine. 'Hurry up and get in, boss. We've a madman to clobber.'

CHAPTER FOUR
SIAMESE TWINS

He is running. He has lived in this place all his life; it has been an easy life to waste and a hard one to like. His city is not a he or a she but an it. Great things do not happen here; there are no striking views, inspiring sights, or experiences you will remember forever, and if there are, he has never been able to see past the weeds to savour them. Untroubled by reflexive animality, at one with his operative level, he is the king of whatever will happen next, observing the swift disappearance of time without ever having known what it was to gaze through the rafters, stare at the night sky, and marvel at the stars, or watch the approval in the face of a stranger presented with an accomplishment no one can take away from him, because everything he has has been taken away. Dream too hard and you'll never wake up, he tells his children; he was always too clever to fall for the traps set by sleep. Better to run and keep going, his failing legs supporting his body like a whisper of a better life smothered under the tumult of reality. He already cannot tell whether it is blood or sweat seeping over his eyes. The force driving him is nimble and selfish, and the beauty is that there is no time to work out what it wants. All he knows is he cannot stop running.

And why would he? There are parts of the city that coaches shuttle tourists through, past floated meadows and through streets with flower boxes that fade before the car parks, betting shops, off-licences and substance misuse services, that constitute the place he knows and joylessly dominates. He has no use for charming edifices and whatever softness sticks to their walls. His place is the chalky sediment that resists nourishment, and his people the bodies that insulate him from the night terrors of Hanging Hill. For however worthless the whirring buzz of small satisfactions are — a pint sunk, a curry finished, a grudge settled — they are all proof that he is still here, and that there is someone his life is happening to. Yet if he is not quick, this precious consciousness that he has sought to make so little of will disappear into the Wiltshire ether, and he will be gone forever.

He is moving with reckless haste. There are few witnesses to observe his charge from Hanging Hill, and those there are recoil in terror as Alvin Lockheart spins his mallet blindly (in truth it is a feeble thing used to nail up calendars), windmilling into lampposts, letterboxes and traffic lights, discoordinately staggering to his feet, a scarecrow that bleeds, blaspheming loudly against divine neglect. He mistakes their fear for mockery — he usually does — who can resist being entertained by a public unravelling on this scale? It was always there, whenever he enters a room, a ridicule spiced with the seasoning of a dead and corrupted love, all for a plain-speaking local hero they're too young to remember him ever being. Besides, his course was set once the irresistible curl of his upper lip issued a fruitless challenge to the world, a cheaply acquired misanthropy he cannot disinherit or walk back. Blame whisky, the enabler of the arsehole within; he cannot remember a day when he has not sought its consultation; dignifying invective as wisdom, confusing spite for insight, turning man into cunt.

A van veers so close to him that he thinks he is dead, but the crash he believes has killed him is just the persistence of his magmatic hangover; this one must be faced like death — stoically and completely on his own. Appreciation of his condition at face value is the deepest thing he can do; his heart is erupting and his wife and son have gone. What did he do with all the time he could have used to say he loved them? For as long as he can remember there were things he thought that were incommunicable, meanings that would not cross realms, ideas there were no sounds for. If he could not say something, it was bollocks — the words that were already there stopped the new ones from coming into being; reality patrolled its borders. The salt water mixes with whatever it is that is already in his eyes. Hard as it is to accept love without having to show it, it is harder existing in its absence; he wants to yell and roar, with all the might left in his lungs, to repeat a word he has heard others use but pride forbids him to utter.

'Fuck,' he croaks. That was not the one he was looking for. It will take something larger than life for him to be able to apologise, to relieve the contradictions encountered within his conflicted past, to occupy the side of things he cannot see, and at this late stage, grow as a human being. He has entered the Blacklight district now, a ghoulish succession of pubs, guest houses, tattoo parlours and brothels, surrounding the approaches to the station. Spitting at his reflection in a window display of antique stamps and lead soldiers, trusting only in the effectiveness of ritual gestures, Lockheart slows down into a menacing canter, suddenly conscious that a running man may look like a frightened one. It has stopped raining and the grass on the bank beneath the advertising hoardings is beginning to stand to attention. The ocean has fallen into the drop. He barges into the doors of the Purple Hearse, prying through them as he would the outstretched arms of his worst enemy, and, losing the hammer, wheezes as the succulent aroma of the pub touches the back of his throat. Sweetly artificial, a space that has changed hands without the proper checks, squalor disguised under air fresheners and magic trees, contamination upon contamination, how on Earth has this place become his local? There was always something sick about the Hearse, as obvious to a regular as a stranger happening on it for the first time, guilty secrets that no one had gone to too much trouble to hide, yielding clues and no confession. He takes his time, relishing their fear, and the silence that can only be broken once. Saying nothing is redemptive; when everything is too much, especially doing anything at all, words rob him of his power. To be God, he must have his own rules and force others to follow them. He revels in moments like this, when they are all finally at his mercy, and his gifts, physical strength and courage, are no longer societal embarrassments.

Marching forward, Lockheart pulls the stool away from a woman at the bar, grabs the landlady by the hair, drags her into in the centre of the pub and, yanking her head back, forces her to look around the room, before lowering her to the floor.

'You know! I know you know!' he shouts, circling round the gap he has swiftly created. 'What have you done to them?'

'Christ, Alvin,' the man behind the bar laughs. 'I never realised blossom turned into fruit.'

Lockheart picks up the fallen stool and throws it at the mirror behind the counter; shards of glass rain over the barman.

'Do you never have enough of yourself?' the barman gasps. 'You could have had my sight.'

Lockheart grinds his teeth.

'Where is she?'

'Damned idiot, you'll bring the police on us all!' shouts the landlady. 'Get out of here! Just get out!'

'Where?'

'You know I can't tell you that, Alvin. No one can now,' says the barman.

The defeated never lose just once, but are condemned to relive their defeat into perpetuity; Lockheart grins and stares round the room at the cowering array of faces. They all have the look of having done something they will regret for the rest of their lives. Failure will always have numbers on its side. Slowly, he leans over the bar and into the barman so his victim has no choice but to acknowledge the eyes that bore hatefully into his own. Squeezing the man's cheeks, Lockheart pulls their faces together. 'Are these peepers going to be the last thing you see, Nick?'

'We don't choose who goes, Alvin. We can't fly, but at least we can swim. Be realistic.'

'As may be. But none of your riddles, Nick. You like your words too much. Tell me where to look. Or give me something to help.'

Lockheart lets go and the barman nods to one of the tracksuited youths milling by a side entrance that leads into an alley. The youngster leans out for something just outside the door, and brings back two small plastic bags.

'Acid Horse,' the barman says to Lockheart. 'It'll show you the way to go. We can't.'

Lockheart grabs the bags and holds them close to his eyes, as if to see them gleam, before pocketing them with a mobile phone the landlady reluctantly hands to him.

'Not for us to grow old in a fug of unspeakable profundity, Alvin,' says the barman. 'This is the only way you'll see them now.'

Back out on the street, Lockheart starts to run again. Life is long, but unless you are busy living happily ever after, never long enough.

*

'We've surrounded the place,' says Tamla, pointing to a badly parked Ford Orion, a hastily assembled blue and white hazard tape barricade, and two worried looking PCs. Beyond them, Orridge stands astride a mini-roundabout, unnecessarily directing traffic with one hand, while stopping pedestrians from crossing the road with the other; his propensity to play the lollipop-lady unlikely to shore up the public's respect for law and order.

'So where is he?' I ask.

'Beats me. If Lockheart's left, he must have used the drains.'

'You think he's still in there, then?'

'Has to be. The florist says she saw him run in like his life depended on it.'

'Maybe it did.' I check my watch, my dad's old Omega Seamaster, covered in dents and scratches and entirely unsuitable to this kind of work. 'How long ago was this?'

'At least ten minutes.'

'And no one has left through a window yet? I thought sound and fury were his style.'

'Maybe he's just popped in for a quiet lunchtime drink...' Tamla says, trying to control the nervousness we are all feeling.

'We come to that point in the job where we can actually get

hurt, again,' she says to me out of the side of her mouth. 'I deal with it by pretending we are in control.'

'Pretending I'm not scared usually works for me,' I reply.

'I'm sorry, sir,' Christopherson says to an elderly man hobbling along on crutches, wearing a battered fez and aviator sunglasses, 'I'm afraid you can't go in there yet.'

'What would I want to go in there for? You're blocking the pavement. That place is for perverts. Let me through, please. I've a heart condition. I was only going in to use the toilets anyway.'

The senior citizen has a point. The Purple Hearse and its environs resemble a medieval canton emerging from a long siege. Plague, famine and the attritional grind of war have marked most of those who have survived with physical or, no less noticeable to the naked eye, mental ailments that set them apart from the ordinary flow of displaced persons clagged up in transit. Extending to no more than a single winding road connecting the railway line to the city centre, and a parallel jumble of disjointed residential streets tailing off either side, Station Row is a thoroughfare commuters hurry through as quickly as possible, their escape route hemmed in by takeaways that offer plastic chairs and tables in the hope of passing as restaurants, and public houses in which it is easy to offend locals offering souvenirs no one wants. Economic cleansing has reinforced the invisible coastline of this island of the void, and it is by the stoical standard of its inhabitants, used to celebrating birthdays on benches and other parts of the pavement, that the Purple Hearse is judged beyond the bounds of redemption.

Tamla pulls off her gloves and rubs her eyes. 'Saying that, I still think it would be best to proceed lightly. Perhaps just the two of you first?'

Christopherson looks sceptical. 'Didn't you say he was wielding a hammer? That sounds a bit dangerous.'

'It's the life we chose,' I say.

'Still. A hammer? I don't know. Maybe we should wait for proper back up, like?'

'Don't worry. If he kicks off, I'll steam in with the cavalry,'

Tamla says. 'But get too many of us in there to start with, and it'll be carnage. Dissuasion is the best form of prevention. I'll be covering the back with this' — she lifts the point of a Taser out of her handbag — 'should he have any ideas of leaving that way.'

'And we need to show this shower who's in charge,' I add. 'And that we don't fear them.'

'Right,' he says, not reassured. 'If you say so, boss.'

I take his arm. 'Come on, I could use a pint. Tamla?'

'Terry?'

'Get some constables who can access the upstairs that way. We can handle the ground floor, but I don't like the idea of having to clear the second floor on our own.'

'Roger that. They can force the skylight.'

At first glance, the Hearse is a tease. Since the mouldering front of the pub collapsed into the main road, a superficial facelift suggests that it may actually be a cut above the competition. Tinted rather than bordered-up bay windows and frilly mauve curtains intentionally evoke an undertakers or genteel funeral home, yet on closer inspection the Gothic schtick gives way to the unventilated seediness of an eighteenth-century Paraguayan bordello.

I know the interior is even less wholesome. Inside, the restoration takes on the aspect of a yard sale for the damned: pairs of wingback armchairs appropriate to a private dwelling habituated by a couple who bond over a passion for serial killing, low faux-leather sofas too deep for drinkers to reach tables, and a column of wonky stools lining the bar the only survivors of Stallones — a mock American diner that closed some years ago — invite revulsion. In the far corner, a spiral staircase leads up to a narrow corridor decorated in sandy mustard checks, the wire carpeting ready to cut the knees of anyone leaving the bedrooms in too great a hurry. These dismal chambers offer intimate massage, hand-relief, two way mirrors to observe a former Member of Parliament sip cream out of a saucer, and occasionally, a disturbed night's sleep for anyone naive enough to take the B&B sign at face value.

In a quiet week, Orridge can always be assured of an arrest and conviction here, and while the rest of us rarely stoop so low, even idealism sometimes needs to be realistic enough to sustain itself. The entire postcode is a societal relief valve, its sadness and waste the milky component of humanism that lends the idea its frailty. For the law, managed containment of Station Row has always been an effective policy. Until now, that is; something that should never have left here has got out, and something that does not belong here has been taken in.

'Looks like we're attracting a crowd,' calls Tamla. 'Don't spare the horses, eh, Terry?'

A collection of hairdressers, tattooists, emissaries from the sex shops, and the impresario of Go Vape are watching us from a cautious distance. In their number is an ex-sapper who runs the Airfix model shop, who, as a sign of the changing times, began wearing a dress a year ago, without forgoing his beard or combat boots. Looking at me seriously, he offers a guarded thumbs-up and squints, transporting me into the film of my life in which I am Al Pacino, and this street is the set of *Heat*. My partiality to fantasy, at odds with a job that requires obedience to dominant reality, is the bashful companion and friend I am ashamed of, creating giants out of windmills ever since I was old enough to daydream. Many detectives who cite 'public service' over a weakness for delusion as the principle reason for joining the force, however much they think they resemble Clint Eastwood, harbour similar fantasies. It has got to a point where, one day, I will have to ask the actors what goes through their minds when they play us.

Stepping through the swinging doors of the pub, I am brought down to the bottom of the canal again. I see myself as I am to these boozers: neither Sherlock Holmes, nor even Morse, but an emissary of the state — a faceless killjoy or, at best, a passing threat. Absolutely no one bothers to acknowledge us, the collective unconscious of this pub exhaling guilt, with an undertow of the same fetid air freshener Eileen Pertwee favours. Once again, the smell reminds me of connections I was about to make, links that would answer questions witnesses cannot, if I could only hold my train of thought and see past the distractions to what I so nearly grasped earlier... there is broken glass on the floor, and as I look down at my over-polished brogues, the adumbration vanishes. Lockheart is not here, a smashed mirror is, and that, at least, is consistent with reports of his recent presence.

'Christ! It stinks, boss,' mutters Christopherson through his teeth. 'Like kennels. At least we're still alive, I suppose.'

'I'll take the bar and ownership. You check everywhere else.'

First I reach for the small awning window, above the dark-tinted one that looks out onto the street, and force it open. I have never been in here this early, and it is a view that would be vastly improved upon by a drink, though I pity any tourist unlucky enough to drop in for one on the way to the cathedral. Right beside the door on a battered couch, eating off plates resting on their laps, are a hungry couple, halfway through a breakfast that appears to be lost somewhere between the continent and a full English, without doing justice to either. They look in a hurry to finish, which is at least rational, one half of the couple wearing a brown leather waistcoat and a cowboy bandana tied round his chubby neck, his partner sporting an unseasonal arts and crafts kaftan and tie-dye skullcap. Neither sartorial combination is favoured by locals. Tempting as it is to assume their innocence, experience suggests they have answered an advert in a Belgian swingers' magazine, and are recouping calories after an eventful night.

'Good cornflakes, *ja*?' asks Christopherson, as the man shovels a folded slice of greasy spam into his mouth, and the woman smiles obliquely at a bowl of Frosties she is tipping evaporated milk over.

'*Ja*.' Her partner smiles. '*Wie Zuhause!*', which is more German than either of us can manage, so, switching the conversation to English, I observe, 'That looks dangerous. Be careful.'

There is an ugly-looking shard of glass resting on the sofa between them, which they affect not to notice, demonstrating an understanding of house rules and local mores. Gambling on other, more cooperative witnesses, Christopherson says, 'Stonehenge is the other way. If you want to beat the crowds I wouldn't hang around. Things are about to get a bit hairy round here.'

But the other options are even longer shots. Stood at the corner of the bar, genuinely unaware of our presence, the day of the week, or the identity of our current prime minister, are three youths in tracksuits, whose unofficial connection to the place extends to dealing drugs out of the adjoining alley. They are fidgety and moving about to music they can still hear from the night before, far in their own worlds, which can become complicated places to retreat to when visitors from other planets come prying. In addition to a lonely drinker in a hoodie trying not to look at us and an elderly version of the same man in a yacht-club blazer who looks like he would enjoy a conversation but cannot break the code of silence, there is an attractive woman with an alarmingly thin face, sipping liquid the colour of cough medicine from a cocktail glass. Her cheekbones and jaw have grown to disproportionate prominence through a mixture of appetite suppression and food substitutes, and while she is far younger than she looks, the smock buttoned at the neck that reaches her ankles implies she is dressed for a different occasion or has woken up in someone else's clothes. The landlady and barman look worried, though, which is good. Lockheart must be close.

'Good morning' elicits no response, and feeling something on my shoulder, I slap it — a fly. A swarm of them have gathered over the league tables being silently relayed on the flat-screen television.

'The kitchens,' offers the barman by way of explanation. 'We've had some issues with the sausages.' It is a man of my own heart who will confess to a lesser crime to deflect from more serious failings. 'What's in the sausages?'

'I don't know, all sorts of shit. The problem is with the freezers.'

'Your problems go deeper than refrigeration. Why not tell us about them and get it all off your chest... Nick, isn't it?'

The barman nods slowly as though he is not really sure he agrees.

'Good, I knew we'd met before. Dexter,' I say to Christopherson, 'why don't you have a look at those kitchens and see if you can find what's exciting the flies?'

'Sure.'

This is no great act of detection as *Nick the Well* is a faithful patron of the bottom tier of this city's pubs, often slowing down traffic as he rolls out of their doorways, though I have never seen him on this side of the bar before. He is not a man well-suited to the world of work, or the kind to dress up for the privilege of drawing a salary. While not exactly noticeable, he is distinct: his lank hair reaches his shoulders, as it probably has for the past three decades, without ever appearing to have been washed or conditioned. As I do not have the time to not judge by appearances, I am surprised he has kept his Fu Manchu moustache, despite my warning that it makes him look intrinsically dishonest, when he was last cautioned for a handbag of heroin he 'found' and failed to turn in. Even without these stylistic hallmarks, recognition was never going to be a problem. His denim jacket, with leather arms advertising his allegiance to rock 'n' roll, has a large enamel badge with '*Nick the Well*' pinned to it. His name, until this dalliance with bar work, *was* his job description. Maureen, the landlady, by contrast, looks like the overgrown child of weightlifters: obese were she not so solid, her hair slicked and ponytailed like the handle of a plunger, squeezing her face back in a way that makes it difficult to use as nature intended.

'Do you want a drink?' *The Well* asks, and avoiding looking at me, produces a brown envelope from under the bar.

'If we have one later, it won't be one of those. Put your bribe away. I don't take money.'

'Dressed like that, you can't blame me for thinking it.'

'Idiot. He's one of the clever ones who's put away all our mates,' hisses Maureen, deliberately not looking at me, 'who's in it for the sheer fucking love of it.'

'You of all people should remember me...' I tell *The Well*.

'Yeah, now you come to mention it, I thought I recognised you. Thought you might have moved to private security though.'

'Not me. Wiltshire Police or nothing.'

There is a dustpan full of glass and a brush that look to have been hastily abandoned, lodged under a stool along with several overfull ash trays. Christopherson, who has returned from the kitchen shaking his head, taps the dustpan with his foot. 'Cleaning up isn't a criminal offence. Hiding proof of your good works?'

Facing me, he adds, 'There's no one back there.'

Maureen and *The Well* exchange angry glances to see who will go first, but before either of them has to embrace martyrdom, the lavatory door is thrown open and a confused young woman, who I imagine is an associate of Miss Smock at the bar, staggers towards us, in the middle of finding something very funny.

Bumping into Christopherson, and waving her fingers playfully at me, she breaks into a second bout of laughter, and hanging on to his neck to remain balanced, buries her face deep in his chest to smother her mirth. In doing so, she is oblivious to the excruciatingly pained faces *The Well* and Maureen are hurriedly pulling, or the way her friend at the bar is trying to pivot her eyes sideways, without moving her head, to alert her to the danger we pose.

With a sigh, she untangles herself from Christopherson and lifts her head so their noses neatly align. Gallantly,

Christopherson allows her to nuzzle him, bravely standing his ground. This second femme fatale is older than her friend and appears to have recently possessed enough beauty to get by on, and may still in a world where standards are relative. Her accoutrements, though, are desperate. Loud colours, teary eyeliner, roughed-up lipstick and mascara that has missed its mark, isolate a human as firmly as prison walls, suggesting she is no longer here for business, but tragically, because she finds the company comforting.

There is a controlled smash from upstairs, in all likelihood our constables forcing entry rather than Lockheart breaking out, but our friend here is not to be distracted. 'Oh boys, you know we have a little ol' tradition every time a handsome man comes into the joint. Of putting a tune on the juke and having little boogie,' she says in a soft Irish accent, and performs a clumsy wiggle that could pass for a fertility dance. 'And I don't mean no show tunes. You know what I mean? I fancy a bit of Bowie...'

Politely, Christopherson replies, 'I don't have any change.'

'Watch the stairs, Dexter,' I say under my breath. 'Someone might be coming down in a hurry.'

'Oh pish to that then, do you boys like to... dabble, you know? *Dabble...*'

Maureen makes a groaning noise that reminds me of a bin full of bottles being crushed in a recycling truck, and *The Well* follows through with a hacking cough that would normally require a respirator being stuck somewhere unpleasant to prevent slow death.

Not to be deterred, our new friend turns to me and says with a confidential leer, 'You see, we have another little tradition in here. We like a little powder party every Monday, you know, to begin the week in the right way... as it *were*.' She taps her nose and eyes me.

'Is that right?'

'Oh it is right alright. I see you!' she laughs. 'I *really* see you... I know you like to dabble. You're notorious! Forget about that ugly prick who was in here earlier. Let's have some fun!'

'You like a party every bloody day, Ava,' Maureen says, her face tense with menace. 'That's your trouble. You need to go home and get your head down before you do yourself a mischief...'

'It's alright,' I say. 'She's gestating.'

Ava pops her jaw at me. 'He knows the score,' she says, and then whispers to Christopherson in a theatrical aside, 'Your friend looks like a movie star. I always appreciate who likes to dabble. I have an eye for actors, always recognise them. You all know how to get rid of that belly fat fast. You know what I mean? A double chin too! I've been in a few films you know. Been on a few shoots, oh yeah. All you fine young men with your houses in the sticks and big hot tubs. I've gone diving in plenty of those.'

'Don't get in your own way, Ava,' cautions *The Well* from behind a glass he is anxiously pretending to clean. 'These men will get the wrong idea about us.'

Not to be deterred, she moves to her point. 'How about it, boys? Both you big handsome men. Don't be shy. Put some money behind the bar and come upstairs and join me and Contessa here for a cheeky line, eh? That's another one of our traditions right there, and if you want to dabble some more we can have ourselves a proper vodka and Charlie party? Come on, I'm feeling filthy!'

Christopherson clears his throat. 'I'm sorry, but I've left the wife and kids outside in the Volvo,' he apologises. 'It wouldn't do to leave them there all afternoon.'

Felled by the blow of an invisible hand, and torn from a dream where reality is whatever one supposes it is, Ava jolts away from Christopherson with disgust, catching her forearm painfully against the side of the bar.

'You dirty, dirty coppers,' she exclaims. 'I can always tell one of you from a human fuckin' bein'.'

As liberating as it often is to be confused for someone else in this job, even if such a mistake lasts only for a few minutes and ends in intense disappointment for all parties, it is time to break cover. 'I'm afraid you're right. We are police officers investigating a disappearance.'

'Aaaagh! I should have noticed the smell...' her voice trails off.

'Could you please put that down?' I ask.

Ava's hand has picked a bottle off the counter. She looks at the object as if it has been planted on her, which in a way it has, and frowns as though it may yet tell her things she has longed to know.

'It's alright. I'm sorry we've upset you,' I say. 'You haven't done anything wrong. Now please put it down.'

'I took you for better at first,' she says to me accusingly, water rising in her eyes. 'You used a big word. And you smell nice.'

'He's one who likes to use big words and smells nice,' says Christopherson. 'We come in all shapes and sizes. Nothing coming down the stairs yet, boss.' We can hear a company of footsteps methodically moving through the second floor room by room, our men and not Lockheart.

Ava drops the bottle, which bounces along the floor like a cheap trophy, and we watch it roll away like someone else's work. Her friend, Contessa, puts her arm round her protectively and glowers at us, which succeeds in teasing out that vague feeling of guilt that usually accompanies my looking for the quality in others.

'It's so unfair,' Ava mumbles. 'All I wanted was a little dabble... oh beautiful world, where the fuck are you?'

If Lockheart is here, he must be hidden in some part of this room that is not discernible to the naked eye, and that means he needs flushing out. Turning my back to the bar, I address the company, 'You know why we're here. We've seen enough in five minutes to make arrests and close this place. Time, I think, to help us with our enquiries. If the man we are after is still here, just close your eyes and blink. He won't know which of you has given him up.'

There are no tutorials on how to talk to a pub full of people who belong in a prison exercise yard, the thin reed of self-belief liable to break at the first snort of derision, which is why I normally like to keep things short and to the point. Christopherson, however, considering this too dry when the occasion calls for going the full Maximus, adds, 'Think about it. What you do next could have consequences for the rest of your lives.'

If that won't have Lockheart running out at me from behind a curtain with his axe, nothing will. But to make sure of it, Christopherson follows through with a clincher: 'Come on, you've all seen him. You know he's dangerous. Why protect a sick psychopath?'

That's enough grapeshot and musket fire for our friends from the continent, who pick up their bags with an intense air of minding their own business, and walk straight out the way we came in. Unfortunately for them, the local contingent have no such means of escape. The all-day drinkers, lads in tracksuits, and to their credit, Ava and Contessa, appear to be struggling with the cornucopia of mixed motivation that makes life so complicated for the genuinely conflicted, who having thought of the right thing to do, wish to track back to a more comforting state of indecision. I have every sympathy for their predicament. They know nature will finish its sentences and clear up after itself without their help, and that anyone ignoring this law of efficiency ought to find another species to drink with. This is not the only pub in the city.

'If you don't know how to close your eyes, I'll accept spoken answers.'

I turn back to Maureen and *The Well*, who, despite looking like they have missed successful careers in mime, are having no more success with speech than sign language. Reluctantly, I force the issue: 'Do you have a licence to sell drugs and sex from these premises?'

The Well turns the colour of a blustery summer sunset hung in the Turner Room of the National Gallery, and pulls at his moustache nervously like one who has long forgotten why he lies and continues to simply out of habit.

'He asked to see the licence, not for you to take all day applying for one,' snaps Christopherson.

The delay is long enough. Responding with the low cunning and offended self-righteousness that defines criminality under any system of government, *The Well* splutters, 'We've jumped through hoops to try and clean this place up, give us some credit. You can't blame us for what goes on here, fair dues. You lot are all over everywhere else — where do you expect the outcasts to go? You know you need this place as much as you need jail or rehab. We're good people here. We didn't ask to end to up as a day centre for pervs and numpties...'

'That's enough,' I say. Allowing a certain type of person to complain increases their self-importance, and *The Well* will believe he is Gandhi if he is not stopped. 'Answer questions or shut the fuck up.'

'Just saying, you should try working here...'

'But we don't; you do,' interrupts Christopherson, 'and under the Sexual Offences Act, this den of iniquity qualifies as a brothel. You'd both be looking at seven years.'

Understandably eager to change the subject, Maureen taps the bar and eyes the door in a meaningful way, before jerking her head down at an angle as if she is trying to get water out of her ear.

'He left that way then?' I ask.

She nods.

'How long?'

She lifts both hands, five ringed fingers on one, four raised on the other.

I pull out my mobile and call Tamla.

'Yeah?'

'He apparently left by the main door ten minutes ago.'

'That would have been about exactly the same time we got here. I didn't see anyone.'

'Okay, start scanning the surrounding streets.'

A constable has appeared at the bottom of the steps, and I put my phone back in my pocket. 'Nothing up here, sir,' he says.

'You'd better pay for any damage,' threatens Maureen.

'You know why he called in?' I say, ignoring her request.

It is too much for her to respond to a question that cannot be answered silently, and nudging *The Well*, she passes the baton to her assistant. He seems disinclined to take it. 'Search me,' he moans. 'I only work here.'

'We know, no one loves you, but the man you're protecting is connected to a serious crime. One that makes what you lot normally get up to look like chickenshit. Do you realise that?' stresses Christopherson.

'So, what were we supposed to do, bar anyone who doesn't pass your good citizen test? We'd be lucky to sell half a pint a week.'

'He chooses this pub, not Wetherspoons, The Cathedral Arms or Pizza Express, but *this pub* to wield a bloody axe or mallet or whatever it was... Come on, help us understand why that is? I mean, it's not for your two-for-one carvery, is it?'

'I've no access to his workings. He came in a funk, broke a mirror and fucked off. What more can I say?'

'Something else,' I reply, 'because you don't want us to come back here.'

'Jesus! Just give them what they want, something, anything, whatever it'll take for them to fuck off out of here!' shrieks Ava. 'They're a disease!'

To his credit, *The Well* looks like he would like to oblige, though there is a hidden difficulty, and without divulging what it is, a simple answer appears to be out of the question. Bringing his hands together, he hisses under his breath, 'I never want to see that cunt again in my life, believe me. I'd grass him if I could, you got to know that. I want him gone but...' — he shows us his open palms — '...there's just nothing there, nothing I can give you...'

'Then tell me what you know about this.'

I hold the bag containing the twisted weeds I found in Nana Pertwee's bedroom in front of him, high enough for the pub to see, and watch *The Well* change colour, again. His lips are not moving, but the noise he makes sounds like the last of the kittens he has swallowed has finally given up the fight.

'Well?'

'Where do... where... how did you find tha— that?' he stutters, his entire body trembling. 'Please. Where did you get it?'

'I've a nose for these things.'

'Just tell me who gave it to you. Please. It's serious.'

'Why?'

'You don't understand, that stuff, you having it. It's not safe!'

'I'd need to know more than that, before you get me as worried as you.'

'Look at the colour on there,' mutters one of the youths, squinting at the bag. 'I've never seen it go like that before...'

'You shut up you,' *The Well* snaps at the boy. 'You tell me what's he doing with it, eh? Eh? Trusting you fucktards! On my daughter's life, I've been a fucking fool to!'

'No, never seen it do that,' replies his friend by the side entrance. 'Too freaky. It's all in bits — look at it!'

'You any idea what's going to happen to us now!' *The Well* practically chokes, raging at the youths, 'I'll tell you, we're fucked. Period. You understand me, right? Fucked. The bitches of the cornhole king! You bloody clowns, you don't even realise what you've done! Messing around with that stuff so the likes of him have it!'

Ignoring *The Well*, and with genuine interest, the teenager by the side entrance sidles over to us and asks, 'Was it like that when you bought it? I know it's a bit off, I mean, we're not allowed to ask you the questions I know, but where do you get hold of a load looking like that?'

I consult my peripheral vision. The wiry clumps have

changed from a greenish brown to ashen-white flakes, nearer charcoal or burnt embers than any drugs that speak to my core competencies. The osmosis must have occurred in my pocket within the last couple of hours. And, trying to disguise my disquiet, I hold *The Well*'s eye, and ignore the boy.

'So are you going to help us or not?'

Christopherson grunts, 'Listen, we're not going to be asked to run a trace and track service for our local drug dealers.' And he gently pushes the boy away from me. Behind him, his friend stands firm, and an ugly little squash develops, neither side having any hope of winning without recourse to overt coercion.

'Easy now,' says Christopherson, 'let's keep this nice and easy.'

Looking to Maureen for support, *The Well* starts to say something to her, but words are inadequate to the crisis, and unable to stop himself, he reaches to snatch the small plastic packet. I catch his fingers with my free hand, and turn them at an angle.

'Jesus Christ! Stop that, please!'

Maureen has reached her limit, her breasts swelling with rage, 'You think they're worth losing everything for, Nick? The coppers are here now. Them others aren't. They'll do for us before those animals will. I'm not sacrificing this place or anything else for them creatures. They've used us like I told you they would, and how long did we have to wait, eh? It's all coming apart already!'

'For Christ's sake, Maureen. There's a limit to what the law can do to us, but them...'

'She sounds like a sensible woman,' says Christopherson. 'You listen to her in the first place and there never would have been any of this trouble, I'll bet.'

Maureen shoves *The Well* to one side and leans across the bar, motioning us to draw close to her. Half-heartedly he attempts to regain his place, his volition impeded by sheer relief.

'*Bizarre Bazaar*, you know it? Top floor of the antique market on St Anne Street, a retro-tack shop, full of old uniforms and record players. That's where you should be asking your questions, not here. We mean nothing.'

'Will the man we're looking for be there?'

'As sure as night follows day, that's where he'll be heading. Everything you want from us, you'll find there.'

I turn to Christopherson. 'It's a ten-minute walk. I'll go. You clear up here.'

'You don't think they're deflecting?' he asks.

I look Maureen straight in the eye. 'No, they're too scared to. They don't want occasion to pick up from where we've left off.'

'Good, clever man,' she says, nodding. 'You're getting it. We want nothing more to do with this. We're the little people, so keep us out of it. You ask there, and you'll find what you want to know. But nothing about us, whatever you do, nothing more about us. Don't bring us in.'

'Of course not,' says Christopherson. 'But if you told us what you're running scared from, perhaps we'd be in a better position to protect you?'

'Ha! You protect us by saying nothing, mister. That's how you protect us.' She slams her hand against the bar. 'And mark me, I warn you now, when you start, don't stop. Whatever you do, don't stop until you've got the real bastards behind all this, you understand? Move quickly, faster than you ever have on anything before, you understand? You relax, just for a second, and it's the end. They'll do for us all. You included. Promise me? I mean it, I value my life.'

'We need more information first. Who do you need protecting from?

Maureen folds her arms and shakes her head, 'Promise me you'll say nothing.'

'Okay, alright, I promise,' Christopherson says, 'we'll act fast and say nothing about you.'

She turns to me. 'And you?'

I nod in assent, slightly bemused.

'Good. Then you'll find what you want from them,' she says. 'They're who you want, not us. You'll get nothing more out of me. You know enough now.'

'I believe that. Thank you. But don't go anywhere. DCI Christopherson will still have to take full statements from you all.'

'Oh sure, whatever,' she says, waving her arm in the air. 'We'll tell you a madman came in here and went straight out again. But the wheres or whys — those answers you need key players for, and we're just the little people, mushrooms kept in the dark. Alive for now and tired of being crapped on.'

I turn to go, but as I do so I catch *The Well*'s chastised eye, and I can't resist it. 'Just one more thing, a question. No, don't worry, I think you'll know the answer to this one. Why do you call yourself "*The Well*"?

Staring at me, with a concentration that almost borders on defiance, he slowly pulls up the zip of his jacket until the leather collar, stitched into the denim, forms a circle round his neck. After a heavy night, it could even look like the outline of a well.

'And I thought it might have something to do with you being deep,' I say, acknowledging the effort. 'Thank you for your cooperation.'

CHAPTER FIVE

PLAINSONG

Out on the street, Tamla repeats, 'Bizarre Bazaar... *Bizarre Bazaar?*'

I stuff two pieces of gum into my mouth and nod, lifting my finger in the rough direction of the antique market. 'Yeah, it's that way. That's where they say he's made for, and where we'll get our answers.'

'Okaaaay. I know the way, Terry, and we have people watching the place waiting for Lockheart to show up right now, but it's a sort of posh-pikey jumble sale, isn't it? Full of flying goggles, feather dusters and old Fairport long-players. What would a criminal conspiracy be doing there, I wonder?'

'So? Where would be more apt, Sports Direct?'

'You know what I mean. It's nearer the posher bit of town. Things get harder to solve there.'

'Play the team in front of us, I say.'

'Mmmm... then again, it'd be ridiculously easy to find out if she's lying to you. I mean, if it were me I'd have deflected as far as Southampton, if I were buying time to hide my misdeeds... not some shithole ten minutes' walk away.' Tamla sticks her hand in my pocket and, removing the packet, helps herself to a stick of gum.

'She's too frightened to deflect,' I reply, covering my eyes from the sun, 'and there's no way Lockheart could have pegged it to Southampton in ten minutes.'

'So you think she's telling you the truth?'

'Not the whole truth, but as much as we're going to get short of breaking the rules.'

'A bit of torture might give us more to go on?'

'If we were the Mafia, we'd have full confessions in five minutes. But as far as Wiltshire Police procedure is concerned, we'll have to make the most out of what she's ready to share.'

'You think it's Lockheart that's giving them all nightmares? Is he what they're so scared of?'

The chewing gum tastes like a laboratory experiment, and I spit it into the gutter, making sure it clears the grating, as public littering will not do. 'It'd be easy if it was. But the way they were, it seemed like they were alluding to *a state of affairs*, not just some crazy guy who'd come looking for retribution. The best thing we can do is follow him, and her lead.'

'And that's another problem right there, Terry...'

'How so?'

'She may have given you the junk shop, but we've lost our man.'

'Lockheart? Someone must have seen him. He was only meant to have scarpered as we arrived.'

'There's no sign of him ever having left this street, or of ever having reached town,' Tamla says, biting her lip.

'So he is still *in the Hearse*? Can't be... They may have been lying, but we looked everywhere.'

'Oh no, that'd be way too simple. They told you the truth alright. He left there just as they say. She at Hairway to Heaven, her assistant, *and* the bloke from Chick O' Land all swear blind they saw him crashing out of the pub in a hurry, just minutes before we got here...'

'They're sure about that?'

'Of course, how could you not be? One hundred percent...'

'So where did he go? I don't get it.' I begin to survey the street nervously, in spite of the presence of police everywhere. 'He leaves and no one sees him go anywhere? Come on.'

'Nowhere... They saw him leave the pub and then nothing. None of them agree on where he went, only that he charged out of the place. They all say he looked so bloody evil that they looked down or away to avoid him clocking them. We're checking CCTV now. Best guess is that he must have accessed one of the houses or worked his way through an alley. But as far as specifics are concerned, we're chasing ghosts again.'

'Lucky we have this, at least,' I say, and hand Tamla the small bag that aroused so much interest in the Hearse.

'Evidence?'

'I hope so. It needs to be sent to Porton Down, today, and broken down and explained back to me. I need to know what it is, and if possible, what it does...'

Tamla takes the bag and, opening it, holds it to her nose with an ironic dignity. 'Eeyooow!' she exclaims, 'have you actually smelt this?'

'I hadn't got round to it yet, no.'

'Let me spare you the trouble. Syphilis, mustard gas and asbestos, all yours in one foul inhalation!'

'That good? Oh yeah, I can already smell that.'

Tamla chuckles and rocks on her feet a little. 'So, you know you think I am an overreaction to life, full stop? Well, cast that to one side for a minute, because this is how I imagine the Battle of Agincourt to have smelt, after the bodies began to turn in the armour.'

She has an enjoyably flustered look, and crossing her eyes slightly, laughs as if communing directly with the contents of the bag itself. 'No, no, too much, this is fucking weird!'

'Go on, give it here.' I reach my hand out.

'Some things do not need to be experienced for oneself...'

'Come on!'

'Your funeral...' she lets go of the bag.

I pull open the polythene and hold the open bag to my nostrils and inhale very gently, braced for the worst. As ruthlessly as truth, the concoction delivers on Tamla's playful warning. I forget myself. It is the odour, somehow separate from the substance, that does it. In seconds it has thrown me over a pyre of human fertiliser, past the lavatories of every junkie flophouse in the city, over the wall of Eileen Pertwee's garden, and into her bungalow, where I take my place next to her in front of the television. Like the subtlest of colognes, the old sickly scent emerges from the rugs and carpets, rising like a mist to reveal things I know I will forget unless I speak of them immediately. With quiet authority, Eileen raises a finger to my lips and turns the television off. The shawl that covers her drops to the carpet, and she stands totally naked before me, bidding me to come to her... Then I am here again, stood on this unloved street, crushed by the restrictive facts of my physical existence.

'Jesus!'

'I told you it was bad.'

'You didn't tell me it would get into my head that fast.'

'Honestly, Terry, I thought a man of your experience could take that much for granted!'

'Oi, you two!'

Rather gingerly for an officer that writes rude letters to lenient judges, we are joined by Orridge, who nursing his tennis elbow aggravated by the traffic cop routine, frowns at us. 'What are you two reprobates playing at? Are we good to reopen or what?' he barks, his voice heavy with disproval.

Still reeling from our herbo-chemical hit, Tamla's eyes search for a put-down, too slowly to stop Orridge revving into second gear. 'And where's our badman, eh? Forty minutes this road's been closed. I tell you, we'd better have something to show for it or else my life will be hell the next time I bump into Councillor Hussein at the Middlemist Golf Club. Traffic is bad enough with works on the Downton Road. Like Piccadilly Circus, this place, but without the language schools or Garfunkel's. Bloody lazy bastards digging the roads. Can't see why they can't work at night and weekends... All this and a madman on the loose, supposedly.'

Tamla and I start to giggle in controlled bursts.

'You're bloody mad, you two. Like little girls... So, where is he? Don't tell me we don't have him yet!'

'Our man is hiding, Max,' I say, trying to pull myself together. 'Hiding and not letting us find him. But rest easy, the good news is that the locals see it as a matter of some urgency that he is caught...'

'That's a bloody relief, because so do I. The sooner we hit this nonsense on the head, lock up this lunatic or, more likely, find out all those poor buggers threw themselves off a bridge in a collective suicide pact, the better prepared we'll be for Her Majesty's visit... and you two, pissing around like this when we're still officially in pursuit. Fucking lamentable, it is.'

I keep my funny reply to myself and try a serious one. 'Easy, Max. Our guy has gone incognito. I don't think he wants trouble now — he's after something else. They've also told us where he might be found. We may even get there before our suspect does.'

'Really? Where's that then?'

'Come on,' I say, taking him by the arm. 'Let us go, you and I, and walk these streets together.'

Orridge stares at me like I am the grandest folly he has ever had to indulge, and we set off.

*

The antique market is thin gruel for those who wish to be stimulated by their surroundings, even for those who have unwisely taken drugs in the line of duty. At best, the walk to get there is flat and colourless, a brittle two dimensionality baked into the very asphalt, rendering hopes of being surprised, enchanted or otherwise seduced by life hopelessly beside the point. This is the hastily assembled scenery of a budget soap opera, a journey across a desolate market town, far too big to be quaint, bolted on to a Cathedral Close so as to bequeath it the 'city' status that justifies its own line of postcards. Divorced from its patrician attractions, crime might be easier to solve if the provincial rump of the metropolis were severed by demarcation lines and checkpoints, so villainy knew where to stop, its presence interrupting the broken eloquence of the ruined cloisters where our investigations peter out into unsolved mysteries.

Perhaps I have the contents of the mysterious bag to thank, but as Orridge tries to keep up, muttering about how we should have already found our man, while showing a puzzling reluctance to reach the place where we might do so, I try to imagine how the city earned the historic reputation it trades on, and to my surprise, I nearly can. The shabby avenues, hemmed in by ring roads, an unfashionable former polytechnic and shopping-villages, were once the fabled gates to the West, through which a traveller would encounter Merlin, clotted cream teas, hallucinogenic mushrooms and the summer solstice. I need only ignore the nondescript bus station, award-less home for the elderly and forgetful, and other tributes to brute function that defy description, to imagine the excitement of the London coach passing through lively cobbled streets, the stones thick with horseshit and hope. All I need do is focus on the sky, my eyes slowly working their way down, filtering out the town planning of the past fifty years that no longer excites even sociologists, the legacy of which so closely resembles other places of no interest as to barely qualify as history. And if I persist in doing so, searching for the missing shadows and shapes that should still be here, I am able to see *her* again. That eternal city on the hill that is always Wessex, King Lear's capital on Sarum Plane, the chill air that carries the breath of winter on its wings the same as that breathed by Hardy, Trollope and Constable.

'He could be anywhere,' huffs Orridge. 'He could be watching us now.'

But if I begin my sensual journey from the bottom *up*, starting from the pavement, matters are very different. Then I see what I observe every day, whether I wish to or not, the unholy blend of about-to-close-and-reopen-under-another-name charity shops that have replaced broken down family franchises and second-hand furniture depots. Not to be outdone, these thrift stores are sandwiched by reviled high-street names that cyclically disappear with recessions, cafes that serve their bacon rare with margarine, and the mobile phone outlets that prove technology makes for poor window displays, the latter the single thriving businesses graced by every sector of society, who in the absence of much to say face to face, passionately communicate it over screens. These reliable highlights would be nothing without their trimmings: the local markets that are outdoor jumble sales, with only the fruit not having come from China; civic buildings that are indistinguishable from the STD clinic and lavatory blocks; a bypass built on backhanders that redirects traffic into the jammed city centre, suffering worse congestion than Los Angeles, without the redemptive consolation of the real estate and Hollywood; and, of course, pubs — more per head than anywhere else in the country, each an entry into a world eerily like its neighbour's. One cannot hate any of this, but nor can one be inspired, and though I failed to notice most of it for the first couple of years, the place and its rituals have entered me and belong as much to my unconscious as they do to themselves in all their gloomy vividity.

'What do you think his game is anyway?' calls Orridge, several paces behind me.

'Hurry up and you can ask him yourself.'

Without considering the city or entertaining it in any way other than having to be here every day, I feel like I am always waiting for it. If I am not dreaming of my life as a writer, I drift through the rituals and circularities that comprise my life and the landscape here: meaningless hallucinations that are obligated to my daily tasks; long, pointless journeys; the familiar but alien lodgings, waiting rooms, interview rooms, empty rooms, interrupted by a little panic and sometimes violence. The series always ends in time for an orderly handover between dimensions, as I climb out of bed and experience it all again, for real. No wonder people are going missing. I might myself if I had anywhere to go.

'Oi!' says Orridge. 'It's that way, isn't it?'

He is pointing at a dry cleaners, which aside from being the establishment I know he takes his shirts to be ironed at, seems particularly off, as the entrance to the giant warren of tat that is the antique market is directly in front of us. By the standards of what has passed, it exudes a fiddly vibrancy, and, being full of peculiar detritus, is at least what it purports to be, the elaborate steel gates leading into a myriad of interconnecting stalls, tightly packed corridors and glorified cubicles. Although there is no formal order to the place, the first floor is dominated by flintlock pistols and sword sticks; the second, curious jewellery and corgi-shaped cigarette lighters; and the third, expensive pieces and more recent cultural acquisitions.

'Floor three,' I say. 'Let's use the fire escape — he would.'

'Shall I wait outside in case he tries to make a break for it?'

'We've PCs following us, Max, and that car over there is already watching it. There's really no need.'

'So they haven't seen him go in?'

'They were looking for a nutter with an axe — all our man needs is a new jacket and a different walk and he's a member of the public again.'

'Bloody hell, this could be dangerous, Terry.'

'It's the life we chose, Max.'

As I attack the steps, Orridge continues to lag behind, making a great show of not knowing where he is going, stopping to examine fire extinguishers and acting as if this building were suddenly created last night, for all he knew, prior to our discovery of it on the street moments earlier.

'Who in their right mind would want any of this stuff?' he huffs as a woman carrying a pile of old video box sets, the most prominent boasting the legend *Garry Glitter's Festive Gang Bang*, squeezes past us. 'This stuff's not even worth stealing.'

'I went from loving and collecting it to giving it all away, without a bit in between.'

'I was *always* at the dumping stage,' says Orridge sniffily. 'I've never liked crap about the place. It's just another addiction, isn't it? Trivial people collecting trivial rubbish that reminds them of when they were young and stupid enough to think a Rubik's Cube was worth more than ordinary common sense.'

'They'd have to be pretty old to remember this stuff from when they were young.' I gently edge a suit of armour blocking the landing out of our way. 'The Wars of the Roses, right?'

'Balls!' Orridge fancies himself as an amateur historian, attends reenactments and works as a volunteer talking head at various festivals sponsored by the *Daily Mail,* so is on home territory here. 'This piece of cast-iron crap was made out of sardine tins in a recycling plant in Lisbon. Full of counterfeit junk this place. It's an embarrassment is what it is.'

'If you say so, Max, *but...*'

'But what?' He cannot help himself either. 'But *what?*'

'It's still the most interesting place to shop in the city once you take Sports Direct out of the equation...'

Reliably oblivious to ironic intent, Orridge snaps, 'Only for people who don't *know* the city, Terry — people like you who just see it as a stepping stone to somewhere else. I'd happily survive with just Mole Valley Farm Stores, Dyas and Aldi. Our general wholesalers are the best in the county. Custard, cider, body warmers, pliers, whatever you need. They've got the lot, and most of it is on offer.'

'That shopping basket sounds hard on your digestive system.'

'I'm serious. Ordinary is good, common isn't common, plain is pretty. It's something any fool who has been to university will never, ever understand, and that, my friend, is why the "blue wall" will never fall between Andover and Grately. People round here have too much common sense. You and your student theorising, you should have heard yourselves earlier. If I want that sort of bollocks, I'd turn on the evening news...'

I clear the last step, slightly out of breath and dimly aware that Orridge is still talking, and that Lockheart must be even more tired than we are. 'We're here. You want to ask the questions?'

He's ready for this too. 'No fear! I'll keep my eyes out for that maniac we're all meant to be in mortal dread of. You lead. They're bound to be more your sort of people here — all bloody mad. You know how to deal with this sort. Let me look round the shop for our fugitive. If he's got here this quietly, he's bound to be hiding in some poke-hole.' Orridge strokes his pocket. 'And I've got nice old-fashioned six-inch cosh in here to sort out his hash if he has any backchat about coming quietly. But you do the talking. This is your world.'

I can see what he means. At the top of the stairs is a long draped curtain, sprawling across the floor, in front of which is stood a naked mannequin in a surgical mask with the legend 'I'll buy that for a dollar' tippexed across its midriff. A leather flying cap is sat atop its head, an old Sten gun, minus its magazine, hanging from its shoulder, and thigh-high silver platform boots, lest he want to take off anywhere, pulled up its legs. To protect the model's modesty, a large and angry print of the Duke of Edinburgh has been plastered over the non-existent genitals, which makes me grateful the place lacks a lift, as no one over eighty could survive the staircase and so waste our time with a formal complaint.

'Disgusting!' snorts Orridge. 'We should have them for public indecency. It's one thing to be showered with disrespect from foreigners but another to have to take it from our own people...'

'Don't worry, Max. Their day will come.'

I haul open the drape, which drags like copper-bearing lead, and we step inside. The view is much as I remember it from the last and only time I was here. Then I was on the lookout for a few old comics to help with insomnia and unprepared for the acres of vintage pornography, theatre programmes, winkle pickers and *Just Seventeens* that awaited me like broken promises to a former self. By the time I reached the till three hours later, I could taste the chocolate spread on white bread, hear the rumble of planes flying over the suburbs on a Sunday, and savour the smell of print as I entered the newsagent for my paper round, the glorious privilege of having encountered all this in real time — duration's consolation prize for having made it thus far.

'Aren't you coming in?' I whisper to Orridge, who is stalling again.

Perhaps it is no accident that I have not been back since. Little suggests they have cleaned up their act. Bizarre Bazaar is still a temple of frozen moments, paths not taken, unrealised possibilities and hopeful speculation, a testament to the future that did not happen, and the past that hoped it would. Maybe that is why I notice a sadness coming off this stuff, not only because it is unwanted but on account of there being something in me that *needs* to want it again, to rescue the idea of value from impermanent becoming and convince myself that *I* matter.

'Strewth!' says Orridge. 'Welcome to the hipsters' landfill. Dog farts and magic tricks. This is even worse than I thought.'

I hardly know where to look to avoid seeing a signifier, an old Christmas gift, or some eerie clue as to how my current sense of self was determined by what happened to be on the cover of the *NME* thirty years before. Besides the expected nods to law enforcement — a poster for Bogart as Marlowe in *The Big Sleep*; Harry Callaghan persecuting hippy serial-killers in San Francisco; and Tom Baker taking a day off from terrifying me to death as a child as Doctor Who, dressed instead as Holmes in a deerstalker — there are the battalions of the rank-and-file goods that help bulk up the true collector's shopping list. Depending on how tenderly an alien visitor regards the stacks of scratched records, football annuals, and browning and yellowing copies of *Whizzer and Chips* and *Warlord*, may be the difference between their annihilating our species on the spot, for making the least of its existence, or sparing us out of pity, for this was the best we could do.

All this, and still no sign of Lockheart.

'Good morning, if morning is still what it is — it's hard to tell from deep within these walls! How can I help you, gentlemen, you distinguished representatives of the outside world, you martyrs to good taste?'

Stood behind the red velour counter at a rakish angle appropriate to a master of ceremonies, the proprietor throws open his palms and beams at us like a welcoming genie, his eyes twinkling madly, which, though part of the agreeable shtick I remember from my first visit, is far too friendly a greeting for two people who may have simply wandered in by mistake. Without a pause, the smile evolves into a throaty chuckle, our arrival at once welcome and even funnier than our new friend at first thought, a performance so divorced from our silent presence that I wonder if it is not being put on for someone else's benefit. Are we being watched? The same thought may have occurred to Orridge, who, ignoring the greeting completely, proceeds with his head down, as if entering a sex shop from a busy street. Once on the far side of the room, he taps a cabinet with the scrutiny of a health and safety official, on the lookout for secret passages or a revolving wall, leaving me to return the pleasantries.

'Good morning,' I offer with as bold a smile as I can muster. Jumping to conclusions, ignoring nuance, universalising off the rule of thumb and embracing generalisations are all part of the job; the ringmaster reminds me of a disgraced public figure on the wrong side of the law. And those who look alike are alike. Was my last visit the only time I saw this man, or do we have a professional connection? The small box room behind him is so overloaded and thick with junk that it has overflowed right up to the counter. If Lockheart is in here, he must be here on the main shop floor.

'I see your compadre knows what he is looking for,' guffaws our friend. 'And what of you, sir? Might you be searching for the same thing or, if I may, something a little different, something a little more peculiar, something wholly *other* perhaps?' His pupils dilate and appear to pop, and he promptly bursts out laughing again. The clockwork jollity suggests cannabis edibles may be behind his mirth, as I would have to go back to being stoned to reference the last time I found everything so funny.

Before I can make a non-committal remark about a fleeing villain to test the water, the shopkeeper starts up again with a vengeance. 'The thing about this place is that the world keeps ending but the young keep turning up! Just as you think all this stuff is really over, once and for all as it were, another cluster of kids pops up ready to rediscover it all again. Once upon a time, not so many years ago, it was just people our age, alright, my age, I see I may have a decade or so on you, but it would have been old timers like us, basically, that would have been the core custom, but not a bit of it now! You'd be amazed, amazed I tell you, simply amazed at the number of teenagers we have turning up asking for stuff even I'd forgotten existed. Amazed! And you know why?'

I am about to tell him that I do not, although I do have my suspicions, but picking up the pace to preempt any possible contradiction, he leaps to the heart of his analysis, 'I'll tell you why, I will, I will! It's because their *culture*, or what passes for culture, is so *fucking boring.* So dull, in fact, that they've been left with no choice! In-no-va-tion...' he rolls this word out slowly as if it took practice to get this part of his monologue right, 'is no longer innovative, or even cultural, or even in the realm of the culture if you follow me? Right? It's all bloody technology. All how and no what. And the music these poor little blighters listen to, on their shitty little phones and tablets and whatnots; well, that's just compressed auto-tune stadium-house isn't it? Even the rappers sound like little girls. Not for me. I remember when rave banged and hip-hop rocked, just like you do. Bet you knew where you were in '92, eh?'

It is time to offer our impresario some unqualified validation. 'Shoulder to shoulder with you in some tent, I don't doubt.'

'Ha ha ha, I knew it, I knew it,' he chortles, practically falling across the counter with unfeigned joy. 'It wasn't necessarily a happier time, but at least we had more time! You can always tell a man who has led an interesting life — they all come in here, you know. They can't help it... can't help it. Drawn towards the place, you all are. Living in the present... who needs it! Because that is the thing, isn't it? There's just that little bit of your life that matters — the part where you might actually do something that interests someone else, and you live that part in real time. Then the rest ambles along off-camera with no one else watching you or the clock anymore. Time doesn't stay still; it just stops happening! Well, this shop is about the moments that actually *occurred*. I like to think I am restoring time to her former standing!'

In spite of my thinking the only state that is fully real is the present, as everything else suffers from actually not happening *now*, and that immersion in it is the only way to beat my sentimentalising tendencies, I nod like an obliging rube, gushing, 'We still have the music; what's gone is our lives!'

'Bravo!'

Unable to help myself, I add, 'As for time being over, I don't think it ever happened. There are no timeless moments because there are no moments. Duration applies only to living matter, not to time. You literally are revisiting the same moment because there aren't any. That's why everything is so familiar.'

'Top-fucking-notch! We've met before, haven't we?'

I nod. None of this has smoked out Lockheart, and as Orridge is now buggering about on his hands and knees, we're running out of places to look.

'Oh, I know that. Recognised you as soon as I saw you. Not so sure about your, er, friend though...' He frowns in Orridge's direction. I look to see where my colleague has got to and catch sight of his arm disappearing behind the tiny changing room curtain. 'He doesn't look like one of my regulars...'

'Certainly not one of your teenagers...' I add helpfully.

Further hilarity ensues, with possibly the slightest hint of caution and rectitude. 'Now, now! That sounds like I think I have proprietorship of those wilful souls who come in, and that I don't. Because we're all free spirits at the end of the day, aren't we, aren't we? Individuals, as it were. Rebels, clowns and loners. I'm Barry by the way, Barry Swillcut. Sorry to be so slow with that. You're right to assume that this is my place — has been for years, what with a little altering here and there, and damnably proud of it I am.'

Swillcut's accent is broad and compatible with any county between here and Shropshire, his smooth burr tailing off like a fondly remembered family pet disappearing into the woods at sunset. With the sandy complexion of a gypsy, large suggestive eyes, bent ears, an oft broken nose, and teeth that look like they are one sticky-bun away from falling out, he is a first cousin of the footpads, highwaymen and threats to a virgin's maidenhood that once terrorised these country lanes, their bodies providing food for the crows on Gallows Hill, Grim's Ditch and other popular places of public execution that are now the province of amblers and doggers. These days the milieu he belongs to moves from respectability to criminality like water through a lock gate, the outward-facing business the insurance policy that their crimes never become too terrible, or worth our bothering with too closely; the respectability of having one foot in the 'legit' world a feint we are all in on. Dressed like a pastiche of an end-of-the-pier fortune-teller, Swillcut's manner has the decorous charm of one who accepts that the assembling and selling on at cost of marginalia is a fair price for the pleasure of meeting such interesting people as us. His thinning and adventurously dyed hair reeks of ongoing sexual self-regard, and I decide I like him, despite my working out who he reminds me of: a disgraced glam rocker involved in a Cambodian paedophile ring, with the most notorious hard drive in recent criminal history.

'I know. I do look a bit like him,' he intuits slyly. Noticing my smile redraw, he quickly adds, 'Don't worry — I can't read minds. It's just that I get it from everyone. Honestly, I wish that bastard had never been born. On to happier things, though. Your name, sir?'

'I'm Terry. My friend is Max.' I do not know whether my intention is to announce us as a gay couple, but then shopkeepers, even ones as friendly as this, do not normally ask their customers for their names, and while I am sure that Swillcut suspects we are police, I want to hold off confirming his inkling for as long as I can.

'So, Terry, buying something for yourself or shopping for anyone special in your life? Maybe you've just met someone you'd like to purchase a special pressie for? Swilly can always tell!'

I am beginning to recognise that Swillcut suggests more than he says, and in his suggestion is his meaning. Together we are embarked on a waltz of coded innuendo, and will dance until one of us cracks and is forced to get to the point, or a fugitive from justice breaks up the party.

'I suspect you use a lot of your own product,' I say, keeping the focus on him, and point to his jacket, which, unlike his clown trousers and battered Hawaiian-shirt, is the work of a once fashionable designer of early nineties boho-chic.

He cannot resist talking about himself and preens for me, 'Oh yes, fetching isn't it? I used to work for them actually, in a rather uncertain capacity,' he laughs. 'All this was mainstream once, you could buy the clothes in department stores. There were record shops on every high street; you didn't need to come into little corners of progress like this to find what you want. All this stuff' — he waves his hands around — 'was everywhere. Yet we keep coming back to it. What part of all this magic, I wonder, could I interest you in, if you'll forgive my persistence?'

'Everything is of interest,' I say, sure by now that Orridge, who has remerged from behind the dressing curtain with a pinched air about him, has not found Lockheart, but has encountered something else that has piqued his curiosity. 'Who is this we're listening to?' I ask, pointing at a speaker.

'Oh, a little-known local band, they don't exist anymore but had their day in the sun when you could still make money out of such things as compulsion, fascination and intrigue. Well ahead of their time they were, well ahead.'

The music is a cross between a fairground din, a Scandinavian troll animation and early techno produced by people who did not understand it, played slow. It is insidious, labyrinthine and highly hypnotic, an effect akin to a favourite uncle strumming his lyre by the fireplace, the danger not apparent until the second you catch his eye, go under and lose control...

'It's sinister,' I say. 'What we used to think music would sound like in the future. Except it doesn't.'

'Yes,' says Swillcut, eyeing the box Orridge has tucked under his arm so as to not draw attention to it, 'the great thing about the past was that we were still able to think about the future; we didn't know what it was going to be yet. And now we've got it, we turn to the past to excite us. Yes, that's nostalgia for you — feast without food... So you don't want anything then, you've just come in here to pass the time of day?'

His eyes are not smiling now; the dance is over.

'No, I'm not here to buy anything.'

'Oh, I must say I am disappointed.'

I turn away from him and allow Orridge to approach the counter, holding the silence. He shakes his head and solemnly mouths, 'Nothing.'

'There is one thing actually,' I mention, as an aside, still facing Orridge and the likely direction of any attack.

'And that was?'

'You don't happen to know whether a Mr Alvin Lockheart has been in for that thing he ordered yet?'

The question has an ugly affect, and suddenly I see another Swillcut: an emissary of the Spanish Inquisition, the crowing torturer stood over the rack, brimming with surprised contempt for our not having found him out before.

'I beg your pardon?'

I say nothing, turn, and look at him coldly, interested to see if any of his warmth will survive this encounter with reality.

'Say, you two fellas, you're not...'

'DCI Balance and DSI Orridge. We've reason to believe a man we're looking for in connection to an ongoing investigation has either already entered here this morning, or will be on his way soon. We want to establish whether you know of his intentions and are expecting him or not.'

Swillcut does not want this to sink in, and, suppressing a snarl, reveals more of his actual nature. Were circumstances more to his favour, I might be about to wrestle a knife off him now.

'You've given me a bit too much to take in there. Your names, his name, whoever he is, police and whatnot. Crikey. You need to give me a bit of notice before coming in with the old one-two.' His voice is softer and less elaborative, his message just for us. 'What did you say this bloke was called again?'

'Lockheart, Alvin, sometimes known as Eddie,' says Orridge, finally entering the fray.

'Lockheart?'

'Yes,' I say, 'an ugly bloke about my height who would have been out of breath and most flustered about something. We had an idea he might be hiding here.'

'Ha!' Swillcut tries to squeeze the cheer out again, the singer in a metal act that cannot start or end a song without cackling at his little in-joke with Satan, but gravity is irreversible, and glumly he concedes, 'No, your honour, that name doesn't do it for me. No bells ringing at all. Have never heard of the bloke. Sorry, there it is.'

At this moment it is rather hard to prove otherwise, in spite of it being impossible for ne'er-do-wells of this calibre and size to not have run across each other in a city this size before.

'Now if you don't mind, I do have a shop to run,' he says, and, recovering quickly, leans over to Orridge. 'You've got something there I can help you with... Max, wasn't it?'

'Yes,' replies Orridge, 'if you could gift-wrap it, please.'

'There are no other exits than the one we came in through?' I persist, glaring at Orridge, the advantage slipping away.

'None, Detective.'

Swillcut ceremoniously takes a box marked 'Giant Bazoombas' and, without the slightest trace of laughter now, stuffs it carefully into a large brown paper bag, whistling the tune to *The Sweeney* as he binds it together with a blue and white ribbon.

Orridge turns to me, ready with a procession of excuses that obscure the actual reasons for a man's conduct: 'For a stag do. My father-in-law is getting married again. Always useful to have a pair about the place on the off-chance that there's another one too. And they're always good for a raffle, aren't they?'

'You know. I thought you boys were either delivery men or police,' says Swillcut, no longer under any compulsion to be friendly. 'You'll be wanting to pay for that in cash?'

Orridge nods and then, to emphasise our changing relationship, Swillcut adds, 'Here, hold on a minute, some comedian came in with one of these.' He pulls an old issue custodian police helmet out from under the counter. 'Take it. This one's on me. It'll go nicely with the tits.'

*

'That was about as big a waste of time as I thought it'd be,' sneers Orridge as he tries to brush away the heavy curtain unsuccessfully, his voice fizzing with recrimination. 'I knew it, knew it from the start that we were writing a crime and then trying to find a culprit. Don't tell me you want to search every shop in this place now, no? I thought not! Honestly, you should have been a social worker, Terry.'

'It was going pretty well until your breast job.'

'Don't you dare try turning this round on me! Would have been a totally pointless trip otherwise...' Orridge scratches at the curtain he is unwittingly standing on. 'Bloody thing...'

My phone plays its music — a message from Tamla: *Suspect absolutely bloody nowhere to be found. Et tu?'*

'Bloody hell! Can someone tell me how this thing is supposed to work?' Orridge curses.

'Allow me, Max.' I tear the cloth impatiently down the middle, and it parts to reveal a statuesque face, as attent and still as a watchful hare.

'I'm sorry,' its owner apologises, exaggerating the motions of appearing surprised mid-movement, 'I was on my way in to ask Barry if he fancied a coffee and a slice of cake for elevenses.'

Cue the laughter, as Swillcut shifts back into his preferred mode of being, 'I think we're running into lunchtime now, Breezy me ol' mucker!' he yells across us to remind us that we were leaving. 'Balls to confectionary — a moist pork pie and a pint is what I fancy! True signs of the superiority of our civilisation over all others.'

'Who are you?' I ask the man he is addressing as a familiar. Until a member of the public knows you are a police officer, many understandably object to having their identity questioned in this way, and I take it as a sign of a restless conscience if they do not.

Accepting my role as interrogator with courtly politeness, the man replies, 'Bertrand Fallgrief, though "Breezy" is all anyone knows me as. I own The Red House Antiques just next to here... over there, in fact.'

'What's the significance of The Red House, Mr Fallgrief?'

'It's the building that stood here before this one,' says Orridge hurriedly, 'the bordello of one of the old bishops.'

'My, that's exactly right,' agrees Breezy, rocking back on his heels to absorb the force of Orridge's knowledge. 'Full marks for swotting on your history. This is where the ecclesiastical tarts were housed. There was actually a tunnel of some kind linking the two sides of Cathedral Street. That's how the cardinal used to get at his fillies unseen.'

'Easy, Breezy. Don't demean those worldly courtesans. They were a refined breed who had little in common with today's sex worker...' chips in Swillcut, wistfully rubbing some dust from his eye.

'Sex workers? Don't make me laugh. Call them whores and have done with it, then we'll all know what manner of female we're referring to,' snaps Orridge.

'Point taken. Sex should be a joyous thing, not something you "work" at. Even if you are having to be paid to for it,' Breezy obliges, winking at me playfully. 'I'm a great believer in the wisdom of whores, as it happens.'

I take my leave of the sewing circle and give The Red House the once over. I do not like it, but Swillcut's neighbour's emporium is clearly a cut above the gauche competition. As one of only three franchises that occupy the entire floor, the other a tiny gallery, it is a proper shop and not a stall or glorified stand. A glass partition reveals a careful and minimal window display, in sober contrast to pretty much everything else in this building, showcasing an austere pair of curiosities. An uncomfortable looking chair, which ought to come with an acupuncturist's commission, sits opposite a very short double bed that appears to have been borrowed from the London Dungeon, with the purpose of punishing sleepers with legs. These are the only highlights Breezy uses to draw in the initiated, the rest is darkness, black cloths blocking out the view into the shop. Doubtless these items are worth a year's fees at Eton, their very lack of utility the salient mark of their true worth to castle-crawlers who appreciate dank and frustrated objects to those that oblige. Yet for all that, I sense The Red House will not be troubling Homebase anytime soon.

'Ahh, you've noticed the old *paillasse*. There's a story behind that which involves an Austrian count, his mistress, Richard Branson and a bankruptcy! Yes, I had to fight to get that piece. Even the shorter version of it would take about a week to tell...'

'I'll look for a space on my calendar.'

Breezy has edged up to me and is beaming with such an excess of helpful goodwill that I resist the urge to turn chippy, as, with the advantages I suspect he has enjoyed in life, niceness may well be another form of condescension.

'Is there much money in this?' I ask, trying to level off the hostility in my voice.

'Far too much! Especially when it's busy.'

'Is this a busy day?' I let my accent be what it is. Competing with his pronunciation would look too much like seeking approval, for although I have been called a chap, fellow, lad and bloke, there is no point in my trying to pass for a gentleman.

'I'd like to say it's too early to say, but Monday's always pretty dismal. Unless a serious collector has booked a viewing, and no such luck at present.'

'Do you actually make or create anything? Or is it all just old stuff that somebody else did that you mark up and sell on?'

Breezy is one of nature's good sports. 'What, engage in genuine creativity? God forbid no! Ha ha, no, of course. I take your point. Let's just say there's a lot more dosh in moving on my kind of cultural artefact than there is in Barry's line, though there's just as little "original" input in my handling early-eighteenth-century walnut sconces as there is in Bazza flogging old *Beano* annuals. All of it some other person's work, of course. We're both a pair of coffin-robbers, basically. It hasn't all been plain sailing, mind. There was a bit of a wobble for a while when everyone wanted to design their own *très moderne* houses and fill them with office furniture lifted off Kilburn High Road, but the reaction to that's already set in, thank God.'

'A return to the old?'

'Oh for sure, yah, you know, rock stars and hedge fund managers that grew up in the suburbs, they like a coat of arms above the fireplace and an old harpsichord in the nursery. Those are the timeless hallmarks of having made it for these types; you've got to be really sure of yourself to prefer the newer stuff. I spend half my life in people's houses helping them put pieces in the right places. Many of them end up friends; it's a way of life really, my vocation. And it's amazing how grateful people are — quite touching, really.'

I bet it is: I come up short in so many ways, but at least I have never compensated for my lower-middle-class banality by nursing a lack that I fill by sucking up to old money or famous people. Those friends I have having only one thing in common: I like them all. Embittered as I may be, the only hard work Fallgrief is committed to putting in is kow-towing to society, cultivating his circle of clients and dazzling buyers with ever greater acts of obsequious self-defenestration. To give him his due, he appears to know it, and he has played down his angular rugby-playing physique with a tatty old cardigan and salmon pink cords that are too short in the leg. He is handsome in a way the head boy from a film set in a 1930s public school might be; a slight chalking at the temples offset by a dark quiff and pleasantly quizzical air which, with his Lennon-specs and Rembrandt moustache, renders him attractive to women who would not afford Swillcut a second glance. I sense these two superficial opposites work in some oblique way together, as a team, and that Fallgrief's sudden appearance for fruitcake and a latte is no coincidence.

'Just the other day I was at Sting and Trudie's place actually, sorting out a dining set.'

'You could have taken him back some of his albums,' chuckles Swillcut. 'I've far too many of them hogging space.'

'Are you two business partners?' I ask.

Swillcut brays like a New Forest Jack. 'My, that was a bit sudden! What a notion, in my dreams, in my dreams! Whatever could give you that idea.'

'I don't know. I'm never surprised to find things where they shouldn't be, or people either.'

'What a thought, Barry, eh? A superb connection, just not one we've ever had the imagination to make for ourselves!' Fallgrief's effusiveness, like his being English, is something that can only be done inadvertently, but his primary quality, the one that reveals who he is, is more mysterious. Despite standing inches from my face, so I can smell rarefied eucalyptus toothpaste on his breath, Fallgrief's charm is at the service of something larger than a single person. As I suspect this entity to be a particular state of affairs relevant to our enquiries, I am ready to see what effect mentioning Lockheart has, when Orridge barges me on, leaning keenly into my back: 'Best be on our way now, Terry. We've a mountain of stuff to be getting on with.'

Ironically for one who expects to be obeyed, I do not like being told what to do, and as I bristle at Orridge's forceful push, Fallgrief's sublime grin, and Swillcut's twinkling peepers, I realise they all know something I do not.

They all know each other.

CHAPTER SIX

CLOSEDOWN

'Listen, Terry, it might not always seem this way, I know, and of course to you I'm simple country plod, but I'm not your enemy. I'm trying to help you, help *us,* from a needless drama that easily could become something far worse if we're not careful...' Max is failing to master the agitation in his voice.

We walk off the stairwell onto Cathedral Street, where a row of dinky upmarket guest houses built into the old city walls curl into the heel of The Close, a celebrated view that always fails to move me, unless I imagine it scooped up and squashed in the hands of a giant being.

'I don't want to pull rank on you, but spell it out, Max. I'm rubbish at nuance and you're doing a fine job of getting in my pubes.' I raise my hand and blink to deflect a whirr of solar-orbs, the sun blazing through the dancing mist and spilling into the street with the luminescence of an astral flare. 'Just get to the fucking point.'

'Okay, okay,' Orridge sighs. 'Frankly, this is embarrassing, but I'll lay it out for you. You don't want to go annoying that Breezy feller. It was alright for a bit with Swillcut, he's one thing, but Breezy Fallgrief is another thing altogether, believe me.' Orridge scratches at his stubble. 'And even if he wasn't, you don't go charging into battle without a nag to ride on! Jesus, Terry, we have nothing! You're an experienced officer, and for all your failings, no, hear me out, because I have never said this to you before, and what I've got to say may surprise you. For all your failings, you're a very intelligent man. Very intelligent. One of the cleverest I've ever met, in fact. And yet you're the daftest clever person I ever met because you're arrogant and flashy and in love with yourself. Just look at you. The way you dress, people would think you were on the take. No wonder you haven't got any money left for anything sensible and can't afford to move back to London!'

'Stay on point, Max. It's not my tailor you have an issue with.' This would be a good moment for Lockheart to reappear though an intervention from that direction looks unlikely; the street tranquil and sedate.

'But it's all part of it, Terry.' Orridge has clenched his fists for emphasis and could quite easily punch me with them. 'Instead of our working well together, compensating for each other's shortcomings as it were, not that you'd admit to any, I find myself having to explain things to you I wouldn't even have to write down for Christopherson. Which makes us so much less than what we could be. You hear me?'

The sun's spots are blending into whatever shapes I want them to make, and I discern the outline of Tamla walking towards us, eating a frosted bun. Christopherson is behind her, staring intently into his phone. Two uniformed officers watch us uneasily from the other side of the road, and it occurs to me that we have been speaking at the top of our voices, shouting even.

'I'm not sure I follow what good teamwork has to do with not energetically pursuing an investigation? You seem scared to do the job, Max.'

'No, you wouldn't see what they have to do with each other, would you?' Orridge points at me. 'When I say that it is time for tact, I don't want you to just say, "Yes, Max", because I know you're the boss. I'm just a DSI, but please just have some respect for my experience and white hairs. That's what being part of a team means. Instead you go hell for leather with that *Hill Street Blues* routine, a regular hard-arse. *Trust* my intuition, as the rest of us have to so often suffer yours, and, don't laugh, trust my superior knowledge of local conditions. This is my ground. I've been on the job here before you even knew where this place was. I was born in this county, Terry. It's my land, my ground. So I repeat, this is not the place for poking our noses carelessly into the perfectly innocent affairs of the doyens of this community. Please, please, believe me. Agreed?' Orridge has actually been tapping my chest to make these points and slowly draws his hand away.

'No, not really,' I answer. 'Not really agreed at all. For an arch empiricist who scorns theory and believes only in first-hand experience, you've a real reluctance to do stuff, Max.'

'Leave it out! We've absolutely *nothing* on either of them, and you know it. We're sailing into police harassment territory. In my experience, that never ends well. What you are refusing to get your head around, simply because you don't want to...' — he is jacked up and talking quickly, in a rush to finish before the others reach us — 'is that most of the time things *are* just what they seem and people *are* just telling us the truth. This isn't some dark fantasy where beneath the surface a fascinating and kinky world of deviants and unholy jokers lurk for us to arrest, and then unearth a giant conspiracy they're all part of. That's just for boy scouts who can't take the world as it is and have to dream up stories to make everything seem more interesting. You go round playing that game, and we cease to do our jobs properly. You're right, I am an empiricist, a pragmatist, a whatever you want to call it, and proud of it. But you, you're setting up a false opposition. Experience is not the *enemy* of a good imagination; it is what keeps it realistic. Otherwise, the ball has a tendency to fly all over the place. Like it does whenever you have it. What I am saying is try and be a real policeman for a change. Just do the job, and stop being so bloody swift.'

'Right. The sort of policeman who thinks things are just as they seem, or worse, wants them to be. The kind that doesn't have any place in plainclothes, that isn't fit to be a detective, that should stick to taking the numberplates of speeding BMWs and enforcing curfews. Be that kind of real policeman? The funny thing is, I don't think you are simple country plod, Max. I think the truth is a lot weirder — I think you just pretend to be.'

'And what the hell is that supposed to mean?' Orridge retorts, his voice tightening.

Usually I fear any sincere criticism of me may be right, and that my counterattacking instinct is simply a way of denying superior adult insight. Orridge, however, is giving me hope that my time may have finally come. 'What's really going on here, Max? For once we're gently ruffling the feathers of an antique dealer instead of making arrests on a housing estate, and rather than run with the wolves, you're...'

'He's nowhere,' Tamla interrupts me. 'Nowhere. We've got people knocking on doors, going over roofs, checking CCTV, and nothing yet... our man's been swallowed by the city. I take it from your aggrieved expressions that you haven't found him either?'

'No,' says Orridge through gritted teeth. 'Lockheart hasn't been through here. We cased the place. Unless Terry has some fanciful theory based on ancient myth in which he's been turned into an antique table, we've drawn a complete blank too.'

'Interesting... okay then. We've gone from killer on the loose to another body being swallowed up by the ether. I suggest you and I go back to school, Max — talk to those teachers and see if they've any views on where the kids might have got to. You two,' she addresses me and Christopherson, already sensitive to my and Orridge's need to be separated, 'should chase the other families. If they actually fear something is wrong, they may be more forthcoming than they've been thus far. Lockheart may be lying low and licking his wounds, but that doesn't mean he isn't still dangerous, so I am going to ask for these streets to keep being scanned and for that entire market to be checked out too.'

'Suit yourself. Those families are where I said we should be looking all along.' Max yawns and, avoiding looking at me, says, 'Well, you said yourself we're not on code red anymore. Whatever that nut's doing, he's decided to do it under the radar. The PCs have it all covered. Let's take a breather for Christ's sake, why don't we? For lunch at least. I'm done in and starving. We've been going nonstop all morning.'

'Care for a bite of this to save time?' Tamla holds the gnawed end of her bun tantalisingly close to Orridge's nose, watching him redden, before tossing it playfully into the air, throwing her head back, and catching it between her teeth.

'Circus, you belong in.'

Tamla wipes her mouth and, leaning against me to adjust the catch on her boot, finally acknowledges my silence. 'Cheer up, chicken. At least no one has ended up with an axe buried in their noggin. Take your lunch break, Max, but I think you're making a mistake. We're in the middle of something here, and this is no time for a siesta.'

'I want tails on Fallgrief and Swillcut,' I blurt to Christopherson, 'the proprietors of Bizarre Bazaar and The Red House. We've reasonable grounds to suspect both are persons of interest.'

'Not this again, Terry,' Orridge groans, a father humouring his still petulant thirty-nine-year-old baby. 'Let's not do this again, now. We've been over and through all this.'

'No. You have, Max.'

Orridge shakes his head — a silverback reluctantly goaded into battle. 'I say this with a heavy heart, because it's like having to read from the *Prayer Book of Common Sense* with you, and I don't enjoy being right,' he sighs. 'And anyway, you and Tamla are meant to be in charge here, but I suppose it needs to be reiterated in front of witnesses. We've absolutely no bloody reason, no bloody reason at all, to think those two men are persons of interest, other than, at best, the indirect insistence of a publican with known criminal connections who was looking to get us out of her pub. And that's it! That's all you have to go on, Terry. However, on the other hand, the one you do not want to acknowledge the very obvious existence of, we have a different seam that you are highly unwilling to mine, probably because it doesn't excite you.'

'Schools and the families I suppose?' I say, grinding my teeth.

'What else? I've worked these estates for years, Terry. I know these families, these clans, the intermarried and the interbred, their histories, their tragedies, their proclivities. I've handled daughters who smoke crack with their fathers, girls prostituted by their uncles, high-risk lifestyles to put it mildly. Folk who consider nothing amiss in not seeing someone they live with for a good month, because if their next of kin was found dead in a Travelodge it'd be preferable to where they'd have expected to find them — in a back alley or ditch, with a needle in their arm. Fertile ground by anyone's standards for a mispers investigation, and yet you... you want to bugger round town in junk shops, chasing fairies and suppositions. To get this thing done, we need to dig deeper into the records of the individual families, their criminal histories, the connections between them. And if you really do think dark forces are at play, and that they're knocking each other off or something of that sort, then we'll at least be in a position to find out about it, instead of being mugged off by Lovejoy and Worzel Gummidge, like we were here today.'

As the only thing I can think of saying is that he was the one that bought the fake tits, I remain silent and glare.

'He has a point, Terry,' says Tamla. 'Until we can find Lockheart at any rate.'

'Good,' says Orridge triumphantly, eyeballing me. 'So unless Terry wants the last word, you and I reconvene here in an hour and a half, Tamla, hot pursuit be damned, and those two can begin knocking on doors whenever they fancy. Until then, I need to find a pasty and someone to lend me a car to kip in.'

*

We watch Orridge walk away with an intent and purpose he lacked on our journey here. Tamla shrugs her shoulders sympathetically, my opportunity to prove that I am right over this finished for now. The failure to have my way would be far easier to accept were it not for the connections I see before me: interlinked regiments of association pouring into a single indissociable totality that binds this morning together through ambitious guesses, fleeting details, half-remembered hunches and, compromised as I would be to put it this way, glimpses of other worlds. Having had to effectively abandon my ego to discern any of this, I lack the proper names, terms and structures to translate my findings into the demonstrable language of evidence. Until the dense complexity of human motivation has been stripped back to reveal a simplicity I have come to appreciate, drawing attention to what might kindly be regarded as my 'instincts' would be all the proof the world requires to dismiss me as an egotistical crank. Thank God no one can hear me think all this stuff. Orridge is right: I am aiming too high.

In light of the dissonant chatter filling my mind's ears, I am surprised that when I speak I hear a single voice, the same one I usually use: 'Stop looking at it. You'll deplete your psychic powers.'

'Just a minute, boss. This will interest you.'

'It'll need to be more than interesting.'

'No, look.' Christopherson hands me his iPhone. The screen is open on the Wikipedia page for a band, Acid Horse. 'Right... you see?'

'See what?'

'Scroll down!'

'What am I meant to be looking for? Here, Tamla, help me out.'

Tamla stands on her tiptoes and peers at the phone. 'No, doing nothing for me either.'

'Come on, guys...'

'This is somehow relevant?' I ask.

'Just read on,' Christopherson orders.

'Okay... okay... I don't *think* I'm getting it...'

'Of course you are!'

'...okay... I'm getting it, I think. This is context?'

'It's more than context, boss. I think it might be the bridge you've been trying to establish.'

'Is that so...'

After Orridge's dour summation of the job, assault on my character failings and usurpation of the chain of command and trajectory of the investigation, Christopherson's smiling puppy eyes suggest that I may have won a convert in the battle for hearts and minds.

'O-k-a-y.' I resolve to reward his faith and try harder, rereading the name aloud. 'Acid Horse... Acid Horse? I heard it in there,' I point to the antique market. 'Yes, Swillcut, one of the owners, he was playing them.'

'No, boss. He was *in them*.'

I examine the list of personnel, 'I can't see him, Dexter. He was called something else then?'

'Further down, not in the first incarnation.' Christopherson lowers his finger on his hand, and imaginary phone, to demonstrate what he has in mind, and Tamla bursts out laughing.

'Gotcha,' I say.

'Recognise anyone else?' Christopherson asks.

'I do. Good Old Breezy. How did you go and put them together?'

'The modern world, boss. You'd do well to join it. I ran a Google search on the "Bizarre Bazaar" and, unsurprisingly, got shit. Then you asked for a tail on Swillcut and Fallgrief. Orridge rubbished it, but I ran another search, and bingo — this came up.'

'Is this what detective work has come to? Fucking about on a telephone?' Tamla asks.

'Don't knock it. It's our first result!' Christopherson exclaims.

'Why didn't you say something earlier, Dexter?' I ask.

'There's no point. You know what he's like — we'd have been here all day. It's easier just to get on with it instead of picking fights with Max, isn't it?'

'You might have a point. I wish someone had told me that earlier.'

'So alright, I know this is not exactly the smoking gun you'd need for the CPS but...' Christopherson allows his voice to trap off.

'It shows a connection,' says Tamla.

'Exactly! It shows a connection. Here they are, look, both of them in a band together in the Eighties, and that must signify something right? I mean, if kids living on the same estates is supposed to be significant, then two persons of interest having shared a history together is at least as important. And the thing is,' Christopherson takes a breath, 'I have heard of these guys — anyone from round here would have. I probably know more about them than I do any other band, even though I never actually owned a record. They were sort of notorious, actually.'

'So why didn't you make the connection when I named the two goons, then?'

'I didn't know their individual identities. I was only very young then. I knew about them through my sisters and their mates. These guys weren't stars like Morrissey or Bowie or whoever — they never were big figures in themselves. I wouldn't have even known their actual names back then anyway. The group was the thing with these guys, not their personalities.'

'How do you mean? They were nondescript?' Tamla interrupts.

'A bit, but on purpose, if you know what I mean. In the first place, they weren't glamorous, more an anonymous sort of band, you know, like Pink Floyd, so you wouldn't necessarily be able to recognise them if they walked past you in the street. And then what made it harder, and this was their image, was that they wore gowns and monks' robes on stage, with all these monikers like *Brother Baker, Brother Robinson, Brother Mason* — deliberately mysterious so you could hardly see their faces, like they were a secret brotherhood of initiates. That was the idea, anyway. A lot of people thought they were pretentious tossers. Even then, though, you wouldn't have known their real non-stage names, not unless you happened to get particularly chummy.'

'Why were they so renowned round here? What was the micro-scene?' I ask. 'I love music and only half-registered the name. I don't think I even knowingly heard them until today.'

'I'm not surprised. They didn't have any hits and wouldn't have been rated in the music press or anywhere far out of this area, apart from Finland or Germany or somewhere like that, I think, where they used to tour. But in those days, you know, before YouTube and the internet, if you had an association with some place, then you owned the place. And not being able to easily hear the records, that was all part of it.'

Tamla takes the phone from me. 'It says here that they met at school...'

'Yeah, they started out as a stoner prog rock covers act at college — a cross between Hawkwind and Genesis. Fallgrief was one of the founders, and then I hear they went quiet for bit, before coming back reinvented as an acidy dance outfit, which is when I first remember them from.'

'And apparently when Swillcut joins them as the DJ element, according to Wiki anyway,' says Tamla giving the phone back to Christopherson.

'That doesn't surprise me, he doesn't seem like public school material. I assume the college they all met at was a posh one?' I ask.

'Chafyn Down: our Eton. No good looking for any of our mispers there — a whole row of houses on Hanging Hill wouldn't buy you a single term at that place.'

'This is the public school near the hospital. It got into trouble for a racist bullying incident that made the news.'

'Yeah, that's the one. It's become a serious playground for the kids of toffs now, but it used to have a reputation for being very arty and right-on. The band did their first gigs there, and the school opened up to the city, which was pretty unheard of in those days. It helped 'Orse, as they were of course known, become huge in the area, for a while anyway. I remember my sister going to a three-day winter solstice festival where they were playing, tied in to druid ceremonies and all that mystical carry-on. And also, later on, big tent raves, where they developed a new following. There was also some political activity on the side as well, Wessex regionalism. They were in with the Marquess of Bath for a while, who gave them a studio on his land. He even got an album on the uses of animal semen dedicated to him. Can't remember the name of it, but it was something naughty and had a memorable cover with pair of bull's bollocks on it.'

'A piss-take, right?' Tamla says.

'Not at all. They weren't exactly known for their sense of humour. It was pretty common for them to dedicate records to natural cycles, old gods, crop circles, you know, all that *Wicker Man* stuff. But it all went a little tits-up when they began to develop a bit of a reputation for seediness. Before that though, they could do little wrong round here.' Christopherson beams. This is probably the most he has ever been able to say to us without gentle ridicule, mild derision and intense scepticism.

'Seediness? How do you mean? Hard drugs?' I ask.

'Yeah, though truthfully, they always had a name for that, and in those days no one who knew about those things honestly gave a shit — our lot included. No, it was more underage sex. They had lots of young groupies. They even had a dodgy name for them, though I can't remember what it was... maybe "the Owlets"? Anyway, they were always a bit on the old side for teenyboppers, if you know what I mean, and then one of the girls started complaining, and then they all piped up about being pawed and groped all the time.'

'Did they go to law enforcement?'

'I can't remember, but their parents were all over the local papers. There was only so much these girls were prepared to put up with in the name of free love and the Earth Goddess, especially when they could take off and watch Ocean Colour Scene at the Guildhall and enjoy being molested by boys of their own age.'

'So no one got into any official trouble, as far as you know?'

'One bloke might have — the singer I think. He went to Thailand, ate his lover's liver or some such, and died of AIDS in the can over there, but the others just melted away. The thing was, their manager, he was more famous than they were. He was a prefect at Chafyn, which is where and why he first started running their affairs.'

'Let me guess: he's Mungo Masters?'

'Mungo Masters. *Mr Toad*. Spot on. What you got to understand about that bloke is he was kind of a cross between Rupert Murdoch, Jeffrey Archer and Andrew Lloyd Webber of this area, all rolled into one, a regular Messiah — making deals, writing musicals, buying and owning companies, shops and all sorts. Rumour was he made all the bad stuff around them go away, but to do it, they had to call it a day as band.'

'But *he* doesn't go away does he? He becomes a hedge funder and financier and massive political donor,' says Tamla.

'For sure. He owns that giant place on the Ringwood Road now, where the neighbours complain about helicopters coming and going. Yeah, he's everywhere but here these days. Not much seen of him at his local...'

'I bet you they could tell you some stories though,' speculates Tamla.

Christopherson nods. 'That they could.'

'The local boy has come good,' she says to me. 'I always told you he'd one day justify his inclusion in the top drawer!'

'As we're in full flight, Dexter, I wonder whether our barman at the Hearse, *The Well*, wasn't a fan or roadie of 'Orse back in the day, or perhaps their tour manager? Or maybe he drummed in the support band? Whatever his story, I'd be surprised if he isn't known to our two chums up there in the antique market...'

'More than likely. He has the air of someone who's been a long time in rock 'n' roll, doesn't he?'

'And while we're at it, Lockheart as well... he may go way back to their glory days too — he's about the right age. A groundsman at Chafyn? A bouncer at one of Masters' Clubs?'

'Why not? There's only two degrees of separation between everyone here anyway. Honestly, boss, this is the way in. I think we're on to something.'

'Our problem is that their connections are with each other. That isn't the same as their being connected to the disappearances. And as there is no reason why they'd be obliged to make their private connections public to us, there's no a priori reason to suppose there is anything suspicious about our not knowing about their past lives... but...'

'It's gut, isn't it?' Tamla says.

'Gut, yeah. It is a very thin line that separates the two worlds. Lockheart looks like the one who might have a foot in both.'

'I bet you if we could just find him, we'd be able to prove it too,' Christopherson gushes. 'Where do you think he's got to?'

'My paranoia is still running riot with that one. I think someone has taken him in and is hiding him.'

'And what did you make of the two 'Orsemen turned shopkeepers? Shady?' Tamla asks.

'Max would tell you otherwise, but Swillcut's a card-carrying jailbird if ever I saw one, and Fallgrief a gentleman thief who'd leave his glove on m'lady's pillow after he's swiped her diamonds. We can't issue warrants on the basis of that, I realise, but with your cultural history lesson, and what I saw of those two beauties, I'd say going in hard with them would be rich in possibilities.'

'What about going back up to the estates?' Christopherson asks.

'No point,' says Tamla. 'Max and I will cover that angle. Just as well to keep him busy doing something he enjoys.'

'I'm done with that line anyway,' I say. 'Fuck it. Questioning families on the estates, the kids' teachers, social workers, the lollipop lady and the bloke that runs the local off-licence — it's all a distraction that will serve no purpose other than giving us more of what we already know, which is great big blank. These disappearances aren't just about themselves. The answer to what's caused them won't be found within the usual ecosphere these people live their lives in.'

'I agree,' says Tamla.

'Think about it, Dexter,' I go on. 'The problems these disappearances pose are simply too weird for us to fall back on experience for pointers, otherwise we'd already have this case. But there are no other cases like this. Pull out any part you like, the absence of bodies, the speed of the disappearances, the fact that all hell is breaking loose and we have people trying to tell us it isn't... that's not county lines, suicide pacts or unreported overdoses. It's qualitatively different to anything we've encountered before. Even if we found that every one of the mispers had worked in the Purple Hearse or that they all knew Lockheart at one time or other, we'd still be stuck at the lowest rung of the ladder. The connection you found might be the first step towards actually scaling the thing. You're showing us where we need to look, but it'll only be worth doing if we move up the food chain.'

'It's an ask though, isn't it? Fallgrief is a proper toff.'

'Yeah. But remember "posh people are taking our children"?' Tamla says. 'If anyone is not scared of upsetting his betters, it's our Terry.'

Christopherson folds his arms and blows through his teeth.

'You know, I don't think I have seen anyone as scared as some of that lot in the pub were. We could get nothing out of any of them. What's new about that? But it was more than their just not wanting to talk to us.'

'It was like they couldn't help you even if they really wanted to?' Tamla says.

'That's it. I don't know of anything round here that scares people like that, or anything round here that everyone doesn't already know about. And I've never seen a victim of a crime act as weird as that Pertwee lady — she was off the scale. We all know what Max is, and I'll be the first to admit I've learnt a lot from him, but I'm with you on this, boss. I think you're right. This case, or whatever it is we're dealing with, it calls for something different in our response, because it *is* different.'

'Which is why there's no point rounding up the usual suspects or digging about in the usual places in the expectation that we'll unearth some small detail that holds the key to the rest of it. I know it's what we're used to doing, but that kind of patience isn't going to get us anywhere this time. We need to be bold, and if we could just establish why Lockheart wanted to make contact with Fallgrief or Swillcut, or more likely, cave their skulls in with that hammer as I think he was planning to do... then... I think we'd be close to prying the lid off dynamite. That's how big I feel this could be.'

'You really think so?'

'Easy, Terry,' says Tamla. 'We all want jobs after this is over.'

'We've got to strike upwards if we want to solve this thing.'

'Sheesh,' she says and grins in childish complicity.

'Jesus, boss. What are you getting us into?' Christopherson laughs nervously. 'I mean, I suppose the worst that could happen is that we knock on a few doors we don't normally go to and get told to piss off and mind our own business...'

'That's not the worst. Don't kid yourself. If we're right, but can't prove anything, which is where we are at the moment, then it'll go much, much worse for us than that. Think of the doors we'd be having to knock on. "Posh people are stealing our children," remember? If we do this, there's no point going halfway and being hung for lambs. We may as well turn the whole applecart over and stamp all over the apples.'

'We've been burnt by conspiracies before,' he objects.

'Those were just accusations dating back however many decades. Now we have missing bodies. The most recent of which did its vanishing turn just a few hours ago, and at the rate they're going, I bet you it won't be the last. Whatever this is, we're in the middle of it, and it seems to be reacting to our probing.'

'Doesn't that make the consequences of pointing the finger in the wrong direction even worse? Because what we're accusing people of is downright bloody sinister. I mean, if I had to say what it was, I don't know, probably kidnapping...?'

'Be honest — it's worse than that. I can hear you thinking it too.'

'Yeah, but even hearing you say that makes me dizzy. The kind of people we'd be going after, I know we laugh about them all being closeted perverts and toilet traders, but we're being serious now. This is serious... They couldn't really be into all that, could they? And still have got to where they have in life... to be where they are, I mean. Important people...'

'Why not?'

'We joke about them, don't we? Judges and politicians and dodgy millionaires... but I don't even know what to call this, whatever it is we're suggesting they're doing. I mean, it's not just regulation Purple Hearse shenanigans... what to even call it, boss? I don't really want to be the one to go first. Ritual kidnapping and execution? It's ridiculous isn't it? It's just *too much*. Once you say it, it just sounds too much to be really true...'

'Not to me, Dexter,' says Tamla.

Or to me either. I recall the exact time of day and spot when I first realised 'too much' *was* the truth. The blade of grass I was concentrating on had not done much that afternoon, yet once the wind changed direction, it was transformed into the tallest tree in the rainforest, a permanent feature of my memory to rival news of my father's accident and the first time I was arrested. Our running gag that the suave bachelor who taught music and ran the chess club was a molester, an accusation invented without our ever seriously believing that our comedic speculations were the shadows cast by a reality too dark for us to recognise, still fell somewhere short of the facts. That day the adult world became as compromised as we had pretended it was, and there were no jokes. I had rebuffed the man's amorous advances with the kind of language that would normally have led to expulsion and capital punishment, with a little spell in borstal in between. Naturally, I was terrified at what form of revenge would be exacted for this rejection, and I waited anxiously for a call to the headmaster's office, despairing of being believed in an 'I said-he did' scenario that an adult would always win. Yet *nothing happened* to me, the incident was never raised again, and I remained at large and unpunished for calling a member of staff 'a dirty cunt'. Both he and I had got away with it, and yet got away with nothing at all. That day I learnt that too much was as great a part of the truth as too little.

'It *is* only *too much* to be true, until we can prove it,' I say. 'Then it'll just be another fact about the world that everyone will pretend to have known about all along. Where we have to be careful is that before we've proved anything, the accusation's worse than the crime, and if we're not careful, we'll be tarred with the stigma of what we're looking for. In a country like this, where we're still encouraged to pretend that six-foot public school boys that blush all the time are the standard of decency we should be held to, embarrassment and shame are the weapons your more refined villain will use against you, Dexter.'

'How else do you think victims are kept in their place?' Tamla says. 'It's an approach that guarantees stability, even if it means the guilty go free from time to time.'

'I'm sure there is even literature out there justifying the outlook that makes all this possible,' I say, putting my hand on Christopherson's shoulder. 'To talk about or acknowledge a crime is as bad, if not worse, than actually having committed it, because it's more embarrassing. The crime happens in private, whereas the accusation occurs in public and so implicates an entire community of enablers. So I suggest, for now at least, we leave any talk of "ritual kidnapping" out of it. We make no references to what we think might actually be happening to these disappeared and restrict ourselves to employing our initiative by asking the right questions very politely.'

'I guess that makes sense...' he allows.

'Anything more than that might be taken down and used as evidence against us. The hardest part is that, whoever we're after, they still have "common sense" on their side. Madness like this isn't supposed to happen.'

'We're not just up against toffs, Dexter,' Tamla says, 'but ways of thinking that have endured for centuries.'

'Can't we get common sense on our side, though?' Christopherson asks.

'Not yet,' I reply. 'People are going missing, but the rest of this story is still in our heads. We're the heretics. Especially if we raise the spectre of the rich being part of a barely concealed conspiracy to steal children from low-income families and magically vanish them. Common sense also has a tendency towards harmless explanations, and benign conclusions, and hates batshit conspiracies. It hopes that eventually, after we've been laughed at and libelled, we'll be steered from the complicated paths we've been down towards the same hackneyed conclusions as everyone else. I'm not saying it doesn't sometimes have its uses — I drive cars and need to buy milk too — but to get to the bottom of how fucked up things really are, you need to get creative and leave sensible procedure dead in a ditch.'

Christopherson strokes his goatee and laughs nervously at me.

'You've thought about this a lot.'

'Trust me. Terry thinks of nothing else,' grins Tamla.

'So what about it?' I ask.

'Don't include me in any of this,' laughs Tamla. 'I'll be keeping an eye on Max and trying to keep him out of trouble. This is between you two!'

Christopherson's worry lines give way to a flash of insolence that holds my eye. 'Shall we pay *Mr Toad* a visit, then?'

'That's my boy, Dexter. Let's.'

CHAPTER SEVEN
THE FIGUREHEAD

Time is inevitability. Old Father Time *is hungry. The more he consumes, the faster it goes. That's why it's so useful to have a bit of it to hand. Like drink, it doesn't affect everyone in the same way; not everybody has to go off the grid, end up in A&E or combust in a puff of smoke.* The Well's *seen some nutters gobble a load and sit in a chair and laugh their faces off — one bloke even got up and drove a car. That's basically the area he's aiming to land in, though if he did end up going the whole hog, or even any hog, and vanished into the tunnel of goats, well, that wouldn't be the worst of all outcomes either.*

Hanging about in the Hearse is in danger of becoming even less fun that the usual average for this time of year, and although he lacks the imagination to visualise exactly how matters could be worse for him at this moment, he has seen things with his own eyes and need only play those back to remember that he had better get a move on if he is serious about switching dimensions and indulging in time travel. Word was that if you pre-empted **'it'**, *you might even be able to choose what kind of trip you had — maybe even making it your own, undoing mistakes and remaking a future in line with whatever you had wanted your life to be in the first place. There were so many legends about this stuff that it was impossible for a gambling man to not want to eventually play the percentages and take a punt.*

That's why he has already had a cheeky little nibble and is now thinking that there may never be a better time to snaffle the bag, though this requires privacy and some modest security arrangements, as it would not do to unravel in front of Maureen, who has been in a raging piss ever since that fruit and nut job arrived with the toy axe and smashed the place up.

The Hearse had cleared out as soon as the law left, and what a fucking awful pair of pigs they were: Nick Cave and Ed Sheeran, the new kind that had watched the movies you hadn't and probably had degrees in psychology and scriptwriting. At least no one had added to the 'he came, he saw, he fucked off' narrative, though with the way shit accumulates, this counts only as a temporary stay of execution. Soon it will all be in the open and, having closed the pub for the day, and maybe for longer than a day, The Well is ready to find out what the fuss is all about. Painfully, the arthritis having set up shop in his hips, and his back aching from receiving confidences over the bar, The Well ascends the narrow staircase, the combination of its steepness and the small treads meaning that he is on his hands and knees by the time he gets to the top. The lavatory in one of the en suite guest rooms is where he will be safest.

Pulling himself up, resting a hand on two signs either side of the narrow corridor, absolute piss-takes both, a 'Love Local, Trust Local' badge on one wall and a plaque pointing towards 'stunning wedding venue and conference rooms' on the other, reminders of more ambitious times. The Well shakes his head at the forlorn hope of ever turning this disaster into a normal pub, where speculative punters of the future might have washed their hands after a piss and asked about specials boards, instead of it remaining what it always was: a hen pen that has successfully fought off successive gentrification drives.

The Well squeezes into his room of choice, leaving the unnumbered door ajar as it is less likely to alert potential hunters of his presence than if he attempted to cover his tracks by either closing or locking it. Though spotless by the standards of the building, it nonetheless reeks of sheets that have never been aired or allowed to dry properly, reminding him of a Gucci case he stole at the airport, only to find it full of damp Austrian laundry. He stumbles over the vacuum cleaner and edges his way into the cracked-tile cubicle that punters usually confuse for an ironing cuddy, which is one way to excuse the fools who have taken a crap amongst the coat hangers and magic trees in the cupboard next to it. Their loss though, because this windowless space is his favourite corner of the pub and probably, for his money, the best shitter in the world, combining remoteness and function, the single spot where no one has yet demonstrated the guile to disturb him. He can take himself seriously here and become whatever he wants without fearing how his metamorphosis will appear to the others.

'Jesusssss...'

The Well does not enjoy recognising the greasy-faced phantom in the silver acrylic mirror sheet, square strips of which are strategically situated through the guest rooms to inspire loving couples to ever greater levels of copulative ecstasy — that was the idea anyway. On the basis of the footage he's observed, stored in the infra-red 'burglar alarms' that double as cameras in every room, this has not quite worked out in practice. Maureen was either too ambitious, kinky or bored to consider standard sexual possibilities; not even the most creative coprophiliac or scat-king was going to enjoy catching their reflection while taking their pleasure over a tatty thunderbox, and what she was doing sticking strips by the plug sockets is anyone's guess. It's just as well he has never tried getting it on here, because his hatred of mirrors is equal to that of any vampire. The Well's problem with looking glasses relates to being the physical subject of his own experience, a relationship he does not like to be reminded of. Usually he knows where not to look, reflexively dodging them at any possible point of contact, but today, in his clumsy haste, he is caught out.

It is too late to ignore the acrylic strip or close his eyes, and, in an instant, he sees his life again: the first time he knew he was ugly, his profile reflected on the mirrored pillars of Topman, Southampton, New Year's Day, 1986; coming up on a trippy pill as his nose melted in a friend's bathroom a year later; the awful ritual of his morning shave, before he let his whiskers go; and so on, the compressed highlights of his tawdry facial history. Hard as he tries, he could never make the person he wanted to be out of the one he saw, his compulsion not to register what others perceived every time they looked at him out of control, as he fled from passport photo booths and avoided group shots with his mates. Finally, the burden of wishing his mug was stuck on someone else's stalk, skulking through adolescence pretending he had no face, gave way to his acceptance that he would have to hide the one he had. And so he created 'The Well': the jacket he can zip up to his nose that has been his shield ever since those difficult early days, his comfort garment and saviour.

Summoning his courage, as if fate has brought him to this point with the specific aim of forcing him to confront his demon, The Well zips the collar right down, allowing the light to glance off his chin.

It is only a face, he tells himself; it is not so bad.

But it is.

What he is witness to is so far removed from even his worst imaginings that he cries out aloud in a bid to wake himself up.

'No, no, no, no, this isn't happening... it can't be.'

But it is. It really is. Unaccountably, his face is no longer there. In an awful reversal of causality, The Well reluctantly acknowledges that, without actually turning his head, he is staring at a reflection of the back of his neck and collar. Incapable of accepting the evidence of his senses, fearing what more he might see if he does not look away, he runs his fingers over his eyes and retreats to the squeaky plastic seat, which slips to one side under his weight like a Frisbee. He is no way in control of himself, that much he might have conceded when he hit the whisky as soon as the cops had left, Maureen coolly telling him that she was finally ready to wash her hands of their association and that he should pack his things and leave.

But it is not the whisky that is playing games with him, convenient as it would be to reach for the materialist explanation. Compared to what he has just seen, one knows where one is with whisky. Could the little bit of Old Father Time, Acid Horse or

High John the Conqueror — *they all belong to the same evil family* — *he munched have done it to him? Gingerly, he rises to his knees and lifts his crown up to the reflecting tape, prepared for anything other than what he actually sees. Nothing, there is nothing there. He reaches his hand out to make sure that he is level with the void, and perhaps to confirm that his head still exists, touching his nose and then the tape, but there is no reflection at all now, only solid air leading back to the peeling grey plaster of the wall opposite.*

There is nothing to do except pretend that it hasn't happened. It has always been an unlucky room, the bog excepted. Twice he has tried to go cold turkey here, both times falling into a feverish semi-sleep, not deep enough to pass out properly, entering into that indeterminate state that is more like madness. He shudders as he recalls the strange and shrill repetitions of words, jumbled entreaties of voices he accidentally stored, crazed ideas and notions that could not make the journey into the pictures he normally saw as he slept that have haunted him within these walls. A reconfiguration of his body occurred too on each occasion, experiencing himself as a battered container tanker sinking in the oceanic depths of his own sweat, trying to set a course and sail to the dry end of the mattress and land on an island he had purchased with his savings, but the promised terra firma was forever out of reach, leaving him shipwrecked on his back with nowhere to drop anchor, and so on into the delirium of withdrawal without end. Such times, such times.

Perhaps this is more of that? He hopes so.

Now where did he put the goods?

Panicking again, The Well's hand shoots into his coat pocket, the torn one. No, he wouldn't be so stupid as to leave it there. He tries the other side — *thank God, thank God. Wiping the tears off his cheek with his free hand, crying periodically now like an athlete trying to catch his breath, relieved that he need only concentrate on what he need do next, The Well clasps the bag firmly in his fist, and then, easing it slightly, examines his treasure. He was right to rid of himself of the remaining packs of*

Acid Horse *but to hold on to this beauty, the thoroughbred alpha dog. Christ, it even looks like it's been delivered fresh from hell, the most potent batch yet, stalks as thick as twigs, the holding bracken dense like a steel afro and the lumps as large as horse turds and heavy like stones.* Payola. Old Man *is stronger than 'Orse. Truly, if the cops had seen this fucker they wouldn't even have thought they were looking at drugs and probably sent the lot off to the Science Museum! He licks his lips, feeling a lift at last, and affords himself an approving grunt. The moment before you do something that will fuck you up is always thrilling, bidding goodbye to one state and awaiting the hit of another. In the spirit of a villain who cannot resist a final speech as he stands over the hero with a loaded gun,* The Well *savours his goods and the moment, picking out and grinding a softish lump between his thumb and forefinger, watching the potent nuggets fall away and gather on his waiting palm like bird food, the process so devoid of the usual encumbrances of being alive that he finds he cannot resist the urge to sing to his redeemer:*

'Oooo, it is a long way to go, a black angel by your side...'

He sounds like a heavy metal chorister, literally long-haired and literally angelic, really he does, laughable as it might be to anyone else to describe him this way. He decides to really go for it.

'The sirens call a sailor to die, enchanted by the sound,

He's turning old, he shall never return, sail on to the eternal reward!'

For once he feels his age without really believing it, unconvinced that he has really spent fifty-six years in this body, relying instead on a certain self-possession, a deliberate attention to things, that will keep him young and take him forward. He has grown and learnt but not really liked how he has grown or what he has learnt, and, in this cramped disrespected space, he will soon forget all that and embrace a vision of himself that will brook no contradiction. The redemptive interval between states, typical of every reprieve The Well *has ever known, must be luxuriated in to the exclusion of all else, his guard included. On!*

'Oh no you don't, my lad. You're not going to pass through my hands so easily!' Interrupts an unwelcome voice.

'Let me explain. Fuck!'

'Can't do that.'

'No, no, no...'

The Well *permits the intruder to get on with strangling him, pinning his head to the pipe, their bodies barely able to grapple in the tiny cubicle, the thunderous eruption of steps and whack of the door being kicked open that ought to have alerted him to the impending invasion of his sanctuary all registering some seconds too late.*

'Never give your enemy the chance to land on your shore. Always defend your perimeter, you 'orrible man.'

'You'll kill me,' he gasps.

'It's the predictability of you, that's what's so inexcusable.'

Faced with such passionate certainty, it is hard for The Well *to disagree, yet even now he clings to a few stubborn reservations. How can he be predictable when he is doing something for the first time? Why is he scared of the marks that will be left round the wrung neck of his corpse? How can a thing be both true and bollocks? He'll have to return to that last one another time, if there is one, as it may hold the key to them all — the rough hands he had hoped to stay a dimension ahead of still wrapped firmly round his neck; the slight loosening he had expected, now that his tormenter had made his point, alarmingly slow to transpire.*

The waves are crashing in. Time is inevitability. Time is eternal. But life, especially his, is not.

*

'How big is the estate, Dexter?' I ask.

'Most of the land we've driven through since we reached the village is his, I think, boss.'

This amounts to a lot of land. The village is an entanglement of former labourers' cottages tarted up into second homes, an ugly prefab shop selling shortbread with a post office window jammed in by the till and a church that catches the light on its mauve windows in a way that is more suggestive of God than anything that has occurred within the building.

'Owning a village, for Christ's sake. Most of us never even get to own a tree.' I tap the window and point to the giant outline of Sebastopol House. 'That thing, I hear it's a health and safety risk, right?'

'Tell me about it. The Parish Council would tear down a guinea pig pen without planning permission, but they bend over a barrel for that creepy monstrosity in a heartbeat. There's asbestos buried all over the property and local builders in every care home who've carked it before their time because they have had to handle the stuff. The bigger you are, the harder you are to say no to. That's life, isn't it? NFW: Normal-For-Wessex. Masters holds a massive garden party every summer. The worthies are invited — MPs, people off the telly. I mean, it's not like the Mafia, but they let him get away with...'

'...murder?'

Christopherson bum-humps his seat awkwardly.

'I suppose that's the question, isn't it? Bit of a leap from turning a blind eye to a toff pushing his luck with agricultural ties to giving their blessings to the ritualistic offing of folk... It's a given you're going to be doing the talking. Right, boss?'

'As Chief Investigating Officer, I can hardly allow you to lead the line. Lurk in the shadows all you want.'

Muttering his thanks, Christopherson catches my eye in the rear-view mirror with the calm of one who suspects the brakes may not work.

'I'm buzzing,' he chuckles. 'They all warned me you'd get me into trouble one day.'

'You? I don't know what I was doing letting you talk me into this, Dexter.'

'Yeah, I should have kept my big mouth shut, eh?'

'Think of it as one for the grandchildren, when you're a revered old man living in a house like that one.'

'Not in this life. I'd rather take my chances sleeping in the woods than upgrade there. Castle Dracula isn't my style.'

The imposing construction looming in the distance seems to surround the countryside it is so well positioned to unsettle, throwing its long self round us like a constrictor about to suffocate its prey. Its prominence differs markedly from its neighbours: stately homes that lack its confidence and swaggering visibility, preferring to wear their privilege lightly and flaunt their treasures in private. These country piles are discreetly tucked from view, reached through unmarked and innocuous entrances, leading through interminable potholed tracks until they finally show off the buildings the approach is designed to disguise. Sebastopol House shares as much with these relics of a shyer era as stuffing money into a mattress does with walking into the Bank of England. It was built as a deliberate statement of baronial intent, a power play cast over the entire area and a challenge to any usurper who might get it into their head that no one deserves to inhabit anything so resplendent and grand. In bad weather, its vast length and girth stand like a flood barrier against the elements, the mansion's outline shaped like a cumbersome devil-bat, the outstretched wings of the building intimidating traffic that passes in awe from afar. In the sunshine, its glass façade catches light, transforming it into a colossal magnifying glass, and can be seen as far as the city, blinding tractor drivers and delivery men to the cost of cyclists and pedestrians alike. The most recent modifications carry the assault further into the sky, its shield of solar panels threatening low-flying microlights that make the mistake of looking down, and the RAF, who redeploy their helicopters over the coast so as to not add to the potential carnage. In a property-owning kleptocracy, this is the spot to strike if I am impatient to begin the novel I will never write and embrace early retirement — Christopherson's get-out: that he had come to keep an eye on a superior he could not say no to.

'It's funny. It doesn't end up looking smaller as you get

closer to it. I don't expect it to *literally* — I just thought it might fit into the scale of the things around it a bit more.'

'It's the whole point, isn't it? It's been made so that it can't.'

We turn off the dual carriageway which connects the cathedral city to a market town that was once notorious for youths ambushing passengers at its bus terminal, the county split into warring fiefdoms that would last until the combatants left secondary school and the sensible ones joined the army or police. The hub is now the fortunate location of an attractive new Waterstones, housed in a former brewery, where the surviving warriors of yesteryear scan staff picks, shoplift stationery and probably miss the old days in their lunch breaks, when life was nasty, brutish and short, but at least their own. For a brief interlude, we lose sight of Sebastopol House. Unnervingly, it feels like the building no longer wants to see us. Our car rumbles over the cattle grids into a phalanx of narrow lanes where our progress is slowed by allowing a four-wheel drive to pass and idling ponies to block the road, the delays informing the illusion that we are going further, and further back in time, than we are.

'Every time a boy racer hits one, it ends up canned in a French hypermarket,' Christopherson points at a fearless pack of donkeys wandering towards us. 'Brexit will put a stop to all that, I expect.'

'Max tell you that?'

'I didn't read it in the *Guardian*.'

'It won't stop the donkeys. Or the boy racers.'

'You know what I mean.'

'I know what *he* means. You've got to start thinking for yourself a bit more, Dexter. Repeating Orridge's nativist war dance isn't going to do anything for your career.'

'That depends which side wins, boss. And a bit rich, coming from you... I mean this — it's not going to help with promotion, is it?'

'Bollocks. It'll be the making of you. What are you saving yourself for anyway?'

'If you must know, when you put it like that, I'd always hoped that I might be in line for your job once you were kicked upstairs and took off back to London.'

'You still will. This will go musically. We're not on a suicide mission, Dexter. Relax. What you are a part of now is the kind of initiative that separates the naturals from the hacks. Grace is on our side here — you heard him earlier. We just need to keep within the bounds of what we know and rattle this Masters enough to provoke him into saying more than he needs to. He'll make a mistake. They all do.'

'Yeah, I know that, boss,' Christopherson replies, convincing neither of us completely, 'but Grace, well, he can be a bit mercurial can't he? Changes his mind a lot. And this bloke may not be the mistake-making kind...'

Running along the byway, the overflown tributaries of the Avon flood the plain, isolating herons on tufty islands of gorse, the buzzards that emerge out of the smoky light hovering overhead like drones while, below them, battered Defenders rust by the side of the road and farm shops selling silk orchids go broke, a slim line of eight-hundred-year-old oaks hemming us in like an armed escort until suddenly we are in open country again — or what might pass as such. Unenclosed bogs, natural lakes and brackish deer trails stretch out towards distant kingdoms and from there to infinity points in the distance, a vast uninhabited wilderness which ought to belong on another continent, yet a characteristically English illusion, as paradise extends as far as the eye can see and no further. Behind the trembling grey smear of the Arcadian horizon lie the overcrowded cities of the south coast, their concrete temples and motorway bone structure.

I scroll thorough my messages. Reliably, my guardian angel Tamla has already been in touch: *'Your guy has gifted enough cash to be a Lord, many times over. But he looks down on Lords because they are cheap. Careful — his head is bigger than yours.'*

'The mound they built it on had to be dug up and carried here, boss,' says Christopherson, 'like Stonehenge or something, because the original Iron Age hill wasn't big enough for General Whatshisname. And Masters has added more bling. I mean look at *that*. What the fuck is it? Unbelievable — like something they pulled off Mars...'

'It must be new?'

'It wasn't here the last time I passed.'

'It's strong. Very, very strong.'

Without warning, a row of baroque classic cast-iron pillars emerges like a hidden army, forming a wall which cuts across the heathland with the ghastly prominence of an outsized radiator that has abruptly metastasised and grown out of all control. Its savage fortifications are topped by tarred razor-wire and steel spikes that rotate sullenly, the battlements of this garrison leading to the first of several checkpoints: a surprisingly small electronic gate cluttered with cameras and various infra-red security devices that presage the dawn of the robots.

'There's a main entrance in a mile or so.'

'This one will do. No point giving them too much notice,' I say, shifting back in the seat.

We are in an unmarked unit BMW with a light bar in the back window, our vehicle a budgetary extravagance that can still lend the job some ersatz glamour and recognisable at once as a plainclothes car to anyone with an interest in these things. I lower the window and flash my badge at one particularly obstreperous camera with a long neck that seems intrigued by me. The gate groans open, and we are in, driving along a steep bridleway, flanked by languorous and slightly bent elms which have lost the will to reach their intended height. The symmetry of the compound is unlovely, spare and sparse, the clean deliberation of lawn, trees and road sweeping the land of its composite character and colour.

'This is going to be one of those very long drives, isn't it?'

'Yeah, it's showing that kind of potential. They'll certainly have time to prepare their stories.'

'How long?'

'At least a couple miles before we get to the house. We just keep going up. I'm starting to think you've never been here before, boss.'

'They're always asking, but I just never seem to find the time.'

'The old trouble, eh?'

'Alright, how did you get on their mailing list?'

'Ha! I've only been here the once, with Max, before that fence went up and when they still had loads of livestock in the fields. So not exactly a regular...'

'What brought the police to Sebastopol House? A burglary? A missing quad bike? Is that why they've become so security conscious now?'

'No, nothing like that. The opposite in fact. It was because neighbours were complaining about the house, the noise from the parties. But rather than send round a PC, Max and I decided to drop in, as he said he'd always wanted to see the place close up, which is typical of his forelock-tugging tendencies. Anyway, when we got here, Max only left me in the bloody car and went in and spoke to the big man himself on his own. They didn't even bring me out a cup of tea, the bastards. So I've never seen inside.'

'He likes to manage things himself, doesn't he?'

'He's Old Father Time. Been here all his life. Thinks he can exercise the most influence by discreet chats, I suppose.'

'I'm guessing the issue was resolved.'

'Well, yes and no. From time to time the neighbours do still pipe up about the noise, and Max has to administer a soft slap to the wrists.'

'To the neighbours or to Masters?'

'A good question. I think it is a bit of all-round community relations,' says Christopherson, scratching his nose.

'That could be his official role if we were to call him for what he is.'

'What do you mean, boss?'

'Our liaison officer with high society and mediator with the ruling classes.'

Christopherson pulls a quizzical face, 'I think it's more that he just knows everyone.'

'Even if he does, how much noise can you make from a *garden party*?'

'It's probably not just those, you hear of other things.'

'Oh yeah?' I press.

'I think there are some soirées that go on late, really late, for Masters' business contacts or out-of-town friends, that the locals probably aren't much invited to. Reckon it makes them feel a bit B-list, if you know what I mean — here's a party for you, and now here's one for my *real* mates. Can't make them feel very wanted, listening to the fun go on from afar... perhaps that's why they get so arsey... NFI, eh?'

'Even so. I'm thinking these get-togethers must be making a fucking powerful racket to carry as far as the neighbours. We're miles from anybody. Makes me wonder what kind of *bunga-bunga* activity is going down round here.'

'Sound carries in weird ways in the countryside. Sometimes it seems like voices are right behind you, other times a bomb can go off and you hear nothing at all. It's to do with the wind refracting, and no buildings as big as this place to block the noise,' Christopherson explains.

'And so, does Max always deal *exclusively* with these complaints?'

'He does, as a matter of fact. This is his turf.'

'Then I don't think he would be very happy about our visit would he?' I suggest.

'Pretty livid, I'd say. If he didn't like you leaning on Swillcut, that'd be next to nothing to how he'd feel about you going up directly to Masters. Still, you're his CO, so I guess he's just got to suck it up, hasn't he? Chain of command and all that.'

'Interesting that you see yourself as next in line for my job when I go, and Tamla too presumably, but not Max, who we know is a keeper. If we're talking about the chain of command, he *is* your senior and has all those years on you as well.'

'True but he's already been up and down hasn't he? And although I'haven't asked him, as who wants to stir up an angry bear, I don't think even he thinks he's ever going to be going up again, not now. He's past that point.'

'He ever open up to you about his adventures on the promotion ladder?' I ask.

'Are you kidding me? It's a sore spot with him, alright. He's more likely to join Extinction Rebellion than talk to me about that.'

'So there's a good story?'

'There are always stories. I'm surprised you haven't asked me about this one before.'

'I had thought about it, but I wouldn't want you to then tell Max that I was petty enough to be gossiping about him, and anyway, until today I haven't been interested enough in him to ask.'

'So what's changed?'

'You go first,' I wrap my knuckles on the dashboard.

'Well... I obviously haven't got this from him, but he's yo-yoed, that's for sure, and not just once: I know he's been up and down and up and then down again.'

'He was busted down twice?'

'Oh yeah. With a few years apart. But yeah, he was got a second time.'

'That would explain the residual bitterness.'

'He likes a good grumble. He's always been famous for that,' Christopherson rocks his head from side to side in what could be taken as sign of someone trying to be balanced.

'Busted down *twice*, though...'

'Yeah, it is odd, I know. Normally, you'd be cashed out or would want to leave after having had that happen to you the first time, but he loves the job, and would probably do it if they made him gargle dogshit. He's your archetypal copper for life, isn't he?'

'That's why his being demoted makes no sense to me, not without knowing more. If it had happened to me I would understand, but him? Max is a professional arse-kisser and a paid-up unimaginative rule-follower, exactly the kind of plank the public likes to think of as your standard idiot policeman, who would be police whether he was in North Korea or the Netherlands. For a man like that to get shitcanned twice beggars belief a bit.'

'For sure. You're not the only one to say so.'

'I can see him being caught on camera enforcing some petty rule that ends up giving a pensioner a heart attack or bothering a black kid on a BMX and it turning ugly, but that's not usually a barrier to advancement in our meritocracy. Do you actually know what he did? Or is it just myth?'

'I've never been able to confer with anyone who knows what he was done for the first time, but as I haven't heard anything too outlandish, my guess is that he just wasn't very good at his job and probably got the promotion ahead of time. I figure the competition may not have been too challenging at that time. Something like that.'

'You need to be more than poor at your job to get busted down, or else we'd have no upper hierarchy.'

'True, but no one has ever said anything about that first time. There may still be a few old PCs who were around then, but if they were, they're not talking, not to a nosy relative newbie like me anyway.'

'What about the second time? You'd have been around by then, wouldn't you?'

'The second time, yeah. That was a proper horror show alright. I did have a moment when I thought "what have I joined up to?" when I first found out about that. Max was just on his way down when I came through the door, so to speak, and God was he not pleased about it. By the standards of this place it was a real scandal.'

'I may have actually heard about some of this... about that IRA taskforce, right?' I wonder if this was where my prejudices against Max first started, or if all he symbolised would have made him objectionable to me anyway.

'Okay, yeah. Max was in a proper pickle, and the way he told it, he had let himself be stitched up, properly like a catsuit, so how much of it was his actual fault I don't know. But he was one of a group that were slung out together, all at the same time.'

'This was a squad of older detectives that had collected here through a process of reverse natural selection right? A couple of ex-military types that Grace ended the career of? This is ringing bells now,' I say, sitting up in my chair.

'Yeah, it would, you'd have heard something about it wherever you were at the time. Max was properly in with them alright, though as a juniorish player, and I think it was a tendency to suck up that got him into the shit, as he doesn't really have it in him to be a proper villain.'

'You ever meet any of these detectives?'

'No,' Christopherson shakes his head, 'but I'm told there was definitely a bad element here then, worse than what was even normal at the time, I believe. A small squad of five of them, including Max, twats and bullies by all accounts, were meant to be keeping an eye on the IRA, as at that time there was a gang working their way through the phone directory to target military families. Anyway, these clowns, our CID, they called themselves 'The Bastard Brigade'. I don't honestly know if they had been soldiers, though they did give each other military nicknames, you know, the Colonel, the Captain, that kind of playground bollocks, and they got to see themselves as something of a law unto themselves, in this area.'

'Strange how that happens...'

'And Max is basically their flunkey, mixing brandy in their coffees and laughing at their jokes. Standard bottom-of-the-food-chain stuff. There was never any real suggestion that he or any of them were actually taking Houston high-fives, but their general demeanour stank. They were at the Beanfield too, bashing travellers with babies about the heads.'

'Nice. I guess they couldn't have had all that much true detecting to do round here back then,' I say, gesturing at a passing chalk combe.

'Spot on. That's exactly it — too much time on their hands and not enough to really get their teeth into. So instead of digging deeper into whatever undiscovered crime there was in the area, they went decadent and threw their weight round the town, loudly. Other branches were nothing to them. The public were all cunts so far as they were concerned, and they weren't slow in saying so to their faces. They kept unpaid tabs at every curry house; any waiter that asked them to settle was a thick wog; barmaids that wouldn't oblige free pints ended up in a lager shower; and any peer in uniform who objected, they were a Code Brown. It wasn't a good look. And God help you if you were a con that complained. One of them, I think, even showed his dick to a WPC and asked her to put arnica on it because of an STD he may or may not have had. You get the idea. You wouldn't want them on a rape case, having your back, or anywhere near the public. Grace was brought in to move them on.'

'Any great event that defined the end of their glorious era?' I ask.

'Of course. The legend is that there was an orgy in the sauna of the leisure centre organised by one of their snitches who worked there. There'd been some dealing going on and I think they blackmailed her into hosting a Saturnalia, got caught, and then tried to get Max to cover it up for them, which he failed spectacularly to do, digging a hole all the climbing equipment in the world wouldn't get them out of...'

'It is lucky he chose this side of the law to operate on — he'd make a shit criminal.'

'Or that's what he'd like us to think! No, I've never met anyone with less of a talent for deception than Max, I mean, he must still be the only person that uses hardcopy soft porn, bought from the same local newsagent he gets his *Telegraph* from every morning, hidden in the supplement for the rest of us to find if anyone needs an emergency toilet break, and I doubt he's ever even clocked it. We used to call his desk *the wankers' lending library*,' Christopherson adds sheepishly.

'So what happened to Max's comrades in arms?'

'The two older ones got pensioned off ingloriously, another was made a Chimp, you know, a Completely Hopeless In Most Police Situations community support officer, and Max was demoted down into the ranks again, stigma and all attached. That marked a bit of a watershed.'

'How do you mean?'

'After that, Grace started bringing more people from outside in. Like you and Tamla,' Christopherson explains.

'So that's why Max loves us so much. A very fruity history for a straight man.'

'Well, you can't really blame him for not wanting to broadcast it can you? Besides, I think there's a consensus, even amongst those of us who think he's an over-fastidious cockwomble, that he shaped up pretty well for all his setbacks, and maybe because of them too. No one knows this area any better, and him going on about it all the time shouldn't blind us to it. The same with the faces and backstories and all the rest of the *Last of the Summer Wine* crap none of the rest of us can be bothered with, until we can, and then we ask Max, don't we?'

I look ahead, unimpressed. 'This has to be the longest drive in the world. Is there anything actually at the end of this? What is it, three miles, head to toe?'

'No. Seriously, boss,' insists Christopherson. 'How many of the rest of us, allowing for cuts, lower numbers and all that, would still walk around a beat on their own all times of the day looking out for people? He has *vocation*. We all know people in this job that could just as easily be receptionists or bouncers, and who aren't exactly in tune to a higher calling when they put on the uniform. But Max doesn't hide in cars or behind excuses — you know that. That's something both of you have in common. For what it's worth, and I am sorry if this embarrasses you, boss, I always felt that if I took stuff from the both of you, you and Max, I would become one well-rounded copper.'

'Thank you, Dexter. That's very good of you.'

'You see my point, though. You and Max, you're poles apart, yet if...'

'I do see. But when I ask Max and he answers, I find I don't buy. He is starting to worry me, Dexter.'

'Seriously?'

'I'm afraid so. Much as I'd like to think he's simply another arrogant officer of limited intelligence, I'm beginning to think we don't really know where we are with him anymore.'

'Don't be like that, boss.'

Christopherson looks uncomfortable; there are certain codes that govern how prescient we can be about one another before we risk breaching the taboo of turning on our own kind, and I am right on the line.

'I think he's alright, boss. I really do. I know how that must sound to you, all the local boys sticking together, but that's really not why. I do think I know what you mean — he *does* get too cosy, and you know, a bit too self-bloody-righteous at times, but at *heart*, he's a good policeman. And a good person too, I think.'

'I hope you're right about that,' I say, convinced that he isn't.

'I really think I am, boss.'

I drop it, for now. The two wings of Sebastopol House sprawl out like the parted legs of a corpse, issuing a sharp challenge to our earlier bravado. Now that we are presented with the object of our journey, I surmise neither of us would be exactly heartbroken to forget the entire thing and drive away, should some excuse present itself on the two-way. The wind picks up on the hill, barrelling hard from behind, clawing the car closer to the giant marble doors, the house appearing to draw us in through magnetic reversal, its very size moving the edifice closer, even though we are the ones in motion.

I play with my seatbelt and try to ignore this projection,

attempting instead to relive the things I have accomplished in my career, those isolated triumphs I remember with pride, the achievements that can never be taken away, even the thin solace of compliments, all a sure-fire sign that I am finally alive to the risk we are running. Heavy with all I have to lose, my stomach plunges and will be in danger of colluding intimately with my intestine if I do not quickly find my game face. There is no more reliable way of being reminded that a taste for adventure is a luxury I cannot afford than feeling my career tilt tit-wards. There is no space left for plans. I am too excited, and the stakes have narrowed time into too tight a corridor of inevitability, for me to do anything other than continue to pretend I know what I am doing. And if I do not, I become a joke to myself and lose everything anyway.

'Here we are, here we are...' I murmur stupidly, murdering the tautology into unmeaning, 'Zero hour.' I feel as I do when I am drunk but want to remain master of my next few moves, knowing that memory loss and embarrassment will instead ensue, however hard I try to hang on. The wind ricochets off the different wings of the house, whistling across the courtyard and through the air ducts of the BMW like a pod of screaming whales fearing imminent slaughter, the high notes creating a lilting crescendo which is all too much for Christopherson: 'What are we doing here, boss? We should...'

'Relax. We can't bail now. They've clocked us, we have to go through with it.'

'Yeah, yeah, I know. I'm just starting to shit it a bit.'

'Don't worry, we're the police. We make the public shit it. Remember?'

Christopherson forces a snigger, stopping before it turns hysterical. 'It feels like the bloody pyramids, looking down at you.'

'Ignore it all. Focus. One foot in front of the other.'

'Yeah, yeah.'

'Here, pull in by that line of cars there, by the fountain,' I indicate.

'One, two... five, six, seven, and that won't include what they've got hidden away in the garage. A car for every fucking day of the fucking week. How the rich live.'

'Tuck in by the Bentley,' I say.

'Words I never thought I would hear. I can't stop my hands shaking. I dent that I die a thousand deaths. You ever forget how to park a car?'

'Every Monday morning, hungover,' is my honest response.

'For fuck's sake, the palms are sweating now. Okay what now?'

'Try switching off the engine, then get out and follow me to the house?'

'So you do want me to still come in, then?'

He would like me to think he is joking, 'I'm not even going to answer that, Dexter.'

'Okay, okay.'

'Be brave. Be British. I'll do all the talking. You can keep your mouth shut and just take everything in.'

At least we are out of the car, and I can rely on my legs to not give me away, even if my stomach still hangs from a thin rope, and my voice shakes like it belongs to someone I know well enough to instruct, but not believe.

'Owwww, that cold's harsh on your ears. A different weather system up here,' complains Christopherson.

'We're closer to the clouds.'

'Can you imagine how much it costs to heat that fucking house? Jesus, would you look at the fucking door!'

The solid steel reinforced doors are covered in marble glass, thick enough for a safe, the chances of a single person prising one open without the help of a team of oxen remote.

'Try to stop swearing, Sergeant. I don't mind a bit of it, but you're taking the piss, and we're about to meet some nice people.'

'I'm not having that. I need a good swear, boss, feeling

this fucking jittery! You'd need the big red key to knock that bastard down. Christ, you'd need it just to push open the fucking letterbox.'

'See, what I fucking mean? You're only fucking enjoying yourself now.' Much as I would like to think that I have caught Christopherson's outbreak of nerves, I know I am feeding them with plenty of my own to spare.

'Who's going to tug that Billy Hunt?'

'King. Fucking. Kong.'

There is an ugly chain hanging slyly beside one of the pillars at the main door, which seems to be a souvenir from some fondly recollected place of torture, the owner wanting his visitors to share his nostalgia for an evening that got enjoyably out of hand.

I give the bell a sharp pull, half-expecting to be lifted back Quasimodo-like over the battlements and gargoyles of Notre-Dame, but instead hear nothing, not even the satisfying clunk of the device catching on its mechanism. The chain slithers limply back up through my palm. And to my shame, I am relieved.

'You want to give that another go?'

'Give them a chance to ignore us first,' I try and joke.

'I'm not so sure, boss. I don't think it's working. It's just for show.'

'It doesn't matter. They know we're here.'

'All those cameras?'

'They saw us coming in their dreams, Dexter. Even the trees are their spies...'

With a speed that threatens to be far-fetched, both doors spring open, as dextrously as swinging bamboo partitions, to reveal a very well-built man, familiar-looking and probably older than he looks, black and absolutely hairless, naked accept for tight-fighting purple shorts and platformed running shoes. I am certain that, at some point, he was the non-singing dancer for a Euro-house act, famous for a Boney M cover, and now a reality television personal trainer, inclined to bully overweight celebrities with his provocative German lisp as they make their way through the Australian jungle in search of deeper truths about themselves. Judging by his formidable lack of clothing, he is above such things as being bothered by a winter in England, or us.

'*The Enforcer*, ja?' asks Christopherson, who looks heartened by this unexpected development.

The man nods, slowly, for he knows who he is and does not want to give us more than we deserve for acknowledging the perfectly obvious.

Making our first positive identification of the day, albeit of a person we are not looking for, appears as good as matters are going to get at this point. *The Enforcer*'s face is so violently unamused that he could be in practice for his next series, his uncurled lip the prelude to a Teutonic tongue-lashing that I can already look forward to laughing about later. Anticlimactically, he raises his eyebrows, folds his arms and hisses, 'So he's in trouble again is he? I've finished with him for the day. Inside, first room on the right,' and without bothering to ask us if we would like an autograph, takes his leave, walking briskly past us into the cold, before breaking into a purposeful jog.

'You know who that just was?'

I nod.

'Says it all if even you've heard of him.'

The Enforcer's directions, though admirably clear and to the point, do not take into account the dizzying scale of our route or the shock that entry into a vault of this magnitude is likely to have on working stiffs raised in terraced housing where the journey from the front door to back could be measured in seconds. A mixture of disbelief and belligerence quells whatever was left of my hyperactive nerves, and before we have the chance to acknowledge that we are both feeling considerably better than we were moments earlier, we have crossed the threshold and the doors have closed behind us.

'Prisoners of Sebastopol House...'

The view before us could take us right back to square one. We are in a palace and not a house as either of us have formally understood the term until now. Everything here, from the structure to the glittering array of items that practically insist upon fawning appreciation, is what and where it is to dazzle and humble guests, who are reduced to the status of 'audience': to be taken aback, chatter excitedly during the interval, and finally lose themselves in multiple standing ovations. I tend to not trust people who do not appreciate the finer things in life, yet this is luxury as a form of pathology.

'I don't want to come over all starstruck...'

'But you will,' I say, trying to play it cool.

'Oh come on, boss! Look at the size of that, that staircase there!' Christopherson points to an ascent resembling the Spanish Steps. 'As if you go up and down one of those every day... I've never seen anything that size that doesn't belong to the National Trust. It's bigger than places you pay to get into. And him, *The Enforcer*, he's a fucking celebrity, isn't he? A star.'

'You think they should be charging us for the privilege?'

'You couldn't blame them if they did. All this, everything here, it's all too big for a house. We could be standing in Trafalgar Square after someone has built a roof over it. The ceiling is where you'd expect the sky.'

'Not bad, I admit.'

'Not bad? It's insane!' Christopherson whispers excitedly. 'No wonder Max wanted to keep it to himself. Disneyland is smaller than this gaff.'

I'm embarrassed, because Sebastopol House is working on me as well, exactly in the way it is designed to, and I cannot help the apprehension that after the fear, which has now passed, comes the trembling and obsequiousness. Our object of worship is the original Georgian show home, an outward-facing conceit staged for the benefit of those looking in, which is what we are still doing even though we are inside. What lies behind the scenery here is anyone's guess, the inhabitation of this august structure an afterthought to the original design.

'Do you think we're meant to take our shoes off at the door?'

'I hope not. I forgot to wipe my feet.'

The terracotta floor, chandeliered ceiling and limestone walls of the Grade II listed auditorium are the stage; its antiques, ornaments and other prominent museum pieces the actors; and we the groundlings, hustling past the cheap seats to fight over standing space, the gap between our lives and all this beauty literally unsurmountable in a nation averse to revolution and civil war. Inequality endures when it is bound up in most people's idea of fairness, however poor they are. Yet even in a property-respecting democracy a blue and white marble staircase borrowed from Versailles, decorated with an ascending line of bronze sphinxes I last saw in Harrods, is enough to provoke a certain puritanism, however well-disposed one is to impulse buying. We are being manipulated, softened up for a great unveiling, the revelatory moment when being addressed by our Christian names, followed by cigars and brandy, causes our professional self-respect to perish in the masochistic face of servile debasement. Faced with that danger, to which even the most dedicated enemy of the established order is capable of succumbing, the most effective way of breaking the spell is to imagine living here and rid myself of the itch of wanting it all.

'Could you ever see all this belonging to you?'

'As it happens, I can't, yet... but I'm having a go.'

'Good luck with that.'

I start by going back to the early days. Once there I observe the masked balls and bewigged-receptions, replete with beauty spots and snuff, the high-pitched laughter of my guests keeping an army of servants on their toes, as we ingest plate after plate of braised quail. Next it is the turn of the shooting parties in which fascist dignitaries decide to carve up Europe with the Tory appeasers, plus-fours and whisky tumblers their props, and finally the dawn of the film companies, *Pride and Prejudice, Vanity Fair, Barry Lyndon,* strict instructions to the crew not to venture into the living quarters of the house or tear up the lawn with the rigging, the integrity of the property coming first no matter whose turn it is to play the game. Throughout it all, what I most dread, irrespective of the period, is to walk down these stairs alone in the morning and face the agoraphobia of all this wasted space, having realised sometime during the night I was not God after all, and in a world where many go hungry, the anomaly of there being room for Nelson's Column by my front door, is a regrettable disgrace. It works: I do not want to be the Lord of Sebastopol House, and care even less if I am in his good graces.

'How are you getting on with your virtual upgrade?'

'Mission accomplished.'

'You've more imagination than me, then.'

'Feast your eyes on these beauties...'

'Whoah!' Christopherson laughs.

We are overtaking a line of ghoulish portraits with the tired air of chronology about them, which stop at the foot of the palatial balustrade. The paintings depict a series of especially unpleasant faces that could, were they not clearly dating from different periods, be artistic impressions of the same man, beginning with a lean hungry visage, developing into a more corpulent version, and ending with a plain weird one, which I suspect is Masters himself, the earlier specimens his glorious forebears, or so he would have us think.

'Someone's crashed the ugly bus here, wheels ah-revolving... I can see why they call him *Mr Toad.*'

'If this is how they look on the walls, I wouldn't want a tour of the attic.'

'*They* were men before their time and we remain children long after ours,' interrupts a voice that sounds used to closing down impertinent speculation. 'Our grandfathers attempted to be wise old seers in their twenties, while we wish to pretend to be irresponsible teenagers into our seventies. So sad, so sad. What can I tell you except, when I look into these faces, all I ask is to be *worthy* of them, worthy of their courage and humility, no more, no more than that...'

Our path is slightly overshadowed by a squat figure of no more than five foot five, robed in a monk's habit, a protruding bulge round his middle, which, with his shaven head, bare feet and hairy toes, and the possibility he may be naked beneath, suggests we have discovered the missing link that connects the Friar of Sherwood Forest to the Shire-Folk of Middle-earth. A stolen peek at his face confirms our ascension to the ranks of pioneering anthropologists will have to wait, for this man is indeed the very likeness of the toadish Squire immortalised in the last picture on our left. As in the portrait, stripped of the artist's mildly flattering licence, our host's forehead is squashed together with his chin; the separating flesh squeezed between a scowl and scorn, with barely an interval between the two, his arms crossed impatiently, with ferocious self-importance, behind his back.

As Masters has caught me in the act of insulting both his person and his precious bloodline, I turn to see if Christopherson can temporarily pick up the baton of civility. Shyly, Dexter smiles, as if we have only just met and he cannot understand what more is expected of him at such abrupt notice, the responsibility of communicating with our compere mine alone.

Masters, meanwhile, will not have his flow checked by anything so petty as our not responding to his musings. 'I see the past is of no great interest to you... no matter, no matter. Though how any *man* can live without being conversant with history and still claim all it has granted him, I will never understand. It strikes me as the supreme act of existential ingratitude.'

This is not exactly the opening I would have settled for. Masters guesses as much, and does not so much speak as icily sigh, 'Personally I regard living in ignorance of history as the equivalent of imagining the world starting when you are born and ending when you die, spending the intervening time intellectually unclothed, wandering round literally naked before one's ancestors...' He pauses, merrily oblivious to the view we have of his densely forested thighs, the flapping sides of his cassock caught in a draft. 'Of course, absence is often as revealing as presence. One can tell a lot, too much even, about *men* with no passion for history and nothing to say for *themselves*...'

Replying to what Masters clearly intends as a statement of fact would constitute a new offence, and I need to start making our affronts count. The smell coming off him is atrocious, an unnatural stench of junk food rotting in hot weather, or perhaps a festering wound turning towards full infection, yet I see no dirt on him, and he does not appear to need a soaping down.

'Such sweet silence?'

At least we have made our intrusion worthwhile for the master of ceremonies, who smiles at his summation, or at least his version thereof, the corners of his mouth standing to attention before reverting to a defensive puckering of the lips so quickly as to bypass gratification.

'And yet, being a mute witness to the great unravelling of time is not so bad. Indeed, there's no shame in it for most people, which, providing you do not mind being *like* most people, is unproblematic. I do mind, though. As unfashionable as an elitist stance is these days, hence that ridiculous malapropism "people aren't stupid", I *mind* being like everyone else very much, and so reject their unthinking attitudes towards the past, and all evidence of their existence in the present, as far as I possibly can, for much the same reason. As the great Sid Vicious once said, "I've met the man on the street, and he is a cunt".'

It is costing us some professional dignity to keep Masters this happy, and it is worth every excruciating second. As we will not be invited back again in a social capacity, or a professional one without a lawyer present, we may as well turn unrelieved humiliation to our advantage, as I suspect his servants are too used to his schtick for him to find them fun, and he would be talking to a dictation machine if we were not here. His predilection for toying with his prey is his weakness. If I were to ask him which, if any, former members of Acid Horse he was still in touch with, it would all be over in a moment.

Yet he cannot resist a bit of rope-a-dope. Despite his practiced baronial gloom, the pleasure Masters takes in emphasising how a once-in-a-lifetime experience for us, visiting his house, is but an everyday occurrence for him, is as good as watching him unobserved through a one-way mirror. That is how I see the murder in him seethe behind his patrician stoicism, like crystals of glass trapped under the skin, his outrage at the outside world and its emissaries second only to his belief that we are unworthy of serious consideration.

'As you appear to be in no hurry to introduce yourselves, I may as well play the white man in this situation. I am, of course, Mungo Masters. Who else could I be? You might well ask. Or to put it another way, I would not walk about dressed like this if I were not in my own house.'

'That is mighty white of you,' I reply, realising I have copied his clipped sonorous drawl, which might be taken for validation.

'Do you both always dress like this for work?' Masters runs a finger up an imaginary line of tape while literally taking our measure, his expression back to one of constipated disdain.

'Every day, come rain or shine. Though we may have made an extra special effort knowing we would be coming here to see you.'

'*Knowing*, eh? Indeed, indeed! I enjoy men who like to plan ahead. It's how you make the gods angry!'

Masters leers forward to relish the pleasure of being far cleverer than I, having successfully gulled me into giving away more than I intended, unaware that this is what I intended, for although we may not be who he was expecting to see here today, or what he was expecting if he knows who we are, he was expecting *someone*, as the badge I showed the camera got us through the gate.

'Your accent... You're not a local lad. Outer London, Slough, the home counties?'

'Harrow.'

'Ah!' Masters exclaims.

'The Wembley bit of it. Then we moved to Croydon.'

'Of course, of course...' Masters nods to himself, as if this explains everything.

'You don't happen to know Silas?' he asks, making every effort to sound casual.

'Which Silas?'

'You know, the one who sent you?'

'We don't take instructions from any Silas.'

'No, I thought you didn't,' he replies too quickly.

'Perhaps you could introduce us. It's always nice to extend the social circle... '

'Come this way, please,' he beckons, ignoring me. 'This hall, for its many attractions, bells and whistles, is a rather impersonal space to receive guests, guests that I have absolutely no recollection whatsoever of my having invited...'

'It's poor form I know, on our part, to not have given you more notice. We know how busy you are and were a little worried you may not have time for us, so we thought we'd best just get on with it, and here we are.'

Masters enjoys this enough to snort at me, 'And so here you are, indeed! This way then, this way. A punt must never go unrewarded.'

We follow him into another vast chamber. My impression is that this one is arguably too reflective of his actual state of mind to greet visitors he gives a damn about in. It is the former ballroom, now reserved for charitable applications, nobodies from the tax office and the occasional role play with domestics who are ready to go the extra mile for a Christmas bonus.

'Please don't mind my friends, they don't bite, however much they would like to if they were still in their natural habitat...'

Running along the sides of the cavernous space are glass cases whose proper home would be a museum of experimental taxidermy.

'Don't be ashamed to stare, most people do. It's what they are there for.'

The display cabinets to our left contain glass cages hung against a sky-blue backdrop, flocks of birds sat across artificial rooftops and chimneys, others gathered and suspended mid-air, or on blossom, twigs and branches, held together by ghostly wires and polypropylene twine, the range and combination of feathered creatures defiantly absurd. Owls hoot at a chattering dawn chorus of warblers and robins, a crow fights over an ice-cream cone with a toucan, and a bald eagle and raven perch next to a budgerigar on a tin foil mountaintop.

In the displays on other side of the room, the composition is a little more respectful to the countryside as it is. A supposedly pastoral wild woodland setting, where a fox on its hind legs keeps a wary eye on stoats, weasels, voles and shrews gathering round tree trunks, wild fungi and dead leaves, adheres to a certain level of realism. Ominously, there is also a hare in a mantrap, numerous skulls and bones scattered about and a line of barbed wire with squirrels wrapped around it. The question as to whether the indoor aviary and its complimentary bestiary comprise figures or figurines is next to unanswerable to the amateur eye, for they are all covered in gold leaf, and so impossible to measure against nature.

'They amuse you, Mr Whoever-You-Are? What do you think of them?'

'It's not what I think of them, it is what they make me think about you.'

'Which is?'

'You're the sort of person who orders badger on room service and asks for the face left on.' This is actually so much less sinister than what is going through my mind at the moment as to qualify as flattery.

'Ha! Most amusing. They were all of the land of the living once upon a time,' Masters laughs, 'and please don't look at me like that. I know how much suburban boys cleave to wildlife. They were all put to death humanely, and none were taken advantage of. By which I mean I didn't sleep with any of them first... as I would never do anything knowingly to upset the RSPCA or B.'

Apart from a wall mural at the far side of the room, above a blast furnace that may also be the log burner, there sits a lonely grey chaise longue that looks uncomfortable enough to be one of Fallgrief's. Beside it is a round oxblood table with an old copy of *Living Marxism* on it, and an enormous hi-fi system that I imagine has seen its fair share of Wagner and Queen, the space otherwise completely bare in a way that intimates this is the point. Tucked in a corner is a portable rack of hand weights and another bearing samurai swords, ready to be wheeled in and out at Masters' discretion.

'Music is the thing in itself, is it not? The one entity that does not need the irritating intervention of words to explain what it is, and yes, my mammalian friends that have fallen foul of Midas are here to remind me of my mortality... of which I have had reason to brood over, of late.'

'I suppose we all have that to look forward to when we're the wrong side of fifty and the hangovers start to kick in.'

'Very droll. I imagine you were quite the cheeky imp before you met your current tailor. I grant you that the afternoon after the night before, especially when that night before still has me in its grip, is the occasion where I grasp extinction all too acutely.'

'Being knocked off one's perch is what they used to call it. The moment when death ceases to just be theoretical.'

Masters' yellowy eyes tauten. Until now he has been

interested in this game of Guess Who in gradating stages, but now his curiosity is genuinely piqued: 'You are right. We do not have to wait for death to know it. Most of us will be consigned to oblivion in our own lifetimes, legacy-less and irredeemable. Life cannot give back what time takes away; the passing years are not the great healer of legend. They are a truth-teller and they tell you that there are certain wounds that will not heal, like life's passing. Yes, if the past is another country, then memory is another dimension, as far away from us as something that never was...'

Christopherson puts his hands in his pockets and glances at the ceiling, implying that there is no point asking whether Masters always goes on like this as he almost certainly does, and is grateful that I am the one talking, not him.

Masters' passion for digression is nothing if not genuine. He taps his head. 'And if memory is not so much unreliable as unbelievable, what value can we place on any life, if the past seems like it never really happened? That is where one makes the existential step, the crucial one, where we cease to ask "Is my life meaningless?" and instead ask, "Isn't everyone else's life meaningless as well?" What, after all, have any of my contemporaries amounted to these past thirty years? I think back to my entire year at Chafyn and it could just as well have never existed! Have these old school mates of mine ever climbed a mountain, crossed a sea, started a dynasty or even got anybody halfway attractive to fall in love with them? How would we ever even know? Honestly, it is like trying to recollect a pack of ghosts... I know only one thing for certain: none of them have remained in here...' He taps his head again.

'Quite,' I agree, never more confident that if there is an answer to these disappearances, then this man knows what it is.

Christopherson is now looking round the room like a policeman and not a tourist, and I watch Masters watch him, out of the corner of my eye.

'That is why you might describe this house as my folly. I would like to think this building emphasises my major traits. It is built to create the illusion of permanence, and resist the sweet sadness of transience. It's why I like the walls so thick...' he offers.

'It must be very easy to delay the awful moment of contact with reality indefinitely in a place like this.'

'A rich man's prerogative. Students ask for safe spaces; men like me live in them.'

I smile ingratiatingly; hypocrisy is self-perpetuating, never allowing you to sin just once, the same situations occasioning the same lies, again and again.

'Draw closer. Come further in.'

Masters turns his back towards us and begins to walk over to the far side of the room.

'Could you be so good as to tell me who you are?' he shouts suddenly.

'I'm Chief Inspector Terence Balance, and this my partner, Sergeant Dexter Christopherson.'

'Yes, the quiet one. I had supposed that I knew you for what you were initially, but I'll admit to being slightly confused, as I was expecting a couple of contractors and police are never so usually elusive as you and Sergeant Silence here.'

'Good afternoon, sir,' says Christopherson, who has been leaning against a wall watching Masters closely. 'I sometimes have my chatty moments, but I do like to listen, most of the time. Please don't think me rude.'

Masters stops under the mural, his back still turned to us, inviting us to take it in. Unexpectedly, I nearly like it. The scene could be from some lost island Darwin discovered on his voyages: storks, pelicans and flamingos all vying for a spot near a cloudy spring, Edenic jets of water blasting from it haphazardly, smaller birds delighting in its plumes and arks; the thoroughly extinct — dodos, Tahitian sandpipers and great auks — mixing it with cormorants and boobies to create an evolutionary mix as to render the painting biblical in scope; an

Arc moored further down the coast waiting to take them to new worlds. Were it to stop at that, there would be no reason why it ought not to feature on the walls of a Pentecostal Assembly, yet the dawn of ornithology is overshadowed by the sky darkening into a demented and grinning being with a black face and red mouth, watching from behind the clouds and licking his lips, the prospect of dinner wetting his demonic appetite.

Satisfied that we have taken this all in, Masters chuckles proudly, 'Human beings did not inherit the planet from evolution; it was given to us and made for us because we are the only ones built in such a way as to be capable of understanding everything in it, while still remaining ignorant of who gave it to us and what we are here for... What are you here for, I wonder?'

'We're enquiring after missing persons, one of whom, Ruth Pertwee, disappeared just earlier today.'

'*Today?*'

'Yes, a few hours ago.'

'Ha! You must be having a very long day indeed, with plenty of distance to still run. I don't mean to tell you your business, Inspector, as you look like the sort of man who assumes to know what that is, but isn't "today" a rather short amount of time to decide whether a person has "disappeared", no? I have friends I haven't been able to track for years, even with the help of the internet and private detectives, and yet I would not have the presumption to assume that they are *missing persons*. They have simply exercised their human right to slip away and opt out.'

'This lady really isn't the opting out type.'

'But opt out she did, Inspector.'

'That would suggest you know a good deal more about her motivation that we do, or even her daughter does.'

'Ha!'

'I think he finds me funny,' I say to Christopherson.

'Oh please, spare me talk on the importance of motivation!' Masters raises his voice. 'Free will and all that humanist mumbo jumbo! It really ought to have been ditched from any intelligent discourse years ago. Who really cares *why* anyone does anything, about what differing motivations they might entertain, what anyone's reasons for doing anything are, when the end result is just the same? The same as it would be if they had done it all for a different reason. I chopped off your arm to save you, he chopped off your arm because he hates you, but the end result is that you are still left without an arm. That is why I find politics pointless. I look to the stars to give me strength!'

'But as to the lady in question...' I interrupt.

'Damn her! I have no idea what this lady's motivation was! All I know is that it is unlikely that she is gone forever,' Masters is furious now, 'the rest is just politics. And indeed, politics is what I suspect to be your *motivation* here, Inspector. Come and annoy a toff and have a good fun watching him squirm, something like that, yes? Do you have any political preferences, Inspector?'

'Left when I can help it, far left when I can't.'

'How intriguing... Yes, in circumstances of privation communism works very well, which is why communism would reduce the world to privation, so as to prove its point and get its chance. But unfortunately there are simply too many nice things in a materially developed society, tasteless as it is, for the poorest to let go and risk it all for a book of bunk,' he says, by way of calming himself down. 'I'm surprised a policeman has any sympathy for the Marxists,' Masters smirks. 'You are, after all, the only public sector workers the public can get away with despising without the slightest prick of conscience!'

'When you are charged with clearing up the system's mistakes, you can develop sympathies in strange places, Mr Masters.'

'Be that as it may, life at the sharp end is a pretty right-wing business.'

'I've had occasion to think the same thing when I've entered a crime scene.'

'Of course you have. I can see you're openly contradictory, Inspector. I like that. We must not reject our contradictions but invite and sustain them; their coexistence in a single person is the mark of genius after all. I have always thought it is in the simplicity and calm of being ourselves that we preserve the unity of the antithetical, and in doing so, can be all things at once. The alternative is to elude greatness by suppressing our contradictions, or simply being destroyed by them: the fate of petty, weak, second-rate men. Society is best understood by those who rebel against it. Even utopia will have its dissidents.'

'Good to know that I'll always be in a job, then,' I smile. 'I was hoping you might like to talk a little more about Ruth Pertwee and these other disappearances.'

'I'm sure you were. But, unfortunately, I have never heard of the woman, which is why I offer you general speculations on motivation and politics instead. Your own line of enquiry is entirely beside the point, so far as I'm concerned.' He tosses his hand away airily and nearly catches a jar of snowdrops, the only fresh flowers I have seen in the house.

It is time to throw it all out there and see what happens. 'How about her grandson? Do you know him?'

'I beg your pardon?'

'Iggy Lockheart...' I let the words stay there to see what they will do.

Masters visibly bristles.

'Perhaps it would help if we showed you a photo of him? My colleague collected one from his aunt's house this morning. He has gone missing too.'

'No, no, don't go bringing out any unseemly snaps. You're looking for faces in clouds, Inspector, but they're just clouds — they mean nothing to themselves.' Masters waves his hands at us in the hope this will stop us talking.

'Clouds are easier to forget than faces.'

'So what if they are. I don't know what you are trying to pull here, Inspector, but I refuse to look at photos of ridiculously named little people that I know nothing about, and in doing so perhaps incriminate myself in the silly stories others might weave around them.'

'I'm sorry you should think so little of helping the police in their inquiries, Mr Masters.'

'No, no. Stop being nice. You have already revealed the real you to me and there's no point trying to walk it back now. I see you for what you are: a false stale blue smell that I should not normally have allowed into the house. Only I showed my one true weakness, which is kindness to strangers and an interest in the free exchange of ideas, and allowed you to take advantage. But enough, now. I refuse to discuss the undiscussable in my own house — especially with a preening narcissist such as yourself.'

'Then we could go to our house and discuss it there?'

'Ha! Are you sure you want to be like that, Inspector? Perhaps you would also like to search my house for this boy, and plough through the grounds for his G-Shock and Air Maxes? Do you have a warrant to do so, I wonder? Or to even be here at all? If so, let me see one at once.'

He holds out his hand with the officiousness of a tyrannical border guard soliciting a bribe, and his eyes twinkle with nauseous self-satisfaction.

'And I would have asked for one earlier if I knew what was in store for me, I might add,' he sneers.

Unfortunately, I am used to suspects being scared of me because I am a policeman. Even innocent people cannot relax in our presence, a guilty conscience can be just as great an indication of fear as it can of genuine guilt, the possibility of losing one's freedom more terrifying to the innocent than a criminal. None of us are surprised that we attract more than our share of power-hungry bullies, hooked on the adrenaline rush of confrontation, emboldened in the knowledge that they are never going to lose an argument, no matter how far it goes or whatever form the fight takes. It is a point the public at large, bar the drunk, stupid or very angry, also grasp, which is why matters accelerate quickly when a civilian does not agree with one of us; all of a sudden an ordinary difference of opinion, particularly one in which the public believe they are self-evidently right, becomes a confrontation between society and all the powers of the state, with a criminal identity to look forward to once the outrage subsides and cell door closes. By inclination I do not like to rely on the collective timidity of those we are charged to serve to get our job done, but it can sometimes be useful, and I know from his smirk that Masters knows this and does not care because he is not scared. He is a true stranger to helplessness and has never been at the mercy of an authority he is powerless to circumnavigate, ignore and dismiss, or a fate that he cannot change with a quiet word and discreet telephone call. The usual logic that our world turns on has been reversed so completely that I fear the power *I* hold over him, and how it could undo me. Perhaps it would be fairer to society if I always felt this way.

'Ha! Check!'

Karmic penance will have to wait, as Masters has drawn so close that were I to lose my footing, assault would be added to his lawyer's charge sheet against the Wiltshire Constabulary.

'Come on, Inspector,' he snaps his fingers at my eyes. 'You'll never make the cast of the next series if you carry on like this! No special dispensation, Officer. Oh no, anything but that. Please treat me like any other suspect going forward. Be strict with me if you need to be. We're all equal before the law, after all... but where the hell is your fucking warrant?'

With brazen self-assurance, Masters edges even nearer me and snaps his fingers again, his other palm still outstretched in mock expectation of a warrant, badge or bus pass, whichever is beside the point now, as this is an invitation to give physical ground and flinch.

'What is it to be, Inspector? Stick or twist! You're finding this difficult, aren't you?'

'If you snap your fingers at me again, I'll take you in. It doesn't matter to me how it changes our lives.'

This works. Masters performs an unlikely pirouette, hopping from one foot to the other, a jester amused to have discovered the immediate limits of his act, while by no means giving up on making his audience laugh. 'I don't like to make the mistake of understanding anything too quickly, Inspector — you may already have noticed that — as I find going round the houses helps me know what they look like, so when I put in my bid, I know what I am getting. But you are imperturbable. That I have to give you.'

'Good of you.'

'So I am just going to come out and ask why you think *I* can help you, why I am the one you are looking for, why it is you've come here asking me questions about obscure individuals with clownish names that I know nothing about... I'm going to give you that even without a warrant because you have amused and interested me,' he preens. 'Remember, these are individuals that I could not be *expected* to know anything about, at least not in the mind of any halfway serious person... no? Lost for words again?'

With a defiant flourish, Masters loosens the dressing gown cord on his robe and breathes out ceremoniously; the sides of the cloth part, and, to my relief, I see he is wearing a jockstrap. Scratching himself suggestively, he continues, 'Why, then, are you not doing what any sensible policeman — I think we still have some of those — would advise you to do, which is to chase the obvious points of entry for a fruitful inquest, which would — if you really need me to tell you your business — be anywhere but here, no?'

'You're a person of interest. That's something for us to determine alone. We are not obliged to tell you why, or take you at your self-estimation,' I say.

'Quite. Though the fashion these days is to be celebrated for who we say we are, and not whatever nature has deemed us to be, but I sense you are not a man to be guided by prevailing orthodoxies. Still, I must insist, Inspector. Why me and not my gardener, milkman or lover? You've as good as admitted that you have discriminated against me because I am rich. Are there any more prejudices of yours that it would be useful for me to be aware of, I wonder? To coax out of the dark as it were? Might there be a little dose of toxic masculinity that you have been struggling with, a partner that was shot dead before your eyes that changed you forever, a girl who thought she could do better for herself than a life with a chump in blue and left you for someone going places in IT? Mmmm?' Masters says, rolling his eyes. 'There must, somewhere, be a *real* reason for why you have decided to ruin my afternoon with your inane cops-and-robbers routine? Please believe me — this is me attempting to give you the benefit of the doubt and help you!'

Christopherson steps up to my side, brandishing the photograph of Iggy in front of him like a cross before a vampire. 'You say you've never heard of this lad, sir. Might you be able to recognise him?'

Masters does not like this at all and, averting his gaze, whines loudly, 'Put it away, damn it! A lot of good you're doing yourselves or that poor boy carrying on like this, least of all yourselves. I know you all have a well-deserved reputation for simplicity, but really, these puerile machinations would bring shame on a scout troop.'

'Have you seen this boy before?' Christopherson persists. 'We think you might have, sir. That he may have been on your staff at one of your parties, or perhaps helped out with catering at a fête you've held. Please humour us, sir, and then we can go away and leave you in peace.'

Christopherson is practically ramming the photograph up Masters' nose, which is very enjoyable to watch.

'A simple yes or no will suffice, sir. Have you ever seen this lad, Iggy Lockheart, before?'

'Inspector, call your dog off!' Masters cries, flourishing the tails of his cassock in the air, so the ends of it fall across my shoulder.

'Yes or no, and then I promise we'll be gone, sir.'

It is Masters' turn to find himself in an impossible position, with Christopherson having forgotten several generations' worth of good manners and deference. Our suspect's dignity, and the fact that I have somehow got hold of and am hanging on to his cassock, prevents him from simply running out of the room, abandoning the moral high ground to us. Yet he will not humiliate himself in front of his staff by calling out for their help either. He has no choice but to cursorily skim his eyes over the offending photograph and sniffily jerk his head ceiling-wards.

'To me, he could be any one of them, any one.'

'Any one of who?' Christopherson counters. 'Young people you've employed here? Or maybe friends of yours, the kind that you never get to know the names of?'

'What the bloody hell you are you implying?'

Christopherson is coming into his own and is not to be stopped, 'I'm sorry, sir, but you *admit* you've seen young people like Iggy here before, yes? That you've invited these young people into your house as guests and not hired help?'

'No! Stop it, stop it at once! I've admitted to nothing of the sort.'

'Then who are "*them*", sir? You said it could be any one of "them"?'

'A mere figure of speech!'

'I'm sorry, I don't understand what you mean by that, sir. How can "them" be a euphemism?'

'I meant simply that he is like *the mass*. You know, the mass. The people, the mob, miscellaneous bodies, the extras! Of course I've seen him before — he is everywhere, ubiquitous in his commonality! That was all I was saying. Stop yourself from disappearing down a dark hole there is no coming up from, get a grip on yourself.'

'I'm afraid I am still not following you, sir.'

'I think Mr Masters is saying that he recognises our misper as part of a generalised abstraction but not as an individual personally known to him.'

Masters resents my attempt to turn translator. 'You speak of generalised abstractions, Inspector! I only wish such things existed. The people, the great *they*' — he motions towards his window — 'can't you feel them, their anger, their unpredictability, stalking civilised beings like hunted beasts, waiting for the next referendum, riot or electrical power outage to make their move? They defy all understanding. You can recognise them, but how do you theorise them? You cannot. No wonder the sociologists are perplexed.'

'I don't recognise them as an abstraction, Mr Masters, I only see a boy in a photograph you are not doing a very good job of claiming you don't know.'

'But that is my point. He is one of them — a mysterious and unknowable force!'

'Rubbish. He is just a person like you or me — well, maybe not like you — but one that thinks and speaks and acts out total bollocks most of the time and then doesn't recognise himself when someone puts him in a book and calls him "the people" and files it under theory. You don't know him or them because you don't want to. You'd rather he remained an abstraction.'

As expected, Masters is excited again, and possibly a little out of control, even by his eclectic standards, 'Ha ha! Indeed, indeed! And he and his kind are freer than I am or ever will be — and more *powerful* too.' He slaps his thigh. 'And do you know why?'

'I'd rather you answered Sergeant Christopherson's question...'

'Because the greatest miracle there is is that everyone produces consciousness!' Masters snaps his fingers. 'The universe's most awesome mystery, that we have consciousness at all, and even the lowliest moron is capable of carrying it like fire in his hand. How do we produce it? By fucking and creating babies. You can't say anything that's more democratic or God-like than that — every one of the herd a potential Allah who can start his own species. Yes, even the most existentially nebulous of them can get their bit on the side up the duff and do what I lack and cannot. I am sterile. I'm less than they are!'

'I am sorry you've got to feeling that way,' I smile.

'And yet *you* come here asking me what I've done with your precious lad,' he continues. 'No, you needn't feel sorry for me. Strong men and women destroy the concept of legitimacy; after them, all that can follow is their descendants and infighting. So perhaps I am blessed after all. That each of us measures all existence by ourselves is as extraordinary as it is inevitable. I can make no one and usher nothing into being, and, between these four walls, I know that. I live here like this for a reason. I detest the world and want as little to do with it as possible. Here at least I am at liberty to exist within the narrow confines of the kingdom you have successfully defiled today, with your impertinence and innuendo. Mankind is unimprovable; all will be as it was. I ask nothing of the world, and you must ask nothing more of me. I'd like you to go now.'

He means it. I do not find it comforting when I am told that progress amounts to knowing better in theory while carrying on as we always have in practice, but having once denied the existence of human nature, I now feel obliged to find out everything I can about it. And take the rest on the chin.

'Just go,' yells Masters.

We have nothing to lose. 'Have you noticed how people are always asking us to leave?' I say to Christopherson, and then to Masters, 'You do know Breezy Fallgrief, don't you? And Barry Swillcut? And you know that they knew Iggy Lockheart, don't you?' I make myself as big as I can so if he wants to hit me, he has plenty of me to choose from.

'Please, you are embarrassing yourself now. I am tired of explaining nothing, who doesn't know Grief and Swilly?' Masters is waving his hands around again, like they could be building up to something. 'Whether I or this Lockhead you mention do or don't only proves that we have lived in this area for a considerable number of years and have thus been unable to avoid two of its loudest bores and detestable nonentities. If I sensed from the start of your interrogation this was the best you could do, I would have dismissed you at once. As it is, I am doing so now. I tried to help you; it did not work. Let us cut our losses. Look after each other. You know the way to the door.'

'Thank you, sir. Of course you don't care who he is, but you do *recognise* Iggy Lockheart, don't you, and that is a decent enough return on our time,' says Christopherson, tapping the photograph against Masters' shoulder.

'Oh bravo, Dr Watson, bravo! Oh do put that dreadful snap away! As I have doubtless demonstrated, life is all about who you become when you can't get your own way. Be creative, Inspector, and tell your dog to be too. I know you have it in you...'

Christopherson makes a whimpering sound, inclining his head between his shoulders like a distressed mutt, and tucks the photograph into his jacket pocket.

'I'm sure you'll make heads out of your tails and sleet out of sunny skies on traffic duty, as the time you have left to solve this particular puzzle is undergoing drastic reduction the longer I have to look at you both,' threatens Masters, shaking his fist.

I turn to Christopherson: 'Good job, Sergeant. I suggest we leave Mr Masters to contemplate eternity with his animals.' And then to our host: 'It's always a pleasure to meet the public. You will be hearing from us again, shortly.'

*

We leave in a respectfully observed silence with funereal faces. Once in the car, we crack up with laughter and relief.

'I tell you what,' says Christopherson, burying his head on the steering wheel, 'that will always have been worth it. Whatever happens next, that will always be worth it. Did you see his face? What was that about? I thought he was going to turn into the bloody Ribena Man he was going so purple.'

'We definitely touched a raw nerve there. You shouldn't have called him "sir" — he didn't think you meant it.'

'He is completely and utterly barmy: a-b-s-o-l-u-t-e-l-y nuts, for Christ's sake.'

'I've never seen anyone that angry that hasn't resorted to violence,' I say. 'I don't know how he stopped himself.'

'No, that isn't his style, he has his driver do his dirty work, and watches from behind a silk screen with his legs crossed.'

'Not a man you meet every day, thankfully. But such style, such class, such elegance... we better get out of here while the going is still good.'

Christopherson lifts his head off the steering wheel, tears of pleasure in his eyes, and starts the engine. 'Let's get out of here before he covers us in gold.'

Weirdness as intense and parodiable as Masters', appreciated from the point of view of a healthy mind, looks stranger than it does to me. Madness is easier to accept as completely unfathomable and simpler to take at face value if you do not have any of it in you yourself. I am too close to Masters' concerns, and susceptible to his weaknesses, for comfort.

'I mean, what was he on? It's a different show, isn't it, before and after he loses control. Like he goes from being this self-loving headmaster completely impressed with himself to something out of a madhouse. Microdosing all day? I hear some of these creative lunatics do that. Appearance and disappearance, living and dying — okay, I followed that, but the rest of it? I mean what the actual fuck was any of it about once he started to go on about "the people" and all that? It was like the Daleks had taken over the Open University.'

'You're forgetting to show due reverence to a captain of industry and pillar of the community. This area's Bill Gates or whoever you described him as.' Predictably, the drive feels shorter now that we are on the way back and the grounds seem slightly less dazzling and worthy of our awe.

'I know that's what I said, but I'd never actually met the bloke before, boss!' Christopherson says, slowing to allow a mob of deer to stroll across our path, 'I mean he's basically paid for everything in that village from a new roof for the church to a sports hall for the local primary school. But, God, I don't know what to think about him now. I'd heard he was eccentric, you know, a bit aloof and sarcastic, but not anything like this. How could anyone that batshit deranged actually be in a position to have a career, far less derail ours? It's impossible, or at least it should be. He's a fruitloop. Should we be worried or what? I mean he was coming out the other end. No one could seriously actually be like that... If I were as weird as him, I'd at least try to pretend to be a bit more normal.'

'He's too powerful to feel the need to.'

'You think he doesn't realise he's crazy?' Christopherson says, as I watch a small group of hitchhikers, possibly lost, scurry into a copse and turn into deer as they come out the other side.

'No, I think he knows. He just doesn't care that he is.'

'That's mad though! Being like that, you could stand to lose everything if your business partners, investors, shareholders, you know, cottoned on to your not being right in the head. All his businesses would collapse.'

'Why? Why should he pay any price at all? The world *is* that mad. Wealth means that it doesn't matter if you wander round your house dressed like a roadie for Sunn O))), spouting precious nonsense to the police. Because nothing is going to happen to you, even if you have the head of every misper in the county mounted on your walls. That's the point about the insulating effect of hard cash — you can afford to be whatever you want. And the world will look the other way and make allowances.'

This seems to have never occurred to Christopherson

before, and he does not like it. His mood slips as only a liaison achieved seconds before an earthquake can, the house collapsing before anyone has had time to get their trousers back on and exchange numbers.

'I know what you are trying to tell me. That while the rest of us are following the rules and being good little girls and boys, weirdos like Masters are doing whatever the fuck they like and getting away with it, but at a certain point that has to stop, right? I mean, sensible boring establishment types, you know, the administrators and bankers that run stuff, they can't let a knobhound like Masters screw everything up and take them down with him. No grown up could have just seen what we have and still take him seriously... Maybe he is actually in the process of seriously degenerating...'

'Grown up sensible people? Which sensible people are you thinking of here, Dexter?'

We ease to a halt and the electronic gate opens slowly enough for me to wonder if it is moving. 'You know, the adults in the room, as it were.'

'Adults?' I laugh. 'What, like the flatterers that enabled an idiot like Bush to get in twice or the good folk that handed Hitler his first term in office? The senators who saw nothing wrong with Caligula marrying his horse or the pacifists who voted for the Iraq War? You've got a lot of faith in the higher-ups, my friend. The lunatics are the front men, your sensible types the enablers, and the rest of us their victims.' I am getting carried away now. 'It all hangs together. They all need each other, and none of them give a shit about the rest of us.'

'Oh come on, boss!' Christopherson says, giving me a little shake. 'I can see how a bonkers clown could manage a band, especially one like Acid Horse, and even run clubs and shops in a backwater like this with some help. But make hundreds of millions of pounds when he can't even dress himself properly? There must be something else going on here, has to be.'

'Why does there have to be? Most of the sensible people I

know are poor. Life is amoral. It looks after you if you channel and spread energy about and doesn't care about anything else. Cunts are running the world, and usually have. Power is not something the good people want because you can't use it without fucking people over and getting blood on your hands, and what nice person wants to do that?'

'Jesus, boss. That's a bit strong. Are you a communist, then?' Christopherson tries to take my entire face in as he asks the question, and we nearly drive up the back of a horse box that has paused at the crossroads.

'No, of course not. Keep your eyes on the road.'

Christopherson's lip trembles. Then he shakes his head and starts to smile again. 'He didn't like it when I showed him Iggy's photo did he? He was jumping all over the place!'

'You did well there. If we survive this day, it will be because of his guilt; and if we don't, it'll be because of his guilt. We have to move fast, though, and hold our nerve.'

'So, what next?' He asks.

'Gamble and bring in an underling, on any bullshit charge. And find out everything they know before Masters gets his lawyers involved.'

'After this it isn't going to be easy,' Christopherson tuts.

'After this we've got no choice.'

'Point. Which one of his happy band were you thinking of?'

'I think it has got to be Max, don't you?'

CHAPTER EIGHT

LOVESONG

'Emphatically no!' Grace says, tossing away the mutilated core of the apple he has made short work of. 'No I am not going to bloody arrest Max. Or let you bloody arrest Max just to keep you happy. What sort of cunt do you think I am? No, please don't answer that. I wouldn't even believe my ears if it weren't for you being the one talking, as I know you are capable of anything, no matter how dark or dangerous. But this? Good grief, you're bad for my heart, no really, you are. My blood pressure and poor overburdened heart. Please stop talking to me. Not another word.'

'I am not suggesting any of this lightly, sir.'

'No, of course you're not. You never are — that's the bloody trouble.'

Grace, myself and Tamla, with Christopherson standing technically out of earshot, while able to hear every word we say, are gathered round 'The Wiltshire Sausage', a Union Jack-emblazoned kiosk run by a Romanian couple with a reputation for food poisoning and hybrid experimentation, sat by the traffic island overlooking the approaches to the railway station. It is a few minutes to six, and the rush-hour train is late. We have taken over the watch from the PCs who have been there all day, in the unlikely event that Lockheart might choose the 6.21pm to Waterloo to make good his getaway.

'There's no point aiming any lower, sir,' I say. 'If we pick up minor players, those at the top will have the space and time to protect themselves, and we'll be nowhere nearer finding the mispers, or at least what's happened to them. The organisation behind this is hierarchal, if you enter one chamber, the one above seals itself off. You know how these things work. If Max isn't the key to all this, he knows Masters is, and is therefore protecting him. I see the first man as the route to the other, and from there we might be able to expose if not bring down their entire organisation.'

'Oh do you? Make mine a pint of blood and tomato juice! "I see the first man as the route to the other"? "The *entire organisation*?" God, strewth, so help me God! Just what planet are you phoning in from, Balance? No, please don't answer that!' Grace undoes his top button and loosens his tie. 'You may as well explain the link between two comets in the night sky, because one being the route to the other is only meaningful insofar as they have anything to do with the potential crime under investigation, and so far the jumble of cockrot, necromancy and sophistry, the pile of hunches and inklings that you would have me believe is an adequate substitute for actual intelligence and evidence, has established no such link.'

'He's in with Masters, sir.' I drive my fist into my hand. 'If you let me have a go at Max, I know we could prove it. I am as close to certain as I can be about this.'

'And so what if he bloody is "in with him", as you put it? At present we have no more reason to suspect Masters of anything criminal, obnoxious blockhead that he is, than we have anything concrete on Max, beyond his being an arse-licker of the first order who enjoys unnecessary visits to the home of the great and good, because that is simply the kind of thing he enjoys doing. A cringeworthy hobby? Certainly, especially when it is on our time. Criminal? Of course not. Yes, he has a spotty past, but I would have thought you of all people would not judge someone on the worst thing they have ever done in their life; and in any case, his former misdemeanours do not make him a candidate for bent copper of the year. Max's carrying-ons are soft porn compared to some of the things I have seen others get up to over the years.'

I hold my hand up to try and slow Grace down, but the momentum is with him now. 'And yet you, Balance, you'd have me believe this is a criminal conspiracy of the first order, though one rather short on actual details, as you admit, which is the problem really, if arresting someone is what you want to be doing, and of course not just anyone, but one of our longest serving officers as well as perhaps the most famous business export this city has ever produced. What's more, you've talked these two' — he gestures towards Tamla and Christopherson — 'into sharing your lively fantasy life and thus possibly ruining them for decent police work in future, which, given their potential, is nothing short of tragic.'

'But sir...' I say.

'Mavericks like you can get away with the odd curveball,' he cuts me, 'but others lack your survival skills.'

'I'm not suggesting arresting Masters yet, sir...'

'Oh no, you're far too measured for that, first you have to beat a confession out of Max, and then you're well on your way up the hierarchy. Yes, I see your direction of travel all too well, Balance. You are nothing if not methodical in your egotism and madness,' says Grace, squeezing my shoulder, not unaffectionately.

I have never minded being jostled or ridiculed, confident that I will always come through in the end, yet hearing Grace's swift denouement of my plan is ending any hope I may have had that he is in my corner on this. 'I appreciate—'

'Shut up, shut up, shut up! You appreciate nothing, Balance. You are a wrecking ball without conscience or concern for the devastation you leave in your wake! Have you even thought out any of the consequences of your proposed inquisition? No, of course not. You are immature and naive enough to believe that you can still control reality and bend it to your will, and everything that can't be shoehorned in must be cut out and discarded for others to clean up and throw away after you. How annoying the existence of other people, vulnerable, tender and open to hurt as they are, must be for you.'

'I think that's a rather unfair characterisation, sir,' I say, trying to make light of criticisms that are probably all true.

'There you go again! You piss-taking, insubordinate, unreliable bastard. And yet, and yet...' Grace strokes his chin and I intuit his bluster is just another stage he must undergo before he can bring himself to admit that he agrees with me.

'And yet there may after all be something, some sliver of substance, in all of this hokum. Not exactly what you say is in it, but something nonetheless.' He nods. 'A life of great belief has to involve great doubt, and your concerns, though formally ludicrous, remind me of the moment in 1976 I was told 15% of City of London Police were on the take, which was formally ludicrous but also happened to be true. I have learnt to dislike coincidences, and there are rather a lot of them in the story you tell too... Too many. I often see things your way even though I know they are not that way, but this time your difficulty is fundamentally practical, Balance: the evidence you wish to obtain from Max is precisely the evidence you would have to possess in the *first place* if we were to have any hope of detaining him, and the simple fact is that you don't have it... yet. It's a vicious circle, and I don't see any way of legally broaching it.'

'That's the point. We can't, and I know we can't,' I say. 'That's why we have to act on the assumption I am right, which will then allow me to prove that I am, once you allow me to arrest Max. I know it is a severe ask, but I can bring it off, sir.'

'Our problem in a nutshell. I'm not a praying man, Balance.'

'Alright; I genuinely believe it is *dangerous* to the public to leave the two of them, Masters and Max, out there. A dereliction of our duty to do nothing given what they are capable of if I am even half-right.'

'Of course you do, Balance, of course you do,' Grace consoles me.

'Isn't it better that I am wrong and we face humiliation and suspension than I am right and another person goes missing?'

Grace covers his face in his hands, gurgles a little, and slowly lifts his eyes above his fingers.

'If only it were as easy as that,' he mumbles.

'Why can't it be?'

Sighing, he says, 'You realise that I have already had multiple complaints about you today? Multiple. And not small ones, no. Nothing but the best for you, boy wonder.'

'Complaints?' I try and soothe the indignation the very idea rouses in me.

'Yes, you heard me. Complaints.'

'Why?'

'Why do you think? Because of your little unscheduled and unauthorised trip to Sebastopol House of course!'

'From who though, from Masters?' I ask.

'No, not Masters personally. Come on, he wasn't born yesterday! No, the mad monk has other people do his complaining for him, and he's not slow to share his troubles with his sewing circle either. Our Member of Parliament, no less an eminence, left a message asking me why I thought it was a useful deployment of my small force of detectives to harass a close personal friend of his, going back to their Oxford days apparently, who also happens to be a pillar of the local community — *wipe that smile off your face* — with obscure unsubstantiated enquiries into non-issues, when we have the Queen's visit just days away...'

'That old chestnut...'

'Yes, the royal cockle-warmer, no less. I got a friendlier version of same from the Chairman of the Rotary Club, who also reminded me of how much Masters does for charity locally, plus, not to be outdone, Lords Radnor, Wilton and Breamore have had their secretaries email me expressing polite disquiet at police overreach, and a local newscaster has asked me for comment on why my men "raided" the home of an innocent member of the public, with abuse, firearms and menaces. Do you honestly know how long it takes to normally hear from all that lot if it was our approaching them with anything we consider to be important?' Grace pulls out a handkerchief and blows his nose loudly. 'Years. But you, you have inspired them all to swing into action in a matter of hours.'

'You're serious?' I am practically dancing with pique.

'Of course I bloody am. You think I'd just reel off the honours list for my own amusement or to scare you? I've never had anything like it in all my years. Everyone from Basil Brush to the Duke of Bognor Regis has a hard-on for you, Balance!'

'Doesn't that just prove my point, sir?' I jut a finger at him. 'Just look at it. As you say, in the time it took Dexter and myself to get back, Masters has only put together a verifiable Band Aid coalition of local power to try and protect him. All of it at the very first sign that someone might be breathing down his neck. They're closing ranks now that they are in danger of being found out. I honestly don't understand how you can't see that?'

'Yes, it means something. Only it may not mean what you want it to mean, Balance. I'm sure you'd have it that this conspiracy of Freemasons, the Illuminati or whatever "cult of the damned" you believe is at work here, have been stung into action by your bold perspicacity and investigative courage, but I'm not buying it. It's more likely that a group of disparate rich people see us acting with undue disrespect for their status. And they may feel that they are the ones to fear a call from you next, not because they are guilty of anything, but merely because they are rich and you think you are Robin Hood. You were, apparently, outspoken in your attacks on wealth and privilege in Masters' company, yes?'

'Complete bullshit.'

'Really? It does sound very like you,' Grace intones.

'Dexter can back me,' I say signalling at Christopherson, who is trying to make himself small.

'So much the worst for Dexter, poor boy. I should never

have paired the two of you up together. You're a school of bad habits.'

'They're going after me, sir. It's a tell-tale indication of their guilt. They'll accuse me of anything to discredit the investigation; this is testing the water and there'll be more heat to follow.'

Grace looks at me, more in pity than irritation, and shaking his head like one who has grown used to being let down, asks Tamla, 'What have you and Max been up to, and how would you read his mood?'

I start to answer her question for her, and Grace lifts his hand to indicate silence.

'Laid back and actually a little cocky,' she replies, grinning at us both, 'with bursts of industriousness and inspiration to show off his range. He took two hours off for lunch, and then said he wanted me to double down on the usual places and usual suspects while he took the more innovative road. He says he's been collecting DNA samples off old clothes from the houses of the mispers, which I suppose might be of some use if we ever find any bodies, and questioning acquaintances. But he's been making out we want to talk to our mispers because they've been witnesses to nasty traffic accidents, and not because they've disappeared. He's at it now. He figures that's a better way of getting people to open up if they know anything or have suspicions than by giving them the truth pure and unvarnished.'

'He may not be wrong on that,' Grace says. 'It's a tactic I've used to downplay serious crimes before.'

'Bollocks. He's stalling and deliberately running down the clock,' I scowl. 'Trying to look like he's doing something useful with his hands, safe in the knowledge that his big backers are on the case now, and you'll be forced to close me down before we can hold his feet to the fire.'

'Control yourself, Balance.' Grace motions me away with his hand. 'Did anyone give you anything we can work with, Tamla?'

'Not a thing. Though our repeated appearances do look to be worrying some people now,' she replies. 'Max will tell you it's the first stirrings of guilt, as he is sticking to his white trash offing white trash story. I think it's only that they're beginning to contemplate the possibility that something really bad has happened to their kith and kin, as us turning up at the door is never good news, is it?'

'At least none of them have complained about you. As to your interjection, Balance' — Grace turns to me again — 'Max may well be playing games, but as I say, I'm not the Ghost Squad and you aren't Internal Affairs. If you want to accuse Max of corruption and collusion in a crime, you would have to go through the official channels with the strongest case imaginable, and as I have already told you, you don't have it. Even if I were to ask for a taskforce to look into police malfeasance, the chances are I'd be given nothing more than what I've already got. And with you acting up as you are, I'm not even sure for how long I'll have you.'

'Then we're not going to bring Max in?' I cry out.

'Thank you, Balance. Thank you for at last demonstrating to me that you have actually been paying attention, and that I have not been dancing with myself.'

'What about all that leave no stone unturned stuff this morning? I heard you say that people will see this as our fault, when we had the opportunity to stop it and didn't.' I am talking too quickly now. 'We're as close to them as anyone is likely to be, and now you are saying that we should back off...'

'Your way isn't the right way to make this right, Balance.'

I say something I should not. 'Why don't you want to solve this case, sir?'

'Don't be such an arrogant bastard, Terry,' he retorts. 'If you want to overplay our hand, you can fuck off to America and join a SWAT team. The way we keep the pressure up isn't through dawn raids and closing down our options but by doing just enough to make them testy, and make no mistake, you've already done that. Then we watch them like hawks to see what they'll do next. That way we actually have something on them when it comes to making arrests. It's bodies versus connections at this stage, and the connections are, as you know, circumstantial as they relate to circumstances that have very little to do with the particulars of this case, which are missing bodies.'

'So what are you suggesting?'

'A more moderate version of what you want, that will probably still be enough for me to be shitcanned, which I don't think any of us can realistically discount. You've already asked for tails on Swillcut and Fallgrief, am I right?'

I nod. 'Yes, because both of them are implicated to their eyeballs.'

'Right, and what about *The Well* and the landlady of the Hearse.'

'Small fry, without a doubt. They're so scared that I can't see them leading us anywhere or to anything.'

'Agreed. In which case we keep Swillcut and Fallgrief under twenty-four-hour surveillance, bugger the cost, and Masters too, but from a very tactful distance, as I'll never be able to justify it, none of it, especially with the Queen coming, if we don't catch them at anything. I'm not going with the other big names because at this stage I've no reason to suspect that anyone else is involved in whatever is going on here; conspiracies work when they don't involve numbers, simply a few well-placed people of influence.' Grace pauses to catch his breath. 'There may be more involved, but for now, God help us if you're wrong about those you have already fingered, as we need our three suspects to commit crimes in the next four days to remain this side of dog food. Once her Royal Highness has come and gone, people will start asking questions again. Until then, I could pretend that this has something to do with Her Majesty's visit if asked, and of course, we keep Max right out of the loop but observed.' Grace backs up and lands heavily on one of the plastic chairs provided for diners.

'Christopherson should do it. He'll look the most innocuous

if Max should catch him at it. If he *is* linked to those others, then the last thing we need is to alert him to the possibility that we suspect him of anything, as we'll need him to go to them — or them to him, if you see what I mean. So if things start to get difficult,' Grace tells Christopherson, who has approached us with a sausage roll and a banana, 'let him get away from you rather than challenge or chase him. I know he doesn't like using phones so keeping an eye on him without going the full AC-12 shouldn't be too hard. And then, and only then, if we can see the unbreakable link that leads us to the mispers, along with some plausible narrative that can actually explain what is happening to them, we can start issuing warrants.' He takes the banana from Christopherson and stuffs it in his pocket. 'Here, you can eat that other thing.'

'Thank you, sir.'

'Don't thank me. For the moment you've put the cart several fucking miles in front of the horse, Balance. So please accept that I am doing far more for you than you deserve, and that I wouldn't even be doing this if my career wasn't so close to the finishing line as for me to see the cream teas waiting for me at my retirement home. And if I lose the police pension, well, I'll still have the army one to visit Poundland with.'

'I appreciate that you are trying to meet me halfway on this…' I begin.

'I am doing much more than that, believe me, so don't you dare ask me to do any more.' Grace glares at me. 'I'm not saying at this stage that if you went to the press you wouldn't succeed in blackening Masters' name a little, showing us up to be ineffectual lickspittles to power and the rest, but we'd never find these kids and this mystery would become your whole life. Sky Crime might want you as a talking head and their resident misper expert — chuntering on about his greatest unresolved regret, the case he could never crack, the mystery that remained unsolved, because he wasn't allowed to lock up the real villains by shadowy forces — that would be you, Balance. A bit of consultancy work on the side to top up your record collection, maybe even a private investigator, given your waywardness, but you would be finished here, knowing deep down you lacked the self-discipline and humility to do anything of consequence as a policeman...'

'Harsh, sir.'

'Everyone has a limited amount they can do in their lives, Terry, but you want to be the one that finds that out for himself, and not have it said about you by others.'

'But what about the drug angle, the stuff I found at Pertwee's and the reaction it got at the Hearse? There is something new on the market and it is linked to this, sir,' I say, woefully aware that it is not a connection I am in any position to explain.

'It may be. The same rules apply.' He looks up at me, waiting for some sign of assent. I nod.

'Good. Wait for Porton Down to find out what it is and what it does. But until you can prove it has anything to with any of the above, keep it to yourself, as while I am sure Masters snorts coke out of his personal trainer's rectum, the idea of him as drug kingpin will only help further discredit you and make this thing look like a bullshit tabloid headline, lacking only Barbara Windsor claiming to have taken Prince Edward's virginity in a caravan to elevate it into a great British farce. I repeat, we watch them and we wait for them to link up. But we do nothing to them directly, and don't even think of getting clever with some kind of entrapment caper, or I will actually kill you.'

Tamla touches my wrist, almost tenderly. 'If they are making moves that implicate them, they're bound to use the Queen's visit as cover — why wouldn't they? But we won't be watching her; we'll be watching them.'

'Exactly,' concludes Grace. 'And then we can finally shed some light on this godawful business. She'll be surrounded by her minders and uniforms, the perfect opportunity for the creatures of the night to think they can go about their business unobserved and plainclothes to observe them. Put our heads to this, and we could yet land the plane in the right place.'

The Waterloo train pulls in and the trickle of commuters leaving the station turns into a human wave, the speed and haste with which they charge towards their parked cars, taxis and waiting children, like the survivors of a great daily disaster, the relief with which they can resume their actual lives a more damning indictment of work than absenteeism ever could be. A smaller flow move the other way to the departing train, none of whom look like Lockheart, Nana Pertwee or any of our other mispers.

'That crack in the world is just getting deeper and deeper,' I mutter, looking at them. 'These are all zombies. Our mispers aren't vanishing by public transport today.'

'Zombies? What a morbid way of describing the foot soldiers of our economy, Balance! I don't see that at all. I see hard-working men and woman keeping this country alive,' objects Grace.

'Ha! We're being softened up for the killing blow,' Tamla snorts. 'And who knows in what form it will come? The Martian invasion, nuclear war, a global pandemic or asteroid from above? One thing Terry's right about is the size of the crack. This lot are exhausted. None of them will cram onto the shame train to defend the existing order when the time comes...'

'Nonsense. Dystopian dreamtime,' chuckles Grace. 'They all make decent livings and know who pays their wages.'

'You think any one of them would lift a finger to save the system, sir?' Tamla asks. 'Think again, they reckon that's our job. The wage slaves will disappear into their boltholes the first chance they get and stay there until they believe it is safe to come out, which will be never...' Tamla makes a falling motion with both hands, the light catching the indented cracks on her nail varnish. 'And then we'll have even more people to look for, won't we?'

'I can't wait,' says Grace. 'Come on. Let the uniforms pick up the nightshift. There's nothing more for us to see here.'

*

Coming home is no longer a metaphysical adventure for me, simply a practical event, which at least puts me on a more even footing with my neighbours, who if bothered by such category distinctions, have yet to mention anything to me. Since the building I grew up in was knocked down and rebuilt as someone else's house, I no longer regard 'home' as a physical place but as an idea that will materialise again if I experience a necessary connection with my surroundings. Until then I live in a converted Methodist chapel on one of the four hills that surround the cathedral city, tacked to the edge of a village-town that has only nearly avoided, by half a mile of woodland, being absorbed into the creeping conurbation that sucks the new developments outwards. The chapel is at the end of a row of subsiding, sloping and formerly swanky cod-Regency terraces, broken up into apartments, all in disrepair, populated by exiles fresh from the economic cleansing of Stoke Newington and Dalston, instigating a further domino run of local banishment as ageing townspeople are driven further west, into NHS funded care-homes or the graveyard of the C of E church opposite.

From my place, the main thoroughfare ambles quaintly past a pub that is so like the living rooms of the houses adjoining that punters assume they have stumbled into a private dwelling, a closed library, shut post office, abandoned pet shop and two other boarded-up pubs, ending up at a rickety bridge where an empty gallery occupies the former tannery that once ensured leather was the town's most famous manufacturing export, before quiet neglect and substance abuse took its place, the odiferous tang of animal skins and urine still present in its walls. I enjoy wandering about the parish and surrounding water meadows, which, without a dog, would mark me as either mad or a criminal were I not a policeman and from London: the locals ready to make allowances for key workers and geographical outcasts.

Inside the chapel the structure of the building is the same as it was when the three rooms were a lively house of prayer. The congregation that shared a wholesome and dignified existence when Methodism was in fashion nearly a century ago, living, singing and believing together, are no longer with us, their observance failing to entice their children and grandchildren, which with rumours the place is haunted, allow me to enjoy an open-plan room with a very high ceiling, a pretty stained-glass window, kitchen and lavatory, at an indifferent rent. As I have never had a religious experience in church or been scared of ghosts, whom I find strangely comforting, there are no unfortunate connotations for me here. And since I could not believe in my own importance if I did not already believe in the existence of God, who provides neither consolation or certainty, simply the best explanation for my meaning-giving tendencies, I have nothing to fear as the nights darken and shadows cluster.

Closing the door behind me, and with my usual complacency failing to lock it, I turn on one of the half-dozen side lamps that I prefer to the industrial-strength floodlights on the ceiling, which illuminate too boldly, and ask myself what did I expect to see, other than a space with no one in it? It is a default setting that will not change by itself, despite my bed being so large as to appear to be waiting for someone else to come into the room to make my arrangements less bereft. Living alone is a kind of act, without a partner to reveal your hidden self, who at least knows who you are most of the time, you are free to project an unchallenged performance, as no one cares enough about you to correct you or set you straight. But after a day in lively company, the emptiness of it can hit me with the force of one year turning into the next too quickly, the usual vision of acute loneliness, built into my natural appreciation of things, impossible to pass off as the ennui common to professionals who live too much in their heads. What I feel at this moment as I survey every empty corner of the room goes impolitely beyond that. Tonight I believe in untidy Platonism; I register it in the hunger of my poor bloody heart: all of this has fallen so far from the idea I had of my life that it is incumbent upon me to do something at once, to cease living in my nightly speculations and change course, so that all this consciousness is not wasted.

Pathetically, I peer into the hollow reflection of my outline in the larger of the two playschool windows that are the eyes of the house, the stained-glass star between them depicting the Lamb of God, and wonder where the lessons of my father and his friends have got me, when the country is quite possibly run by demonic fornicators and agents of the Devil. Despair as an impetus towards action is always followed by the even firmer resolution that I have what I deserve and I am fortunate to have even that. It is a pattern I have been trapped in the negative feedback loop of for years, triggered increasingly by the realisation of how poorly I have fared next to less talented, generous and public-spirited individuals, who bathe in rose water whilst I make do with the soap suds from last night's washing up.

I groan loudly, daring anything to hear me.

What a predictable catalyst visiting Masters' lair turned out to be, opening up too many unfortunate and glaring points of comparison: we are both preposterous egotists who live in elegantly under-furnished monasteries, my own version thereof a squat next to his fully realised ideal; the Linn turntable, my dad's old Heals furniture, a silver-mounted photograph of my parents in their prime, the model soldiers and Penguin classics stacked along the pew, all supposed to cover my nakedness before creation, and usually do, are basically the cut-price take on Masters' grand aesthetic. The pitiful pride I try not to take in them emphasises how unlikely I am to travel as far as he has in life, whatever good I might try and do or code I uphold, and that my hating the bastard will not make this knowledge any easier to bear over the coming decades. Slowly, I take off my jacket and undo my tie, the conceit that saves me from jealousy unable to take the sting out of the chasmic distance between this rented God-shack and the pagan ebullience of Sebastopol House.

'*Tumphhh, tumphhh...*'

There is something at the window: a scratching sound. I am so used to noises here, the grinding of pipes and cawing of crows that fly in by mistake, that I would normally wait for an explosion before worrying, yet as I have not exactly been forging powerful new alliances today, caution kicks in. I wait for it to happen again, which it does: possibly stones, several small ones, being scattered lightly against my windowpane, the intention not to break the glass but to unnerve. I pull out my cricket bat, an old SS Jumbo, which lives under the bed, and edge towards the window the noise has come from. Its edifice protrudes over the street, a couple of feet above a diminutive stone staircase that rises from the pavement to the two interlocking blue doors that kept the eager faithful at bay every Sunday, sat like nostrils on a punchable face. The other window rests over the street on the other side of the entrance and is just as exposed to passing interest. If whoever out there has come mob-handed, and decides to take both windows at once, I am done for, and that is before they discover they can simply walk through the front door. I look to the back entrance in the kitchen, which leads straight into the garden, stretching out unfenced into a large moat with public access. Should my assailants know anything of the terrain, I cannot look to escape that way either...

Recognising that I am running away with myself and creating *The Long Good Friday* out there, I clear my throat and cautiously peel back the thin net curtain. Standing under the mottled glow of the old street lamp... is Eileen Pertwee, only her face visible, her sleek running gear blending predatorily into the night. Seeing that she has got my attention, Eileen rolls back her shoulders and pulls up her top.

'I bet you've been thinking about these all day, you fucking pervert!'

Unfortunately, they have not been the only things I have been thinking about. A car that I thought was empty turns its lights on and quickly pulls away from the curb, leaving Eileen in a cloak of exhaust, and me with the near certainty that every move I now make is being watched.

*

He lives in real time and treats everything as important, despite knowing none of it is serious. Here in his bath, 'The HMS Invincible', a battleship worthy of inclusion in Jellicoe's fleet at Jutland, Masters has attained the serenity it would take most tyrants a lifetime of global decapitation to even approach the sublime heights of. From the mentholated depths of his steel tub, he glares up through the conically aligned glass ceiling, allowing the weather, surrounding planets and cosmos into the room, without the inconvenience of two-way exposure to the elements and nature protruding beyond her station. This observatory and chamber of contemplation are Sebastopol House's crowning achievement, and when he is anywhere else, this is where he yearns to return to. The Takahashi TOA-150B F/7.3 Triplet Ortho Apochromat Refractor Telescope, his current favourite for spying on Saturn's rings and Jupiter's moons, lies jettisoned by a pile of towels, a metal penis which having achieved perfectly realised thing-hood through the performance of the duties it was designed for, is satiated and entitled to rest. He cannot believe he only paid £2,000 for it, or would have, had he not been gifted it for a load of balls he spouted at a charity lunch about a space programme he has no intention of ever launching unless matters really get too hot for him down here. If only everything could be so easy to get away with. At this he gurgles playfully and wipes the bubbles off his chin, a baby-man free from the reach of the adults, because truth be told, he would find life even more prosaic than he does if things really were that simple.

Masters squints and concentrates on a star: his old favourite, Sirius A, the Dog Star, the brightest collection of burning dust and gas gathered in the Northern Hemisphere. Incredibly, he was once romantic and ignorant enough to believe this evolving nebula held a personal relationship for him, based on some rot his nanny said about how the luminous orbs in the night sky were the souls of his dead ancestors. Every one he could spot was meant to be a signal from heaven indicating good luck, the astronomical equivalent of catching a falling leaf, and if he were to spot a shooting star, then his future wife would be thinking of him as well. Future wife! Any wife? Horse crud and specious nonsense! If only the activity of interpretation could be so transparent. He chuckles into his flannel, because of course, he does not really want the story to be decipherable, distrusting pat explanations and anthropomorphic balderdash that is only the wish fulfilment of a particular species that cannot stop talking about itself. Still, good fortune has been his, in a way, though calling it good ascribes it a moral character that may be a little too ambiguous to be approved of in the pulpit of the cathedral, should the bishop want to look too closely into his affairs.

Music wafts up the spiral staircase that connects his observatory to the master bedroom occupying most of the floor below. Every note he hears was worth his considerable investment in its reproduction: the Métronome Technologie CD deck from Paris, £70,000; Continuum turntable from Melbourne, £80,000, with Koetsu cartridge and stylus from Osaka, £2,400; darTZeel preamplifier and power amplifier from Zurich, £28,850; Magico speakers from Berkeley, California, £58,000 (the £200,000 Wilson speakers from Utah are still with GBS); interconnect and speaker cables from Transparent of Maine and power cables from Crystal Cable in Amsterdam, total £18,000. Grand total £257,250, or £457,250 with the Wilson speakers. And add another number to the total for the Naim all-in-one streamer fresh from the factory production line on the Southampton Road — investing in a local business, really they should be honouring him with the keys to the city! All of it money beautifully spent, which is more than he can say for the other things lucre can buy. He is of course listening to Roxy Music's 'Avalon': Ferry's greatest achievement to make the rich seem interesting. Visualising the equipment downstairs, his bedroom a verifiable shrine to high-fidelity, encourages an unexpected twinge in a part of Masters' personal technology that has lost some of its old single-mindedness of late. It is in an intriguing development.

'Now, now. It's been a while, Leviathan. It has been a while, so it has...'

Masters touches his penis, and then dismisses the thought at once. He simply has too much respect for reality for so absurd an activity to fly, being too grounded to literal truth to pull the thing off. Instead of seeing the object of his desire as he closes his eyes, he cannot get past the reality of a middle-aged man that he does not find attractive wrestling with his organ in a bath, and there is nothing to sustain arousal in that. Alternatively, going downstairs and actually masturbating over his speakers and pre-amp might work, yet he feels a little uncomfortable about doing so: another invisible line transgressed that could one day bite him in the back.

Clear-sightedness has always been his curse, and while it has also forged a path for his many successes, seeing them for what they are has rendered them mostly unenjoyable and often unsatisfying. The trouble with seeing through things, other people most of all, is that there is no one left of his own calibre to share his many insights with: he has driven the good ones off and is tired of the rest. The detective from earlier, amused and dangerous, had the potential to be a real friend, but friendship can be an addiction, sentimentality will fill the gap left by truth, and sentimentality is not an emotion the future understands. No, he cried that rot out of his system long ago. Too many false alarms: candidates who appeared to be real companions, until he let his guard down and discovered that he had offered the tit to envious coveting threats, who under the guise of pretending to worship him, had their sights trained on their own interests after all. Although he has an address book that includes everyone who is anyone from Lake Geneva to Wick Lane, his lack of personal ties is his security *against seeing things from anyone else's point of view. He, Mungo Masters, is the person he has always intended to become, and now that he has become him, occupying his ultimate essence, he must seek new challenges. The only way to do justice to the past is to exist entirely in the present. How, now, to exceed oneself, to move beyond the paltry facts of his physical existence, transcend the units and figures and present God with his unfinished work? Stick or twist? The questions are not theoretical. The policeman was an emissary and harbinger of a possible future, an ugly projection in which the howling mob have caught up with the Overman, discovered his secrets, and stopped his fun. The point about neurotic obsession is that it should never seem as important to anyone else as it does oneself, yet more and more bodies are being caught up in his projects and experiments, and it is not altogether clear how long the consensus he has established over his merits will hold, for even armour rusts and gaps appear. They are on to him.*

Masters opens the tin on the bath rack, and removing a gnarly grey substance, breaks it up in his palm and releases the crumbling flakes into the water, quickly changing its colour: a thick brackish blood-red released from the hissing fragments. No one understands anything until they get their first glimpse of infinity. Yes, he knows something of the loneliness of God. A shadow gathers over the wall, it would be unwise not to test it. Taking only the very merest of sniffs, as if to test the temperature, Masters submerges his head, swallowing a mouthful of foaming liquid, and vanishes deep into the bowels of the tub. Far above his palace another meteorite shower passes unnoticed by a woman he will never marry, and belt of clouds, black as his ancestors' blessings, settles over Sirius A, wiping the shine off the Dog Star, until it too blends into deep existlessness, with the twilight approach of dawn.

BOOK TWO

There are more things in heaven and earth too than truth.
William Faulkner

Let us guard against saying that death is the opposite of life; the living creature is simply a kind of dead creature, and a very rare kind.
Friedrich Nietzsche

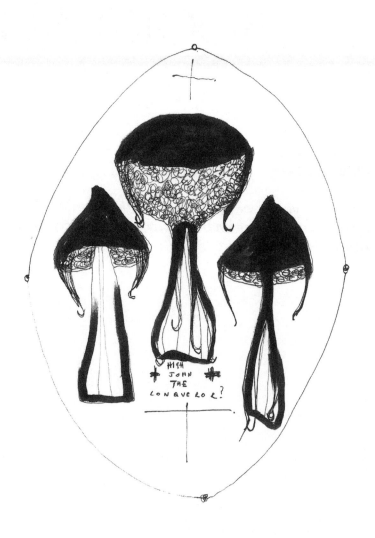

CHAPTER NINE
A STRANGE DAY

For the next three days, no one sticks a bomb under my car, strangles me in a doorway or drops anything heavy on my head. Despite several hours of near-unbearable tension, what I am most afraid of happens, which is nothing. The plumber has come to my house to fix the leaking tap only to discover the flow of water is working perfectly, so the fault must lie with me, the man who reported the fault. Every morning I wake to a county made up of model citizens. No one else goes missing, the morning skies are full of the golden smoke of early spring, diurnal sunshine filtering through the mists on the water meadows, as the bunting, banners and flags go up to herald Her Majesty's visit at the end of the week, now just thirty-six hours away.

Playing his part to injured perfection, Masters has not so much as left his mansion, at least not by any visible means, as although I am supposed to leave him alone, we have all taken turns watching his place; while Swillcut and Fallgrief have not put a foot wrong either, both assiduously following their ordinary routines like the unsung heroes in a film that has threatened to run over budget. Of course there is always a hidden cost: Nana Pertwee has not been found, Lockheart is still missing, as is every other misper we have failed to find, and there is a potentially lethal unidentified drug doing the rounds, our usual informants having reached new heights of collective inarticulacy on the subject. But the problems of one small city are as remote as civil war in Syria, a coup in Myanmar or famine in the Yemen, next to the excitement generated by the Queen's visit. It is in bad taste, if not breaking an outright taboo and disregarding form altogether, to raise anything that could sour the magnificence of the visit. What has already happened has gone; the past is an impossible emotion, and my credibility now rests on the following: the entire population needs to be snatched from their beds for me to not look like an overreacting bedwetter. Whereas all my doubters need is for a corgi to show up and snaffle a commemorative sausage roll to enjoy complete vindication. And as with so many of life's sweetest injustices, it is an incumbent's game to lose. With open eyes, powerless to prevent the inevitability of the narrative, I have cast myself in the tiresome role of the detestable challenger, who unable to leave well-adjusted people alone to enjoy their fun, surfs the light fantastic of conspiracy theories, fed by personal bitterness and a chip on each shoulder.

Besides, Orridge has been busy, drip-feeding findings that are intended to firm up his preferred account of events: all the missing persons were engaged in high-risk lifestyles or are the children of parents who are, and those that are not are known persons of interest in unsolved crimes ranging from smearing a Range Rover with butter to leaving a tub of urine in the library. Furthermore, the old Pertwee woman was heard to say she would rather kill herself than waste away with dementia, and as a crowning achievement of baseless hearsay, a serial killer is back on the loose, according to a nameless informant who once shared a cell with him. It is a powerful assemblage of invention, dug out of a box of dead ends, encompassing a bit of everything with one notable absence. There is no mention of posh people kidnapping children, which we seem, by anything but mutual consent, to now be too embarrassed to mention without evidence, despite there being nothing to substantiate a single rumour Orridge has spread.

To make matters even terser, I have information, confidential to a point where I have had to swear to take it to the grave, that makes me more certain than ever of my obsessions. Christopherson has told me that a parent who does not want to be named has complained about a cheerful copper known to us, who has been doing the rounds of the estates announcing there is nothing to worry about regarding the kids who are vanishing, hers especially, as they have been seen living it up in a commune in New Cross, even though the women has yet to report her boy missing. Contrary to our friend's intentions, these glad tidings of comfort and joy feed a genuine and growing fear amongst the people who do not count that something really is going on, which all the blue, white and red confetti in Britain will not charm away. Max's rupture with his own inglorious past is not looking so clean either. Orridge has confided to a few of the divorced constables that he has squirrelled away his pension in Porkies — a bar in the Philippines run by one of the ex-cops that was busted from his old squad — encouraging them to invest similarly, the promise of a rosy retirement replete with fanny and free drinks for all who take the plunge.

As for Masters, here the pain is concentrated most acutely, because as sure as I am of his place atop of this cesspool, deciding who goes and who stays, I am also sleeping with a witness whose pillow talk is inadmissible evidence. I have fallen so heavily and carelessly in love with Eileen that even if she were feeding me a wealth of lies, I would seek a reason to excuse her. Mere mention of her name causes me to smile, and I find myself trying to bring her up in conversation, only to find that I am unable to share anything she has told me, far less confess my feelings towards her. Through her I have learned that Iggy attended a large party held at the house of a local bigwig, as have many of the other adolescents who have disappeared. Exactly what they did there, where the house is or who owns it, is admittedly beyond her brief, yet even the feeblest of inferrers could follow the smoke back to Masters.

Yet no one is willing to come forward to testify — not even Eileen's daughter, who was sounded out for an event herself. Leading the charge with any of this would erupt in my face. Witness tampering would be the least of my problems; Orridge would have a field day with the manner in which I have allowed a manipulative suspect to make the most of my conceit, elope with me to deflect suspicion from herself, and deflect it onto a poor worthy whose only crime was to ask unemployable pond life to help out with the canapés of an afternoon. Like the self-righteous cop who laughs only once in a film, and then only at his cosmic bad luck becoming even worse, I am for the moment damned if I act, and a witness to my own irrelevance if I do not.

There is banging on the car window. Tamla is wearing her hair in minuscule Yorkshire-Heidi pigtails, drumming her knuckles on the glass with the impatience of a youth who wants to share their parents' drug stash.

'Sitting out here on your own, lonesome as a cloud?'

Despite having pulled in ten minutes earlier, I have not had the heart to get out of the car and join my colleagues in the trailer. Encouragingly, a local artist has sprayed 'Who's offing our kids?' on the side of our catering Winnebago, though in the current climate, I am not sure this is the intervention my cause needs. I can also hear Orridge singing 'Buffalo Soldier' loudly, and I really do not want to know what has occasioned it.

'Yeah...'

'I think I am conversant with the problem,' I say.

'How could anyone not be? It's difficult, isn't it?'

'Difficult to be in the same space as Max? Yes, as our new trainee is discovering for himself. The poor guy's just reported in and happens to be from Nigeria, hence Max's Bob Marley rendition.'

'That should make him feel right at home.'

'At least it stopped Max from gloating on about how the Conservative majority here will never be trimmed to less than fifteen thousand, or a one-five-treble-zero cushion, as he likes to call it. At which point I had thought, *how I really wish DCI Balance was in here to say something funny to that*, because I really cannot be bothered to speak truth to power today...' Tamla coos.

'As you say, it is sometimes difficult to be in the same space as Max.' My partner does not appreciate that I am not in the mood for talking or cheering up.

'And that's before he gets going on those BT shares you should have bought in the Eighties. Here, let me get in next to you. I've something to share.'

'Please no more indifferent to middling to shit news,' I say flatly.

'What are you really in the market for, then?'

'A partisan miracle that shows divine favouritism would do me nicely.'

'Ohhh, that sounds very specific and a little bit technical.'

Tamla slips into the seat next to me, bringing the fragrance of creosote shrubs, pinyin pine and the rest of the cosmetics counter at Liberty in with her. 'Let me first start with a warning, Terry.'

'God. What have I done this time?' Having crossed a line that could end my career, I do not think it unreasonable to be scared all the time.

'Quite. I came over to yours the day before yesterday to cheer you up with a spliff or two and saw you letting in a woman old enough to be my mother, give or take a couple of decades. Ring any bells with you perchance?' Tamla asks.

I say nothing, and she continues, 'That woman is Eileen Pertwee, isn't she? So, not to be deterred I came over again last night and I saw you had your blinds drawn, which as an advocate of natural light you have never been known to do, so I am guessing that she was with you again and that you now have a *thing* going on? Don't bother lying to me, it won't be helpful. I'm not being nosy, only looking out for you.'

Tamla has always been able to move from using the element

of surprise to complete victory, bypassing a bloody struggle, attrition and counterattack, and rather than responding by asking what bloody business is it of hers, I reply, 'She's not that old. And she was with me the night before the two you're talking about too.'

'Three visits on three consecutive nights? Jesus Christ, Terry. That's a little bit Romeo and fucking Juliet, isn't it?'

'She's... a bold woman.'

'Last of the great romantics, is she? So she led it, yes? Good, I'm glad you're not that stupid.'

'I don't know about that.'

'Stay clear of suspects, Terry, for fuck's sake. That grave, head-down martial seriousness that's great for getting mixed-up social workers to abandon their best instincts and develop a crush on a detective isn't going to wash with a civilian that could be implicated in the biggest shit-show this dump has ever hosted. If I can see everything you do, it isn't going to pass unnoticed by others for very long in a goldfish bowl like this, is it?' Tamla gives me a hard nudge. 'And in case you were otherwise occupied, there are people here who have a hard-on for discrediting you, the size of which you could not even believe. Unless you have an uncle you've never told me about that is actually the commissioner of the Met, you have your work cut out for you to just stay un-shitcanned, and that's if you're tactical and sharp, which I don't suppose there is any chance of you being whilst you are in the grip of hard-dick insanity.'

'I am not looking to defend myself, but it...' I mutter, knowing how bad this looks, and in fact is.

'Then don't.'

'It, it just...'

'Don't tell me, it just *happened* right?'

'It did. It was a surprise.'

'But it isn't a surprise for me. How could it? You men, it doesn't matter how the years add up, you just can't keep it in your trousers. You see opportunity everywhere even if you don't think you do. I mean, what's wrong with having a good old-fashioned fling with a colleague for a change?'

She is joking. It might have happened if Tamla were not my ideal fantasy when I was twelve — the peroxide blonde singer of a jingle jangle band, stood in high heels and wrapped in a scarlet napkin — or I her preferred father figure when she was nine, the man in a suit and tie that never walked through the front door with a reassuring tread, representing a security she never knew, to read to her before bed. These fraught and deeply unprofessional associations came out early on our friendship, and even earlier in our lives, pouring cold water over our libidinal potential, so when the moment of truth came one night, we fell about laughing instead.

'So you're never going to see her again?'

'Is that an ultimatum?' I ask.

'Well?'

'I think we're already past that point, to be perfectly frank.'

'Because she'll draw attention to your association in a way that'll mean curtains for your career?'

'No, she wouldn't do that.'

'Why not, who are you to her, Terry?'

'I, I mean, *we*, her and me, we really like each other. No, it's more than that — we've fallen in love.'

'Oh God.'

'Yeah.' I rub my eyes.

'Well, you've got me there. She at least shared anything with you? That you didn't already know?'

'About love or this other drama?'

'Try and be serious.'

'The community know someone powerful is behind these disappearances,' I say, 'the same as we do. It's where the posh people accusation came from. She says lots of local kids have been approached by middlemen to take part in parties, her daughter included, but none of them will say shit when asked — same as our experience. But what we know about Masters...'

'Which is not as much as you think we do, Terry...'

'Okay, what I think we know about Masters is the missing piece they, the families and victims, the ones this is all happening to, don't have.'

'So you mean they can't name him for you? That's not very useful for your theory is it, Terry? If Masters really is a cross between Lord Summerisle and Dracula you'd think some scared villager might have the goodness to say so?'

'If you'd met him, you'd *know* he's the one behind it. He *is* a self-styled Prince of Darkness, for Christ's sake. His whole place is adorned with trophies that sing of his villainy. I mean, I genuinely think he is taunting us, and that part of him wants to get caught. That's how blatant it is. Christopherson even told me his neighbours have complained about these happenings, and Max — Max, for fuck's sake — is the one that goes in to deal with these complaints! Any kid who has been to one goes missing sooner or later. That's the basic maths involved.'

'Sure, and we have everything except proof.'

'If I'd been allowed to question Max...'

'Yeah, that would have been a classic of its genre!' Tamla shakes her head dismissively. 'What you have, Terry, is the greatest circumstantial evidence ever assembled in one place, but still no killer link that shows these parties are the ones the Pertwees learned of. I so badly want to put a smile on your face, Terry, but you're still at square one.'

'If we could piece together what we "suspect" with what these kids know, but won't tell, then we'd have him. I just need to find the right kid in the mood to talk. That'll come once they know we're on their side. At the moment they don't think they can trust us, or anyone else.' As I say this I know that if it was so easy, then it would have already happened, and that I am in no position to talk about trust.

'Even in the event of that happy day, and one of these kids mentions Count Masters by name, we'd still be dealing with their word against his, which brings about its own problems, doesn't it? We'd need a score of them, an absolute score, before we could set about building a credible case, and the trouble is none of them, none of them at all, are talking. She got a theory about why that is?'

'Not a theory — she says they are absolutely terrified.'

'Hmmm.'

'Why not? If there really is a creepy cabal of kid-eating lizards out there, who've infiltrated us and have links all the way up to the upper echelons of society, you'd keep shtum too, right?'

'Only if you buy into all that Illuminati crap, which I of course would not blow my nose on.'

'You don't have to. The cloak and reptiles stuff gives real conspiracies a bad name, and worse than that, it allows the real bad guys to operate in plain sight. I don't for a minute think aliens, the ghost of Denis Healey or any of the science fiction bollocks on YouTube is behind this, no more than you do. But some of the kids might.'

'Indeed. And what *do* you believe, Terry?'

'I think whatever Masters is up to, alone or with others, is stranger and more mysterious than any paranoid bullshit you could pull off the internet. It's why he has a hold on these kids, and that hold means he can use a threat a lot worse than being battered to keep a lot of people who normally enjoy talking quiet. It goes to the heart of what's going on.'

Tamla puts the tin of lip balm she has been playing with onto the dashboard, takes a colourless swab of chewing gum out of her mouth, wraps it in a piece of tissue and throws it out of the window.

'Why their lips are sealed, that is admittedly hard to fathom... one of them would have let something out by now if only by the law of averages. That's the way it always goes. The more of these little brutes that know about something, the more likely we are to; they can't help themselves once they think they know something we may not. It's the perfect bargaining position.'

'Like she says, they're terrified.'

'I agree that they must be scared. But mightn't that suggest that they are actually *implicated* in some way, and what they are afraid of is that this is going to come down on them all if it comes out into the open? It could be a classic case of victim guilt, but on such a scale that it's way off the scale...' Tamla points her finger upwards.

'You're saying that they could all be accessories to the crime?' I reply.

'Not exactly. I am trying to be a bit more subtle than that. It could be like the girl who thinks she had it coming because she was wearing red knickers and a short skirt, or the kid who thinks he deserves to be bullied because he doesn't fight back. Yeah? Look at history — it's full of examples. The inmates that take gassing as the punishment for forming orderly queues to the chambers. You see what I am getting at, don't you?'

'There are no successful crimes without some cooperation from the victim. Real or imagined,' I say.

'Spot on. These kids, they may believe, however wrongly, that they are somehow involved in the actual disappearances themselves, either through association or collaborating with the real perpetrators to gull others in, no? It's got the best explanatory potential of anything we've discussed. If they all believe they are complicit, either because they made it too easy for the predators, sent out the wrong signs, or did nothing, or even didn't know what to do, and only found out later, then the wall of silence starts to make sense.'

'That might be a part of it.'

'Sadly that doesn't make it any easier to break down — harder, if anything,' says Tamla.

'Unless we were able to get one of our own, I don't know, a younger trainee that could pass for a teenage waster, to go deep cover and be picked for one of these shindigs, then...'

'Behave, Terry! This is you all over! Think about what you're saying. Have you any idea how long it would take to plant a naked cop in this community unnoticed and then wait for the villains to actually come to us because they've run out of other candidates? It's not exactly sympathetic to the timeline we're working on, is it?

'So, is this the good news you had for me?' I ask.

'You're a victim of your own wishful thinking, I never said my news was going to be good. In fact, if anything, it's set to make life even more complicated.'

Tamla pulls her iPad out of the scarlet satchel she affects instead of a handbag. 'Though if we're looking for a way in, then I may be able to offer you a better path than deep cover operations involving teens. But this is strong stuff,' she warns, 'hold on to something and prepare to not believe your eyes.'

'What am I supposed to be watching here?' I ask.

'You'll see...' Tamla switches the device on and clicks on one of two MP4s that sit amidst the clutter of her desktop. 'We'll do this one first. Keep looking at the rat with the white stripe down its back. You can't miss him, he's a sweetheart.'

'Rats?'

'Three minutes of laboratory film compressed from over forty-eight hours of footage.'

'Glad the distributers spared me the director's cut.'

'Cutting and splicing is what these guys do. You won't be bored.'

We are watching a large cage with four rats in it and a number of rodent props that allow them to while away time constructively, or at least that is the idea, as only three of them are engaging with the boredom breakers: one spinning in a wheel, another climbing ladders on an assault course and the third rolling about with a ball. The fourth, a chunky slob with a white skunk stripe running the length of his ample body, is slumped dozing in a corner. A number of sequences quickly pass, the time in the top right-hand corner whirring away, without this essential formation changing until things slow down properly and we watch the big one stir, as if awakened from a coma. What he does next is consistent with any grouch who has just been disturbed. Showing his teeth, he makes a display of anger to his three hyperactive mates, shrieking at them. Then, in a sudden movement, he leaps on the rat closest to him and tears at its head. For the next few seconds he chases the other two round the cage, cornering one and scratching it to pieces, before rolling the other on to its back and biting messily into its chest.

'He got up on the wrong side of bed...'

'Look now, see what happens.'

Twisting about in the innards and remains of his companions, the surviving rat gets onto its hind legs and, for a second, standing on two feet like a man, seems to address us, staring straight at the camera. And then he is gone. The camera is still running, the cage and the corpses of the others are still lying motionless, but our lead actor is nowhere to be seen.

'You see that?'

'Is that a trick, of the camera?' I ask, not knowing what to make of this at all.

'No.'

'Run it again. Now, now stop there. Close up. He's there...'

'And then he isn't.'

'Go again. That bit again.' I try to work out what I missed, the telling detail that will explain the mystery.

'By all means. But this isn't ordinary police work we're watching.'

'There, again, what the fuck? Are we missing a bit of film?'

'No, no editing out. He just vanishes, poof, like that.'

'Let me see it again.'

'You really need to?' Tamla asks.

'One more time, please.' Not being able to believe my eyes, I am convinced the fault must be found in me, and not the footage.

'Performing the same exercise and expecting a different result is the textbook definition of madness.'

'Once more,' I insist.

'Okay, but I've seen this a dozen times at least already. You're not going to spot anything you missed before.'

'You sure there aren't any other clips?'

'Positive. It is just as we see: fatso is in slumber, fatso wakes and kills the others, then fatso disappears into thin air whilst still effectively trapped in a cage. No camera trickery, no one in the lab doctored the film for a laugh, there were no trap doors or false entrances. The boys in Porton Down are scratching their heads as we speak, but like us, they've been told that with Her Majesty coming tomorrow, there are to be no distractions. The local news can live without *Dynamo*, the amazing vanishing rat story, especially as no one wants to get into why this particular rat was being filmed in the first place.'

'Porton Down? They gave that rat whatever it was I found in Nana Pertwee's bedroom?' I say.

'Just as you asked,' replies Tamla. 'They tried to analyse it first, of course, see what it matched or might be a distant cousin of, but drew blanks. It wasn't consistent with any plant or chemically created substance they knew of, so wanting to see what it could do in practice, they decided to dose our four-legged friend with the entire clump, expecting heart failure, a little inertia or possibly nothing at all. And instead we get the full Houdini.'

'So what the hell happened to it?' I ask.

'I don't know, they don't know. It is what it is.'

'*It is what it is* and *Keep Calm and Carry On* have never struck me as realistic maxims, and now I feel utterly vindicated. This thing just vanished in a finger click and they don't even have an inkling why?'

'No, though we can return to that. Watch this first. This is even better than the rat.'

Tamla hits the next MP4 and we leave the laboratory for a dim and grim street corner, the grainy footage of a CCTV camera capturing drizzle, depravation and the emptiness of late Monday morning, according to the time and date in the right-hand corner. The screen then breaks up into twenty-four boxes, each segment displaying the different sequence of the street under surveillance.

'Is this where the rat shows up next?'

'He'd have had to have discovered time-travel. What we just saw was from this morning. This is from three days ago.'

'So what am I meant to be looking for now?'

'Just wait a sec, and you'll see.'

'Hang on, this is the railway approaches, isn't it?'

'You got it. And can you remember why we were there on Monday?'

'Lockheart... and that's the Hearse. The side entrance is that door right up there in the corner.'

'Bingo. Our old friend's last dance.'

Lockheart crashes onto our screen, springing from the box in the far left-hand corner, charging through the sections next to it, down into the next line of frozen moments, and, on reaching the second to last shot, he pauses. Lifting his head up to the camera so we can see into his sunken red sockets, and raising his arm, either waving or drowning, he gestures to us. And then he disappears.

'No. Not again. Don't do this to me.'

'Too late.'

'Is he in the last frame?'

'Uh uh.'

'What about cameras set up elsewhere?'

'This is all we have. We've pored over every other angle on the adjoining units, and all we got was him leaving the pub. The link-up shots of Fisherton Street and the Old Mill show nothing. Nothing from the one off the approaches either. This is it.'

'How do we know we're not a couple of frames short of the full picture?'

'Terry, we *have* the full picture. It isn't the fault of the camera that he doesn't show in the last frame. He doesn't show because he's not fucking there!'

'Couldn't Lockheart have moved into another space in that time that the camera might have missed?'

'Possibly, but you know how these systems operate. They're pretty exhaustive, without many blind spots. Not one big enough to miss a giant like him, anyway. I don't blame you for clutching at straws, but the technology isn't the problem. I wish it was.'

'So we've a vanishing man, and not one that has simply gone missing, but one we see dematerialise before our very eyes, to add to the list of the others missing in action?'

'And don't forget the rat.'

I lean back into my chair and gaze hopelessly at a battered A to Z of Cardiff, tucked behind the rear-view mirror. 'Please tell me what the fuck is going on.'

'I know it's not easy. But we're going to have to think about this like rational grown-up detectives for a minute, and try to forget that what we've seen doesn't make any sense.'

'I am all ears. I am only ears.'

'The CCTV lads, they call this the ghost in the machine. It sometimes happens — figures appear from nowhere, others vanish in a finger flick — they really weren't that fazed. It's not uncommon, and really, they're too used to it to give a shit about the metaphysical aspects of the problem. The scientists are another matter. For them, this is the Bermuda triangle of intriguing mysteries — spontaneous combustion without a body, molecular hypertrophic disintegration, anti-matter particle reversion — they'd happily do a TED talk on it now, but as we don't let the talent write the cheques round here, Grace has ordered them to be quiet for the time being and also asked me to not show the CCTV to anyone else, yet... because what could we say if we did? That our mispers are literally, *literally*, vanishing, and that we don't know how or where!'

'So you showed him first? Grace?'

'Had to, no offence, but we can't form our own secret society here, Terry.'

'And he told you to show me?'

'Of course. He gave you some credit, said that you'd be able to draw solid conclusions that we could act discreetly on.'

'And what the hell is that supposed to mean?'

'Some leeway, I think.'

'Good of him. Amidst the slings and arrows, a vote of confidence at last.'

'You could look at it that way. It was also a given no one else would know what to make of it.'

'You can't blame them.'

'I wouldn't. Most people aren't going to get past utter disbelief. I think the only way we're going to take advantage of the confidence placed in you, Terry, and not throw our hands up in sheer despair at the freakiness of this thing, is if we try and get beyond the *Close Encounters* aspect. If we *can*.... which of course isn't going to be easy with this challenging just about all we know regarding the natural order of things, but...'

'But there's always a practical angle, right?'

'There's always a practical angle, right. *If* we can find it, then from there the rest of this might slowly shift into explicability. Least, that's the hope.'

'So proceeding from the wobbly assumption that what we're watching isn't magic, which would be the simplest explanation, let's face it. What do the two clips have in common, asides from the vanishing trick performed by man and rat in plain sight?'

'Sticking only to appearances? Not much. Anger followed by an absence of a body in both cases? Apart from that, I really don't know. They don't even share a species.'

'And what about what we *can't* see?'

'If you mean an underlying cause, we can assume the rat's deranged ferocity was caused by the dose given to him in the lab. In Lockheart's case it's not so easy to explain what's going on under the bonnet, it could be anything. I mean, we know he's a nasty guy, so it's not like he needed much provocation to be any meaner.'

'He might have had it though, the same as the rat had.'

'You mean the gear?'

'That's got to be the link. We know the rat is on that stuff, only a sniff of which had us in the sky on diamonds. Remember? Imagine a much higher level on a smaller body, and what that might do. Also Lockheart's in-law's bedroom is where I first found the stuff. Exactly the same bundle they gave to the lab rat. Perhaps the old woman was also with the programme, or at least administered some without her knowing? We haven't been able to find her yet or work out how she got out of her house. The gear, this mysterious drug, is the link. And I wouldn't be amazed if it weren't involved in some way with the other disappearances too.'

'One thing at a time. Let's leave the old lady and everyone else out for a moment — there's enough in the mix as it is. You think Lockheart was under the influence in the clip?'

'Yep.'

'And on a much more extreme dosage than the rat?'

'Absolutely I do. It would explain how they were both able to vanish in one go... if we accept that's actually what happened.'

'What do you mean?'

'Living beings literally vanishing is not the most "practical" of angles is it? Perhaps they both attained temporary invisibility or some resistance to being picked up on camera...'

'Are you serious? Listen to yourself, Terry!'

'Why not?' I know I sound mad, but I want to make the most of my changing view of reality, whilst the inspiration lasts. 'It'd mean they'd still be wherever they were...' I point at her vape on the dashboard. 'But no device could actually see or record them because they'd entered, for however long, a parallel dimension of some kind?' I tap the window, which is where this dimension may be found. 'It's how a lot of people think about ghosts, you know, switching between their spatial zone and ours...'

'Christ, gimme a break! You're not following the data, Terry. Lockheart hasn't turned up anywhere else since he was captured in this footage, and that rat didn't show in another part of the lab for afters — it vanished good and proper. The grandmother too, if you want to include her in this circle of love.' Tamla grabs her vape, gives it a stare, and thrusts it in her bag. 'When you go, you stay gone with this thing, other dimensions or not.'

'The mispers may stay disappeared, but they're not the only ones interested in the drug we could talk to,' I argue. 'The wasters in the Hearse recognised the lump I showed them, were intrigued by it, and knew exactly what it was. If we can find where they've gone to ground, and more of this stuff too, then we may be able to work out what's happening to the bodies. But more importantly, I could have enough—'

'To draw your link back to Masters?' Tamla sniffs. 'I know you think all paths lead to the Count. Perhaps they do. In a place this small any great dramas are usually connected. But a smoking gun? Not yet. We haven't even got past the *Close Encounters* aspect yet...'

'Why do we have to? Masters' guilt is perfectly compatible with our not having an answer to any of this madness yet. It doesn't matter if we can't explain why a portal to the Bermuda Triangle opens on Fisherton Street every time a maniac charges out of a pub. Masters is controlling the drugs in this city for some purpose and all these missing people are the pieces he's either discarded or doesn't care for. I *know* it.'

'Back to your supersensory powers again. You're nothing if not persistent. Maybe you're right, and he is involved. But after watching this, how can you believe it's still all about him? What's beginning to worry me is that we could be looking at *anything* here, and the part we're looking at may be the least important bit of it...'

'I thought you weren't one for conspiracies?' I say.

'I don't mean conspiracies. I mean genuine mysteries we've been drawn into without realising. We're coming at this reductively — we have to, that's how we work — but what if this really is something for the boffins and witchdoctors? I appreciate your Masters obsession, I really do — you're a brilliant detective with brilliant instincts — but there is a part of me that thinks we could have inadvertently strayed out of our domain. Masters may have too. This might not be simply a police thing anymore, Terry.'

'How so? Whatever else is going on, crimes have been committed, Tamla...'

'Don't be self-righteous. My point is that what if the crimes, or whatever the hell they are, are only a small part of a mystery bigger than missing kids? That these missing kids — I don't know — are the tip of an iceberg, and that this drug that makes people vanish is our real story, and Masters is just a sideshow...'

'So what?' I say raising my voice. 'They'd still be crimes no matter what they're ultimately part of. It doesn't matter whether they're being committed by a mysterious "entity" or a stick-up artist. Lives are still being destroyed. People are still being extinguished. So far as I am concerned, your mystery *is* part of the crime; solve it, and we have a criminal. It's all one thing, even if all we have now is fragments. We've seen physical beings disappear before our eyes, we have the footage of them doing the disappearing — that's evidence, right? No one has to take our word for it! And what are we supposed to be investigating if not missing people? We've even got a hypothesis as to how they vanish. It doesn't matter if we can't explain how they have yet. It won't make those responsible for putting this stuff out there any less guilty. Jesus, if we can't square the circle on this, we should retrain as crash test dummies...'

'I'm glad you've got your passion back, Terry. I'm only reminding you that we are still driving blind, even with footage. It's crazy, yes, but it doesn't offer us a way in.'

'I'm sorry, I have got to take this.'

'Still in the honeymoon stages... Be careful. You don't mix up wanting to see her with solving this investigation.'

My phone is ringing and 'Sister Midnight' — the name I have given Eileen Pertwee in my contacts list — is bringing light to my screen.

'Is everything alright?'

'Yes and no. Though that doesn't really matter. I've met someone who can help you.'

'Help me?'

'Yes, you.'

'How?'

'You know how. Help you to be good at your job, help you become an important man, help you save the missing kids, help you. Meet me at the Saxon Gold in an hour. I'll be the pretty one sat next to the crazy bitch, you can't miss us.'

Eileen hangs up, leaving me smiling appreciatively at a plastic cellular lump that was briefly thrillingly alive.

'That was quick. That her?'

I nod.

'What's she offering today?'

'A way in.'

CHAPTER TEN
THE SAME DEEP WATER AS YOU

I do not have far to go to find Eileen and her contact. The fear that I will lose everything, her included, if we do not solve this case, is even now not quite as great as my excitement at seeing her again. Sat over the road from my chapel, issuing a permanent challenge to those moments when I wonder what it would be like to never drink again, is Saxon Gold. It bucks the trend of public houses being turned into private ones, having started life as four tiny homes separated by three walls, and completed its evolution on the cover of *The Wyrd Britannia Pub Guide*. The inauspicious and deliberately ignorable exterior, lacking the historical pedigree of the showier abutting properties, is part of a short line of 'double cottages' whose previous occupants, through some subtle process of pushing their luck, converted all four houses into a pub one weekend in the nineteenth century — the name a joke in a village that never cared which set of invading usurpers their ancestry could be traced back to.

There being no sign outside the place, 'Saxon Gold' is painted in faint and faded yellow letters across the front of the buildings — a frosted glass chamber pot in the middle of the door and a bench and table sat on the street outside, the only visible clues these cottages are a tavern. As a consequence, there is little passing trade, with only a sprinkling of curious hipsters and class tourists tipped off by its cult boozer status treating it as a destination in its own right. Instead the pub enjoys a reputation as a locals' 'social', drowning in the hoppy ale supplied by an award-winning brewery on the trading estate, the inspiration for barefooted men to walk across the cracked raven-oak floor and leave coin offerings by the mounted walrus head: a shrine to the ineffable feeling that kicks in after a few drinks, and a deterrent to those too nervous to pry further than the front door lest they be confused for burglars.

Further in, the very minimum of arrangements have been made to transform the atmosphere into one fit for the general public. The main bar is one long room leading straight out to the weedy rock garden, the tables a succession of tiny booths lining the walls stretching crossways, while another egress, by the entrance, leads into a cramped chamber with a barrel table at the centre of it, surrounded by stools poised to splinter painfully, a small service hatch connecting it to the rest of the action. This is the 'Athelwulf Room': an exhibit in a museum of vanishing rural life, with just a few battered Caravan Club paperbacks, prints of biplanes and an old photograph of the 1913 floods evincing the existence of the last century. It is also where I spot Eileen Pertwee and her friend, cramped close together: Eileen busy acting out the performance of waiting, head leant forward to anticipate my arrival before the rest of her body can, her ringed fingers drumming away on the barrel in time to the speed she would like the seconds to move at; the companion taking Eileen's distracted silence for rapt attention, murmuring on at her in rapid and gassy bursts. My heart has accelerated dangerously. Eileen has too great a hold over me and I need do no more than admire her hair to be reminded of that grip and the ensuing blindness it engenders.

Drawing in so I can fit through the narrow doorway, the face I meet first is 'Shrek', the giant bald landlord, fresh from an argument with his Siamese wife over the Pad Thai menu, whose grand launch is again delayed. He hands me a pint of the usual: usually a glass of anything going, on the tacit assumption that I ignore the noisy lock-ins, Transits parked on the pavement and the near-riot when he closed early on New Year's Eve so he could watch *The Great Escape*, permitting, meanwhile, the hinterland of this glorified workingman's club sovereignty to resolve matters that occur within its own borders its own way.

Worn down with the understanding that there is a necessary level of corruption in any free and open system, I mostly look the other way. And in about thirty years, if I am still here, I will have my own mug hanging above the bar.

'*Summer Lightning*,' he announces solemnly. 'Inspector Balance.'

I fear the local beers, all of which are deceptively easy to drink and loaded on percentage, though long ago gave up on insisting on lager, having decided there was no point going out of my way to show weakness.

'You'll need a knife and fork to get through this one.'

'Thank you.' I survey the bar: all locals. If I have been followed or I am being observed, it is by someone I think I already know, as everyone watches each other all the time here.

'Don't bother. It's been up on the bar so long, I was about to sing it happy birthday.'

I take the first incriminatory sip and turn to let Eileen know that the moment is upon us again. She is making a show of pretending not to look at me, and for a horrible yet entirely convincing instant — because it is the thing I fear most in the world: that I have actually presented my cards to someone who does not want them — I wonder whether she is waiting for someone else. Have I been trapped or humiliated, or subjected to a karmic helping of both, to be taught a lesson in humility? My fear fills the moment so completely that if she were to get up and go to the lavatory, I would be sure that she would not come back, and that I would be left here on my own. Instead she breaks the rising tide of panic, which thankfully was hidden in an expression I have spent years trying to iron every emotion from, and shouts, 'Here he is: trout-in-traction!', which is a regrettably accurate depiction of the face I pull. 'God, I hope you don't try and look that inscrutable every time you walk through a door... I'll never let you take my heart alive if you do!'

'Inscrutable?'

'You know what I mean!'

Eileen tries to slow the acceleration of her smile into hysterical laughter. I recognise that my response is exactly the same as hers. Knowing we share a connection so fundamental that anything short of it is a transparent attempt to walk back nature's grandest achievement — the union of souls in telepathic communion — becomes funnier the more aware of it we are; language operating at a far lower evolutionary level than love at first sight.

'Come here. Sit down, sit down. There's someone I want you to meet,' she says, patting the stool next to her effusively.

'Pleased to meet you. I'm Terence.' It is difficult for me to pay attention to anyone else when in the presence of Eileen, but I try.

'Detective Chief Inspector Terry of the Wiltshire Sûreté, to give you your full title!' Eileen says. The delight in her face encourages the presumption that she is proud of me, and I fight the urge to actually kiss her eyes.

'My, it's a pleasure to meet you Detective Chief Inspector Terry. Eileen is right — you are *very* striking.'

Eileen's companion offers a hand, which I am not sure whether I am meant to shake or kneel down and kiss. She has delivered her greeting in the voice of a Marilyn Monroe impersonator, and seems quite capable of singing 'Happy Birthday, Mr President' if asked. I am not sure if she is playing me for laughs or possibly a little touched, and as there is nothing to do except allow her to give me more to go on;

I smile stupidly and squeeze in next to her. Middling mental illness seems a likelier explanation for her behaviour than a poor sense of humour, as she continues in her best Norma Jeane, batting her eyes ridiculously. 'I do so appreciate a man in uniform, even when he isn't wearing one, no, *especially* if he isn't wearing one! It just makes a girl feel so safe and so protected, and I don't care what these bitter feminists say — every *real* woman will tell you that is exactly what she wants in her life... someone to look after her and be there for snuggles!'

Eileen is rolling her eyes and mouthing 'bear with', while I am overcome by the slightly malarial nausea that I always encounter when I am holding back from doing what I want, which in this case would be moving to another table.

Not breaking out of character, Eileen's friend continues, 'Oh mind my manners, won't you just, Mr Inspector. I do keep doing it, assuming everyone must have heard of me. Here, my card. How rude of me to not have introduced myself properly — I am Amanda Baal. You might have seen my art displayed about town, but I am mainly into taxidermy...'

'I understand that you might have some information for me...'

Ignoring my request, she replies, 'Oh please, not Amanda, call me Fluffy, Mr Detective Chief Inspector! It is a liberty I permit my close friends and intimate initiates.' Amanda is not exactly fluffy, though I can see why the sobriquet might fit, as it is not so different from its more muffled and less cuddly cousin — flaky.

'A name must suit a person — don't you think? Like yours does you. And I have never felt like an *Amanda* or, God forbid, a *Mandy*. Although the different names we could answer to do seem to address different parts of ourselves, haven't you found?'

'I'd never thought about it like that before.'

'Oh don't talk such piffle! Of course you have, an intelligent bright young man like you. You don't fool me!'

Fluffy is certainly a marriage of many forthright 'parts' that do not necessarily belong together on the same person. Her hair is dyed in a snow-white bob, cut with extreme precision, leaving her oblong and heavily made-up face, carrying at least two coats of orange blusher, too bright and artificially swollen for such a careful outline. 'Terry's a hopeless one for small-talk, Fluff. I think he'd be interested in what you told me earlier, though…' Eileen says, a gentle reminder to Fluffy that rather than listen to her thoughts on gentleman callers and the kindness of strangers, there was a specific purpose to our rendezvous.

But Fluffy is not ready for that yet. With masterful concentration, she lifts a heavily scented handkerchief to her nose, sniffs deeply and then waves it vigorously over the table as if to banish evil spirits and malign smells. There is an essential disproportion of elements about her: tiny hands on long arms, narrow shoulders rolling out into a generous midriff, and a stately chest that looks uncomfortable wrapped in the too-tight kaftan smock she is bound in. But behind these colourful distractions, I feel the gravitational draw of her kaleidoscopic lenses — the contacts I saw Eileen in that first day — and behind these the steely calculation that has got her through life's slow erosion of hope.

'Eileen did mention that you might have some useful information for me?' I repeat.

Childishly pleased that she has my attention, though still not interested in obliging, Fluffy ignores my question and continues, a little short of breath. 'Art is only my passion, Inspector. My day job is being a white witch. I pick herbs and use them to create natural remedies to help people suffering from this stressed-out existence of ours.'

'I see… I wonder if this is this related to the information you might have for me?' I press.

Fluffy taps her glass. 'Would you like a drink, Inspector Terence?'

'No.'

She smiles at her glass.

'But let me get you one,' I say.

'That's very kind. We'll share a bottle of, oh I don't know, maybe 'Breezy Wind'? Yes, I think that would hit the spot most nicely, thank you.'

Eileen whistles; 'Breezy Wind' is a sparkling white grown locally with the aim of knocking champagne off its perch, and retails at £50 a bottle in a pub. I am guessing that this is the going rate for spilling the beans, but I needn't have worried because as soon as a fresh glass and ice bucket are deposited near her, Fluffy, with the confidential look of a seasoned old pro, gets right down to it.

'I believe you were — oh, how could I put it — admiring some of my work just a few days ago? A little bird tells me. I do so like that expression. You'll think me silly, but when I was little I actually thought one existed. And yet I could never quite picture what it looked like in my mind... a little bird, I mean.'

'Your work? I was admiring it?' I have no idea what she is talking about, but sense that she has got to the point at last.

'Yes, two examples of it as it happens. Birds and that which cometh from the ground...'

'I'm sorry, it's been a long week. I'm not following...'

'Taxidermy and the demon weed, Terry,' prompts Eileen. 'Stuffed animals and drugs.'

I sit open-mouthed, feeling not at all clever. 'Of course.'

'Of course,' says Eileen. 'You wanted the piece of connecting string, and Fluffy is it. She has just been a bit shy about coming forth, is all, haven't you, Fluff?'

'Terry,' Fluffy necks her glass in one and taps the bottle. I refill the glass. 'We've both done long service in hard stations and know the only idea in this world that means anything is you scratch my back and then I'll run my hands down yours. We're not two little girls playing footsie here. You're in a position to set things right for me, and I want to help you. I know *what* you're looking for and *who* you are looking for.'

'Then you already have a considerable advantage over local law enforcement, Amanda.'

'Fluffy, please, Fluffy.' Except she is not Fluffy anymore, the steel has risen to the surface, her *Suddenly, Last Summer* routine nowhere to be seen and an avaricious smile has replaced the clueless pout. 'And as for the police. Well, yes, of *course* I know that! They couldn't help a girl across the road without calling for backup, far less have the brains to understand my particular problem!'

'I guess you have been conferring with Eileen?'

'Oh don't blame her, she only wants what's best for you. As do I. You see, we both know you are deep up to your neck in it.'

Eileen takes my hand. Tenderly, she says 'She needed to know some things, Terry. You were flailing about on your own, and as you said, even your friends on the force weren't supporting you, didn't believe you, thought you were mad...'

'But Fluff knows you're not,' says Fluffy.

'How much did Eileen tell you?'

'She didn't need to say much. As soon as I knew she and you hooked up — now don't look like that; you should know there's no secrets in a place like this — I said to myself, I said, Fluff, here is the answer to your prayers. *He* is the answer to your prayers.'

'But how are you the answer to mine?'

'Ha! I knew you were a bright one the moment I saw you waltz in here, Inspector! Everyone here knows about, how should I put this, "our *problem*" — shall we call it that? — in this area. Yes, it isn't the first time "our problem" has occurred, and God knows the police aren't remotely up to doing anything about it in any way, shape or form. They never were.'

'So why are you coming to me if you know I'm part of that useless tribe?'

'You're not a typical policeman, are you? I am giving you the benefit of the doubt, Inspector Terry of the Sûreté. Because I think you're an ambitious boy who is a little different and doesn't care who he has to throw over to get to the top. And as Eileen has said, you aren't scared about blowing this thing wide open, no matter who it involves, which is why I'm going to tell you all I know. And in so doing, I hope to remove a very considerable thorn that is growing into my side at such an angle as to make life frankly impossible for ickle ol' me...'

She pulls out a ball of rolled tissue paper and opens it.

'Here.'

'Alright. So it *is* this.'

'Oh it *is* this alright! You've been looking for it, for more of it, haven't you now, Inspector?'

'That was the general direction of travel, yes.'

'I knew it!' She thrusts a tusk-like odorous clump of herb, reeking of the same foully savoury musk that I noticed first at Eileen's, into my hand.

'Typical plod! The stuff has been rife everywhere in plain sight these past few months, doing the rounds and the proverbial foxtrot and fandango, and yet here you are again, the very last of us to even cotton on to its existence!' Fluffy squeaks, enjoying herself. 'Bet you don't even know what it *is* do you? All your fancy labs and forensics and what not. Oh, Inspector, all that infrastructure and taxpayers' money, and yet you need to be sat here in Saxon Gold with me, silly ol' Fluff, to even get your bearings!'

'You're right. I don't know. We, the police, don't know. But I liked you more when you were being Fluffy. Now you're Spiky. Soften back up a bit, Amanda. No matter how far ahead of the game you think you are compared to us thick idiots, you need my help. And you must need it very badly to risk Fluffy PLC on a gamble like this, so ease on the taunts. They don't suit a nice lady like you.'

'Ouch! I'm surprised at you. Can't you take a little gentle teasing?'

'And another thing: I am guessing that you could have cut

in with your assistance and know-how any time these past few months as these kids were going missing, one by one, but you didn't, did you? You waited until now because it simply didn't suit you to be the Good Samaritan any earlier.'

Fluffy folds her arms, disappointed once again by the cynicism of her fellow creatures.

'You waited as you knew the information you were sat on was only going to accrue value as the human cost grew higher. You're in this for what you admit are the most selfish of reasons, and that doesn't sit well with me. In fact, that alone is enough for me to take you in. And seriously, Fluffy, were it not for the fact that there are worse beasts out there, that you of course are going to lead me to, I'd probably be handcuffing you to a tree by now.'

'Charming! Call yourself a gentleman.'

'I don't, actually, not even almost one.'

Fluffy has gone the colour of a pink rabbit that I once won at the fair and slings her wine down in a contemptuous gulp, our love affair well and truly over. 'Don't push me, Inspector.'

'I won't have to if you get on with it.'

Eileen pinches my knee. 'Easy, ladies. We're all on the same side.'

'So what *am* I actually looking at here, Fluffy? Other than drugs of some kind.'

'*High John the Conqueror*, Inspector.'

'The what you what?' I ask.

'*High John the Conqueror*. Special Wiltshire and Dorset Edition, sometimes also found in parts of the New Forest, so I suppose Hampshire can take some credit too.'

'And what is he supposed to conquer?' I ask her.

'Our minds, our bodies, our lives.'

'Not much, then. But what exactly is it?'

'Not plant or mushroom, but a bit of both: part mycelium, part herbaceous — a genuine hybrid and a one-off. Which is why your lab coats won't have known what to make of it.

But those of us who have long abided in these parts, who understand our history, who *share* a history, we do, we know.'

'You may. Yet I'm not feeling the local connection...'

'How's that?'

'*High John the Conqueror?* Since when has that been the exclusive property of the south west of England? Isn't it supposed to be some kind of health supplement? From maybe an American or African plant root, I think? And used in voodoo too, Dr John, Gris-Gris, drums and cowbells and crow's feet, all that Mardi Gras vibe?'

Fluffy nods patiently.

'That would make it pretty ubiquitous, right? So what's to stop me from buying it in liquid form off Amazon, supplied straight from a vegan cafe in Ibiza that sells the stuff for fun? Most things are legal nowadays with loopholes that can be exploited, or at least available on the dark web.'

'Oh, nothing could stop you buying it. I'm sure you could if you so chose.'

'Then what's so special about yours, if we're talking about the same stuff, the same family tree?'

'Right. First things first. What you're making allusions to, Inspector, is *Jean de Conqueroo*: love potions, spells to get your willy hard and win hearts — they're related to our friend here, but he isn't that. Look at it carefully, Inspector. The hocus-pocus rubbish you're talking about on the internet, that they use in ceremonies with old Creole fortune-tellers and flog as an aphrodisiac, that snot and this have the same relationship to each other as Dr Pepper does to crack cocaine. They just don't play in the same leagues. Just look at it, for God's sake. Can't you feel its strength, its latent power?'

I take the silvery root in my hand. It is stronger and more completely formed than the variation I have encountered before, with a flat-knotted head weaving down into two curling strands, bunching together like the chalk testicles on the Cerne Abbas Giant.

'So our variant is unique, is it?' I say, eyeing it warily.

'Absolutely. That other stuff you've heard of is just for voyeurs and supplements junkies. A mild buzz, a little tingling, and then it's over.'

'Whereas this takes the top of your head off?'

'That much you do already know, I believe!'

'I'm guessing your close acquaintance with this is connected to your witchy activities?'

'Of course. I am a watcher and a picker. Snatched at the optimum time, this stuff is dearer than truffles. To the right people, anyway.'

'What's the optimum time and how do you know the right people?'

'The optimum time is every forty years.' Her eyes flash and change into several colours I cannot name. 'And I know the "right people" because that's my taxidermy you saw in his house.'

Fluffy has scored the winning goal and I feel my recent despair reach the next stage of its journey: the spiritual lift afforded by sudden vindication.

'Of course, I knew it. I fucking knew it!'

'Yes, I thought we'd be friends again, Inspector! We'll do well to return to him later. Let's leave the best till last.'

'I bet he understands the optimum time is worth waiting for too...'

'Of course.'

'But every forty years? What's with that timeline? And how did *he* find out about it?'

'Nature. In a word, nature. That's just the way nature wants it.' Fluffy reaches for my hand and squeezes it. 'Any more than that would be chaos. You've already seen something of what *High John* can do, Inspector. Would you really want that growing seasonally, an annual perennial? Can you imagine the hills, dales and plains alive with the stuff? Why, it'd bring the sky down on our heads! How it comes to be, exactly, I can't say any more than I could tell you why we're here — I'll admit that — only that it makes the journey over from the other side very rarely, whatever the scientific reasons for that may be. My guess is that it's just too damned dangerous to share what it knows with us any more regularly than that. And that's mighty thoughtful of it, because being what it is, we can only handle its truths every few decades or so. Once you've eaten it, its work is done for a generation. It doesn't want to reproduce in you like your usual fungus might. All it wants to do is to take you *back over* with it. And if it can't, then it's up to old *High John* himself to make sure you make the journey.'

'I'm not following you now,' I say.

'I'm saying *he'll* come for you.'

For me to use any of this, it has to make sense to me first. 'Now I'm really not following you. And not only not following you, but I don't understand where you got all this information from. Who made all this supposed knowledge available to you?'

'A mixture of folklore and experience, what's been passed down by mother to daughter through the generations, and what I've seen myself with my own eyes. This county is rife with legends of what this stuff does, real legends, not the stuff you get in a National Trust or English Heritage gift shop, or what they pipe through your headphones in museums and guided tours of stone circles. I'm talking about real oral traditions that the people who belong here, who were here first, know all about, Inspector...'

'Have you ever heard of any of this?' I ask Eileen. 'Do you know what she is talking about?'

Eileen smiles goofily, and I realise my love for her is not because she is a missing part of myself that could make me whole but the lost part of herself that keeps me company in my incompletion, our sudden interdependence as inevitable as pain.

'I don't know as much about it as Fluffy, but of course I have *heard* of it being spoken of, and Fluffy did give me a tiny bit for my mum, which is why I suspected it might be the stuff you were talking to me about.'

'Your mum? You mean you medicated your mum on that stuff deliberately? You never said anything about that to me before...'

'You didn't ask! And anyway, lots of people do use it to control their pain. How was I supposed to know that was significant?'

'You're the one who comes from here and has heard all these stories! If you believed in them, then of course you knew it was significant!'

'Well I'm sorry, Terry, but I'm not the detective here! I hadn't heard *all* the stories, just the ones that said it had magick properties and could help you if you were ill, you know, that could put you out of your misery altogether if you had enough of it...'

'Jesus Christ, Eileen! Don't tell me you took it into your own head to instigate euthanasia on your own mother! Because you thought this stuff was some kind of right-on hemlock?'

'She wanted to go, Terry. Begged my daughter to smother her with a pillow! She had every cancer going, couldn't tell the difference between her hands and a set of keys and shat blood into a bag. What's so wrong about dying in your own house instead of having it drawn out so you end up in a ward that stinks of bleach, surrounded by masked faces!'

'This just gets worse and worse...'

'Oh the worst is yet to come, Inspector. The worst is yet to come...' chuckles Fluffy.

'You look like you need this!' Shrek has appeared at the service hatch with another pint of *Summer Lightning* and I begin to wonder if I have not been spiked, and whether all these people were laughing at me before I got here and will be laughing as I leave, wrapped in a carpet and left for dead in the woods.

'There you go. Careful to not spill any over your nice tie.'

I accept the drink and swallow a deep draft, too late to forget what I have just discovered. Wiping the beer from my mouth, I try and summon the remaining vestiges of my professionalism. 'Let me take this one disaster at a time. Fluffy, you're saying you knew of this stuff's existence through the tales passed down by your ancestors — I get all that — but also through experience? What experience are you talking about? When and how did you first come across this stuff first-hand and see what it could do for yourself?'

'Why, the last time it grew here, Inspector. I know about it because I was there. It was the winter and spring of 1976. My mummy found a crop quite by accident when we were out foraging for wild mushrooms. She was a hippy, my dad a biker, and pretty soon the boat we lived on was rammed with *High John*. Wild it was, until my uncle overdosed on the stuff, and we realised the legends were true...'

'What happened?'

'We're still looking for him.'

'You're serious?'

'Oh yes. And after that, people started disappearing willy-nilly! I told you this had happened before. Except then it was all done through innocence, there was no manipulation, what happened then were genuine accidents, fools messing with what they didn't understand.'

'Unlike now, that is?'

'Let me put it this way, there are still fools messing with it, but I wasn't the only one waiting for it to come back, and the other one who waits, he's no fool and no innocent. You know that.'

'Our man with a penchant for taxidermy?'

She nods.

'Why can't you say his name?'

'I need to know I can count on you before I do.'

'You can count on him,' says Eileen.

'I need to hear him say it.'

'You can count on me.'

'Masters. There, there it is. You know him already for the bastard he is. He has everyone living in fear of him and his henchmen, creatures of the night that they all are, but I don't fear them, I despise them,' Fluffy looks like she is about to spit on the floor. 'He, though, he is another matter. He was there with us back then, hanging on like a tick, trying to get as much of the stuff as he could with that sad band of losers he was "managing"; he offered Mummy a small fortune for her stash, but it had all gone by then. He didn't like that at all. And so I made me a mental note. I thought, there's a man who is up to no good, and there is a man who will pay anything to get hold of *High John*. And I swore then, that if and when its time would come again, then my time would come again! There would be a fortune to be made if I could remember the places, the exact spots, where it grew, so I made my little maps, and checked and waited and checked and waited, every year, like *The French Lieutenant's Woman* waiting for her man at the end of the pier, waiting and checking and preparing for...'

'The moment it grew back?'

'Exactly!'

'So the cycle has started again. Then what do you go and do?'

Fluffy pours the rest of the bottle into her glass and the glass down her throat.

'This part isn't so nice. I'm not proud of myself, you must understand. I knew the window is small, that it'll have gone the way we all go by the summer, and that I'm not the only collector out there waiting for this moment. So I moved quickly.'

'This is in the last few months?'

She nods. 'Ideally, I'd have let it mature in the ground for longer, but I couldn't take any chances, what with others getting their hands on it first, not after how long I had waited. No, it was my birthright. I had to have it, Inspector, so I got straight in there, and, well like I say, I am ashamed of this, but I knew *he*, his nibs...'

'Masters?'

She nods again. 'I knew this was the epoch, the coming, he

was in preparation for it too. You see, I had trailed him all these years, never let him off my radar. I mean, he didn't know it, but I've cleaned in his house, framed and hung pictures for him, even massaged the evil prick. And when I had finished the last of those stuffed bats and whatnot you saw in the cases, I led him on into a conversation that he thought he had led me on to...'

'Yes, I can see you're good at that.'

'I have to be in my line of work, Inspector. I allowed him to believe he was playing me, and I innocently mentioned to him that I have spied something in the woods, and he takes the bait, and says he wants some of it if I can get it. And then I tell him well he might, but it's going to cost him what it cost me waiting all this time, and then I have him by the nose, well and truly hooked, because he doesn't know which woods I'm taking about, what with the entire New Forest staring back at us and blinking. So then I say, I already have a huge third-party client that buys in bulk, such as it is, because there isn't enough of *High John* to fill more than a few suitcases. It's not like the stuff you see packed in boxes or barrels on television; this is a serious luxury product. And I say I am selling all this stuff to the third party, and he says, to hell with him — I'll gazump the bastard and offer five times whatever he's giving you. And so I name my figure and he says fine. And there we are, Inspector. That brings us up to the beginning of the year, and I am starting to finally become a rich lady.'

'But you're still a white witch with a conscience. And you can tell something isn't right?'

'Yes, that's the regrettable part. Something wasn't right. Something was wrong. The bit I am not proud of. When I start to see that the disappearances are starting again, but it isn't Masters that's doing the vanishing, it's kids off the estates, I start to worry a bit and tell Eileen and a few others that posh people are taking our children.'

'And what good did you think that would do?'

'Well I hoped someone like you might put two and two together, and that you would then work your way back to Masters.'

'Of course you did. What could be simpler?' I turn to Eileen. 'I know you've given some to Mrs Pertwee here. Is there any more of it that didn't end up in Masters' hands out there that we should worry about?'

'I could use another drink, Inspector.'

'Not yet. How much more of it is in the community? And how much more is in the woods or wherever else it grows?'

'In the community a little — I did sprinkle a bit here and there you see, to spread the love around as it were, in small doses strictly for friends. They're nothing for you or the law to worry about.'

'You're a martyr to the cause of friendship. And what about out there in the wild and all the other places it grows, how much is still growing?'

'That's just it!' Fluffy hisses. 'It's all gone! Oh, that bastard is no fool. He got his goons to tail me and follow me to my patches, tracking me until they were confident they knew all my spots, until they had basically got my map in their heads, and then they took the lot! Just snatched it like thieves in the night! Everywhere I went back to, there were these great big bloody industrial holes in the ground. In one place they even used a digger so there's no mistaking or leaving anything behind. They were taking no chances, they left nothing, even pulled out trees in some places, by the roots, taking every little bit of it they could find and then some. Devastation it was, Inspector. They took chunks out of the landscape, leaving me with nothing, nothing at all.'

'But leaving them with enough to disappear a small city.'

'I suppose so, if they wanted to.'

'It doesn't quite explain what they're up to with it though, does it?' says Eileen. 'Okay, they're vanishing our kids in some weird kinky party games, but what's their ultimate purpose?'

'Knowledge,' says Fluffy.

'And you find this knowledge as you hallucinate that you are actually disappearing, maybe actually somehow vanishing, yes?' I gesture to my empty glass.

'That's right. But not hallucinate. You do vanish, literally and "somehow".'

'Where, then, are you actually going to? Are you talking about a person taking a journey in their own mind or something else? And can you come back? And how can you be sure of which outcome it'll be?'

'There it's a bit like all drugs, only more so and more potently. The quantity you take, how mature and ripened it is, when in its life span it was picked, all that affects the user. And the trip they take. You can't know for sure how it'll go. It's a dangerous game of trial and error. That's all part of the fun for these freaks, Inspector. And where you're going is another realm, a different physical space, like I say, it's a real journey, not an imagined one.'

'And not everyone makes it there?' I am thinking of the boy who started our search, Iggy Lockheart.

'No, not always. Far from it, in fact.'

'And this is an actual place they visit?'

'I keep telling you, yes, absolutely, not some psychedelic bullshit in the mind of a druggie, oh no.'

'I'm going to try and accept what you are saying for a moment, that users make it over and see whatever is there to see, but some physically remain here, and for whatever reason fail to make the full journey...'

'Yes, the poor sods...'

'Then does the drug slowly poison them, make them disappear that way? Or do they vanish in stages?'

'They're *High John*'s. They're his responsibility then.'

'And who's he? A euphemism for the drug itself, right?'

'No, I mean the spirit who watches over his produce and that does its bidding. He can toy with you, scare you, and eventually, he'll take you.'

'No. I don't get it.' I push my glass away. 'What are you

talking about, Fluffy? Are you asking me to believe there is an independent entity that is separate from the drug and its effects that stalks users like prey?

'Of course.'

'For Christ's sake, are you having me on? Is this a fucking piss-take, is that what this is?' I snarl.

'Don't be ridiculous, Inspector. Don't doubt my sincerity.' I have hit a wall and that wall is her pride.

I turn to Eileen. 'I don't know... I don't know what to make or do with this, what to believe...'

'You're not trying hard enough, Inspector!'

'It's one thing to believe a person can vanish into thin air, maybe they can, but another to sign up to monsters. And this is what you'd have us believe has happened to Iggy Lockheart and all these other kids?' I say to Fluffy.

'Of course.'

'Jesus. Where the hell am I going to go with this?' I sigh.

'Easy, Terry.' Eileen touches my wrist. 'You don't have to accept Fluffy's story, but it's important that you understand it, see what it is she is trying to say.'

'So what am I supposed to be understanding here? That a creature of some kind, presumably an aggregate of plant and pure spirit, is able to come and physically vanish people that the drug hasn't already made disappear, at first time of trying?'

'Something like that, yes,' says Fluffy. 'I've never seen it happen, I'll admit that, but then I've never known anyone left behind either. When he comes for you, he leaves nothing behind.'

'And this *High John*, is he like you or me, a properly real being?'

'Oh he is real alright, but not like you and me.'

'No, that would be too easy, wouldn't it? So although you are asking me to believe in ghosts as a precondition for accepting your story, we don't know what this thing is? Who would we be looking out for? I'm thinking of a woodland version of

Swamp Thing at the moment, or should I be envisioning an old bloke with a beard that dwells deep in the woods?'

'He's a great king, that's all I know.'

'A king? Like Arthur or Alfred?'

'I expect so.'

'Except he doesn't sound noble or benevolent. The way you describe his role is as a supernatural insurance plan that the drug keeps in reserve to clear up all the loose ends and leave no witnesses. If the plant or drug or whatever we're going to call it can't get you first, he'll get you next. That's the idea, right? Where's the greatness in that? It's like something from a nightmare.'

'Greatness is in the eye of the beholder. There is no sense in denying the sinister side of this, all things of value possess one. What you have to remember is that he can't let anyone live with the knowledge of what they've seen and still remain on this side — it'll be too much for them and us, you see? Protecting the two individual spheres is more important to him than sparing the lives of the silly and curious. Sometimes the truth is a nightmare, Inspector.'

'With the risks so high, what's the attraction, then? Why would anyone do this to themselves? What's so good about this knowledge?'

'To break on through to the other side. Just like we always have with drugs. On the other side there's enlightenment. The meaning of life and the secrets of the universe — they're all there to be answered. The adventurous are always going to want a piece of that.'

'What's the use if you're dead?'

'Ahh, you might not be. There's even immortality for some. For those who see and exceed the knowledge.'

'A place at God's right hand?'

'Don't tease me, Inspector. I'm being a good girl and trying to help you understand.'

'Police are supposed to use their imaginations, but as a breed, we tend not to be very sympathetic to the stuff we can't see or fingerprint. You're insisting I take a metaphysical position, Fluffy, that would be laughed out of every police station and court in the land.'

'I guess it's like all religions, Terry, you just have to take the experts' word for it,' Eileen offers. 'It's not like anything Fluffy is saying is crazier than what you would read in the Bible or see on the wall of a temple, is it?'

'I think that might be my problem with it, or with her, I mean you, Fluffy...'

'How so, Inspector? I thought we were friends again.'

'Let me put it simply. Along with fulfilling our spiritual requirements, religion also meets our need for pomposity and self-importance, even though it should be the last thing that does so...'

'And you think I am the self-appointed cardinal of *High John the Conqueror*?'

'I consider it a possibility, yes.'

'Ha! Another farty woman who is making up stories and inventing her own bogus religion so as to feel slightly important for once in her silly life? I don't have time to revisit old arguments, Inspector, but I think it is organised religion you are talking about. I deal in the real thing, and if I am anything I am *High John*'s John the Baptist, not St Paul. The world is too mysterious, but also too simple, for the ordinary religions to have a hope of understanding it... of course, I know you are worried that if you share this conversation with your bosses you'd be certified. But I have tried to tell you everything as honestly as I can and be as straight with you as possible. It's not my fault you're surrounded by closed-minded berks!'

'Terry,' says Eileen, 'perhaps the most useful way of looking at this is that you don't need *everything* to solve this case, just a bit of it would suit your purposes, am I right perhaps?'

She is right. My priority is to link Masters to the disappearances, not to solve the secrets of the universe in the form Fluffy has presented them.

'No one else needs to know any of this stuff, at least not to begin with. Do you see what I mean? Maybe just the bits that will suit you and help stop the disappearances.'

'You mean just enough stuff to put away Masters.'

She nods. 'Let them think it's an ordinary drug, and flag up Masters' involvement. You can't arrest a plant or its spectral enforcer. But you can a man.'

I turn to Fluffy. 'I'm going to take what I've heard as a full witness confession to Masters' guilt in receiving and distributing drugs. That's nothing compared to what I think he's done and doing, and nothing to what I hope I might get him on later, but that's okay. We can park the rest of this occult stuff for later. All I need is a chance to get into his face.'

'Good luck with that, Inspector. But what I have said is for your ears only!' She scoffs. 'I am certainly not going to be appearing in any courts or signing any statements or any of that legal to-do. Good God no. You must think I am mad to agree to any of that! That's not what I am saying. This is for you to do on your own!'

'You what?' I lean over the table.

'You heard me!' She retorts, not to be cowed.

'This is a joke. What did you tell me all this for if you're not up for doing anything about it?'

'It's up to you to do the doing, not me!'

'You wouldn't be in any trouble yourself, though. For picking or supplying, we could bury all that, you'd simply be witness for the prosecution. I could even fix it so you don't have to appear in court, if that is what you're afraid of...'

'Really, Inspector. I wouldn't have thought a man like you could be so unworldly, or maybe you're just too hopeful to see what should be plainly obvious: it's not you or the police or the courts I am afraid of, it's him!'

'What, this *High John?*'

'No. Bloody Masters, that's who. I don't want to die! I've already made my confession — what you do with it is entirely up to you. But I am sure as sure can be, that you'll not find me signing anything or putting my name to any official statements. No fear!'

'Your confession is worthless to me, Fluffy, unless you're prepared to swear an oath that it is true, otherwise it's all just pub talk so far as the law is concerned.'

'What I've told you should be enough by itself. It's up to you how you use it — that's your job after all. That's what Eileen said you were supposed to be good at. Me? I'll be lucky if I make it in one piece as it is.'

'What makes you say that?'

'Why do you think! His goon squad, of course. I'm halfway sure they followed me here as it is. I seem to be bumping into them everywhere, the confectionary isle of Waitrose, buying a coffee at Stable and Wick, out on the street — you name it. It's intimidation, and it's working.'

'Which goons? Have they formally approached you?'

'They know they don't need to. They're not that stupid to cross the line. They're his usual faces, you know 'em all: Swilly, Breezy, the gimp from behind the bar at the Hearse and, of course, your boy...'

'My boy?'

'Yes, *your* boy.'

'You don't mean...'

'No, she doesn't,' says Eileen. 'Not that kid, Christopherson, you turned up with but the other one, the old bloke who looks like a nodding dog.'

'Orridge?'

'Yes, that's him,' says Fluffy. '*Uncle Silas,* they call him — their man on the inside. A nasty piece of work and always has been.'

'Christ.'

'You might well say, but what you do about it is up to you. Just make sure you do something, go about it quickly, and don't involve me when it goes down, there's a good inspector now.'

'You're cutting my legs away here.'

'They'll grow back!'

'What are you going to do?' Eileen asks. 'You've got your proof now — you know he's guilty. Surely it can't be that hard?'

'I've never doubted he's guilty. But if none of this is being put out there officially, then I can't do anything official with it. This was already an insane stretch when it was just Masters I was considering, but you throw in Max, and the fact there are no drugs out there anymore...'

'Mycelia plants, Inspector.'

'Okay, whatever, but that mix, even if Fluffy here was ready to testify, which she isn't, all of this would be the sell of the century to the CPS, and that would be even without my trying to persuade everyone I wasn't on a load of this *High John* myself. Plus, of course, I still can't prove shit if my only witness isn't talking.'

'Don't give me any of that "my hands are tied" stuff, Inspector. I didn't think you were that weak. You're resourceful. You know there are *other* ways. Brainstorm, think aloud, seize your chances.'

'Suppose I get into his place and find this stuff,' I say, 'the *High John*. He'll get off on a technicality, or see me behind bars for breaking and entering. Anything short of somehow catching him red-handed doing evil with it, at his ceremonies or orgies or whatever they are, is no good. Unless I can see how all this works in practice, then knowing everything I do is still useless.'

'So think of something else, some other way. Go on. I know you've got it in you.'

'Tomorrow is Queen day. There isn't going to be any appetite amongst even the people I trust to pick any of his goons up. The lawyers will be there fighting their corner as soon as I lay a hand on them. And that goes a million times over for him, their master. Which means I've no choice now... there's only one way I can go...'

'You mean you're going to give up? I expected better!'

'No. When you attack you have to go for where they're strongest and feel safest...'

'Meaning, Inspector?'

'Meaning that if Max doesn't like me now, he's going to like me even less tomorrow morning...'

'That's my boy!' says Eileen, sliding her hand between my legs. 'We'd best all enjoy our last night of freedom, then. Here's something I didn't show you when I cleaned Iggy's caravan!'

'What, more of that stuff? Eileen, I've got to be able to trust you...'

'No, you old woman.' She hands me a small paper wrap under the table and whispers conspiratorially, 'Coke! No, don't look at me like that, we've all been round the block here and your career's likely to be toast before your next drug test is due anyway! Go and powder your nose and make sure you leave some for the rest of us. It won't take you over to the other side, but it will allow us to pass the next few hours most pleasantly!'

'I don't do powders,' sniffs Fluffy. 'Only the natural stuff for me.'

'Great, more for the rest of us. Best foot forward, Terry. You've a big day tomorrow!'

Spontaneity, in a life overruled by patient calculation, can be enviable, and as I have been looking forward to the next few hours with Eileen since I went into work with a painful erection at 6am, I am ready to consider breaking the law.

'I can't take this either,' I say, motioning with my eyes that it is time for us to leave.

*

Being in love helps you notice things that have nothing to do with love. There is a thunderstorm in the night, but I do not hear it at first because I believe Max is in the room with me and has been sat by my bed watching us, breathing beer and sandwiches over my quilt, for some hours. I overhear him say things addressed to me that he wants other people to believe, deflections and excuses, some clumsy and others modestly self-serving, his voice and face eventually blending into that of my father, at first as I remember him, and then as Dad, not a representation but how he really was and still is in heaven, where we can choose the bodies that were the most accurate picture of our souls in life, the embodiments we occupied when we peaked and felt most ourselves... *yes, yes, you were my dad, but that was a long time ago...* and then I am with Max again, who actually apologises as he knows he is not who I want to see, though now he is here, I repeat some of the lines I have prepared for him tomorrow, which sends him away sharply, before I hear Dad's approach again; his steps, the way the pavement sounds under the tread of his well-polished brogues, his very presence that can be no one else's, and that lean, interested face that watched me grow up, coming to my door, and waiting, yet we both know I cannot let him in, because I am in charge now... *life isn't long enough for me to have forgotten you; and if I can't forget you, I can't miss you...* I hear him walk away, slowly, and it breaks my heart because I could have used his company even though when you are in command you are on your own, and it is Grace telling me this, spitting biscuits all over my shoulder and growing dangerously mauve because he has mixed red wine with cheese and this always leads him to overheat, before Masters himself is standing at the foot of my bed in his dreadful monk's habit, grinning diabolically and waving a golden blade in the air, singing too of '*the possessed sword of a thousand deaths*'...

Eileen watches him, impossibly serene in the face of potential death, which means she obviously knows something I do not or has learnt something new while I was looking the other way, as I am raising my voice at Masters, threatening him with the puny force of the law and trying unconvincingly to yell, as to actually do so would mean waking up, which I do not want to do, my rare bursts of sleep too precious to risk, warning him that the will of the people always catches up with you in the end, and that he should bugger off before he gets his nose broken, yet we are in his house, not mine, and that impossibly I am having sex with someone who I hope is Eileen but is actually Fluffy, my orgasm the sort that takes you suddenly and by surprise, allowing you to see things you did not expect in its aftermath: the disappeared, our vanished teenagers, all of whom are proceeding in a line up a steep grassy incline, while I ask God to love them like he loves us, the scrawny teenagers turning their backs to me as they approach the old hanging trees on Gallows Hill; parts of me vanishing as they fall over one by one, like they were old friends of mine dying, and it is true that the soul remembers what the mind forgets, the distilled essences of the past, and I am all at once alone here, standing naked amidst the nettles and brambles. Alone with my abiding fear that I will one day lack the motivation to collate all the different clues and act on them or do anything at all except stay in this copse, frightened, bruised, will-less, not even confused but resigned. These experiences filter up into ideas and then back down into experience again. I cannot wake up, all this is really happening to me and sleep cannot render it less real, I cannot let anything go, I must always force the issue, I have never let a sleeping dog lie, my life would already be nothing if I had not met Eileen, I must tell her, I cannot find her, I wake up and she is here on her pillow next to me, still serene and asleep.

Then I hear it.

The heavens opening up, the rain falling so hard it could chip the tiles off the roof, gutters gurgling with such violence that I imagine frothing rivers of freshwater carrying livestock, Range Rovers and pianos down the street past Saxon Gold, the deluge released by a force too great to resist, so powerful that I do not *have* to worry about tomorrow. To worry is to blaspheme, while to lie here and accept the storm is the only effective protection from it, of accepting God's comfortless existence, of his being awake and everywhere so I can sleep at last, my troubles smothered by his heavenly envelopment and attack. I do not have to wait for him: he is already here. When I wake and resume my small role in the universe, I will know what to do, and do it without thinking. Who, after all, can spend the night in the world of sleep and not wake up a little changed?

CHAPTER ELEVEN

COLD

There are mornings, and this is one, when the police ask other policemen for their identification in an orgy of officious self-reference that revels in the absence of exceptions, Her Royal Highness's imminent arrival here bringing together the aspects of my profession I despise most with those of society at large: the Royal Family, celebrity culture and deferential obsequiousness masquerading as public service. Most of the people out here today are police, the streets leading to our trailer encampment are teeming with them, and those that are not stood po-faced against threats real and imagined are waiting their turn to.

'Excuse me, sir?' The PC barks my way, in spite of his knowing full well who I am.

I touch my badge, attached to my belt, which admittedly I feel exposed without, and receive the surreptitious nod and wink of acceptance. To be accepted as a policeman by other police is not the same as having to show any aptitude for the job, though reassuringly the two are not mutually exclusive. As a detective, my uniformed colleagues and superiors must feel comfortable in my presence, whereas all that is required of them to fit in to our state-run cosy club is to conform to the pack behaviour of a closed shop.

Walking past the phalanxes of officers and flags, in this usually deserted space, ignites many of the inescapable debates I prefer not to dwell on, lest I throw my badge into the River Avon. There is not a despotic regime in the world that cannot rely on its police force to defend it to the death. Even that other mob, the army, is more likely to contract emancipatory insanity and join in with the freedom-loving hordes than any of our number. We reflect our governments more than we do our societies, and the worse our rulers are, the nastier we are. We cannot help ourselves — we attract those who obey and who want to be obeyed. That can get in the way of the other half of our job, which is to contain human nature, clean up the mistakes of the economy and preserve and save life. Those that hate us pretend that this part of the job, contrary to whatever they would do in danger, does not exist, and there are those amongst us that wish it did not either. It shames one side to acknowledge the duality of our role, and the other to perform it. Yet if I were a victim of crime, used to waiting until it is too late for the sirens to arrive, I would lose my breakfast over the street today.

'I'm sorry, you can't, ahhh... apologies, as you were, sir,' says a uniformed sergeant that I could probably remember the name of if I thought about it. In places, the line of police is already two uniforms thick. Motorbikes and cars are parked as badly as their riders and drivers are able, drawing as much attention to our presence as possible.

'Thank you, Sergeant.'

For us to stand bluffly in public view, safe in the numbers we do not always have, taping off ten times as much public space as we need, stopping people we know are perfectly harmless to inform them of the gravity of the situation, have the odd helicopter up there in the clear blue, with constant backup from other forces on overtime, with less personal risk than being injured in a dream, passes as our version of the Royal Tournament, and the joke is on the ones clapping. Seething behind this eager jamboree are the same impulses that would in different circumstances flatten and arrest the very crowds that applaud us — and maintain they started it. I take ownership of both traditions. You cannot separate our good from our bad because we carry the original sin of our cause in us: crime. We exist because it does. As it ought not to exist in a perfect world, because nor should property, nor should we, our continued presence a societal embarrassment that no amount of copaganda or good works will ever be able to exorcise.

I knew all this at once without ever having to be told, finding goodness in its elemental form too shocking a force to survive very long without institutional assistance. Where else could I have gone, if I wanted to be one of the good guys, who exist, however seriously we take our politics, now that the cowboys have been found out as Indian killers, other than the police? Every work of critical theory excoriating the state could be right, yet a policeman responding to a single distress call has already done more for the needy than a militant on a demonstration, the writer of outraged pamphlets, or the chorus on multiple rallies ever could, or so I believed. The police were my trade-off between cynicism and decency, and in me they saw what they needed too: the kind of recruit that could become a poster boy for crime-fighting in the twenty-first century.

Today our journey of mutual convenience has finally run out of road. Having risen as far as I can on reason, novelty and prematurity, to qualify for the next level I must show the Neanderthal characteristics of my enemy, which is perhaps what my colleagues saw all along: my patient career arc and compromises simply the superficial concessions of one holding his nose, whose real self was basically indistinguishable from their own.

'Do you mind if I see some identification, sir? Spot on, go right through.'

My first surprise is that Orridge is looking more than ready for me. He is the first thing I hear and see: mansmelling, manstale, manspreading and mansplained, an adoring crowd of uniforms huddled round his corner of the trailer, practically fawning over him with relief.

Tamla brushes past me and whispers, 'God help us. He's been a busy boy.'

'That can't be good?'

'Roger that.'

I have committed the cardinal error, again, of believing I am the only one who can make plans, and as I catch Orridge's leery and bloodshot eye, I know that my response to whatever he has pulled will determine which of us will look back on these next few minutes as the beginning of our glory years, or their end.

'Ahhh, we've just been waiting for you, Terry. Fashionably late to the party as usual!' Orridge calls.

His posture and tone would be right for the closing act of a heroic bender; he is dressed in his old tweeds, when I expected him to show up today clad as a Beefeater, resplendent and royal-ready. Instead his soiled shirt is unbuttoned, tie unknotted, and in place of his loafers are scuffed and muddy walking boots. All this while I cannot remember him looking more triumphant or sure of himself. Swallowing uncomfortably, I feel the fear of failure narrow my trachea. My foremost hope is that this curious display of nonchalance is a signal that he has finally gone mad.

'Where is Grace?' I ask hoarsely.

'In a briefing with the Royal Security team,' replies Tamla. 'Just to clear the roofs of snipers, probably.'

'Forget the chief for once!' Orridge belches, beckoning me towards him.

'He can't claim credit for this one, oh no. This is Max's contribution to the party, Terry!'

The air is fetid with the silty stink of a dried-out caffeine river, the cigar Orridge holds aloft like Liberty's torch, a soggy fat stump that several have sucked on. 'Sorry, Terry. Would have saved one of these beasts for you. Cohibas. I know you like a smoke, but we didn't know when or whether you'd show up.'

'I'm here now,' I say too quietly.

'Then welcome to the war, though just like the Yanks, you're already too late for our finest hour!'

I wince. 'Yank' was a nickname he tried on me for a little while hoping it would catch on, after I had foolishly lent him my box set of *The Wire*.

'And, as a Yank, you can't really, not this time, take credit for the lion's share of the glory. Though, granted, you've grafted a bit.'

The small crowd of uniforms around him chortle moronically, and I rule out a nervous breakdown as the cause for this latest twist in our fortunes: Orridge is in full possession of the initiative and the room.

'I know you've been "burning the midnight oil", Terry, we'll always have to grant you that, but you haven't been the only one who has this time.'

'What Max is trying to tell you—'

'Please, my dear' — Orridge signals for silence with his cigar like a conductor controlling an unruly string section — 'this isn't *your* good news to tell, Tamla, not this time. This here is Max's baby, and I say when it cries and when it goes to sleep!'

'Good to see you enjoying yourself, Max. They've decided to give you a knighthood at last?' I ask.

'Very funny, Terry! Very funny. No, not this time. This time I've gone and cleared up that mystery that seemed to be evading the best detective minds of our generation and the next! Yes, that had us chasing dragons and pointing the finger of blame in all the wrong places, that frankly, was making fucking fools of us all... some of us more than others... heh heh...' He winks at his fan club. 'Yes, you might say that I've just gone and done you a favour, though knowing how uptight you college types are about real teamwork, you'll probably not see it that way...'

My stomach is contracting and my voice cannot help but follow its example; I feel like I am losing control. The trouble with control is that it is difficult to believe in once you have lost it that first time; the blabbering anger, the uncontrollable self-pity, the cascading fear of not being properly understood all seem like the truth. And control? Control feels like a con.

With difficulty I ask, 'What are you talking about, Max?'

'Sorry, Terry. I can't hear you?' Orridge says as loudly as he can.

'What are you talking about, Max?' My voice is shaking, and I make a feeble effort to stand to my full height.

'I am talking about what is so.'

'This is getting very Kipling.'

'My favourite writer, Terry.'

'I don't think this is the occasion for our first literary discussion.'

Orridge laughs, in my face. I can hear in my voice that forced attempt to maintain grip when I over pronounce my words, which is always proof that I am frightened, my skin simply the seal for the shaking liquid vulnerability beneath that is the real me. 'What's this about, Max? Oblique isn't usually your bag. I thought you'd be waiting at the city limits for the royal cavalcade, not buggering about in here stinking the place out with your cheroots.'

'I'd love to be thinking of just Queen and country today, Terry. Nothing would have given me more pleasure that that — I'll tell you that for nothing. And if I hadn't the misfortune of clearing up the messes, hiccups, and shit-shows others thought they could handle, I'd be all spick and span now, all spit and polish. But when the self-appointed specialists aren't up to the task, it often falls to ordinary blokes like myself to show up, and show the show-offs how it's done.'

'Why don't you stop beating that chest, put the shirt back on, and tell me whatever you have to tell me, then?'

'Said you wouldn't be happy, didn't I?' Orridge winks. 'Your least attractive quality, Terry — an absolute absence of humility in any way, shape or form. Well, isn't it obvious? What else do you think I could be talking about here? What else have you and her and poor old Dexter too — God, I should never have let you get him involved in this mess, but it's too late for that now — what *else* have you all been rabbiting on about nonstop for the last however long?'

'You tell me, Max. You're the one relishing the moment.'

'Your *mispers*! Your mispers of course! What else could I be bloody talking about? Well, I've only gone and practically solved the whole thing for you, haven't I?'

'Scale back that sugar rush, Max. You've—'

'Come on, Tamla. Be a big girl about it — I succeeded where you failed, and it's driving you mad with professional jealously, end of!'

'Oh grow up!'

'No, why the bloody hell should I? You people are too used to having it all your own way! Face it for once and take a dose of your own medicine if you please! You can't handle being bested by an old-fashioned copper who doesn't give a monkey's cuss for your theories, reading lists and pals on equal opportunities commissions! Who just wants to get the job done the way we used to do it, before we had to worry about all this rubbish you get these days...'

'So what is it, Max? You're drifting. Back on point please. A group shot in Ibiza? A barn full of captives? Your gang theory? What? Don't hold back. If you're right, then I am undone and ready to bow to the better man.'

'The serial killer, of course, Terry. The one explanation it was always most likely to be once we had ruled those other ones out.'

'You *have* a serial killer? Are you serious?'

'No, not yet, but I don't need one, not as proof that I am right anyway. It's only a matter of time before we or someone else will get hold of the bastard, and then you better hold me back, because I'll tear him from his guzzle to his zatch.'

'Then what do you have?'

'What I have, is what *you've* been looking for.' Orridge jabs his cigar at me. 'Bodies. Bodies of course. I have the mispers, or what remains of them, the poor sods. I have your *bodies*, and now we have our crime. We know what we are dealing with at last, thank God,' he says, addressing our audience as much as me.

'Easy, Max. Aren't you over-egging the pudding a little...'

'You be quiet, Dexter,' Orridge points the cigar at Christopherson, who is lurking up the other end of the trailer. 'I've been good to you, but you misstepped. This has got nothing to do with you now.'

'When did this breakthrough occur?' I ask. 'You might have thought of telling me in real time.'

'I tried that, but your and Red Riding Hood's phones were turned off.'

'It's true, Terry,' says Tamla. 'I just needed the sleep.'

'This is last night, then?'

Max nods. 'Last night, yeah.'

'What happened? Take me through it.'

'I got a tip off, not one of my regular sources, a voice I don't recognise on a burner mobile...'

'I thought you knew everyone?'

'I do. But I can't be expected to remember them all, especially if they're trying hard to not be recognised, which this particular voice was. Gave me nothing but a location, a copse off a drove way that runs behind Wick, that tiny hamlet near Downton, joining it up to Whitsbury. Mainly used by off-roaders, farm vehicles, the occasional fly-tipper, but a nice and deserted spot. Anyway, he says...'

'He?' I ask.

'Yeah, he was a man — I could grasp that much. Woke me up, he did. I was all settled for an early one because of today. He says there's a decomposing body halfway down the track by a burnt out old Outlander, just tucked into a little woody bit between the two main paths, and signs of fresh digging too. Well that was all I needed for the alarm bells to get going...'

'Haven't we had any teams search down there?'

'May have, may not. There's been a lot of ground to cover and we haven't had the men or time to get everywhere yet.'

'He's right about that,' says Christopherson. 'There hasn't even been any public search parties organised.'

'And now we don't need them, thank God,' says Orridge. 'This spot, and I take no pleasure in saying it, is journey's end for our mispers. So anyway, I got on straight down there. It was as the source said. A body, quite fresh I'd say from the state of it, and then shallow graves, a few just covered in branches and leaves, no big effort to disguise anything, not rushed either — you get the feeling he was confident about not being caught. Which made me think there may have been something in what you said after all, Terry...'

'Very generous of you. How do you mean?'

'I give credit where it is due. Whoever offed this lot didn't think we were going to miss them enough to look very far or thorough, that's true, as whoever did it didn't bother to go very hard covering their tracks. Like I say, my guess is that he either thought he would get away with it, or didn't care if he didn't.'

'So what exactly do we have?'

'One fresh kill and bones, lots of them, taken apart by animals, foxes and what not. In a terrible state most of them are, and they're spread all over the place. I only picked up a small sample of debris, not half of what was out there.'

'You shouldn't have picked up any of it all.'

'Easy to be wise after the event when you were safely in bed. What if our chum came back and moved the lot while I was away, because he'd been watching me all the while? You have to trust instinct.'

'What about the body? Not long dead you say?'

'A bloke. Maybe a week or so since he was in the land of the living. A bit of his dick is still there. But with half his head sliced off, which doesn't exactly help with a positive identification if you're about to ask me who he is!' There are knowing laughs round the room. 'And the other half the birds have had a go at, crows I'd say, carrion scavengers, clean eaten most of the remaining face, bleach poured all over him and no hands to fingerprint, lopped off at the wrists, all rolled in a carpet. Very nasty, cause of death could be anything. He's resting at the morgue at the hossie now. And the bones are with forensics for all they can do with them. Looked to me like our suspect could be some kind of cannibal. Some of the bites on that body might have been made by a human, if that's what you'd call the animal who did this, though that's for others to determine. But a pal I have up there, that was the first thing he said when I showed him the marks.'

'You have any idea how many bodies might have been left in the wood?'

'God knows. Could have been a Civil War battlefield for their ubiquity.'

'And "headless" — he's at Odstock now?'

'Safe and sound at last, cold packing in the ice box.'

'Jesus,' says one of the uniforms, 'it's just fucking beyond the pale, isn't it?'

'Yeah, sickening is the word, most absolutely bloody sickening,' Orridge adds, looking at me meaningfully, his tag-line for *South Today* safely laminated, 'a horrific and completely unforgivable crime.'

'What do you think?' I turn to Tamla. 'Shall we have a look?'

'Have to,' she says.

Orridge stirs in his chair, suddenly agitated. 'Best cremate the lot in time I say. There's no helping them now. Or making sense out of that jumble.'

'Now, now, Max. It is far too early to jump to conclusions.'

'But I saw it all. You didn't!'

'Which is exactly why I'm on my way to the hospital now...'

'Save yourself the bother. There's bound to be more of them popping up now we've found the first — you know how it goes.'

'I do.'

'So what's the point of going now?'

'As you say, Max. Instinct.'

'Good luck to you, then. A complete waste of time I say.'

'You're coming too,' I retort, 'unless someone you know has already gone on and squeezed our corpse into an oven with last night's dinner.'

'What the bloody hell do you mean by that? There's no point now, we've got the Queen and...' Orridge starts to his feet and looks genuinely discomforted at the thought of losing more of his day to this relative triviality. '...I mean...'

'He's there, isn't he?'

'...Who?'

'Your half-headless corpse,' I say.

'Of course he is, but I need to get ready for the Queen, you know. We've put this thing to bed for the moment, parked it as it were, and it can be revisited later. But the Queen, she's only here for one afternoon...' Orridge obfuscates.

'We've plenty of people to turn up for her, Max. She's a popular assignment, whereas we're the ones that do the jobs the other fellows can't, aren't we? What could be more important with a serial killer running about than tying up loose ends, lest something happen to Her Majesty?'

Orridge looks about the room, but there is no sympathy for his predicament, only the curiosity of the vacillating centre that cannot wait to find out what will happen next. He is coming with me and he knows it.

'Max, there is a kind of view of policing that sees some crimes as so traumatic that it doesn't matter who you catch for them, just so long as they go away, bring closure, and then never need to be thought of again. You might think this is just such a crime. But that doesn't just show contempt for the victims; it shows solidarity with the criminal, because then you and he — are on the same side.'

'What bollocks are you spouting?' Orridge splutters.

'I'll drive,' says Tamla, pulling open the door. A current of clean air sweeps purposefully through the trailer with the briskness of a new invention, and I see something in Max's eyes that reassures me as nothing else has.

Panic.

*

Eileen has never been the sort of woman who thinks she has closed a door only to find it open, and nor is her daughter, who is her twin sister in practical matters. The front door, never the most robust of objects, has been forced off its lock and the mechanism broken. It has also been shut in such a way as to look closed until it responds to her slightest touch, and pops back all too readily.

She knows at once that it would be safest if she walked straight back down her path again and checked in with her cousin who lives on the opposite side of the road. The woman is already looking after the Pertwee children, martyr that she is, and she would doubtless tell Eileen to call the police. But since Eileen has fallen in love with a policeman, she does not know where she stands with that organisation anymore, if ever she did, and she does not want to get her lover into trouble by bringing attention to herself, especially not today, so whatever is going on, she realises, must be faced by her alone. Eileen drops her overnight bag by the door, leaving it ajar, and steps into her house. Inside everything is as it should be, or at least as it was when she last paid any attention to it, and she is about to grasp false consolation with both hands, gratefully, as she has a shift starting in four hours and all she desires now is to sleep, when she hears a fit of giggles coming from her living room, complicit and secretive, malicious and uncaring, and careless in regard to its discovery: whatever is making this noise knows she is listening and enjoys that knowledge.

Eileen understands she should really turn tail and run now; there is still time to make a clean break to the door. Every instinct of hers loudly announces this course, all save one: her pride. To be driven out of her own house, in light of what she believes has happened to her family and to others, is an impulse that would have her hiding for the rest of her days. It would be better for it to all end suddenly on a high, for she has never been this happy before, than sully the last few days by becoming a self-identifying coward. God knows, she has met some pleasant snivelling weaklings in her time, but you always despise yourself for ever trusting one, making plans with them or waking up in their company.

Very slowly, Eileen enters the living area, resisting the spur to simply call out and challenge the intrusion, which is always a sign that, beneath the bravado, you are bricking it. Although there is no sound now, she is undoubtedly in the presence of others, she can feel them there waiting for her. In her hand is a can of Mace her lover has given her, and she has faith in the damage it can do to the first wave of an attack, after which she has her entire body to fall back on, before she has to contemplate anything so desperate as screaming for help.

Disconcertingly, though she is positive she heard the laughter coming from here, the living room is completely empty, and just as she is about to check the adjoining kitchen, which really is too small to hide anything, she notices a trickle of liquid gathering at the foot of the drawn curtain, which is the way she leaves them when she goes out these days. The curtain shakes a little and there is more suppressed laugher. Eileen has seen and smelt so many things that do not exist lately that she can hardly believe her eyes, as she watches a small pool grow in volume, to the accompaniment of the same idiot laughter, gruff and disrespectful, no longer willing to even contain itself. Tearing the curtain right off its rails, she drags it away from the windows, back over the sofa.

Standing there, carelessly urinating with diabolic smirks on their faces, penises pointed towards her, are two well-built, but short, young men in their mid-twenties, recognisable to her as the beaters on a local shoot, also faces on the bare-knuckle boxing scene, failed suitors to her daughter and occasional visitors to Iggy's caravan, now ransacked and torn to pieces in her garden. Fortunately, the curtain has absorbed the initial force of their collective trajectory, and despite their cheerful jeering, by the time they register an angry woman brandishing a can of tear gas, their jet stream is no more than the trickle of a pair of ineffectual shower roses.

'I know you two cunts!' Eileen shrieks.

'Easy now!' one laughs, conspicuously not putting his penis

away, rather looking to manually harden it into a more statuesque posture, his brother more warily shifting his out of view.

'You filthy pigs,' she says, shaking the can hard. Eileen is not going to make the same mistake the big talkers do in the films, chattering away a prime opportunity for effective violence that might settle things in their favour, and taking aim, she sprays point blank into the first one's eyes, his brother foolishly staring at her in disbelief, and so wide open for the same treatment seconds later.

Eileen drops the can, somehow she has already emptied it. Both men are on the floor at her feet cursing her loudly, and that is before she takes the opportunity to stamp on one set of fingers, and grind down on the other, quickly stamping on the ear of the boy closest to her, and kicking the other in the neck. The woeful noise they make could even call in the cavalry, and Eileen is about to congratulate herself on a job well done, when she feels fat sausage fingers grasping her throat from behind, squeezing dangerously, and the stench of rotting vines and unwashed stone floors overpowering her will to resist.

'Dear, oh dear,' says Swillcut. 'You've met my nephews, the most unfortunate of boys at the best of times. Only look at them now! Hopeless, absolutely hopeless!'

Eileen's disgust, outrage and cold fury has passed into the hands of brute inevitability, wielded by one who offers no choice, to resist is to die. There are no odds now, she is their prisoner and she must make plans as a captive would. Life is too good to fight to the death over. She does not want to quit at the top or go out like this. She only wants to see Terry again — and to do whatever it takes to make that happen.

'Wait until we dose you up,' chuckles Swillcut, dragging Eileen out through the back door into the garden. 'Old John will wear you, wear you and your mind!'

*

'Why did you do it, *Uncle Silas*?'

'What?' Orridge barks back.

I let the question sink in before repeating it, angry that I could have been frightened of anything so farcical. 'Why, *Silas*? You were coasting, playing nice safe shots. All you had to keep doing was sit tight and let your mates take care of everything. Just keep playing dumb, throwing the odd red herring into the mix and generally getting in our way without looking like you were. No more than the usual. But this? Acting on your own initiative has never been your bag. What a fuck up to start thinking otherwise now.'

We are stood over what remains of the remains of *Nick the Well*, the corpse easily identifiable by his badge and the rump of the jacket, which though a bloody shredded mess, still boasts the unique hallmarks that once made it so unmistakable in life. In the interests of privacy, and so as to not distress anyone called in to identify a deceased loved one, the body has been laid out for us in the secular 'quiet area' beside the hospital chapel, lending the corpse an arid dignity that its former owner struggled to reach in life.

'What the fuck? What're you on, Terry?' Orridge barks through the handkerchief he is affecting to hold over his nose, lest our close proximity to murder threaten to overcome his nerves.

'The mother of all unforced errors, Max! You should know — you're the one who made it.'

'Speak the English? I don't understand bullshit.'

'This is a fucking mess isn't it, Max? Or *Silas*? Which is it, which one is the real you? And I'm not just talking about the body here, I mean the whole shoddy hole-ridden thing. Really, it's so poor I'm actually shocked you had the brass balls to try it on at all.'

'For the life of me, what's he on?' Orridge appeals to Tamla. 'I have not the foggiest fucking idea what you are talking about!'

'You heard me, I'm embarrassed for you, Max, plain embarrassed.'

'Has your friend gone completely mad this time? He needs his head checked,' Max tries to grab Tamla's arm, who brushes him off.

'You can leave us now,' Tamla says to the embarrassed student nurse, who, having led us here, does not need to be told twice. 'What was that you were saying, Max?'

'He's mad!' Orridge says gesticulating at me wildly with his handkerchief. 'Finally totally lost the plot and his marbles into the bargain! I don't need to stand around and hear this shit.'

'Oh you do,' says Tamla. 'Best humour him until he's finished.'

'I know Wiltshire PD can be pretty sloppy — Christ, you know that too — but even our lot would have been able to see through this mess,' I say. 'How did you think you were going to get away with it? No, don't tell me, you actually thought that your friends in high places would cover for you? Was that it?'

'He's bloody mad!' Max enthuses. 'He needs a full fucking medical!'

'What gets me is how you failed to identify this corpse as Nicholas Toll to start with. *Nick the Well.* One of your snitches, isn't he? That's a pretty glaring omission for someone with eyes and a memory.

'For Christ's sake, Terry. Look at the bloody state of him! Who's going to recognise that poor sod from this mess...' — Orridge points at the corpse — '...and it was dark, I told you... and I didn't get to see him this end. I was busy with the paperwork...'

'Come on, Max. There's a badge on that jacket that is as good as his name, rank and number.'

'There wasn't time for that! We needed to bring him in before the foxes got to him again...'

'Serial killer, Max. I thought it was a serial killer that did for him, not a fox.'

'You what?'

'A serial killer. Remember? A serial killer who murders a herd of victims who all happen to know each other, who live within a mile or so of each other, and who doesn't care if he's caught, and yet is still uncatchable? You hadn't really thought through any of this had you, Max?' I say leaning into him.

'Oh sod you. It was better than anything you or Miss Marple here cooked up.' — Orridge spits — 'A big nothing is where you lot had got to, until I came in and sorted things out for you...'

'Sorted things out? Yeah, we've listened to that story. Save it for people who don't know you, Max, who don't know what you're really like.'

'Put yourself in my shoes, how the hell was I expected...'

'That's what I am trying to do, Max! I'm trying to see the world through your eyes. That's why I have to return to it; how did you think you could get away with this? It worries me, it really does, how anyone this formally bad at what they are meant to be doing could try something this ambitious!'

Orridge stares back at me with the kind of hatred that is closer to destroying the bearer than the object of it.

'This *is* ambitious,' says Tamla. 'Very bold of whoever did it...'

'Of course it's ambitious. Max has only bloody gone and killed someone! But I can't be disingenuous with you. I think I can see why you thought you'd walk off scot-free, Max. You just looked at our government' — I point to the ceiling, — 'and the President of the United States, the idiots on *Good Morning Britain*, Assad and Kim Jong-un, and think, yes, I'll have a bit of that! If they can get away with it, why can't I? You look at their example and you think why not you? Idiocy and evil is openly rewarded wherever you look, and you, you're just stupid and arrogant enough to think you'll have some of it as well, and get away with it too... why not when others have got away with so much worse, eh? Is that it? Perhaps you thought you were just following in the footsteps of an honourable tradition...'

'You're mad. Plain stir fry. A nut job, totally tied to your own fantasies. I told you, I'm off. I don't need this,' Orridge makes as if to leave.

'You do need this, Max, because even in your hour of triumph, you were bricking it, weren't you? There was a nagging doubt in there somewhere, Max. You wouldn't be human otherwise. The fear you were going to end up a stooge, the fall guy, a patsy? A misgiving that this wasn't going to be the crowning achievement of your career after all...'

'What the hell are you on about?' Max turns to Tamla again. 'Have you two been on the marching powder and wacky baccy again? You mix that and this is how it turns out! I haven't served thirty long years to be dressed down by the Glimmer Twins!'

'I'm trying to see it from your side, Max,' I continue. 'You know, here you are, true blue, holding the line, etc., a true servant of power and footsoldier of special interests, and for all that you expect, at the very least, a Christmas bonus and an invite to the yacht on Capri once all this blows over... but do you really think this is just going to go away? You really think it'll be shooed away quietly without a culpable party left with his dick hanging out to carry the can? You stupid bastard. He's you. You are that guy. You're the can-carrier.'

'I don't have to take this from you, Balance.'

'You're never so vulnerable as when you think you have the entire thing stitched up.'

'I don't have to take this from him,' he says to Tamla. She smiles and pulls the sheet back up over *The Well*'s reduced head. 'So leave then.'

Orridge looks like he would like to do as she suggests, yet stays rooted to the spot, his mouth bent open slightly. It would be cruel to say it, but I do not think I have ever seen him look uglier or less intelligent.

'Don't be an even bigger mug than you are, Max. This is a crime that calls out for a scapegoat. And now that you've royally screwed things up and actually gifted us with a body, we've got a full-blown murder case on our hands. So unless you've already got someone that you want to frame, which you might have, though you'll want to move pretty fast with that one if you do...'

'You realise that this farce could let a serial killer off the hook, Balance? For God's sake, you're playing with people's lives here. This isn't a game between you and me anymore! Try and get past yourself for once.'

'You may think you've got the perfect answer to this problem, your serial killer theory, Max, but you haven't taken into account that your handlers don't need him now, have you? They already have their answer to this problem: they have *you*. You've taken the heat off whatever they wanted to keep in the dark, and instead brought it all on yourself. Nice one, and very noble of you too — I hope they appreciate your sacrifice.'

Under this harsh light I watch the last of the blood leave Orridge's cheeks. Incredibly, the possibility I have outlined does not seem to have occurred to him. Now that it has been spelt out, his posture has moved from defensive aggression to naked injury.

'Who are you working for, Max?' Tamla asks, resting her hand on his arm. 'Because it isn't the people of this city or law enforcement, is it? You've sort of lost sight of your base, haven't you? And then gone and had your head filled with stardust and big ideas? You can't blame folk for beginning to wonder whether you are any kind of policeman at all... I've always known you're a little bit partial, Max, but never this crooked. What happened to you?'

Max twists, and practically snarling, mutters, 'Fuck off. Fuck off the pair of you. I don't need this.'

'I know, you've already said that,' I tell him. 'Look at it this way. It's already a given you'll do time for one murder. Your handlers have done their homework and measured you right. But they and I will give you credit for one thing, though. You know how to keep your mouth shut. You've been silent this long after all. You're not some junkie punk who'll give them up...'

'Christ, Terry! Switch *Radio Balance* off for a second and look at it the way a normal human being would!' cries Orridge. 'A known drug addict is dead, a complete piece of shit in a doorway, for crying out aloud. He is found dead, and there are a million ways in which he could have died, and yet you, you have the effrontery, the sheer effrontery, to accuse me, an officer of several years' service, of, well I can hardly say it, of actually offing the wretched low life! No one will believe you! No one could take such an accusation seriously, it'd be... it'd be unheard of.' Orridge stares at us for emphasis.

'You have to take it seriously, Max. You have to, because you know I see you, see your true colours that you hide under that bluff normal bloke bollocks,' I say, leaning into him again. 'There's already way too much in the mix for you to get away with a slap on the wrist. This won't just be a case of you doing a couple of years behind barred ones in an open prison playing ping-pong with Jeffrey Archer — it's already way too serious for that. No, you've been to the rodeo before. You know you'll have to pack more than an overnight bag, that you'll be going away for a good long stretch, don't you? You'll have to be locked up for that long, otherwise it'll look like the cover up that it in fact is. And what with your name destroyed, as it would have to be, let's face it, because we already know they're going to take advantage of your loyalty, and no pension, you can forget that now...'

'You shut your bloody mouth!'

'And your future prospects fucked, as not even private security would touch you after this...'

'No! That's not how this is going to play out!' Orridge yells.

'And with all that and not much time left on this planet, as none of us are getting any younger, and with no one wanting to know you even if you get out of prison in one piece, because we know a lot can happen to you in there, don't we? Face it, Max, by the end there'll be nothing left of you to parole. Your life will be finished.'

'Just shut up. Just stop talking.'

'Nothing... expect whatever little modest standing order they have waiting for you in the Channel Islands, fixed up on the side, probably not even accruing interest — just the sort of one-off payment they keep for their injured gamekeepers or butlers that have twisted their ankles.'

'Fuck off out of it! That's not the way it's going to go down, Terry!'

'Isn't it? There'll be enough money, maybe, to cover that airfare out to the Philippines, but even your bent ex-cop mates aren't going to want their names sullied by association. Think about it, after all, you're a kidnapper, a murderer and a pervert all rolled into one — and by your own lights, probably a serial killer too!'

'I want a lawyer.'

'I thought you would,' says Tamla. 'Here, call one. You know the numbers.' She hands Orridge her phone and he stands there just looking at it.

'You've as good as admitted your guilt, Max. That we can work around, but hoping for a better outcome really is naive. You've drunk the poison and you are going to be the one who is going to die.'

'You're lying.'

'Why would he lie? You'll see it like we do one day,' intones Tamla softly. 'So why not see things as they are now while you can still save yourself?'

'I've nothing to say to you, dolly bitch.'

'That's not very nice, Max,' says Tamla. 'Especially as you'll have a lot to say about it in twenty years, I'll bet, all alone in your caravan,' Tamla tells him. 'Then I bet you'll be ready to confess to anyone who'll listen to you, about the great conspiracy you served: the names, the titles, the lords, the ladies, duchesses and dukes, the rock stars and their managers and PAs that you covered for. But by then no one will be listening to you because you'll be just another ex-con protesting his innocence after the fact. Good for the odd *Sun on Sunday* exclusive, maybe...'

'But basically soiled goods,' I come in. 'And even if they do reopen the case again, it'll come too late for you, Max. Your goose will already have been cooked several thousand Christmases earlier, old boy.'

'You know he's right,' says Tamla. 'We've got plenty of time, so stop sweating and looking at your watch. Forget about the Queen, that was all part of another life. This is all you need to think about now. Let the ones who put you in this position take responsibility for themselves for once. You can't look after them forever. Why should it always be your turn to suffer?'

Max takes off his tie and stuffs it glumly into his breast pocket. Staring down at the plain white sheet that covers the mutilated corpse, as if for answers, he mutters, 'Neither of you have any idea, no idea at all...'

'And nor had you. It's amazing you didn't look this far down the road... which actually makes me think we are alike after all, Max.'

'Uh?'

'Shit or bust, putting all our faith in a full-frontal attack in the daring hope that it would be enough to save everything. You know what I mean. It was what I was going to do myself this morning, but you moved first, and to be honest, in doing so, you have made things ridiculously easy for me. Previously it was all looking rather difficult, I'll admit...'

'You always were a jammy bastard, Balance,' coughs Orridge hoarsely. 'The buttered toast landing the right side up for you every time. I don't think you have ever had to graft for anything in your life...'

'Don't take this personally, Max,' interrupts Tamla. 'It was difficult not to screw up in your position. Being a crook is harder than being a cop — there's so much more that can go wrong for you. I don't know what Kool Aid you'd been drinking, but Terry's right. You've been playing against type and have gone well out of character. Acting impulsively, instinctively, passionately... you haven't had time to consider all the variables. You're a people pleaser at heart. All you wanted to do was save the day and impress your exalted mates. Was that it? Maybe so they showed a little more respect than they're used to doing and actually owed you one for a change? And then look at what went and happened!'

Max remains sullenly inside himself, his expression an empty mask of forgone calculations, too early and too late to find their way into the present and rescue him from his tormentors.

'Here, Max. Have a chair.' I pull up a stool. 'This'll be easier to take sitting down.'

He sits down as if commanded to.

'You know she's got a point. Your mistake here was to kill *The Well* on your own initiative. I can't believe anyone else could actually be stupid enough to ask you to do it! You weren't reading the memo properly. All you were probably told to do was create a diversion and direct the finger of suspicion elsewhere, not bloody chop some poor cunt to pieces and blame Hannibal fucking Lecter for it, you silly sod.'

'I didn't do it on purpose,' Orridge blurts. 'It wasn't murder.'

'Of course it wasn't.' I glance at Tamla. 'We know that already, Max. You're no killer.'

'Tell us what it was then, Max?' she asks.

'I knocked him about a bit, that's all. I was angry and he was the weakest link. I needed to stop him from taking that stuff and... we all know what happens to people who take that stuff...'

'*High John the Conqueror?*'

He nods, 'Yeah.'

'Have you been running it for them, Max?'

'No fear! I wouldn't even carry that stuff in my pocket. I'm bloody terrified of it! You know what it can do. It's a bloody horror show. I know you've watched footage...'

'So what happened?' Tamla presses. 'How did it go wrong?'

'Like I tell you, I was just trying to scare the bastard is all, and he *was* scared but not scared enough. I'll tell you what, he was more scared of you and what might happen to him if he started to get the blame... for all the other stuff.'

I nod. 'You didn't trust him to carry his own water then?'

'No chance. You know what he was. That kind. He could see the score for himself. Jabbering and blabbing. It would have only been a matter of time.'

'So you knocked him about a bit. Fair enough...'

'I had to! He showed me no respect, no respect whatsoever. Anyway, I tapped him a bit harder than I meant to...'

'Relax, Max. We've all been there. It happens.'

'He made me so bloody angry you see!' Orridge protests. 'He was pathetic. I hate pathetic people, weaklings who are all soft inside and out...'

'So he's on the floor...'

'Yeah.'

'And he stopped breathing?'

'That's how it was. That's what happened.'

'So then what did you do?'

'Looking at him lying there, you know, looking at him, I thought...'

'That you could deal with two problems at the same time?'

'Yeah.' He nods. 'That's it. Birds and stones. I thought I needed to make it work to an advantage. Take the situation and turn it around. To make it look like everything, the disappearances, the vanished scumbags, to make it all look like they were all killings, you see?'

'Of course.'

'And *Nick the* fucking *Well*, well worthless vermin like him, a packet of human dust who'd never contributed anything or done any good to anyone — who'd miss him? I saw it then, that he fits the profile of the mispers pretty good. If he was found dead, then maybe that was how they all ended up. Why not? Birds and stones, like you called it.'

'And you've been steering other birds towards your handlers too, haven't you, Max?'

'What do you mean?'

'The mispers, you've been curating on behalf of your boss, your real master, haven't you?'

'Or maybe procuring would be the more correct term,' says Tamla.

'No. Neither of those. Vetting, vetting is more like what it was.'

'Call it what you want, Max. I'm sure you were only one talent scout amongst many but an important one nonetheless. That badge, it's a priceless commodity on the open market.'

'Yeah, you can say that again. I gave them something they otherwise wouldn't have had.' For a fleeting instant Orridge looks mildly pleased with himself. 'Well, I had opportunity, you know. And a lot of experience. I know these kids — they don't trust us. We're the last people they'd go to for help, so they don't come to us when things go wrong. And if they do, no one is going to notice an interview that goes missing... I already had a foot in that world, knew my way round it, so to speak.'

'And there's so many of them to start with, isn't there? These kids. Fresh meat.'

'Right. You know how they breed them on the estates, and they all bloody look alike too, even their parents wouldn't be able to tell them apart, boys and girls, pasty waxy greasy stupid faces, all of them looking for a little excitement and dosh.'

Max actually smiles at me, and I recognise where I have seen the reflex before: in the faces of every 'unwilling' criminal, all of them convinced that what they were involved in was never so simple as a crime, the relief of confession too deep and quick and sudden for their responses to cope with, the liberation — now that the lying is finally over — absolute.

'Okay, so much for that. There's a person behind all this that we need you to name...'

'Say what?'

'The one who you were rounding up these poor unfortunates for. Him. Not to be too melodramatic, the boss. His identity — not the guests; they can come later — their host.'

Max changes colour again, a radish-red rash emerging from under his floury skin.

'You don't know what you are asking now.'

'Believe me, Max. I do.'

'Not so simple, Terry,' Orridge says, covering his eyes with his hand.

It is not only fear that is holding him back but the shame of admission. He is not yet ready to see himself as he actually is, different from how others see him, and the way he would still like to be seen, even though he never was this person. Despite his will being uncoupled and undone, his mind has yet to catch up with truth. I am ready to give him one final push. Tamla understands this too, 'Max,' she starts. 'I see your problem even though you can't yet.'

'Eh? How could you?'

'Oh it's not so hard. Nothing is harder to kill than the desire to think well of yourself.'

'Easy for you to say, stood there.'

'Your trouble is that you still think you are a policeman, and that's good in a way, because it's what's protecting you from reality, helping you to deal with the shock of the jig being up. But the fact is that you stopped being one a long time ago. If ever you were a real one. You may have fitted in alright, but who you fitted in with, they weren't really police either. They were bad actors, like you, a chorus, decoys that are there to make up numbers and reassure the public, while those of us who can really do this job go about our business. So let it go, and accept what you are. It'll be good for the soul.'

'You know she's right, Max. I wouldn't want to have taken

this away from you, but you've already taken it away from yourself; why do you think you never made it past sergeant?'

'That wasn't my fault — you know it. My mistake was I was too loyal to others...'

'And that's still your mistake, Max. It's still your mistake! Masters and his happy band, they give as little a fuck for you as they do those kids they vanished. What are you still protecting them for?'

'That's not true. Look, look at this, he gave me this.'

Max pulls off a £140 quartz battery *Citizen* diving watch and proudly brandishes the back of it. 'Look, it's even inscribed.'

Tamla takes it, raises an eyebrow and hands it to me. On it in scratchily engraved letters is the legend *'Don't let the bastards grind you down.'*

'Very thoughtful. Some people buy presents for their pets at Christmas too.'

'They respected me, Terry. You never saw that.'

'Yeah? I bet they never even let you into their parties. They didn't, did they?'

Max bows his head and I wonder if we're going to have to watch him cry as well as lie to us.

'You don't understand. It wasn't my place to take part, you know, in that kind of carry on they got up to at the parties, orgies or whatever they were — it wasn't my thing. My job was to patrol the perimeter, police it, make sure there were no gatecrashers...'

'And that no one could get out. *That no one could get out.* Don't forget that part.'

'They trusted me! Believed in me completely...'

'That I know, they trusted you to know your place. I bet you didn't even know what was going on in there, I bet you still don't, do you?'

'I didn't want to!' he cries.

'Yet you were ready to hand-deliver other people's kids to these scum,' says Tamla, slapping his ear. 'You must have known there was something very off about the way these boys were literally vanishing into thin air. Please tell me that you did?'

'The less I knew the better! We were all agreed on that.'

'Hear no evil, see no evil, know no evil. I'm disappointed in you, Max,' she says, holding on to the ear and talking into it. 'I thought you at least might be man enough to take ownership of the horror show you're a signed up member of.'

'You don't understand. There was a division of labour. I was never involved in anything that happened... inside.'

'Just out of interest, Max. What *did* you think was happening to all these mispers? You were keen enough to cover up and pretend a serial killer was behind it all, so I am guessing you realised the truth was even worse than that. Am I right?' I ask.

'I don't know,' he says, and I believe him. I nod at Tamla and she lets go of his organ of hearing.

'I didn't know and didn't want to know,' he practically shouts. 'Some crazy occult carry on. I'd heard the stories of a monster coming over from "the other side", kids vanishing in the morning mist, all that. Well, it's not my bag, so...'

'But it is your bag, Max. And the only thing that'll make it better is you giving up names, all of them, and the biggest one first...' Tamla reminds him.

'Jesus,' he says. 'There were so many faces. You'd know some of them — you're bound to. That woman who does the countryside programme, you wouldn't believe what she's really like, dirty she is; that chef from the telly, the bastard, well he's a bastard in real life too; and that rugby player with the cauliflower ears that pundits on the Six Nations, he's up his arse, he is, and everyone else's... There were so many faces. It was hard to believe they were who they were— if you see what I mean. You wouldn't expect to see them there involved in all that...'

'You're wasting time now, Max. The host... the master of ceremonies...'

'It won't bring anyone back! There's no coming back from where they all are!'

'Name him, for Christ's sake.'

'You already know who he is!' Orridge cries.

'And so do you...'

Orridge hesitates.

'Let it all out, Max. Make it good!' whispers Tamla.

'It's not as simple as that,' he says. 'Perhaps I should... perhaps I should have my lawyer...'

'Don't say that again, Max! Don't throw away this one last chance to still be a policeman.'

He looks at the floor and then they come, the tears. It is now or never.

'Be a cop, Max. Be a cop this one last time and that's how everyone will remember you — the way you want to be remembered — not as some errand boy for local crooks, but the brave man who repented and blew this whole thing wide open...'

'God, Terry. It's so complicated. None of this is the way it looks...'

'No, it's simple. The good guys and the bad guys. Be a good guy, Max.'

'But it's too late — can't you see? Don't you realise? I'm fucked, fucked already!'

'No, Max. You have a second chance, right here. You can still be the white knight.'

'You... really, still?'

'Of course.'

'But...'

'But nothing.' I lean forward so our faces are practically touching. 'We're alike, you and I. You've always known it. In our hearts we both have. Neither of us really gives a fuck about the rules. We go through the motions, but really we make it up as we go along. We're old-fashioned lawmen and meaning-givers. Others need laws; we don't. We live on the fly. It's why we understand the criminal mentality and why we are so good at keeping the peace; we're right on the line. That's what creates the tension, though, and that tension is what is pulling you apart.'

'You're right,' he says through his sobs. 'It's fucking killing me!'

'So say his name. Say it, Max. Say it. It's him, isn't it? Him. He's your master...'

'Yes.'

'Say his name.'

'Yes!'

'Say it!'

'Yes,' he says, 'yes, it's Masters! Masters!'

'At last!' whistles Tamla and bursts out laughing.

*

The door swings open, and Christopherson barges through, breathing heavily.

'They've broken cover!'

'You what?'

Panting, as though being a harassed, sweating mess is something to be proud of, he gasps, 'There's been some movement, boss. Something's happening. There's been movement.'

'Well, we could have told you that,' Tamla says, and indicating with her head our unfortunate colleague on the stool, adds coolly, 'It's been all go here too.'

Solemnly, and carefully avoiding Christopherson's eye, Orridge shuffles round on his stool so he is facing the wall and looking away from us, so as to better disguise his collapse.

'What happened to him?'

I point to our colleague. Orridge is sobbing to himself quietly and not in a position to contradict my optimistic characterisation of the last ten minutes.

'That's a long story, but the short of it is that Max has come clean with us and we have a full confession.'

'You're serious?'

'Perfectly,' says Tamla. 'He's been working hand in glove with Masters, luring the mispers in, at the very least. There's probably all sorts of other horrible things too, but we'll have to wait for those.'

'He admitted that to you?'

Tamla taps her phone. 'It's all on here. I recorded the whole thing.'

'Still, will it stick? I mean, he could say anything happened in here — you held a gun to his head, you know what I mean...'

'Max,' I call over to the forlorn figure, who so little resembles the man I met in the trailer earlier that I have to remind myself that there is no such thing as victory, 'are you listening to us?'

Without turning round, Orridge grunts in the affirmative.

'Is there anything you have said to us that you would not be prepared to repeat on oath, Max? Do you take anything back?'

'No,' he says quite clearly, 'nothing. You'll get it all again.'

'How did you get him to...?'

'Never mind that. What are you so excited about?'

'Our tails on those gimps. They've reported movement at last.'

'You mean Swillcut and Breezy?'

'Yeah, Breezy left home very early this morning and went straight over to Masters' place...'

'Why are you only telling us now?'

'Be fair, boss. There was quite a lot going on this morning. Not the easiest thing to do to get a word in or command your attention with all that other excitement.'

'That might have been the point,' says Tamla. 'Max here was supposed to create a diversion from the main event?'

'I doubt that. I don't think they trust Max enough to let him know what they're really up to and coordinate. But it does show they've been gearing up to something. Is Fallgrief still there now?'

'Oh yeah, Breezy hasn't left since he drove up.'

'When was that?'

'About 4.30am.'

'What was he driving?' I ask.

'His wife's Mini Cooper,' replies Christopherson.

'So there's no way he could mug us off with some story about making a delivery of any of that old shit he peddles then...'

'Absolutely not, unless it was something very small he was carrying...'

'*High John the Conqueror* is not exactly big,' says Tamla.

'Maybe. Whatever it is, it's not exactly a sociable hour for business either.'

'Not unless you're one of the undead.'

'So that's Breezy. Why the rush if this is old news? Swillcut just dropped his trousers to the Queen?'

'Him exactly, boss. He's gone plain weird. He leaves his place very early too, but drives up into the Hanging Hill estate...'

'Why there? What's there for him...?'

'We don't know, his tail was redeployed to form part of the Queen's security detail, so we don't know exactly where he got to.'

'What, redeployed at the precise moment he actually goes somewhere?'

'About then, yeah.'

'I did that.' Orridge adjusts his stool and, still facing away from us, tells Christopherson, 'Do you want to finish this or shall I?'

I motion to Christopherson to go on. 'It's alright, Max. You'll have your turn again.'

'He disappears up there into Hanging Hill. We don't see any more of him, until fifteen minutes ago. I called you but your phones were off...'

'Yeah, we have an unhelpful knack of doing that. Go on.'

'So I came straight over instead. Swillcut, he's coming into town, and very quickly, at high speed, right off the ring road and into the centre. Breaking the speed limit, dangerous driving, mounting the curb, all sorts.'

'No one stopped him yet?'

'Haven't tried to. Waiting to see what you'd say? But if we don't act quickly, the Queen's security detail are likely to get involved.'

'So he's driving straight into the centre of town, suicide-bomber style, right to where the Queen's due? Towards the station?'

'Right.'

'I can't see him wanting to watch her come off the Flying Scotsman, can you?'

'That's because he doesn't want to, Terry,' says Tamla. 'I don't think he wants to get into town at all, he wants to get *through* it.'

'And he can't take the ring road...?'

'Because it's blocked off and closed — as is every street connecting the city to the rest of the county, all the short cuts, the main bypass, and all other entrances and exits. All except for the very centre, the actual route the Queen will be travelling along. That's the only route left open, boss.'

'Can he double back on himself? I'm just thinking this could be another play?'

'No way. His way into the city from Hanging Hill will have already been blocked off by now if that was what he was trying. If he wants to get to Masters' gaff, which I think is a reasonable best guess, then his only way there without taking a massive detour through Wilton is right through the middle of town before that's shut down too. He's basically got to do it ahead of the Queen.'

'When are we closing it?'

Christopherson checks his watch. 'In about twenty minutes, boss.'

'So he could be trapped in town if doesn't hurry up?'

'Not at the speed he's going. He'll just about make it I reckon.'

'Can we call ahead?'

'They'll be able to hear anything our people can, Terry,' says Tamla. 'They'll be all over our radio. I'll bet they know what we are doing before we do.'

'Then we need to catch him before the road closes. We as good as know where he is going, the question is what's he doing crossing town only to cut back through it in the first place?' As I say this I realise I know what the van was doing in the area, the answer so obvious that I can ignore it only by pretending that we are dealing with different people from those we are.

Orridge laughs unpleasantly and, turning his head to the side so we can see half his face, chuckles, '*Hanging Hill*, Terry. Are you really trying to tell me that you don't know what lives up there?'

'Terry,' says Tamla. 'Easy now...'

'You can do better than that can't you, Terry? Someone very important to you can be found touching her toes and watering her garden up there...'

When I next become aware of what I am doing, I have Orridge pinned to the floor by the neck, his bloody face already struck by my hand. Tamla and Christopherson are attached to each of my shoulders in a belated effort to restrain me, and slowly I stop trying to strangle him.

'Why?' I ask, loosening my grip to allow him to speak.

With the fatalism of one who feels that the horrors of hell are about to be endured with one other, Orridge croaks, 'We're both fucked, Terry, you and me. Masters isn't going to let you come out of this unhurt either. He hates you as much as you hate him.'

'Why Eileen?'

'Insurance. Of course. Insurance against you making a move against him.'

'She's in the van?'

'Oh yeah.'

'They don't care if they get caught anymore, do they?'

'No. This is all going somewhere really special, Terry.

Somewhere where the likes of you and me have never gone before.'

I let go of Orridge's collar, and I am already at the door when I look back and yell over my shoulder, 'What are you waiting for? Call ahead. Tell anyone who's listening that stopping that van is a priority.'

'What about him...' says Christopherson, pointing to Orridge. 'What do we do with him now?'

'He's coming with us. Aren't you, Max?'

'No fear!'

'Don't be like that, Max m'boy — get him on his feet. We're about to experience the value of real teamwork.'

'Fine, Terry. But just one thing...' says Tamla.

'What?'

'I'm not allowing you anywhere near the steering wheel...'

*

Tamla crashes through the provisional barricade, traffic cones scattering in all directions like skittles struck by a sledgehammer, our speeding car pivoting onto the pavement and back into the street again with a painful scrape. All around us horrified members of the public duck for cover, cowering in doorways and diving behind bins and benches, our howling siren a portent of doom for our prey and careers, unless I have a trophy mounted on my wall by nightfall.

'Shit!' Christopherson cries, defending his head with his elbows and arms in preparation for the crash we have narrowly avoided. 'Careful, Tamla! There are people everywhere.'

It is true that the streets we are careering through are already, if not teeming, then generously lined, with our Majesty's happy subjects, some of whom have decided to film us on their telephones before the main event.

'We're fucked anyway. Makes no odds if we die like this. It'd be better, if anything,' groans Orridge, who seems to be making peace with the new direction his life has taken. 'It'll be easier this way.'

'Tamla?' I am sitting next to her, riding shotgun, the BMW gathering such momentum along the narrow city street that if we knock anything living, it will have transitioned to the next stage of decay by the time the ambulance arrives.

'Terry?'

'Thank you for this.'

'You've got to dream, haven't you? We get there, to that roundabout' — she points directly at the over-runnable chalky lump in the road that we accelerating rapidly towards — 'before Swillcut has cut across town, and we can block his path...'

On cue, we watch a grey Ford Transit hurtle across the mini-roundabout at a speed as lethal as ours.

'Oops, there he goes.'

'Fuck's sake,' through gritted teeth I bark through the two-way radio, 'Grey Ford Transit, moving at high speed over station roundabout, past water gardens to intersection opposite Cathedral Close, to all units, prevent progress of this vehicle.'

'See it coming now,' a voice answers. 'Blocking with bike.'

'Oh no you don't...' shouts Grace over the intercom. 'Consider Balance's request overruled, on the highest authority.'

The car skids to a halt, Orridge, who is unbelted, flies into the windscreen with a crunch as the glass cracks, the rear of the vehicle bucking round so we complete a semi-circle. I notice none of this, as I shout desperately over the radio, 'We're in hot pursuit of known felons. What's got into you, sir?'

'Better out than in! I'm saving this city from humiliation...' his voice crackles. 'I'm not having you and the filthy crew you're chasing jamming the works with the Queen arriving in only a matter of minutes! Take it outside the city limits and deal with it yourself, but not right here, not now. Over and out.'

My passenger door is pulled open and an unfriendly non-uniformed face asks, 'Could you please get out, showing me your hands first?'

Orridge slumps back, exhaling, and is pulled out of the rear door along with Christopherson, Tamla already staggering ahead of us with her hands above her head.

'Okay, put them down, you're not prisoners of war,' says another voice. 'Please try and be as normal as possible, if that is possible. You're attracting attention.'

Our car has been catapulted beyond the roundabout, into the advertising hoardings, and we are now being led through the very corridor the Queen is due to proceed down, escorted by half a dozen worried-looking plainclothesmen, who I assume are her personal bodyguards.

'What are you bringing them up here for? This is the station!' cries an agitated ham-faced figure in a Barbour jacket, blocking our path. 'She's just getting off the train now! Take them somewhere else, for Christ's sake! At the bloody double!'

Belatedly, I notice that either side of us crowds of expectant faces, plastic Union Jacks at the ready, are eyeing us with a mixture of disappointment, confusion and growing worry, our wobbling crash-shocked frames not what they left the house to come and see this morning.

'Look at that man, Mum,' says a boy pointing at Orridge. 'He looks like he's been in a fight.'

'All of you, get down on your knees, right away!' The man in the Barbour jacket screams suddenly, 'she's coming through now, on your knees, double time!'

'Are you mad?' I say. 'We're police officers!'

'I don't give a toss if you're SAS. Do as you're told and hit the deck, and empty your pockets, quickly, on the street in front of you. Do as I say!'

Unfriendly hands force us down, and we lay out our offerings in front of us: keys, chewing gum, a battered wallet — pavement tributes to Her Majesty as a roar goes up, and an old lady crosses the street directly in front of us, looking down with some concern as she is not used to seeing her subjects in so craven a posture, not since the Middle Ages, the local paper snapping our sheepish and agitated faces for posterity, loyalty to the Crown a matter of record as I wait for the relief of sweet submission, only to encounter deeper reserves of defiance instead.

I stand up, ignoring the grumbles of the plainclothes handlers who, I realise, are not going to shoot me or send us to the Tower for this crass indiscretion.

'Fuck this for a game of soldiers,' I tell Tamla, who is also on her feet, pulling down the torn hem of her skirt. 'We need to find another car.'

'You clowns are for the bullet!' roars the red-faced handler. 'Never in all my years with the Royals have I witnessed anything so reckless. You're meant to be police officers! Trust me, I wouldn't want to be in your strides.'

'Or I in yours,' I reply. 'Apologies for ruining the moment and all that. Here, something for the corgis,' I point at the half-eaten bacon roll Orridge has removed from his pocket and left on the curb. 'While you're here with that intercom, tell them we need another car please, one of the fast ones.'

Amazingly, having glared at me for an appropriate amount of time, the royal handler does as I ask and repeats my request into his mouthpiece, the crowd's attention having moved to Orridge. Our colleague in crime prevention has hauled himself up, using Christopherson as a pivot, before stumbling sideways and collapsing swan-like in the middle of the road — from his injuries or from the thrill of it all, it is hard to tell.

'Rule Britannia!' Tamla smiles, flashing a V for victory sign at the apoplectic handler. Brazenly, she hands me Orridge's chewed and turd-like Cohiba Panetela that he was brandishing earlier. 'Don't worry — I don't want you to light it. Just guess what this smells like?'

I hold it under my nose and inhale. It is not strong, yet there it is: traces of the sulphurous reek of *High John the Conqueror*. 'If he had puffed it to the juicy bit,' she adds, 'it would have been his cyanide capsule.'

'So he was ready to make the supreme sacrifice?'

'Not at all. The box these were in was sent to the trailer this morning as a personal gift to Max from an unknown admirer. Max thought they were a gift for a job well done.'

'He give one to anyone else?'

'No, the triumph was his alone.'

'Look lively!' shouts the handler, tearing off his headset with perplexed irritation. 'Clearly somebody up there likes you — I have no idea why. This isn't over yet, not by a long shot, and we will have plenty to talk about later but...'

'But?'

'There's the car you wanted. Now fuck off.'

CHAPTER TWELVE

PORNOGRAPHY

In the end it is easy; we follow the milk float in through the gates. There are just the two of us in the car — Orridge stretchered off to hospital with 'shock and concussion'; Christopherson remaining behind to explain what is happening to an incredulous Grace, who, when it came down to it, decided a kidnapping in progress required a response after all, albeit a more modest one than the fanfare accompanying the Queen to the Cathedral Close.

'That wasn't so hard.'

'Still early days.'

The back seat of our department's only Lotus Evora, our consolation prize for being right, is loaded with a brand of pepper spray Marines shower in each other's faces for laughs, and a pair of Taser Pulses: souped-up hairdryers that could barely check the trajectory of a dangerous dog. The prospect of coming up against firearms, having scaled the great wall, is daunting, yet solving the first problem by simply following the dairyman in, as even a monster like Masters likes his tea with milk, means we now only have the weapons to worry about.

'I've seen more backup assigned to lifting a drunk off a bench.' Tamla squeezes the steering wheel. 'I mean, we're in a hostage situation, one-two-three — multiple ones at the very least.'

'They have their priorities clearly mapped out today.'

'Evidently. But the Queen... it's not just her is it?'

'How do you mean?' I ask.

'You know, she's not the only reason we find ourselves out here by ourselves is she? Her being here doesn't do any harm as excuses go — it's a great one. But it isn't just *her*... She's not the only reason we find ourselves flying solo.'

'There may be something else.'

'Ha! You know it. No one else really knows what's going on, do they? That's why we're here on our own. Why they elected for speed and stealth and not numbers. Grace is playing both ends with us. His superiors, and their superiors, they don't want anyone else to know about any of this — no more than they can help anyway. I'm not saying they don't want this fixed — of course they do — but they'd be happy to be spared the grizzly details.'

'And for the press and the public to be spared them too.'

'Exactly. Which makes me wonder whether there's a cover up already in the offing?'

'They've checked Eileen's house — she's not there — they can't cover that up...'

'No, I mean once this is over, covering up the *whole* thing. All of it, from the first mispers to right now. Everything and all of it.'

'You can see why they would. No one comes out of it looking good... though we end up looking a bit better than everyone else.'

'A bit better than everyone else? Come on, Terry. Give us our due, for fuck's sake! We're crusading heroes compared to everyone else!'

'If we're heroes, we're the kind of heroes that make the jokers who claim to be heroes look like cunts. I can't see them lining up to give us medals for showing them up for what they are — not when the alternative is pretending there was no case to solve in the first place.'

'Well, they'd better reward us well for our silence then. A nice big cover-up like this one will have to be massive. As key players, they need us to keep mum. It's definitional. We're worth our weight in treasure to them. I'm through with this shithole, Terry. I want my own modern pad overlooking Canada Water and a nice fat promotion.' Tamla's voice is trembling slightly.

'Let's get through today first...' I say.

'Oh, for God's sake. You're hopeless. Bring it on, I say, the confidentiality agreements, the offshore bank accounts, that pointy little witch's hat the commissioner wears... that's just the right shape for my head....'

We overtake the float and rev up the drive, the choke of the Lotus's engine and scraping of its wheels over the gravel, generating the effect of a mechanical charge. Packs of frightened young deer stare curiously at the sports car that has interrupted breakfast, accelerating out of the lingering mist like a noisy midget stacking plates in the middle of their meal.

'I'm thinking that getting us here might even be the point. If you set a trap this obvious, you can't be all that bothered about getting out of it yourself...' I say.

'He's been so careful about deflection so far... I agree it's weird.'

'Not if this is what he's been building up to all this time — a grand finale featuring his favourite drug of choice... and least favourite policeman. It's why Grace has got it arse about tit. He seems to think we're going to interrupt Masters taking tea with the vicar, all Kipling cakes and cucumber sandwiches, with us looking like the insane conspiracy theorists. But I don't believe Masters wants to rejoin the community and pretend that nothing has happened; I think he wants to leave it for good.'

'It would explain why the van headed here in plain sight....'

'For sure. He's decided to go big or not at all. Look, it's there.'

We pull into the forecourt where the Ford is tidily parked next to the usual motor-show pieces. Cutting the engine, we stop the car in front of the giant doors and turn to face each other. Tamla takes my hand. 'You're going to have plenty to write about now.'

'Why do you say that?'

'You told me you always wanted to be a writer. Talking isn't the same as writing. You're all in here — that's where your writing is.' She taps the side of my head and brushes my hair gently. 'Too far in for you to be able to reach it. But now you're going to have material to die for, Terry.'

'Material isn't my problem... it's more that—'

'Okay, Terry. Whatever!'

She smiles with brazen impatience and slaps me affectionately on the leg.

'Just trying to give you a vote of confidence. Don't overcomplicate things!'

Quickly we get out of the car, Tamla cramming the Tasers and sprays into a large Swindon Literary Festival tote bag she has found by her feet, and I gripping the T-baton that will have to pass for a lance if we are to stand a chance against Masters' dragons.

'When we see Eileen Pertwee next, please be cool, Terry...' Tamla checks to see if I have understood, and I nod. Without Eileen my existence will be unendurable, and I have no interest in still being alive tonight if she is not. My partner knows this. 'It'll be okay, but they're using her to fuck with you, so don't make it any easier for them.'

'I know,' I admit, overcome by the strength of my feeling and the accompanying vulnerability.

'It would have to be this quiet,' says Tamla, thoughtfully changing the subject.

Although we have given pursuit, we both sense that it is us who have been chased here by those we followed. The details I recognise in the forecourt seem to belong to a past more distant than the beginning of the week, when I first laid eyes on this worm's lair. An implosion of déjà vu, the auto-fateful variant, grips me, and memories of falling and being pursued seem less like the terrors of early childhood than traces of past lives and earlier existences; my certainty of dying in a dream the parting gift of the life before this. For a sickening instant I know these formative nightmares will come true today. There will be no rubbing of my eyes under a duvet with the reassurance that none of this happened. I have unwittingly met one of my life's goals: to live in the glorious finality of real time. The second passes, but the dark conviction that I can now count my life out in minutes remains.

'Hurry up, Terry, and give me a leg up. I think we're going to have to try and force a window.'

'They'll take some forcing.'

'There's no point knocking on the door asking if he is in is there?'

'Stop. We don't need to worry… look.'

The doors are once again drawing open, and in the finest traditions of the old West, Swillcut strides out before us, a porkpie hat atop his head. He is chewing a matchstick and brandishing a Russian Saiga-12 shotgun, powerful enough to shoot straight through a line of roe. Without weapons of equivalent lethality, Tamla and I are helpless spectators unless we can push him further than he thinks he can us.

'This far and no further, gents,' he says out of the side of his mouth, more solicitously than his commanding position warrants. 'You've got off one stop too far, methinks.'

'I could say the same for you, Swilly,' I reply wondering what it will take for him to pull the trigger.

'That's a matter of opinion, Inspector,' he replies, and from behind him, having waited there in single file, step out two burly young men, one of whom looks like he has been crying, the other with a swollen face, so that the three of them now form a line in front of the door blocking our path. The first of his adjacents carries an old side by side 12 bore gauge, the other a samurai sword, probably lifted from Masters' collection. Neither appears intent on forcing the issue too quickly, but nor, judging by their stance, will they get out of the way by our simply asking them nicely.

'I hate pigs,' the one with the enflamed face hisses, the utterance rendered slightly pathetic by his faux-Chicago delivery.

'Are you sure you want to kill anyone today?' asks Tamla, stepping up to the lad. Surprisingly, he actually stumbles back and, while pointing the gun defensively at her, does not seem inclined to use it without greater provocation. 'I warned you,' he says, this time in the rolling vernacular of the region, 'I hate pigs!'

'Oh, I am so warned!'

'What should I do?' he calls stupidly to Swillcut, who has retained nothing of the charm of that first meeting in his shop.

'What you asking me for?' his uncle replies. 'Consult your common fucking sense.'

'What *should* you do?' Tamla repeats, smiling. 'It's the question of the day really...'

'Use the butt on the bitch!' Swillcut advises sharply.

'Go on then. I'll put you down.' I point the T-baton at him, pretending that it is a Glock so that there is a greater chance that he might believe it. 'The week I've had, I'm looking for the least excuse.'

'He means it! He's going to shoot!' shouts the lad, throwing his hands out to prevent any flying bullets from reaching him, and so dropping his rifle. 'This wasn't my idea! Okay?'

Tamla calmly picks the gun off the floor and glancing at Swillcut, who is still glaring at me, checks to see if the safety catch is on. Finding that it is, she thumbs it off.

'Easy now,' says Swillcut. 'We're not mucking around with toys here.'

Pulling the gun up so it is resting on her shoulder, then taking careful aim, Tamla shoots Swillcut in the foot. He merely looks surprised, and bends down to check what has happened. Before he has had a chance to register the damage done to the limb, Tamla drives the heavy shoulder of the gun into his nephew's hip, sending him keeling over in agony, and from her position above him, to the youth's surprise, shoots him straight through the arm at near-point-blank range with the second round.

'Tut-tut. Raising loaded weapons at officers with menaces and lethal intent. Most unwise. Really, what did you boys expect?'

Both men are now making a lot of noise, writhing about on the floor ineffectually, leaving the lad with the katana, whose blade is almost resting on my nose, albeit rather hesitantly, as the only threat still standing.

'This is harder than you think.' I tell him. 'Isn't it?'

The question is rhetorical but he seems to consider it. Scrutinising me, then inspecting Tamla, before glancing back at me again, the young man lets go of the sword and, barging past us, charges into the courtyard without looking back.

Tamla takes Swillcut's gun off the floor and, checking that it is loaded, says, 'After you.'

'You can't leave us to die,' Swillcut screams as I accidentally catch his chest with my foot on my way through the front door.

'You'll make it,' I reply. 'Here...' I kick his porkpie hat to him. 'Use this to stem the bleeding.'

Inside the house the decor is not as exact or curated as I remember it from my first visit. In fact, it seems as though a team of light-fingered vandals have had the run of the place — the furniture pressed against the walls and piled in corners so that a smooth passage has been cleared between the entrance and many intervening rooms, pantry and kitchen that lie between it and the enormous back doors that open onto the rest of the estate. Elsewhere, ornaments have been pulled off tables, fittings tugged off sockets, drawers left open, candles and effigies strewn across the floor, and paintings turned back to front on walls.

'The mob have stormed the palace. That looks about the

right way to me.' I point to the perfect through-view, leading to the conservatory and the gardens beyond. 'Whatever is going on, is going out there.'

'You anticipating the arrival of more trouble?'

'Not that lot...' I point at two young men in their underwear, potential mispers who have narrowly avoided their date with *High John,* or yet to partake of the herb, bolting up the main staircase.

'That was right out of the John Rambo playbook back there. I knew you had it in you... still...'

'You saw the odds.'

I catch my foot against something sharp and nearly slip. 'Fuck... there's shit on the floor, careful...'

'What is it?'

'A *beak* I think.'

'Beak?'

'They're stuffed birds. Somebody has smashed the cases and played football with the lot...'

'I'm glad that one was dead before *that* happened to it.'

Tamla nudges a tawny owl out of the way, with a small dildo stuck out of the back of its head, and I step over the torn remnants of a murder of crows. There are shards of broken records and crumpled inlay sleeves mixed in with the avian debris. The giant hi-fi has been dragged into the hall and toppled, along with the floor-standing speakers, which lie in pieces like a broken roadblock.

'It must have been quite a party.'

'I don't like it; it's got that last-days-of-Ancient-Rome vibe.'

'Come again?'

'The slave owners get drunk, shag their charges, and then slash their own wrists in the communal baths.'

'Point.'

'Ahhh! That *smell.*'

Although the gate-like entrances at both the front and back of the building are agape, ushering in a wintery chill, the reek along the connecting corridors is as foul as what we have come to expect from *High John the Conqueror*. The usual blend of putrefaction acquiring a new onus, nearer to whatever kind of rich stench plants produce when they make love than to the sweet and meaty aroma of yore. If anything, this is worse than the former pungency, the stench so noxious as to be very nearly edible.

'Yeah, it's been here alright. I'd say they've had a *High John* party, and haven't spared the horses.'

'It stinks like they've used it to supplement the garlic in the cooking. It's coming off everything.'

'Let's pick up the pace, I can't take any more of this without hurling...'

Tamla does not move, her twitching nose mouse-like in the presence of danger.

'What is it?'

'This'll sound mad.'

'Go on.'

'It feels like the stink can see me somehow... there's a mood in it... I can sort of see it myself, like this stinking thing has a face...'

'Stop breathing, Tamla,' I warn her. 'The fumes are probably toxic. That's why. Strong enough to work on us without our even needing to ingest any of the shit. Ignore everything you think of, and try and hold your breath until we're outside. Come on, quickly.'

I struggle with my own advice. These corridors resemble the pointless places I visit in my dreams, their true character tunnels which invisible assailants stalk me through, endlessly and without interruption, until I forget who is chasing who and we start all over again. Words are as dangerous as people now, and I do not stop or speak until I have reached the threshold of the garden and allowed Tamla to catch up, realising that I have sprinted the remaining distance.

'Sorry. I'm anxious about her. I am so anxious about her.' It would be better for me not to think of Eileen until I can actually see her — my hope that her value to them might at least be half as great as hers is to me.

'I'm sorry, Terry. But I can't move any faster in these things,' Tamla pants. 'They still rub.' Her box-fresh chestnut Dr. Martens are covered in droplets of melting ice, having crossed the dividing point where Sebastopol House's stone floor gives way to rye grass, snowdrops and coltsfoot.

'Jesus...'

'I know.'

'I'd do nothing here, just look out all the time... you couldn't get used to it, could you?'

'You can get used to anything...' I begin. 'No, you're right. It's too much.'

Before us is a bifurcated view of breath-taking splendour. Our appreciation neither adds to or completes its achievement: mankind's total dominance over nature, a victory that does not so much improve on whatever God left there as dispel the thought that anything existed at all, before Masters' landscapers got to work. As with all of Masters' accruements, we are invited to react as sun-worshipers, our rapture alienating us from the grandeur, so as to establish the proper power relationship between the guest and owner.

To our left lies Wiltshire: here we take in a scene of sculptured sparsity; pruned copses, a quartet of diametrically squared lakes, attendant grottos, a smattering of giant oaks, mock rolling dales, shady avenues, elegiac glades, fauns, centaurs, a Temple of Apollo on an artificially piled mound, and statuettes of nymphs, fairies and giant toads, so hopelessly mismatched that they destroy the idea of criteria itself, stretching out upon hundreds of acres of silence. To our right, by way of contrast, is Hampshire, and no view at all. Instead there stands a signposted entrance that reads 'The Folly', marking an imposing high-hedged maze, no more than a few feet away from the back doors, its stout walls an entwined and impassable tangle of yew, boxwood, holly and hornbeam. This is too tall to peer over, preventing us from seeing beyond the formidable frontline of the cultivated entanglement, blocking any sense of perspective going forward.

'Do you hear that?'

'I think so... yes,' she says.

From deep within the leafy construction, there are faint notes of music, which with small clouds of smoke, are drifting over the bottle-green labyrinth and harmonising together in the hazy mist.

'It's Minotaur time, isn't it, Terry? This is a crap game for the visiting team.'

'We've got no choice. They got here first.'

'There's two separate paths right from the off. What do we do, stick together or spilt?'

'You serious about splitting? Or just pretending to be brave?'

Tamla curls her bottom lip in a sarcastic imitation of a chastened toddler.

'I thought not. Together's the only advantage we have. And of course — you have the gun.'

Tamla kisses the barrel, and bending down onto a knee, tracker style, runs her hand over the grass. 'The path going out that way, it looks more used to me. Do you see?'

'There's scraping and marks all over the ground where it forks off. People have been shifting gear along here.'

'Yeah, recently. I say we just follow the marks and ignore the other turns. It's all too fresh to hide... maybe this isn't going to turn into the test he's hoping for.'

'I don't think he means this to be a test, only to look like one.'

'You still think he wants us to find him?'

'I do. The rest of this is enough of a challenge to throw off our hardworking colleagues if they had got here instead of us. But you and me? He expects *us* to clear the hurdles. That's what he wants.'

'Careful, Terry. You don't want to go thinking that you and

him have a special relationship or, God forbid, respect each other's abilities — that way the path of true delusion lies.'

'It's not like that. I'm not saying he sees me as his great foil, Holmes to his Moriarty, pitting my wits against...'

'Aren't you?'

'Okay, maybe I am a bit. He's a lonely weirdo, on the lookout for random soulmates he senses a connection with. Even one like me.'

'No offence, but he must be fucking desperate to pick you.'

'That's the point. I present a kind of challenge or threat to him... which is the exciting part for Masters, how he gets his libidinal bang,' I suggest.

'Shhh...' Tamla cups her ear. 'There. We're getting closer, aren't we? You hear that? Sounds like someone is drowning the most unusual cat in the village.'

The music is growing clearer, an odd and discordant collection of noises, nearer animal communication, meowing, cawing and mooing, than humans performing for one another with a view to beguile or entertain. The path has also ceased to split rhizomatically and abruptly turns a corner, joining an avenue that leads straight across to a small portal gateway cut into the hedge.

'This is the way; step inside.'

'After you. He'll be disappointed if he sees me first.'

We break into a clumsy jog, unable to stop ourselves, the equivalent of tearing through a report simply to get to the end, wanting to know what happens last and not next, careless in our haste and urgency. We do not notice the silhouette follow us through the gap and into a centre circle: *The Enforcer* — clad in the fitted special-forces fatigues he wore on his television contests in the jungle, his Excalibur TwinStrike crossbow pointed at our backs.

'Oh shit. What is this?'

'I don't know...'

The pantomime in progress is enough to floor any hope of a tidy or simple resolution to this puzzle. With whatever is the opposite of synchronicity, events conforming to my foe's will and not my own, the first person I lay eyes on is the author of the dark charade, and not the woman I have rushed headlong into danger to 'rescue'.

'Believe your eyes, Terry. I see him too.'

Masters is dressed as a Roman centurion, replete in a bronze breastplate, leg armour and hobnailed caligae sandals, his Praetorian helmet weighed down ridiculously by a taxidermied trumpeter swan strapped to the plume. Beside him, two seniors I recognise as ageing disc jockeys are clad similarly, gladius swords resting ominously in their scabbards. Both are swaying incense thuribles, alternatively singing incantations and chanting, a stork tied to the head of one, floppy and loose, evidently a fresh kill, and a bolt-upright bustard glued to the other's crest, the weight of the bird forcing him to crook his neck dementedly. Although some ritual is evidently underway, there is a rushed and improvised feel to proceedings — a pile of shiny tracksuits lying in an untidy heap by a restaurant trolley laden with bronze bowls and goblets.

'Please tell me this is a wind up...' whispers Tamla.

'No, it's something worse than that. It is real.'

The three classicists are far from the only eccentrically clad actors visible to us, and possibly not even the pick of the crop.

'My, oh my. All our Halloweens have come at once... I feel like I've stepped in dogshit,' mutters Tamla. 'I'm spoilt for choice. Where do I point the gun?'

'I'd need weeks to work that one out.'

'What the actual fuck are they doing over there?'

Overseeing ceremonies at the centre of a small stone circle — a collection of misshapen rocks and menhirs that could be taken for a Pagan temple, at a stretch — Masters points heavenwards and shouts something in a dead language, provoking a subdued cheer from his audience. Some of the flanker stones have been laid on their side and are serving as benches, which a few shivering masked individuals have gathered on. These are mispers, huddled together unenthusiastically with only swimwear, panties and loincloths for warmth; their faces hidden by surgical masks, executioner's hoods and bandages, turquoise ink covering their exposed limbs. Whether they have been held here for weeks or gathered in an overnight swoop is unclear, but any initiative or resistance seems to have absented itself from their pusillanimous mood and passive demeanour. One of them could be Iggy, the boy who inspired this great search, or none of them could be. If any of us are still here in an hour, I might ask.

'Look, over there,' says Tamla.

At the centre of the megalithic ring is what I presume to be a sacrificial stone: a thin totemic plinth painted in green and purple stripes — the same eyes and tongue that I saw in the painting in Masters' ballroom, leering over the pattern. Resting on the stone, which leans at a slight tilt, is a naked woman, tightly wrapped from head to toe in blood-red muslin cloth, bound by weeds and gorse. She is absolutely still and at the very least drugged. Only the outline of her breasts and knees protrude against the covering, and I recognise them at once as Eileen's. I am too frightened for her to feel any of my own fear now, the danger she is in rendering me calm and implacable.

'I see her too,' says Tamla, adding, 'It may be too late.'

'Don't say that. Please.'

'I know. Sorry, Terry. What about them?'

'They're probably harmless. Hopefully.'

Stood at the edge of the circle are a motley collection of near-pensionable musicians, of varying types and tendencies, swaying out of time to music that they barely appear aware of playing. A hairy, wild, ancient festival-fodder from the days of crust stares angrily at a coronet that his withered dreads keep getting in the way of, as the other part of the brass section, bank manager-like in a suit and bow tie, wrestles with his saxophone, slobbering haplessly over its mouthpiece. Neither they nor their bandmates seem excited to be here, or surprised to see us. Despite our gatecrashing proceedings, the small group grimly persevere with their diabolic improvisation, a triangle and harp clanging purposelessly, an electric bassist with a generator grinding out a few death-metal notes, and a lifeless bongo player, a beat or two behind the rest of the passionless cacophony, following from the rear. A few sport token efforts at fancy dress: bonnets, capes, a strap-on plague doctor beak, and a hockey mask, but also walking boots, Birkenstocks and Karrimor anoraks, which betray their sensible daily existences. The bassist misses a chord and, rubbing his ears, pulls up the battered hood of his monk's habit. At which point the performance clicks, and I know who we are watching.

'Acid Horse!' I say to Tamla.

'What?'

'Acid Horse: Masters' old band. They experimented with *High John* back in the day. He was their manager. I don't know what they're doing here, but that's who they are.'

Conducting the orchestra of the half-willing with one hand, and also blowing rather half-heartedly into a flute, is Fallgrief, clothed ludicrously in puttees and a hooded Panama hat, carrying a Smith and Wesson weighted barrel, which he is using as a baton. Gamely, he issues shouts of encouragement at the melee, glancing nervously at us and grinning awkwardly, as if to suggest that none of this is really his idea — which it might not be. Towards the back of the circle, stroking the foot of a large statue that I presume is of *High John*, is our old friend Fluffy. 'Sorry,' she shouts defensively, 'I had no choice. I needed to meet him again! I love him more than you. I love him more than anyone!'

High John, if that is who we are facing, is a dishevelled specimen of monsterhood: an arts and crafts yeti built out of bark, with a bracken mohican, conkers for eyes, and cones and twigs hanging off his chest like a neglected outdoor toy at a garden centre. I am sure that in motion, dosed up to the eyeballs, the effect of his advance would be menacing, but stood here in his own version of the Burning Man festival, the effigy displays a tackiness I associate with all religions: their plastic saints, garish stained windows and many-limbed deities — concepts better imagined than observed.

'W-h-a-t a joke.'

'Careful, he might hear you...'

'I don't care if the muppet does.'

For the first time since last night, I smile; yet whether it is the wind moving his eyes, or my exhaustion taking pictures of my unconscious and projecting them outwards, I see *High John* watch me and take my measure. And I know something then of what it is for this mossy incubus to be the last thing a true believer sees in life.

'All of you...' I try to shout, but my voice is hoarse and strained, barely carrying over the din, and Tamla looks at me to signify that if I have no chance, nor will she. Our effort to interrupt proceedings has had one effect on the audience, though. Another attendant has decided we have come far enough. Approaching us in plus-fours and the smock of a New Forest snake catcher, as indignantly as if we had sabotaged a carefully prepared shoot, is Masters' gamekeeper, foaming at the mouth and carrying a large net that he appears to view us as the right fit for.

'You better not be scaring no pheasants!' he yells. 'Better not have no dogs with you neither!'

'I've had enough of this...' says Tamla.

'Try and give him the benefit of the doubt.'

'I know you gypsies! Better not be scaring no birds with those dogs!'

'Can't afford to give him a chance, Terry.'

Tamla's shot hits him in the groin, the buckshot spreading randomly, as she is no longer taking careful aim. The man squirms as if impaled on the cathedral spire, his thrashing legs and the net brought together in a flailing human web, worthy of a gladiator's final moments in the Colosseum. That stops the music. Slowly, Masters ceases to swoosh his arms in giant figures of eight and allows them to fall anticlimactically to his sides. With impatient scorn, he surveys us, and seemingly deep from within a haze of pain, cries, 'You arrive at last! Yet persist in defiling what is holy, and treating us, *his* children' — he points to the sod-work sculpture of *High John*, which at least is no longer staring into my soul — 'as outcasts! Who, like women of the night, are liable to vanish before they expire!'

'Jesus, Terry. I'll never accuse you of exaggeration again.'

'This is nothing.'

I scan the crowd, and in spite of the numbers present, and array of dangerous weapons assembled, there is a susceptibility to extinction about those present. No one appears ready to join the gamekeeper for a spot of instant martyrdom. Summoning my voice, so as to be heard above the injured man's cries, I yell, 'Let's start by letting anyone who wants to leave, leave.'

Masters lifts his head heavenwards in search of divine confirmation of our imbecility.

'You understand nothing,' he snorts loudly. 'You are a natural conservative, Inspector, with rebellious tendencies. I offer you the chance to become a true revolutionary, to embrace the only reconfiguration that counts!'

Tamla lifts the gun straight at him. 'A lot of people have been hurt already. Don't let any more be.'

'Or face more violence at your hands, *Agent Starling*? Is that your answer to everything, you police? To maim, belittle, harm and destroy? What indelicate creatures you are. Small wonder you have as little reason to remain in the world as I have!'

'Don't be a bigger dick than you are,' warns Tamla. 'I've never shot anyone in my life before this morning, but that's three in the last five minutes.'

Waving her intervention away with a contemptuous flick of his hand, Masters calls over to me, 'I'm not little people that can die a statistical death. I am happy to take a chance on this tiny woman's temper. There are certain things you need to learn before you can judge me, before anyone can judge me.'

I begin to move towards him, my hands feigned reasonably in front of me. 'Of course we can't shoot you,' I say, and then to the ensemble who are gazing herd-like and open mouthed at us, 'He's right: he's too important to shoot. But you? You good people aren't even worth shooting, so far as he is concerned. Don't worry. That doesn't mean we are going to kill you, only that he doesn't care if we do.' This elicits a round of concerned murmurs. 'So please sit yourselves down, and keep out of harm's way, while I and... the Hip Priest here, drink a long draft and sort this mess out between us...'

Masters sneers at me but cannot resist the prospect of public debate, even in front of a crowd like this, who, having flopped to the floor as I advised, are beginning to stare wondrously at their hands and hide behind them giggling like children.

'You may not credit it, Inspector, few do, but something nice happened to me long ago, a happiness that I could trust, that remained after the moment's passing.'

'That sounds very pleasant. For you.'

'Don't humour me, man. You owe me more than that. Don't you wonder about the true character of what you have been so inexpertly groping towards?'

'Of course, all the time.'

'Perhaps if your capacity to learn was equal to your dispensation to mock you would already be stood here beside me, instead of being a hitman for the bumpkin flying squad. You must realise' — Masters removes a lump of *High John* from his toga belt — 'that once we would have had to endure almost another hundred years of frustration for this opportunity to come again, yet now, thanks to Mother Nature's daily savaging by our species, I only had forty years to wait before the glorious rebirth of *High John the Conqueror*! You see, the planet *had* to yield its gift before it was too late for it to do so... before there is no planet *left* for anything to grow from. Hence the shorter cycle... biological self-defence, Inspector, the planet doing what she needs to do to survive. She could not afford to sleep another hundred years for this' — he lifts the generous sample of *High John* in the air provoking an awe like sigh from the crowd, and then, alarmingly in light of what we know of it, triumphantly drops it into his mouth and swallows — 'to grow again!' He chokes, pounding his paw in the air.

'I hear the news from the polar caps isn't encouraging. Maybe you'll have even less time to wait for your next crop.'

'Of course, Inspector,' he coughs. 'At last you begin to see... I scoured the Earth for forty years searching for new growths, risking my life on every toadstool and spore I found, but thanks to our onslaught against the environment, mankind's that is, it will soon be only a matter of a decade to wait before it grows again, then five years, then an annual harvest! The plant must keep apace of our attempts to destroy its natural habitat, to grow faster than we can destroy the conditions it requires to exist. Soon it will appear in our cities, between the cracks in the pavement, in the walls of our houses, becoming ever more lethal, and ever more *irresistible* to a species that seeks consolation in mind-altering substances! *High John the Conqueror* is nature's answer to us, her way of saying enough is enough. Surely you must see that by now?' Masters loosens the strap on his helmet and, with a turn of his head, allows it to slide off onto the grass. His chanting centurions appear to have other things on their minds than our conversation, one now cowering warily under the shadow of a passing cloud, the other licking his lips hungrily as he stuffs a handful of daisies into his mouth.

Masters laughs at them benignly, and wiping the druggy crumbs off his lips with his fingers, sucks at them.

'You say the planet is *protecting* itself by producing this... drug plant.' I take another step closer to Masters, Eileen as motionless as the surrounding slate. 'Is that because it sees us humans as dangerous, something that needs to be wiped out in a zero-sum game with nature?'

Masters nods eagerly.

'If that's the plan, then why doesn't nature just send an earthquake and a couple of giant tsunamis instead of an *Alice in Wonderland* trip?'

'Because it is us that has forced the issue, Inspector! The planet is forgiving and would rather still give us a chance. *High John* is that chance, though be under no illusions, humanity will fail the test, just as surely as it has every other opportunity for its salvation! Your cynicism is not lazy; it is hard-earned. Surely you must agree?'

'Humans are adaptable. I'd never bet against them. And I thought *High John* is supposed to be a source of knowledge for us, not our enemy?'

'Knowledge for a few chosen individuals, yes, but no longer for us as a species. Unfortunately, you are at least forty years out of date on that particular hope! Of course, we were once able to exist as its neighbours. Then, back then, it was our friend.' Masters wipes the phlegm from his mouth, fighting down his rising excitement. 'But what was once an aphrodisiac, a sensual intervention, a political vision or whatever nature required its most intelligent life forms to see and to be, has now become a path to lead us out of the world itself...'

'The shit has got stronger, you mean...'

'Oh yes,' guffaws Masters, his stomach shaking with maniacal joy. 'The shit has got stronger all right, man! The crop has metastasised. It used to want us to dance with it; now it wills us to disappear, to vanish, to be gone. Because we, Inspector, we have become the problem.'

'I know the formulation, man's the disease and all that.'

'What, and you honestly don't agree?'

'No. We're not perfect, but nothing is,' I reply.

'You are absurd!' He genuinely looks worried for me.

'Green misanthropy doesn't appeal. I like people.'

'This species? You cannot be serious. We're a cancer!'

'Easy now, this is looking bad enough without adding genocide to the charge sheet.'

'Ha!'

I am now within striking distance of Masters' throat, but, sensing danger, he inches back, without interrupting his flow. 'Nature, she is most munificent, Inspector. We may harm her and torture her cycles in the most gruesome ways, but at least she allows us a glimpse of enlightenment first: to be at one with somewhere happier and more complete than the cave we dwell in. She reveals the objects that cast the shadows on the walls — our first actual sight of reality, Inspector. Answers at last! *High John* is her gift to those of us who have not given up on her truths.'

'Are you talking about the stuff that grows in the ground or the beast behind you in the nightmares?'

'They are two parts of the same sentence, different descriptions of an identical entity. He is our dark enlightenment, nature's *instrument,* the one that effects the dimensional switch, the guardian and living embodiment of the crop, both her effect and her policeman! Yes, I thought you'd like that, Inspector! A copper — just like you!' Masters indicates to the statue, and bows his head with deference.

'Through him I was able to see past all this dredge,' he continues, 'into an existence more beautiful and true than these passing shapes and impressions... he is the chosen means that nature uses to communicate with us, that protects her secrets from exposure. Who kept me company in all those years of waiting, of living in the present by default to insulate myself against the pain of that moment having passed...' his voice stutters, and I feel a passing pity for Masters — his friendless evenings, the children who never taught him to love, a wife that did not miss him, his only comfort the insanity that was responsible for all this loss, on the promise that one day he would be so out of his mind he would not even notice it, and confuse it for redemption.

'"The stuff that grows in the ground",' he continues, 'as you indelicately put it, is what "the monster" is made of, Inspector — his flesh made real! So join *us*...'

'Us?'

'Oh yes, *us*! You didn't think I would really rely on my powers of eloquence alone to entice you to enlist? I honour this woman to become a creature of eternity again, and enter the Now-Nowever...' He clasps his hand on Eileen's shoulder, rocks her a little and pinches her skin. She remains motionless and I experience a sickening mix of jealousy and helplessness: Masters is close enough to touch her; I cannot. And for this alone I hate him. I thought my life was simple before, but it is even simpler now; the only thing I care about is saving Eileen.

'I honour her with this invitation to come with me and know more than God, and I could honour you too... Inspector. You too could feel the triumph of *High John*'s eruption in you. But you will have to hurry. I first ingested of his fruit at dawn, your female companion partook over an hour ago, you have a lot of catching up to do my friend!'

'Don't you dare!' shouts Tamla at Fallgrief, who has leopard crawled up to me while I have been trying to flank Masters, with a feral stealth worthy of his public school's Combined Cadet Force training.

Looking rather embarrassed, Fallgrief offers the pistol he was carrying, the wrong way round, to Tamla, who motions him to drop it. Through chattering teeth, he apologises, 'Can't blame a cove for trying. Can't—' He abandons the sentence, a presentment of the psychedelic abyss opening before him. 'God... I don't remember it being this... *much*.'

'You should know your limits,' says Tamla.

Controlling my desire to lunge wildly at Masters' leering face, I ask, 'Why give me the honour of accompanying you on your journey? I'm an insignificance and an irritation.'

'Stop fishing for praise, you tart! We lack the same belief, you and I: the ultimate faith that this is all there is. I have intervened once to show you were right. Now your superiors will know that you were the genius who saw it all, and they the craven fools that could not. Isn't that what you wanted all along? Admit it! There's no shame! None of us are without our egos, Inspector. So come for the rest. I promise you once you have, you will not care who or what you are anymore; you will only have eyes for *forever*.'

A player in the band kicks back into life, making a burping noise on a gong that transmogrifies into a submediant fart. I hear Tamla hiss behind me, 'He'll be heading off into space next... Be easiest if I give him the next barrel, Terry.'

'He's unarmed and there are witnesses, Tamla,' I explain.

'Enough,' Masters says. 'Their debt has been repaid.' He waves at the musicians and, drawing closer to me while still blocking my path to Eileen, winks and adds quietly, 'They, and these other "experiments" that I took under my confidence, have drunk of a soup of mushrooms. Others have been given just the tiniest touches of the real stuff. They won't know the difference. To start with, they will believe that they too are on the journey of *High John*, but they will not be going anywhere but here. They have what they need, not what they want, and they are lucky to even get that.'

Two Acid Horse veterans have begun to slap each other in the face. A centurion is lying on his front, sicking up over the sandalled toes of his companion; several mispers have risen and are wandering round the stones, whispering to themselves mysteriously, as others jump out from behind them to surprise their friends. Everyone is out of their minds.

'Imbeciles,' mutters Masters. 'A perfect microcosm for the entire species.'

'Can you tell me how I can get home?' one girl calls to Tamla.

'Maybe we should all put down our weapons to talk about this properly,' suggests Fallgrief helpfully, striking his fist into his hand, 'Jaw jaw, not war war.'

'I don't want to hurry you, Terry, but I don't like how this is developing,' Tamla says. 'It's unravelling, and this gun is getting kind of heavy.'

'Why involve them all in the first place?' I ask Masters, edging closer again to the stone Eileen is propped against, to try and lever between them.

'Because *he* needs food,' says Masters, 'and I need the collaborators to help me provide him with food.'

'The mispers were *food* then? I don't get it.'

'Naivety does not suit you, Inspector,' smiles Masters. 'No one is fooling anyone else here. I have no need to recount the gory details. These useful idiots here had to be strung along with the promise of what I genuinely offer you... the others, the "mispers"; well, this is not costless. For every soul that crosses over there is another that needs to be taken by him,' — he points to the statue again —'eaten and replanted.'

'But you were the one who took them; they weren't eaten by any monster. You gave them the drug, by force or by lies. It's on you, not the New Forest Godzilla, Masters.'

'More mockery!'

'Your monster — if I credit it with an existence of its own — it didn't bring these kids to your parties, feed them full of the drug and then watch them vanish into thin air as part of some mystical experience you think you could benefit from.'

Masters lifts his finger to my face. 'Oh, I gave them access to the "drug", as you call it. I do not deny it. Why should I? But this is history without context! Your victims, the missing persons, they are no more than the carrion of the estates and scum of the shires. The first ones who vanished, they were the trial: guinea pigs for I and my chosen initiates to learn from. I had to see how it would work in practice after all these years. After all, the Sixties were a long time ago, and it is fair to say the effects of *High John* have always been, how best to put it, slightly *uneven*. Without thorough testing, how was I to ensure and determine what were safe levels to experiment with? The amazing thing is that you have focused entirely on these nobodies, the very last thing I had expected law enforcement to do, to tell you the truth! No one seems to have cottoned on to the disappearance of certain higher profile names...'

'What?'

'A Christian light entertainer that has not been seen in

the public eye for over a year, a soap opera actress and an anchor for a popular quiz show that are said to have eloped... a cricketer that went missing before a tour supposedly suffering from depression: all of these were personages who I thought might attract your attention first...' Masters states.

'Right...'

'So in light of those early losses, drafting in expendable replacements was, if you'll pardon the modern crudity, a no-brainer. Using the human waste your colleague Orridge, *Silas*, scooped up for me, I could determine the rough amounts of *High John* that would produce transformation and disappearance, and what quantities would leave the user in a loony bin and, crucially, observe the different effects *High John* would have on different minds, personality types, characters and souls, without worrying about losing names off my shrinking Christmas card list...'

'That's mighty shitty of you,' I interrupt.

'What choice did I have? *High John* is a great discriminator and not all outcomes are the same. An identical dosage can lead one man to madness and another to the silvery Thanatosphere. There are those of us who trust him too little, or are too trivial to accept his challenge, and those that soar. And for the cretins who cannot or will not make his journey and fulfil the true purpose of the plant, there is but one fate. He will come for you and dispatch you himself. They are his food.'

'So that's a full confession then?'

'Please don't blemish this moment with earthly concerns that will soon be of no interest to us! I freely admit that I have administered usage, and introduced the "drug" to the *Untermensch* you care so deeply for, but sadly I cannot take responsibility for those poor specimens that left in one piece and returned home to their former existences. Nor take credit for the way they then spread and disseminated a gift they had no business taking with them, putting *High John* in hands even more careless than their own. Those idiots at the Purple Hearse, for instance. And your Iggy too.'

'What did you do with him?' I ask.

'Nothing. Neither I or my charges came for him or took any of those sad individuals. We eliminated no "evidence". We did not need to. It was he, *High John,* that did that.'

'I see. Back to the monster.'

'Think about this, Inspector. Why, at this stage would I actually lie? I had no need to kidnap or dispose of anyone who lacked the iron will to make the journey over to enlightenment. It would have been a pointless risk to expose myself too, especially as they had all come here willingly and of their own accord, and were certainly too terrified of what they had seen to speak of it.'

'Not to us anyway...'

'Especially not to you, a police force who would have given short thrift to accusations involving their social betters and, wait for it, monsters! I repeat, *High John is* the "drug", Inspector, but also the "monster". The plant that causes you to disappear and the spectral manifestation that comes for you are the same thing: one part works bio-chemically and the other on the imagination. The result is the same whatever way you look at it — you either disappear gloriously at once, or over time and most horribly... but vanish you will.'

'Nature's crime and crime-scene cleaner,' I venture.

'Except that it is no crime. *We,* the human race and its tiresome condition, are the crime!'

The centurions that may have been 'guarding' Eileen have passed out, covered in each other's breakfasts, and the nearest member of Acid Horse is banging his head, methodically and hard, against a menhir, crying softly to himself. I edge another inch forward, tingling with pent-up adrenaline, which is nearly disabling in its intensity. Masters makes no movement back, but instead pulls out a pouch from his belt and dangles it in front of my nose. I am a centimetre and a second away from doing something: part of me thinks I have already done it; part of me cannot imagine doing it all.

'Everything you need is in here!'

'I don't think so.'

'But I do, I do!'

'No...'

'I am he as you are he as you are me, and we are all together!'

I try and lift my hand and cannot. To my horror I realise that he may have been trying to hypnotise me, and that I have entered some kind of trance — my thoughts having switched from saving Eileen to securing the bag of *High John the Conqueror*.

'You've only the last yard to complete! It's perfectly simple, Inspector. What else can *High John* do with those who have only peeked instead of jumped, scratched but not sniffed? The stubborn, the foolish, the hedge-betters and the truly terrified? Those whose brains are too small to proceed to the light? They always warned us that there was never enough room in heaven for everyone, well, they were more right than they knew! All of this is a process of "parabiosis", where the young and ignorant provide blood for the old and wise. Like any good mycelial system, *High John* makes tomorrow's crop out of the rest: either he will destroy you at a chemical and molecular level and remake you as a dimensionally free being, or recycle you as next year's manure, to feed the next growth. Not all lives are as important as others, we know this.'

I shut my eyes and try to break Masters' spell.

'Don't play the hypocrite, Inspector. Your whole life is a half-measure. It took nothing less than becoming a cop to repress who you truly are. Nothing else would have worked. Time to kill the cop. Look at her. That woman is full of the stuff, an immaculate dose no less!' He gestures at Eileen. 'So am I. I am swimming in *him*. It is your time to partake, to be free, join her, join me. What else is left for you but to rise to the level of God?'

'You don't want to join God; you want to be him.' I

understand for the first time in my life what it means to want to die for someone else. The question is whether my sacrifice will have to come too late.

Masters starts to laugh shrilly and offers me his cheek, rapping it with his fist, leaning forward and screaming, 'Peasant! Go on, chin me! See where it will get you! She and I will be in paradise, and you'll be left here with an awful lot of paperwork and explaining to do!'

My punch catches Masters square on the jaw with such force that I feel the lower structure of his face shatter and disintegrate against my fist. For a second I hope I have knocked him out, but he is making a gurgling noise and scratching at the sword in his scabbard, his fingers trying to loosen the buckle. I grab his staggering body and throw it against a rock, ready to swing him back up and catch him with another punch if the first was not enough.

A projectile whips through the air.

Tamla screams.

The crossbow bolt has slashed across her hip and stopped in Fallgrief's back. Another makes the same journey, arriving in the same place. Fallgrief collapses against me gently, whispering quietly into my ear as he slumps to the ground, 'That bloody hurts, old boy. That bloody well hurts!'

Without bothering to reload, *The Enforcer* casts his crossbow across the centre circle and, tearing off his smock to reveal a perfectly toned upper body, shouts at us:

'You have breached the Temple!'

I know what he means without agreeing with him, and I do not have the energy to argue. With extraordinary athleticism, he takes a running jump and launches himself into the air with the intention of falling combatively in our midst. Unfortunately for *The Enforcer*, he misjudges his landing. Tamla kicks both her legs up from her place on the ground and cartwheels him over her into the pointed 'altar' stone, his head bursting open on impact and knocking the entire monolith edgeways.

'My, this takes me back to the old days!' Fluffy calls from the pillar she is wisely taking cover behind, 'I want everyone to know none of this had anything to do with me! I'm only here to get paid! I never hurt anyone... none of this was ever my idea, it couldn't be, I never have any!'

An excited misper rushes up to Masters and splays across him protectively, shielding him from my fists. 'I will save you, Master! Save you from the Babylon.'

Pushing the boy out of the way, I clutch a handful of air. Masters has pulled himself free of the rock and drawn his sword from his scabbard. Stupidly I expect him to try and make an escape, and instead watch him lift the blade to my neck, so that its point is pressing against my flesh. Leaning into it with his weight, my skin pops and blood trickles over the hilt.

'You can't like that?' he drawls in a thin, painful after-voice. 'Can you! The truth is more interesting than a lie. Willpower hedged against nothing... I hoped I might have had a friend in you. Go on, laugh at me...'

Out of the corner of my eye I notice the red muslin wrapping turn, wriggle and tear, ringed fingers and painted arms pulling apart the cloth prison and breaching the vine bonds.

'Save it,' I whisper, the tip of the sword slowly cutting a line up to my cheek. 'You don't always have to have a prayer or song. I advise divine silence. Everything you are is not fit for public consumption.'

'You really have no idea what is out there, have you, Inspector?'

'No more than you. All you know is you want to go. The rest is dreams and supposition.'

Above the twisted mush of his lower jaw, Masters' eyes burn with the grief a son feels for a father who has wasted his life playing a role.

'You are a profoundly silly man, Inspector, but at least you are not petty, I will give you that.'

With a finger flick, the sword briefly leaves my cheek,

arriving again at my earlobe, which Masters slices cleanly off, smattering the shoulder of my suit with blood.

'I can't stand up, Terry,' calls Tamla. 'I've turned my leg, kicking that heavy fucker. It's a fifty-fifty, no one is going to tell tales. Kill the bastard if you can!'

The point of the sword lands again, this time between my eyes, Masters pointing it against my glabella with the consummate skill of a seasoned fencer.

'I don't know whether to give you a last chance or not,' he spits, broken teeth and bloody saliva oozing out of his mouth. 'After all you've done to me, why should I?'

I close my eyes and wait for it. I will not beg.

'Open them, Terry.' Eileen stands perfectly naked before me, Fallgrief's pistol pointed directly at Masters' temple.

'I wonder whether your *High John* works when you're already dead?' She says to him, and lowering the gun into the gap in Masters' armoured pelvic girdle, pulls the trigger.

The shot is sucked into his body with a muffled clap that reverberates off the stones, and Masters drops the sword and hops backwards against the sacrificial slab Eileen had been rested across.

Masters tries to lift one side of his body up to rest his elbow on the stone, but it is already dematerialising before our eyes and his. What remains is pumping out a steady jet of ichor over us both. 'You bitch,' he froths. 'You've made a stat of me... an inescapable fact!'

'Christ!' shouts Tamla. 'You got him just in time, he's... he's going!'

Masters' head rolls off his vanishing torso and watches the rest of his body disappear without it, its eyes wide open, all-fearing, all-knowing and, in seconds, all-dead.

'How much has he given you?' I gasp, drawing Eileen into me so that our faces are pressed together.

'Too much,' she whispers back. 'Enough to disappear a small house, Terry.'

'We can call an ambulance. Pump your stomach. It's not too late...'

Eileen shakes her head and rubs her face into my chest. 'Don't kid yourself.'

'I'm not. We could have you in ICU in half an hour. They deal with overdoses all the time! It's not too late.'

'It is, Terry. We both know it is. I've been given too much. If I don't vanish, I'll be for *High John*. You know what happens next.'

'We don't know if there is any *High John*. It could just be people driving themselves mad. The monster may just be more bullshit...'

'Come on, Terry. We know.'

'No! Get a grip, Eileen! I'm going to get you to Odstock.'

'*Come on*, Terry! I *feel* it. At the top of my soul I feel it, it's *happening* to me. It's *filling* me, and then I am going to overflow... without you.'

We both look down at Masters' discarded bag, lying by our feet, and whether it occurs to me first or not, by the time our eyes meet, we are both thinking the same thing.

From behind us Tamla calls, 'It's too late for her, Terry. Whatever else we don't know about that stuff, we know it works. If she doesn't go now, she'll go badly later. The worst way. Leave her be. It's the kindest thing.'

'No.' If I cannot save Eileen then I will join her.

'There's no other way, Terry.'

'I'm sorry Tamla. I'm going with her.'

'Are you fucking mad?'

'No. I am not.'

'Please, Terry. Please don't be mad! You'll kill yourself!'

Eileen crushes my hand in hers and we breathe together. With embarrassment, I recall the opportunities I wasted, the interested faces I ignored, the intimacies I saw as weaknesses and my failure to realise that I need someone else to complete me and dignify this splintered existence.

'You won't leave me?' Eileen asks.

'Terry, for God's sake, don't be a bigger fool than you are,' Tamla shouts. 'You take that stuff and you're in the lap of the gods! Just think about what you are doing!'

I think about what I am doing: the unrepeatability of every moment, the resolutions I patiently waited for, the relationships that were certain to come, properties not of eternity, but of situated, exact and vanishing instances. There to be enjoyed at the time, or rued evermore. With colossal arrogance, I rejected life's gifts for the unfulfillable promise of future perfection: I was alone once and cannot be again.

'I *am*, Tamla.'

It was this life or the next, and I chose the next. For entirely different reasons, I am now about to again.

'You're not, though! Be sane. Please!'

I pick up the bag and tip the entire contents into my mouth. Dry particles of stalk, gritty heads and seed stick to my throat. Eileen, who has been massaging my neck, hands me a goblet of mushroom juice she has picked up from the stone table, and I swallow the rest of the grit down.

'Careful not to vomit it,' she says. 'It's foul.'

'Terry!'

'I'm sorry, Tamla.'

'Oh Christ, Terry.'

'You know I think you are great Tamla... I've always thought you are great.' I am actually crying, the effect of *High John* of this potency instantaneous. 'Better to be cooked together, than be left on my own. I can't let her go. I'm sorry... I don't want to leave you, Tamla, but I love her too much.'

'You silly sod.'

'There's plenty of this stuff here, you can...'

'No, Terry, I can't. Someone has to stay here and wear all the medals.'

I look back and blow her a kiss. Tamla is as lovely as ever, lying on the grass rubbing a leg, her limbs curled protectively round her like a discarded golden fleece. Elsewhere a misper is trying to fly off the ground on one foot, to escape gravity and the comedown of a journey home. His friends applaud his efforts and attempt lesser voyages of their own, tripping over the corpses of Fallgrief and *The Enforcer* as they stagger into the maze for games of hide and seek. The violinist of Acid Horse has picked up his instrument and is striking it with passionate determination, his bandmates taking to their knees to pay homage to their God, *High John,* who having stepped off his plinth, is roaming about gobbling souls and toppling stones, crowned in a burning plume of fire, the midday sun filling the circle with its entropic energy.

'I wish you luck, Tamla. Please take any credit and leave me with the blame.'

'Have no fear of that, dickhead. Your legacy is fucked with me.'

Eileen's bare arms are draped round my neck. I could tell her everything; I would be equally content in her silent presence. Dad walks out of the maze and asks for a quiet word; the place I am going to is not for him; it is his father's house, and he would rather stay put and mind the garden, but at least he understands why I am the way I am now and nods approvingly at Eileen, the sun growing ever more blinding, a path out of the maze literally burning through the foliage, my steps moving from earth to air to fire, as more of me becomes nothing and my ears fill with the noise of atoms breaking, fizzing and dissolving, the brightening particles of my soul emptying into the breeze, blowing through my being, cleansing me of my attachments and accomplishments; I know the sensation well, I remember it from runs in autumn, fires in winter, falling asleep in summer and waking in spring, it is always with me, it was already here, accessed at strange moments that I quickly forgot about until they came again, and I have never felt so reassured.

'Come on,' says Eileen, pointing. 'We're out there now.'

I gaze up at the sky and see ourselves from above, stood under the extended black arms of Sebastopol House, the three counties joined together again in a single ancient kingdom, gleaming in fiery golden light.

'I'm still your unfinished work...'

'Who are you talking to?'

'If you can hear me, it doesn't matter.'

'I can hear you,' she replies. We lock shoulders.

And then I hold my nerve before heaven and wait.

ACKNOWLEDGMENTS

Thank you to my excellent editor Tom Bromley who suggested I make more use of the first person, to Matteo Mandarini for checking to see whether an early draft of the novel was attached to the rails, to copyeditor James Hunt who sets new standards for thorough scrupulousness, proofreader Josh Turner whom nothing awry gets past, Polly Penrose for her characteristically bold artwork on the cover, Johnny Bull for the design, Jess Wadsworth for sharing her experiences and knowledge of police work, Christiana Spens for her haunting illustrations, Eddie Otchere for taking brilliant photos of an ageing subject, Phoebe Matthews for going through it all one last time, and my wife Emma for bringing me to where the action in the novel is set. Thanks also to my children Lola, Spike and Titus for taking the same amused interest in my professional life as their grandfather did, and to my mother, to whom I owe my keen appreciation of things that go bump in the night.

ALSO BY TARIQ GODDARD

AND AVAILABLE FROM REPEATER BOOKS

**HIGH JOHN
THE CONQUEROR
AUDIOBOOK**

NARRATED BY THE AUTHOR

THE PICTURE
OF CONTENTED
NEW WEALTH
AUDIOBOOK

NARRATED BY THE AUTHOR

"An ingenious take on the gothic novel that forsakes cheap thrills for something far more interesting — a lucid exploration of good and evil and the meaning of faith."

Daily Mail

NATURE
AND NECESSITY

"There's a ferocious energy here that will keep you reading through to the bitter end. Goddard has reinvigorated the country house novel."

The Guardian

A wild reimagining of the nineteenth-century realist novel, a story of siblings battling for survival and supremacy, a war story without armies, and a warning that even the most promising and prosperous of lives can be crushed by the fear of uttering the confession: I love you.

THE REPEATER
BOOK OF HEROISM

"An unashamed celebration of the everyday heroic. Read and be inspired."

Bobby Gillespie

In these personal, provocative essays, the authors behind the uncompromising project that is Repeater Books come together to redefine the idea of the hero for a twenty-first-century public which desperately needs something to believe in.

THE REPEATER
BOOK OF THE OCCULT

"A highly recommended and exquisitely curated collection of occult stories that elevate horror to sublime philosophical contemplation."

E. Elias Merhige

Edited by Tariq Goddard and "horror philosopher" Eugene Thacker, *The Repeater Book of the Occult* is a new anthology of horror stories that explores the ever-shifting boundaries between the natural and supernatural, between the real and the unreal.

REPEATER BOOKS

is dedicated to the creation of a new reality. The landscape of twenty-first-century arts and letters is faded and inert, riven by fashionable cynicism, egotistical self-reference and a nostalgia for the recent past. Repeater intends to add its voice to those movements that wish to enter history and assert control over its currents, gathering together scattered and isolated voices with those who have already called for an escape from Capitalist Realism. Our desire is to publish in every sphere and genre, combining vigorous dissent and a pragmatic willingness to succeed where messianic abstraction and quiescent co-option have stalled: abstention is not an option: we are alive and we don't agree.